Helena's Inherit

Christ

1

Acknowledgements

I have thoroughly enjoyed writing this my first ever book. They say everyone has a book inside of them and, I hope this one isn't my last. There are, as is customary a couple of people I would like to thank, my husband John for supporting me in this little venture, for making the tea and his researching skills. Obrigado!

Thank you too, to those who read my early drafts you know who you are! Also, a big thanks to all the friends I have made since moving to central Portugal five years ago, which provided the setting and the inspiration for the book. Lastly to my good friend Gady Rui Santos whose lovely painting provided the front cover, it is beautiful.

For Mum and Dad with love.

Table of Contents

Elizabeth was almost ready for her first client of the day. A young woman who, just happened to be her one and only goddaughter Helena Stratton. Having watched Helena grow up, and knowing all too well her god daughter's personal traits, she knew, with the certainty that comes with familiarity, that Helena would not be late or early; in fact, she would walk through her office door exactly on time. Glancing at her wristwatch, and taking a deep breath, she sighed contentedly, knowing that she had precisely twenty very precious minutes to herself. Behind her heavy wooden desk, she let herself lean back into her old but extremely comfortable chair, as she contemplated the coming encounter with an almost childlike delight

Handling Helena's case, had turned out to be so very different from the routine cases that a provincial solicitor normally encountered. Elizabeth, thanks to her goddaughter had, over the last three months, experienced one of the most unusual and satisfying cases of her career. It had been remarkable and also completely unexpected, at least in terms of what she and her goddaughter had discovered. Indeed, Elizabeth herself struggled to think of the single adjective to describe the journey she had been on, let alone Helena. But today when Helena walked out of Elizabeth's office at the end of the meeting, it would symbolise the termination of this part of her god daughter's journey of discovery; but, and more importantly it would also mark the start of the future, and that no doubt would signify a momentous change in Helena's life abut also that of her father William too.

Helena had matured into a striking young woman, medium height, curvaceous in the right places, with an unruly wavy cascade of golden blonde hair, with subtle hints of red. In September she would be thirty-three years of age. She had inherited her mother's square facial features, and well-defined cheekbones, though her green eyes and hair colour came from her father, she was also lively and intelligent.

Helena obtained a degree in Horticulture from Exeter University which was swiftly followed by a master's degree in Viticulture. Following this she had tried a few different jobs before eventually at the age of twenty-seven applying for, and being successful, in obtaining a manager's post in the USA. Her boyfriend Tom had followed her, and for the last five years or so they had worked together managing a vineyard and winery, in California, for the De Bretts.

Consequently, Elizabeth hadn't seen much of Helena for around six years. Then and completely unexpectedly last summer, she received the devastating phone call from William, that her best friend Helena's mother had terminal cancer. Elizabeth had done all she could to support both William and Helena through Sofia's illness, but it had still been a bit of a surprise to receive Helena's call in January, just eight weeks after her mothers' funeral.

As she thought about Helena, Elizabeth reflected on how much she looked like her mother, they looked like peas from the same pod. Leaning her head backwards against the headrest, she closed her eyes, and her mouth curved into an involuntary but slight smile as she remembered her first meeting with Sofia, when they were both fresher's and had turned up for the university hockey team trials.

They had never made the heady heights of the first team; they forever languished in the third, with an occasional outing into the second. However, they did discover that they had a lot in common; a love of real ale, that they lived relatively close to each other, one in Coventry and one in Warwick, but most serendipitous of all, they found out that they both had Portuguese family, and they hit it off straight away. Over the years since they left University, they had remained good friends, and whilst the friendship inevitably took second place to their respective families when their children were young, in recent years they had become closer again. That was, until last summer, when out of the blue Sofia was diagnosed with cancer, which quickly proved terminal, and ended the friendship forever.

As she reflected on a future without her, her secretary 'Bells' entered with a mug of tea, and placed it down on the desk. Bells handed over the days mail, and placed on her desk the Guardian newspaper. They spoke for a few minutes about the mornings appointments, before Bells hurried back to her own office to answer the strident call of the telephone. Elizabeth cradled her mug of tea, and walked to the window that afforded her excellent views over the city centre from her tenth-floor office. Coventry had been her place of work for more than thirty years, and during the last two decades she had been privileged to witness the second transformation of the city centre skyline.

The first of course, followed the brutal devastation of the incendiary bombs dropped by the Luftwaffe in November 1940. These raids destroyed many of the city's historical centre, including its late 14th century Cathedral, and many of its medieval streets and buildings. Today, all that remained of the old Cathedral were the old walls, which lay adjacent to the new Cathedral which had been designed by the modernist Basil Spence. The new Cathedral consecrated in 1962, was located directly opposite the administration building and student hall of the old Lanchester Polytechnic. As you excited the polytechnic the beautiful statue of the Archangel St Michael on the exterior cathedral wall, was the first thing you saw.

Elizabeth had often walked inside the old Cathedral walls viewing the huge cross of nails, and trying to imagine what it must have been like before the war. When she exited the ruins and walked the few metres from the old cathedral and entered the new one, she always felt the solitude and peace that connected the old to the new. Often, whilst sitting quietly inside, a holiday she had taken to Berlin fifteen years ago inevitably popped into her thoughts. Whilst in this lovely city, she had made a special point of visiting the Kaiser Wilhelm Gedachnis Kirche. Allied bombs had destroyed the Gedachnis Kirche during the Second World War, and the cross of nails was sent to them from the cathedral in the sixties as a gesture of reconciliation, and when she saw it, it had moved her more than she had expected.

Following the end of the war, the rebuilding of the city began quite quickly, but by the late 70's and early 80's's many of those buildings were looking increasingly grey, and dated. Now, as she gazed over the city, she saw a skyline that was transforming. The Three Spires for which Coventry was well known remained, but they were now hemmed in by many new buildings, most of which were owned by Coventry University. The University had come into being in 1992, when the former Lanchester Polytechnic, whose campus was centred around the old and new Cathedrals, had received its charter. In the years that followed, student numbers had grown significantly, and consequently the campus had had to expand to meet the demand.

This growth in educational facilities fuelled investment in more buildings in the downtown city area. Even today, new buildings were still rising on sites and streets which had formally been post war builds. These streets were no longer favoured by todays fashion conscious retailers who preferred to be in the new indoor Shopping Malls. Even the few older 20th century buildings that survived the bombings, but now sadly stood empty, were not escaping the bulldozer. Fortunately, they had had no real architectural merit, but they did tell the story of the city, and Elizabeth was saddened to see these last vestiges of buildings that used to house cycle manufacture and small-scale engineering disappear

From her lofty position overlooking the city centre Elizabeth continued to witness the transformation on either side of the cities ring road. High rise cranes moved in a slow dance, as they effortlessly moved steel girders into place for the new offices, and additional halls of residence. This morning the backdrop to this activity was a brooding sky, various shades of grey mixed with the odd spot of bright blue, rain was coming, and she was glad she was inside warm and dry. As she watched the changing shapes of the scudding clouds, the buzzer on the desk sounded. She returned to her desk to answer it, it was Bells her secretary, who asked her a couple of questions, received the replies, and then told her Helena, had arrived. Elizabeth put the phone down and turned around reaching into the cupboard for the Stratton file whose contents held all the information she needed for Helena's visit today.

She thought back to the phone call she had received from Helena in early January, after Helena and William had begun the sad task of clearing out Sofia's personal possessions, so they could be given to Oxfam. However, Helena had told her that they had been distracted by Sofia's keepsake box, inside which they had discovered an old envelope languishing in amongst the Christmas, Valentines, New Baby and birthday cards that spanned decades. Inside the envelope they found a letter written by Helena's grandfather to her mum many years before. The letter appeared to indicate that the family might own a small rural property in central Portugal. Also inside the envelope was a separate hand-written note dated 1918, which contained the names of Sofia's great grandmother and great grandfather, as well as an address of a solicitor in Maçao, Portugal.

The contents of the letter were a total surprise to Helena and her father. Together after some days of reflection and a great deal of discussion over glasses of red wine, they had decided to seek Elizabeth's view. Elizabeth invited them around for a drink and whilst sitting in her capacious kitchen, Helena had passed her the letter which she read a couple of times. She admitted to herself and to them that she was more than a little intrigued, and agreed she would check it out. The next morning Elizabeth asked her secretary to check if the solicitors still existed, and twenty minutes later and much to her surprise Bells confirmed that indeed they did. Elizabeth wasted no time, she had immediately picked up the telephone and called them, just ten minutes later she was directed to call another set of solicitors in Coimbra. That telephone call led to a train of events that none of them could have possibly foreseen. Eight weeks later, and following many such conference calls and a business trip to Portugal; Elizabeth had been able to give her goddaughter some rather extraordinary and exciting news. Helena was about to inherit from her great-great grandmother Sofia, a Manor House and Quinta in the small village of Ameixeira in central Portugal. However, that wasn't the end of the story because subject to some further verifications, she was also entitled to a substantial inheritance from her great grandfather Luis, Sofia's son. As the story had unravelled itself, they were astounded to discover that these two inheritances were not, in any way, related to the inheritance that was alluded to in her grandfather's letter. Her great-great grandmother Sofia had, in the 1950's given that property, a small old house and some scrubland, away to a second cousin.

Today's meeting with Helena, was one of the last they were to have together, before she embarked on her journey to Portugal to take possession of the Manor House and Quinta. Elizabeth was delighted for her, though this was bitter sweet, knowing that Sofia, one of her best friends had never known about it. With a small sigh of regret for that single fact, she pressed the buzzer and asked Bells to let Helena in at exactly ten o'clock.

Helena, who hated being late for anything, had arrived with ten minutes to spare and was now sitting in the modern and functional waiting room, she felt a frisson of excitement, knowing that after today everything was going to be different. She thought of her life as before and after the letter. Deep down she knew this change was going to turn out to be transformational, leading to a future she could never have envisaged when her father opened that envelope. Glancing across at the photograph of Elizabeth, which was displayed on the wall along with those of the other partners; she pondered and not for the first time, what it was that her mum had seen in this purposeful woman, that made them become such firm friends. To her they had seemed complete opposites. Her mum had been vivacious, outgoing and whilst academically bright, she wasn't at all ambitious. Despite obtaining a good degree in biology, she had subsequently chosen to train as a nurse, a career she loved. Elizabeth on the other hand had been both super intelligent, and exceptionally driven. Physically, she was tall for a woman at five feet ten inches, she was possessed of a long face and a high forehead, from

12

which her straight shoulder length dark grey hair hung like a curtain. With her large but sunken blue grey eyes, and the two dull red spots on her cheeks, the result of a patchwork of broken capillaries, and thin bluish lips she reminded Helena a little of a bloodhound.

It was an ordinary face, not one that would give you a reason to stop and take a second look. Looks though, as the saying goes can be deceptive, because Elizabeth Briggs was a very competent, efficient and successful solicitor, the oldest child of three, from the marriage of her Portuguese father, to her Scottish mother. Schooled in Warwick, before reading law at Cambridge, Elizabeth was married to a fellow solicitor in the well-known Coventry practice of Gamp, Briggs, Briggs and Jones. So,, when Helena found the envelope it was logical to turn to Elizabeth, the fact that Elizabeth spoke fluent Portuguese was to prove to be a bonus.

Helena herself, was still amazed and shocked by what Elizabeth had uncovered after being passed from the initial solicitors, to the second firm in Coimbra. This second firm of solicitors had informed Elizabeth that they were the administrators of the estate of Sofia de Jesus Silva, who was Helena's great-great grandmother. The revelations didn't end there though, as they went on to inform Elizabeth that additionally they were, jointly with the descendants of Rafael Alencar de Mascarenhas Silva Brás Noronha e Alencar overseeing the Trust fund set up for Sofia's son Luis. It transpired her great grandfather was his son, from the long-standing relationship he had had with Sofia. Moreover, he was, at that time, a Count and therefore a Portuguese aristocrat. Helena was sure there had been some enormous mistake, how could she be related to a Portuguese aristocrat?

Surely if her grandfather had known anything about this, he would have said something much earlier. In the end she had eventually been persuaded that no mistake had occurred, and so she and her father began to come to terms with this momentous and completely unexpected revelation. After that matters moved very quickly; firstly, various proofs of identity were requested, including birth and death certificates for Helena's mother, grandfather and great grandfather. This proved to be slightly easier than expected, because her mum had kept all her family documents in one place, along with her life insurances and very oddly her school and University education certificates.

At this point the true nature and size of the inheritance began to be revealed, as the next request came from the Count's family solicitors, who asked Helena if she was prepared to undergo a blood and DNA test. Whilst the request surprised her, Elizabeth had subsequently explained to them, that the Trust set up to manage Luis's inheritance had, decades before, collaborated with Sofia to protect both parties.

At the time, Sofia didn't know if her son was alive of course, but she hoped he was and that he had married and had children. Against this backdrop she negotiated a deal with the Alencar family that included a very clever clause. In essence, the clause set out that in relation to both her own, and Luis's inheritance, any legitimate heirs coming forward, within fifty years and one day of her own death, would inherit. But if no one came forward then the capital sum plus any growth, would revert to the Counts family, along with Sofia's own legacy. To be certain that anyone coming forward was a legitimate descendant, it was further stipulated that the best available technology of the time should be used to help establish a familial link if possible. When Sofia died DNA testing had not been available, however she had had the foresight to give a sample of her own blood. Moreover, the Alencar family were also required to co-operate. The resulting testing proved that Helena was familially linked to Count Rafael Alencar de Mascarenhas Silva Brás Noronho e Alencar from his relationship with Sofia de Jesus Silva. As the Count had publicly acknowledged his son in his Will, and his only marriage had not produced heirs, was a matter of record.

For Helena and William, what had started out as a tenuous search to discover if her great-great grandmother had owned a small house and land, that she may have left to her son Luis, and ultimately to Helena's mother, ended up being an inheritance which proved to be much more extensive and complicated.

This morning's meeting, with Elizabeth was to resolve any remaining outstanding issues, and to receive confirmation that the arrangements for her trip to Portugal were in place. Helena's meeting with her Aunt was scheduled for ten am, and at exactly ten am Helena entered her office. Elizabeth gave her goddaughter a hug and a kiss on both cheeks, before sitting back behind the desk and adopting her usual and efficient manner, she opened the file on her desk turned to Helena and said, 'If you're ready Helena perhaps we should make a start? Sitting further back in a chair, which was rather less comfortable than the one Elizabeth was sitting in, Helena replied

'Yes please, Aunt Elizabeth, I am keen to know the latest news.'

To an interested outsider, anyone viewing this meeting and not knowing the pair would never have guessed that they were Godmother and Goddaughter. They liked each other, but the generation gap, and life experiences operated to keep a little distance between them.

Elizabeth leant forward slightly smiled at her Goddaughter.

15

'I spoke at some length yesterday with Senhor Gonçalves, and he confirmed that everything is arranged for your visit to the Quinta das Laranjeiras. He told me that he is very much looking forward to meeting you in a couple of weeks' time. No doubt that meeting will be more than instructive for you. He has managed to process all the paperwork we sent through, and is now ready and able to hand over to you your great-great grandmothers estate. There are though, a few outstanding issues to resolve in relation to Luis's inheritance, and he will continue to work through these over the next few days or so. He will confirm to me that all is good to go by Tuesday next week.

He noted your request to stay in the house, but he has advised that although the buildings structure has been maintained the house is not, and never was connected to the national grid.'

Elizabeth looked up and grinned at Helena.

'Apparently, the plumbing system is archaic, water is drawn from wells, pumped by a generator that hasn't been used since your great-great grandmother died. He couldn't vouch for the water quality, so he wouldn't want you to drink it, until it has been checked out!

Senhor Gonçalves took some pains to convince me, that I should convince you, that you might be more comfortable in a guesthouse or hotel nearby.'

Helena who had been expecting something of this sort simply smiled at her and replied

'Please thank him for his advice Aunt Elizabeth, but I am going to spend my first night in Portugal in the house, even if afterwards I follow his advice! Perhaps you could ask him if it's practical to arrange for a bedroom to be made ready for me? I am happy to reimburse him for any costs of buying a new mattress, and bed linen, torches etc. I assume that at least there is an indoor toilet, which

16

is functioning, and if not, well perhaps he could organise for a portable toilet to be available. It might sound like over kill, but we will need one of those if work is to commence on the house. We can't have the workmen inconvenienced, can we?'

As Helena said this she laughed, Elizabeth who had caught her drift laughed back. The rest of the conversation moved on rapidly, and before too long Helena was outside on the pavement, feeling both apprehensive but excited. She looked up at the sky, the grey scudding clouds that were evident before she had entered the solicitor's office's, had now turned black and leaden, she could smell rain in the air. Briskly she made her way back to her car. Spring, despite having formally arrived, was nonetheless still cold and depressing. Her trip to Portugal would bring with it the added bonus of a mature spring, and hopefully warmer temperatures.

Three days later Elizabeth called her at home to say that a bedroom would be made ready, and that the downstairs cloakroom would also be cleaned and hopefully would be functioning. Helena allowed herself a small smile of satisfaction, that was tinged with anticipation. Elizabeth also confirmed that Senhor Gonçalves himself would be at the house to meet her and show her around. He would be the one to pass onto her the basic facts about the Manor House and Quinta's estate.

Helena wondered for the umpteenth time, what details of the Estate really meant, after all it couldn't be that big could it? Apart from a few old and decidedly grainy photos of the front of the house and the GPS co-ordinates Helena had little concrete information about her inheritance. She had asked several times if there was more information available, but her Aunt had replied that Senhor Gonçalves was in the best position to explain it all and he felt it would be better done in person, so with good grace, Helena acquiesced.

On the penultimate day of April, Helena hugged and kissed her dad goodbye, confirming that she would meet him the following Tuesday at Lisbon airport. Then she, along with her packed mini cooper, set off on the drive to Portsmouth where, after an overnight stop in a hotel close to the ferry terminal, she would board the early morning ferry that would arrive approximately twenty-four hours later in Santander. She knew she was embarking on a life-changing journey to a country she had never visited, despite her Portuguese ancestry; but she was excited and looking forward to whatever it was going to bring her. After all that happened to her in the last six months, it could only be an improvement. The hotel she had booked into was comfortable, and she had a meal and a couple glasses of wine before falling into a deep sleep. The next morning, after a large and delicious English breakfast, she checked out of the hotel and made her way to the ferry terminal.

As it turned out, rather unfortunately for her, and even more so for her solicitor Senhor Gonçalves, the journey to Portugal, and the Quinta das Laranjeiras in Ameixeira was not to run at all smoothly. Firstly, the ferry's departure from Portsmouth was delayed by four hours due to deteriorating weather conditions in the Bay of Biscay. Helena had phoned Elizabeth's office from the ferry and asked her to forewarn Senhor Gonçalves about the delay, which was significant. Instead of arriving at the acceptable hour of five in the afternoon, it was more likely that Helena would arrive after nine o'clock in the evening. The crossing was uncomfortable as the storm swells in the Bay of Biscay whilst, perhaps less ferocious than had been previously forecast, still caused the ship to roll a little. In the end Helena was delayed by a total of six and a half hours, because as she waited in her lane to exit the ferry in Santander, the motor home directly in front, would not start. Therefore she, and all those behind her in the line couldn't exit until a recovery vehicle arrived to tow it out of the way. Helena by this point was beginning to wonder what third piece of bad luck would strike, as in her view bad things always came in three's.

However, once free of the terminal buildings the satellite navigation system purchased in the UK, proved to be an absolute godsend. Largely, because she not only had to get to get to grips with driving on the right-hand side of the road, but doing so in a left-hand drive car!

If she had tried to negotiate her way out of the busy city using road signs and a map, she thought she might still be there! But with the sat-nav on, and with only a few wrong turns, she found herself on a major road heading towards the Portuguese border. Six hours later, and after just a single loo stop, and driving on what seemed for the most part unencumbered motorways, and 'A' roads, Helena closed in on her ultimate destination.

However, by now it was almost eleven o'clock in the evening, her eyes were scratchy, and she was very tired. For the last half an hour she had been driving on poor quality roads headed for Cováo; this was because the hamlet of Ameixeira in which the Quinta das Laranjeiras was situated, was not recognised as a location on the sat-navs system. Consequently, Helena had punched in the village of Cováo, which was where the local freguesia (parish council) was based. If she found Cováo, she hoped it would be of sufficient size to have a café or restaurant open. Helena's original plan, which was to simply stop and ask directions, was now at eleven o'clock at night, looking increasingly unlikely to bear fruit.

Still, she had no choice but to find somewhere to stop, as the sat-nav continued not to respond to the inputting of the post-code or Ameixeira: nor had she seen any road signs that would point her in the right direction. To make matters worse her back up, the Michelin Map of central Portugal was devoid of a large number of villages that Helena had already passed through! On entering Covào she wound down her window and scanned both left and right for signs of life, but the silence that greeted her was deafening. Only the amber glow from a few street lights showed that the village must be inhabited. Slowing right down she eventually saw an old and battered sign that pointed to the main praça (square). Turning right, she found herself in a small central square, devoid of cars and people and dominated by an enormous Willow tree. Fortunately for her a building that proclaimed it was Café Central, still streamed light out into the road through its single door. Helena quickly parked the car right outside and went in.

It was immediately clear that they were in the middle of closing for the evening, as only two people were visible. At the counter a middle-aged man with a grey flat cap on his head, was seated on a barstool; a small nearly empty glass of red wine reposed in front of him, and at his feet lay a small black and white dog that, on seeing Helena, demonstrated a proprietorial air, and closed in on the man's dirty brown boots.

Behind the counter, a woman with curly brown hair, and an open face, was wiping down the coffee-making machine. Helena walked up to the counter, and in her best and rather un-practiced Portuguese said,

'Boa noite Senhora, (Good evening Madame) I am so glad to see your open. I need some help; can you tell me how to get to the village of Ameixeira?'

Helena continued, explaining to the now smiling faced woman that according to her sat-nav and her Michelin map the village didn't exist. This caused the woman to

20

broaden her smile, and putting down her cloth on the bar, she pronounced that Ameixeira did indeed exist, and was actually quite easy to find. The man who was listening intently gave a snort of derision, and said it was late for lone women to be wandering around, then he bade them both good night, and left the café with his little dog in tow. Once he had exited the woman proceeded to give Helena directions, ending up by confirming that it was less than a ten-minute drive away. Having thanked her for her help, and the offer of coffee that she had refused, Helena was on her way again.

By now the clock on her dashboard was indicating it was close to eleven fifteen, and any expectations that Senhor Gonçalves would still be waiting, had long since vanished. Helena, was fully resigned to have to spend the night in the car, she had brought with her own pillow (she never travelled anywhere without it) and a duvet in case of an emergency like the one she now faced. At least she would be warm, if not entirely comfortable until daylight returned. Following the directions, she drove on a deserted and largely unlit road, passing through several small villages. Pines and eucalyptus trees that edged the twisty road swayed in what was clearly a strong breeze. Eventually she saw a sign for the village of Vinha Velha, and two hundred metres after that came the turning on the left, where the road sign pointed to Ameixeira. About a kilometre further on and after passing a few dark houses, an old barely readable sign loomed up from the darkness that indicated she should turn left for the Quinta das Laranjeiras. As she turned she rapidly discovered the tarmac had ran out, and she was on an unmade road, her car began to bounce up and down, and so she plunged her foot on the brake, slowing right down to avoid the pot holes and ruts she was encountering. About three hundred metres further on her headlights, picked out from the gloom a large pair of open entrance gates, flanked by a pair of sturdy stone pillars.

As she passed through them, she saw the driveway was edged on either side by a series of trees, whose leaves and branches were swaying slightly in the wind. A thrill passed through her, she was here; and even though the house and its environs were enveloped in darkness, she felt energised, she wanted so much to laugh out loud and shout 'this is mine', but of course she didn't. As she approached the end of the drive, and the outline of the house came into view, she saw, much to her surprise, that there was a car on the right-hand side of the driveway. Pulling up ten metres from the rear bumper of the already parked car, she put on the handbrake but left the engine on. A light suddenly came on inside the car, and Helena saw in her own car's headlights, an older man exiting the driver's door. At first, she wasn't sure whether to get out of the car or not, but as he walked towards her car she could see he was impeccably dressed, and carrying a briefcase and her reservations diminished a little. Helena opened the window, in time to hear him say in perfect, if heavily accented, English 'Miss Stratton?'

'Yes, that's me.' she replied, her voice sounding loud in the still cold air.

'I am relieved that you found your way here, my name is Senhor Gonçalves I think you were expecting to be met.' Relief flooded through her, she turned off the engine, opened the door and exited the car, proffering her hand.

'Olá Boa Noite' .– (Hello good evening.) she said with clear relief

Senhor Gonçalves shook her hand with quite a firm grip., as Helena continued.

Senhor,'I am both relieved and surprised to find you still waiting for me at this late hour. I was resigned to sleeping in the car. I am so very sorry, I do hate being late for anything.'

'It is of no matter.' He said waving his hand in the air as if to confirm it.

'Maybe though, as it is so late, I should take you inside and show to you your room, and point out the cloakroom on the way, and perhaps the planned discussions could wait until tomorrow at ten am. I am sure your very tired after your journey.' he gave her a small smile, 'I know I am.'

Helena immediately felt guilty at keeping this elegant older man waiting; and for her foolish wish to spend her first night alone in an unfamiliar and isolated house. But she quickly agreed, and lifting her suitcase from the car she followed his lead. A torch that, until now she hadn't noticed was in Senhor Gonçalves hand, suddenly lit the way, and the outline of the large house came into view. As they walked towards it Helena realized with a shock that it was much grander than she had previously imagined, the photographs she had seen made it appear smaller. It loomed over them, and for the first time she saw that the drive way curved round into an oval, at the centre point of which a number of steps led up to an ornate veranda, and beyond it a pair of doors. She followed him up the steps, once at the top Senhor Gonçalves pushed open the left hand of the two doors, and without any ceremony she entered the house of her ancestors.

If it was dark outside, then it appeared to Helena that it was even darker inside. Once inside she stopped, and a variety of odours assailed her nose, old wood, and a faint smell like musty old clothes, along with a strong disinfectant. The torch beam was casting strange shaped shadows around the walls, and Helena was beginning to think she had perhaps been more than a little foolhardy to insist on staying here on her own, when her flow of thought was interrupted by Senhor Gonçalves pointing out a door that led to the cloakroom. He then used the beam of his torch to point the way to the staircase that gave access to the first floor. Placing her left hand on the wooden stair rail, she climbed the stairs slowly, her every step echoing on the old wooden treads, at the top of the stairs Senhor Gonçalves turned left, and left again, before stopping at a large wooden door, which he opened with his left hand. The beam of his torch gave her glimpses of a large room, lit by an oil lamp from a bedside cabinet, that cast a circular pool of soft light around it. As he lowered his torch she could make out the outline of a large ornate bed.

'This is the bedroom prepared for you, I hope you find it quite comfortable Miss Stratton.'

'Thank you I am sure I will.'

'Maria has, as you can already see, lit the oil lamp by your bed, there is a torch too, over there in case you need the cloakroom in the night.'

He pointed the beam of his torch in the direction he was indicating, and as he did so the beam did a side-to-side jiggle.

'Also, over here, you will find a cool box with some food and drinks in case you are hungry, you will meet Maria tomorrow. The jug has fresh water in it for washing, if you need to use the bathroom, just retrace your steps down stairs and the cloakroom is the second door on the left in the hallway. Maria and her husband Manuel are staying the night here, in the old cook's bedroom, down on the ground floor.

On hearing this Helena felt her anxiety decrease, and Senhor Gonçalves, who had noticed the change in her body's stance, smiled.

24

'I thought it would be nicer for you to have someone else in the house tonight. They won't disturb you, but if you want them just pull on the bell by your bedside and they will come. Now, if you don't mind it is quite late, and I have an hour or so still to drive before I am home, so unless there is anything else…. I think that will be all until tomorrow. I have a spare key so will lock the front door behind me, so you don't have to follow me back down. I hope you sleep well Miss Stratton, until we meet again, good night.'

And with that he shook her hand, gave a short nod of his head, and then quietly turned around and left.

Helena sat down heavily upon the firm bed, after only a few moments she heard a car start up and drive slowly away. Suddenly, the adrenalin that had sustained her thus far evaporated, and she was overcome by tiredness, but she needed the toilet, so she picked up the torch and made her way back out of the bedroom. It was pitch black apart from the light from the oil lamp that spilled out into the doorway. Very carefully she found the balustrade and made her way downstairs. Her footsteps echoed on the stairs and on the tiles, she found the cloakroom and opened the door. Inside it was as dark as dark could be, and she realised that the smell of disinfectant she noted on entering the Quinta, must have come from here. She felt around and located the loo, and a small sink. Having seen to her own needs, she found the flush and left. Retracing her steps back up the stairs, she looked around slowly, but it was so dark that she couldn't see very much, exploration would have to wait until the morning.

Once back in her room she opened her suitcase, found some pyjamas, quickly undressed and got into the bed, placing the torch on the bedside next to the oil lamp. Her feet wriggled down the bed and then they touched a hot water bottle, she leant down and pulled it up to her chest and thought what a lovely gesture that was. The mattress was firm but soft, the sheets and duvet cool, and she thought that the bed would prove to be comfortable. Turning to the oil lamp it took her a few seconds to figure out how to turn it off, the flame died slowly, and then she lay in the dark hugging the hot water bottle. As her eyes adjusted to the dimness, it was comforting to know other people were in the house, even if she hadn't met them yet. She pulled the duvet around her, and much to her own surprise, she felt her eyes closing, and very shortly afterwards she fell into a deep and largely untroubled sleep.

It was morning, and she was almost awake. Helena knew this for two reasons: firstly, she could hear the unmistakeable and steady beat of rain on the Quinta's terracotta roof tiles and secondly even with her eyes still firmly shut, she could see shadowy morning light filtering through the window. Something had startled her awake, what was it?

Perhaps it was her own imagination, so she prepared to snuggle down inside the bed again, only to be disturbed a few seconds later when she heard the sound again. Someone, clearly deranged, was pressing on a car horn and holding it down several times over, and it was coming from somewhere close by. Was someone trying to attract her attention? The bit of her mind that was conscious, was telling her that it wasn't likely, as no one knew she was here, whereas the other part of her brain wasn't quite so sure. Minutes later the sound of a vehicle driving away made her slump rather dramatically back into the embracing arms of her oh so comfortable bed. As she did so, her leg touched the now tepid hot water bottle, and she pushed it further down the bed away from her feet. After remaining where she was for a few minutes longer, her sleep deprived brain suddenly kicked into second gear. What an idiot, of course someone did know she was here, three people knew that she was here in the Manor House of the Quinta das Laranjeiras. Despite feeling a rising inner excitement, a stronger pull of inertia pinned her back in the warm bed, she was faintly conscious that her back ached, probably in protest at the long drive from Santander; and she could hear, albeit faintly the odd movement that comes from being in a house with other people in it, as occasionally a word or two filtered through on the air. Helena felt the same heady mixture of apprehension, anticipation and excitement that she had first felt weeks ago, on learning that she had inherited a Manor House, and land in Portugal. Those initial feelings though, were nothing in comparison to how she felt this morning, now that she was, at last, physically here in the Quinta, laying in this comfy bed, warm and fuzzy brained. Her mind seemingly of its own volition, drifted back to that extraordinary January day, which had been the catalyst for all that, had happened since.

It was just six weeks following her mum's funeral when she together with her reluctant father, resolved to sort through her mums' wardrobe. They were not doing this because they wanted to, but because they had made her mum a solemn promise only weeks before she died, that they would. The weight of that promise had kept her awake for several nights, and in order to try to get a half decent night's sleep, Helena had persuaded her father that they should carry out her wishes. Her mum had pressed them on several occasions to make sure her clothes went to Oxfam. She was quite particular about it; Helena even now could remember the conversation.

'No other high street charity shop please, only Oxfam, I don't want them sitting in the wardrobe for months or even years. You have to move on, and seeing my clothes, or staring at the wardrobe without opening it, won't help you to do that.'

Trying as she always did, to hide the pain she felt, Helena replied with a false cheeriness.

'I will mum, but it is going to be some time yet, can we get through Christmas first.'

Her mum, who was now painfully thin, moved uncomfortably in her bed. Helena used a couple of plumped up pillows to help prop her up, but it seemed to her that each movement she made was difficult, nonetheless despite any pain Sofia was feeling, she gave her daughter a stern look.

'Promise me now, that you will have given them all to Oxfam within a month.'

So of course, they had promised. In the end her mum didn't make Christmas, only a few weeks after that conversation, she entered the hospice, and just a few days later died peacefully, in early November.

Now, they were about to carry out her wishes, albeit a few weeks late, and it was a task that neither of them really wanted to undertake. They had decided which wardrobe they were going to tackle first, and it was the one in the spare bedroom, so with mugs of tea in hand, they crossed over the threshold. Whether by unconscious design or not, they were immediately distracted by the sight of her mum's keepsake box, which sat on top of the wardrobe.

The box was round, large, and covered in a chocolate brown silky material. It had a large and ornate ribbon which was attached to the bottom half and came up and over, to tie in a bow on the top. However, the bow had come undone, and one side of it was now hanging in front of the wardrobe doors, and it seemed to them both that it was trying very hard to draw attention to itself.

As she remembered, that she had given it to her mum full of delicious chocolates for her birthday more than ten years before Helena's eyes prickled with tears. Between the three of them they had eaten all the chocolates, and subsequently it had gained a second, and perhaps more useful life, as the place where her mum began to save all her cards and memorabilia, her Keepsake Box she called it. Helena, guessed that her dad William, preferred to postpone the wardrobe clearing out task, and so he needed little persuasion to go and fetch a chair, and bring the box down. Once it was down, William placed the box in the middle of the floor, on top of the faded pink carpet. Both arranged themselves on either side of it, in the space between the bed and the door. Helena undid the already half undone bow and took off the lid. Inside stacked one on top of the other were cards covering every occasion. She picked up the top one, which was a Christmas card from the previous year, from Sylvia one of her mum's friends from work. They worked through them silently for a few minutes, then Helena's father William picked up one, and smiled. He showed it to his daughter, it was a card Helena herself had hand made for her mum's 35th birthday, and she smiled at its simplicity. She had drawn herself and her mum by a swing, and had hand written 35 in the top left-hand corner, before covering it with silver glitter, much of which still remained. For the next half an hour or so, they ploughed steadily through the cards, talking quietly, and sometimes even laughing about the memories they evoked.

About half way down the box, it was her dad who came across the faded envelope with Sofia's name on it. William at first thought it odd, and anomalous to discover this old envelope addressed to his wife, in amongst a box of cheery cards and precious keepsakes, but he kept his own counsel. The envelope was old and not sealed, so he opened the flap and took out the contents, and began to read them. Helena who had looked up from the card she was reading, studied his face; his features showed a mixture of surprise, and then clear puzzlement as he continued to read, when he came to the end, he was shaking his head. Without saying anything he silently passed the envelope, and its contents to her. It's reading had set of the chain of events that only a few months later had brought Helena here, to this bed, in the Manor House that she had inherited in central Portugal. Her eyes, which were still tightly shut prickled once more with tears, and try as she might she couldn't stop the other, less than happy memories from resurfacing. Succumbing to the inevitability, she let herself tumble through all that had happened over the last eight months. Unhappily, and very much regardless of her attempts not to remember some things, these memories seemed to have a life of their own.

She remembered with complete clarity the conversation Tom and she had had only ten weeks ago. Perhaps, not surprisingly, the memory of it still made her irrationally angry. She recalled that she was not really looking forward to receiving Tom's call that day, as their recent conversations had been a bit awkward, and if she was truthful far from normal. However, this call was bad on a level she could not have envisaged, even recalling it now, months later made her livid; she was at the family home in Hobs Hill, Lincolnshire when he phoned.

With the benefit of hindsight, she realised that the meat of the phone call was not entirely unexpected, however her reaction to Tom's dismissal of their five-year plus relationship had completely surprised her, and looking back on it, she behaved like an out of control banshee, and it was all a tad dramatic.

So much so, that she was embarrassed to think about it. Did she really tell him to go boil his head in a vat of wine, whilst at the same time making it very clear she thought him a low life, and one without the balls even come to England and tell her in person that their five-year relationship was over?

Was it really, she, the normally well-mannered and controlled Helena Stratton who screamed at him down the phone, that he had been, and still was, a selfish pig with the morals of a hyena? Was it just a touch theatrical to make it very clear that she would never forgive him for not coming back to the UK to support her dad, and her as

31

they grappled with the reality of her mum's terminal illness.

Throughout her ramblings Tom was attempting to speak over her, continually trying, and failing, to justify his shabby behaviour. But by now, Helena had the bit between her teeth, and she just wasn't going to let him walk away unscathed, after all the things he had, and hadn't done. When the call had finished, she thought back over the previous six months, and reflected on his increasingly infrequent telephone calls; which when they came, had become all too predictable. For example, she remembered all to clearly that when she had almost begged him to come home and help her with her mum, he had simply said

'You know I am no good around ill people. I hate it when you have a cold, let alone handling a terminally ill woman. I would embarrass you.'

Several times, he even had the gall to say,

'Besides, the business needs me to be here right now Helena, it's our future I am trying to protect.'

Helena told him so many times to stick the business somewhere dark and smelly, and that she never wanted to see or hear from him again.

But Tom being Tom though, did what Tom did best; he put his head in the sand, and blithely dismissed her rants as the product of stress. He continued to phone occasionally, but always failing to ask more than a desultory question about how her mum was. In reality most of his calls centred on the viticulture business he was managing *'alone'* what progress he was making *'alone'* and how good the sales were looking, even though he was *'alone'* etc. Helena, even had to remind him that it was *'they'* that managed the business not just him.

She could hear him now, in that soft Irish accent of his,

'Of course, of course, that's why I need to stay here, because it needs my attention, until you come back of course.'

She couldn't get over his selfishness, she needed him too, to give her some emotional support, and a degree of unrestrained physical contact, but he clearly didn't require the same from her.

As her mum's health declined it seemed to Helena that his calls became less, and less frequent, though she was so wrapped up caring for her and holding her dad up, that she probably was grateful, because half the time she didn't have the energy to speak and make small talk. Though she remembered all too vividly that when she called him in floods of tears to tell him her mum had passed away, he didn't offer to come home on the next available plane. Looking back on it now she was positively sure he was trying to find a good excuse for not coming at all, by then though, Helena was so emotionally drained that she couldn't have cared less if he came or not. He finally turned up five days later, and was about as much use as the proverbial chocolate teapot.

The day of the funeral dawned, and somehow, they got through it, her father said some beautiful words about the love of his life and his soul mate Sofia. He talked quietly, about how they had met, and fallen instantly in love, and were married within nine months, followed by Helena their only child eighteen months later. Helena couldn't stop herself from chuckling at some of the tales he told whilst all the time, trying to stifle her sobbing. The church had been full of friends of mums from the hospital where she worked as an orthopaedic sister, and of course Aunt Elizabeth and Uncle James, were there too. This increased the numbers in the church by 95%, as they had little family of their own to speak of. Helena's Mum was an only child and her dad who was adopted might as well have been. He and his half-sister had been estranged since their parents had died. Both sets of her grandparents had died within the previous ten years, so the only family mourners were her, and her dad, and Tom and his parents, who Helena had always liked very much. Tom flew back to California two days later promising to call her every week, a hollow promise she somehow knew he would never keep. Eventually, he had called, but with the sole intention of ending their relationship, he wasn't even very interested in the letter she and her dad had found. That call on top of everything else, would be the catalyst to change the direction of her previously reasonably straightforward life.

A week later Helena gave the de Brett's formal notice of her resignation, and although not a vindictive person, Helena secretly hoped this would backfire on Tom, because the original reason they were employed had been because the company had wanted a couple, with at least one having a Viticulture degree, and that was her. Tom hadn't got a clue, but of course over the years he had learned, so maybe they would keep him. Meanwhile she had decided to look into the letter; if nothing came of it well that would be that. So she told her dad she was going to pursue it, and then if nothing came of it, she would look at France or Australia as potential fertile ground for work.

As if a switch had been flicked, Helena's mind then turned to memories of her grandparents. On her dad's side, they were Hugh and Brenda Stratton, both came from Selby in Yorkshire, her father was adopted as a baby, though Helena wasn't told this until she herself was eighteen, and it explained many things. Soon after adopting her dad, grandma found herself pregnant with her own child and Aunty Linda became the apple of their eyes. Helena's granddad Stratton was the branch manager of Barclays Bank in the town. Her grandma, meanwhile had never worked, she kept the house and played hostess to granddad's colleagues when required. When she, and her parents visited the house, it was, as always, immaculate. Helena and her mum had never felt comfortable there. Painfully, Helena remembered that she could look at the books and ornaments, but she most definitely was not allowed to touch them. Unhappily her memories of them both, were always tinged with bitterness, and regret. They say children remember injustice, and unfairness more strongly than adults, and she remembered the time, when she was playing with a little black and white Staffordshire pottery dog, which she had taken down from the mantle shelf in the best sitting room, and then, much to her dismay, she had accidently broken it. The consequences were horrible, she was banished to her room for the rest of the day, without lunch, because her grandma told her *'little girls who touch things that don't belong to them, don't deserve lunch'* Her mum having spent the morning out with William shopping in Sheffield, was absolutely mortified when she got back to find Helena sobbing in her bedroom, without having had anything to eat or drink since breakfast, she herself was only eight at the time.

On her mother's side, she never had known her grandmother da Silva, who had died when her mum was only ten years old, but her grandfather was just lovely, his home was always a place where she could play without fear. Her mum's parents had been born in America, in Pennsylvania. Helena remembered with fondness his wonderful accent, for a child growing up in a midlands city and having Birmingham with its strong regional accent as a neighbour, her grandfather's American accent had seemed ever so exotic. Helena could not remember her granddad ever speaking much about his parents, let alone his grandparents, and she now thought that perhaps he knew very little of his own family history. Her mum had, at some point, mentioned that her grandparents, and therefore Helena's great-grandparents were called Eleanor and Luis. Luis's parents were from Portugal, his mum having emigrated to America when he was a small child. Eleanor's family were of Irish descent, and that was as much as she knew. Eleanor and Luis had met and married in the USA in the 1920's. After they married Sofia's dad was born at the end of 1928, and he was their only child. Apparently, they idolized him, and they both worked hard to earn enough money, so he could go to Pennsylvania University, where he read mechanical engineering. Helena's granddad then married her grandmother who was also an Irish American girl, Anne Clarke in 1959. His parents were both pleased and proud when he obtained a senior post at the Jaguar Car company based in Coventry, which saw them emigrating to Britain in 1961.From what Helena knew it seemed they only went back to America a few times after that, and then only for the funerals of their parents.

Helena's mum always said that her mum, having agreed to come to England, wanted to put all her energy in to the future. Both had European ancestry, and so America never felt like home. With the Second World War had come the loosening of family ties, and people seemed to prefer to think of brighter futures, rather than to dwell in the past. Coventry was where they decided to make their home, and to grandma da Silva, America was the past and as such, all their focus went into making Coventry the place to settle down and raise a family. Helena's mum was born shortly after they arrived in Coventry in late 1962, in the Gulson Road maternity hospital and she was named Sofia Anne de Jesus Silva. Granddad had said Sofia was a family name, belonging to his grandmother. Granddad de Silva never remarried, and Helena had loved him very much, and she knew she was very much loved by him. In his retirement years until he died in 2003, he lived in a small village just outside of Coventry, in a cottage with a thatched roof and lots of small but cosy rooms.

Throughout her early childhood she would spend as much of her holidays, and weekends with him as she could, and it didn't take much to persuade mum or dad to take her. Avô (grandfather) was the person who taught her to speak Portuguese, and they would spend many summer days learning the names of the vegetables they picked, before plucking handfuls of sweet smelling sweet pea flowers for her to take home to her mum. As she got older, Helena rarely visited Selby as her dad and his parents just didn't get on, and these occasional visits were always strained affairs, best avoided.

Helena's tumbling thoughts veered off course yet again, as her mind wandered back to one particularly horrendous Christmas at her father's parents, she guessed she was about seven years old. It was Christmas Eve and Helena was on the verge of drifting off to sleep waiting for Santa to come, when suddenly the sound of raised voices coming from her dad and grandfather Stratton woke her. Half an hour later, her mum was in the bedroom getting her dressed, telling her that they were going home. Helena had cried and cried, saying they couldn't go home because Santa wouldn't know where to deliver her presents to, but her mum soothed her tears by telling her that Santa and his reindeers knew where every child in the world was, and so she was not to worry. Even so, whilst she was in floods of tears the car was hurriedly packed, and in short order Helena was laid on the back seat with a blanket to cover her up, and they were on their way back to

37

Coventry. Santa of course did know where she was and the next morning she was delighted by all the presents he had sent her.

When Helena grew up, she came to understand what lay behind the difficulties between her dad and granddad, and it was heart breaking to see two proud men unable to bridge them. All of these memories had been running through her mind like a slow-moving black and white silent movie, and she knew all this reminiscing was making her maudlin. It would be unwise to stay in this cosy cocoon much longer, and with some trepidation and a deep breath, she opened her eyes.

What she first saw was a wooden ceiling with a carved central rose. From the rose hung a large metal chandelier with eight arms, it was green in colour and hanging here and there were broken bits of ancient cobwebs. Helena's eyes strayed to the wall in front of her which had a fresco painted around its four edges. It was Art Nouveau in design with sinuous, organic lines, leaf tendrils, and tulips, linked together with highly stylized birds of some sort. Most of the once vibrant colour had faded, but the essence was still there, and it was quite beautiful.

In the centre of the wall was a huge mirror, with a flowing frame made of what she thought was wrought iron painted green; she thought it was again, an Art Nouveau piece. Inside the frame the mirrors silvering was decaying in places, but in no way, did it detract from the overall effect. Two large windows on either side of the handsome mirror had their internal shutters open, leaning back into the recessed alcoves in the walls. Under each window was a marble topped crescent console table, again that unmistakeable Art Nouveau signature was all over them, on one was a porcelain pitcher and bowl and on the other an incongruous pale blue cool box.

Her now semi-functioning brain kicked into third gear, how could she have forgotten. Helena pondered on her amazement at finding Senhor Gonçalves still waiting for her last night; despite the fact it was past eleven pm, especially as she had long since resigned herself to sleeping in the car. Remembering now the short conversation, the detail came back to her easily. Senhor Gonçalves had told her about the cool box, and that a Maria and Manuel were in the house, and that any conversation they might have had would have to wait until the following day. He also told her the pitcher was full of clean water, and she wasn't to use the water from the taps in the cloakroom until it had all been checked. Now, brought into the present, she marvelled that despite the strangeness of the house, and the lack of any external light, she had slept well, that is until that unknown sound had woken her just thirty minutes or so ago.

Now fully awake Helena checked the time on the mobile, discovering it was 9.20, she admonished herself out loud, 'Oh Hell, come on Helena, you need to wash, dress, and eat something before Senhor Gonçalves arrives.'

She pushed her legs over the side of the bed and stood up stretching her limbs, and saw for the first time for a while, her own reflection in the mirror. She acknowledged she had lost a little weight, and thought it didn't suit her. Green eyes stared out at her from the blue grey smudges underneath them, and she realized that mascara, which hadn't been removed before she got into bed, was now spread under her bottom lashes. Helena moved towards the pitcher and poured some of the cold water in the flowery printed bowl, next to it was a small bar of soap, which she unwrapped. It was lavender scented, a smell that fleetingly reminded her of France. Giving herself the best wash she could in the cold water, she next hunted in the wash bag for a toothbrush, finding it easily, before realising with a sigh that she had forgotten to pack any toothpaste.

She thought to herself that a brush with water would have to do for now. Helena rummaged in her suitcase and found a clean set of underwear, a pair of jeans, and a string top. Next her hands found the sage green woollen jumper with an envelope collar, studded with a dark green button that used to belong to her mum. Pulling it over her head she smelt the faint but lingering spicy fragrance of Opium by Yves Saint Laurent, her mum's favourite perfume. Helena felt a tear forming at the back of her eyelids and said to herself that she wasn't going to cry. Instead she looked out of the window and said out loud.

'Mum you will never guess where I am; I wish you could be with me to see this, you would love it, but I promise I will do all I can to preserve it. If I make contact with any family we may have here, I will make sure they know about you and granddad too, love you.'

Then she gave an involuntary shiver, smelt a brief whiff of Opium and was consoled by the thought that her mum knew. Quickly, she opened the cool box found a bottle of water and a banana, which she ate before stepping out of the bedroom door.

The bedroom opened onto a wide but still dark landing, with a corridor running both left and right before both turned 180 degrees, ending up at a flight of wide stairs leading down to the ground floor. She walked all around it, with only the light from the windows in her bedroom to guide her. On the landing she counted seven doors plus her own. Each one was made from a soft golden wood inset with marquetry in a sinuous leaf design, and large gilded curvaceous handles. Helena was sorely tempted to open them all, but when she tried to open the one nearest to her, she quickly discovered that it was locked. A brief moment of frustration, followed by curiosity, brushed across her mind, before she rationalised that locking individual rooms was probably a necessary precaution, in a large and empty house.

Standing at the top of the stairs, she glanced downwards, and then made her way down the wooden steps to the hallway. Here she stopped again, her eyes, which were now used to the low light levels, made it easier for her to see what she hadn't been able to the previous evening. She found the cloakroom and went inside, a small window high up had been cleaned and opened, and she blinked in the light. The loo was clean, but she noticed the water from the flush wasn't totally clear; it had a faint rusty iron colour, which probably accounted for the water stains in the loo's basin. After washing, and then drying her hands on one of the small stack of paper towels, she re-entered the hall, having left the door wide open to provide an additional smidgeon of light into the hall. Having done so, her eyes were immediately drawn to the pair of magnificent entrance doors. The previous night she had had no real opportunity to take in the size or style. With her footsteps echoing on the hall tiles, she

41

made her way to the door and ran her fingers over the glorious dark wood, she marvelled at the hinges and the intricate brass lock. Most of her friends would have found this style unfashionable, but she adored the architecture of the Edwardian period and couldn't wait to see more. She was taking in all the details, when she heard the slow approach of a car, checking her phone for the time; she noted it was almost ten o'clock.

She put her hand on the door handle and tried to turn it, hoping that Manuel or Maria had unlocked it. It was, as it turned out, surprisingly difficult to open, and it took her a few attempts, but eventually it came out of its frame. Through the opening Helena could see that the heavy rain she had woken up to, had now slowed to a light drizzle, and the cloudy sky was more white, than grey. In the drive Senhor Gonçalves had pulled to a stop in roughly the same place as he had been parked the night before. Helena though was slightly puzzled, as she didn't think he was driving a sports car the previous night, but she couldn't be sure. Though she did think a sports car was a little odd for a gentleman of his age and profession. Helena stood on the top step out of the rain and under the cover of the veranda, whilst she waited for Senhor Gonçalves to get out of his car. Five minutes later she was still standing there, her arms wrapped around her chest, and her irritation was inexplicably rising. He must know she was there waiting for him but, it was clear that he was making no attempt to get out of the car, and he seemed to have his mobile glued to his ear.

Recognising that her normal patience was wearing thin, she told herself she must still be feeling tired, and had just resolved to return to the house when the driver's car door opened.

However, it wasn't Senhor Gonçalves her solicitor that got out. Instead, Helena found herself staring at a

42

remarkably handsome, and much younger man probably in his mid-thirties. He wore a pair of well-cut black trousers, black loafers, an open necked white shirt over which was a deep red chunky cardigan. He reached into the passenger seat and retrieved his briefcase, and walked towards her. Helena guessed that he was more than six-foot-tall, with broad shoulders, and a mop of curly blue/black hair. As he advanced up to the top step he held out his hand and said in English.

'Good morning Miss Stratton, my name is Senhor Marco Gonçalves; I have the pleasure of being the estates solicitor. I believe you met my father last night?'

As he spoke, he gave her a light smile but when Helena failed to respond to his greeting, or his question he continued speaking.

'I am sorry to have kept you waiting, but the call I was taking was from my father. I also ask your forgiveness for not being here to meet you personally last night, but I was detained in Lisbon a little longer than I expected, and my father offered to come and meet you instead.'

The intensity of his gaze increased, and his eyes seemed to be boring into her as he gestured to the front door and said

'Miss Stratton shall we go in, it is a little damp out here.'

Galvanized by his comment, Helena shook his proffered hand, and felt an alarming bolt of electricity shoot up her arm, shaking herself she turned, and let herself in before holding the door open for him to enter.

'It's me who should be apologizing,' she said quickly.

'You probably think I am a total nitwit, but I was expecting an older man, not that I mind that your younger of course,'

And then realizing what she had said, her voice trailed off, before she managed to stutter,

'Please do come in, I am sorry it's so dark in here.'

43

Marco brushed past her and waited for her to close the door, which much to her chagrin wouldn't close, despite her shoving it hard several times. After watching her struggle for a little while, he raised his right eyebrow in a faintly amused way and gesturing at the door said,
'Please let me do it, this door has probably only been opened a couple of times in the last forty years, and last night's rain may have made it swell a little.'
Putting down his briefcase, he moved towards the door and with a determined couple of pushes it closed. They stood looking at each other a little uncertainly, until Helena broke the mood.
'We could find a place to sit, but all the rooms appear to be locked do you have the keys Senhor Gonçalves?'
'Actually no, Maria and Manuel have them, we gave them the only complete set, so they could open up the house a few days ago to both air the building, and prepare a room for you. They should be here any minute, as I asked them to meet us just after ten am. My father said they stayed here last night, though normally they live in the small white house with the yellow door and window surrounds just down the road, you will have passed it on your way in last night'.
Helena, who had wrapped her arms around her own body once more, responded in a defensive tone.
'Oh, I see, actually I didn't notice it, or much else to be honest, as you know I was very late, and it was very dark. I really wanted to apologize properly to your father. I kept him waiting here all that time, he must have been frozen, and I feel so guilty. But you see I assumed he would have left, and I was so surprised to see him here, that I really didn't get chance to apologise.'
'You mustn't worry; my father spent the evening very comfortably in the house of Maria and Manuel. Although my father normally works from the Lisbon office, he had a

client to see in Coimbra yesterday, and as he only visits that office occasionally these days, it was lucky for me that he was close by. So when I rang him and said I was running late he offered to meet you. Obviously in the end I could have met you as you were delayed, but we didn't know that at the time. By the way Maria and Manuel are well known to us, and I believe they all three came here together just before you arrived.'

Helena heard him say all of this as if listening through cotton wool, and so the first thing that popped into her head was that she didn't know anything at all about Coimbra, other than it was the site of Portugal's oldest University, and possibly one of the oldest in the world, but she felt strangely compelled to respond to him, so she said the first thing that occurred to her.

'I have never been to Coimbra, though I believe it has a very fine and ancient university. It may be surprising to you to know this is my first ever visit to Portugal.'

Marco Gonçalves raised his left eyebrow, but continued on as if she hadn't said anything.

'My father came to wait for you here, only when he knew you were close by.'

Helena gave him a confused look.

'How could your father possibly have known that?'

'I believe you stopped at the café in Cováo to ask for directions? Alice, the owner knew you were expected so she called Maria, who in turn told my father. As you will discover, if you intend to stay, this is a small community, everyone knows everything even if it's meant to be a secret.'

He smiled which lit up his face; Helena saw that he was even more handsome than she had originally thought. Looking at him properly, she couldn't help but notice his eyes were a deep dark liquid brown, and his eye lashes were long for a man, like her, he also had square bone

45

structure to his face, with broad cheekbones and a manly jaw. A voice inside her head, told her to get a grip he is your solicitor, not a potential suitor, and he is probably married to boot. Helena was saved from any further disconcerting thoughts by a sudden movement from somewhere behind them.

Before she had had an opportunity to say anything else, a middle-aged couple came towards them from the rear of the hall. Helena assumed that they were Maria and Manuel; they looked shyly at her but also with some curiosity, before moving themselves towards Senhor Gonçalves. Maria kissed both of his cheeks and gave him a hug, whilst Manuel gave him a hearty handshake and a further bear hug, a quick and friendly conversation in Portuguese followed. Evidently, they were pleased to see each other. A minute or so later, Senhor Gonçalves turned to Helena, whilst continuing to talk to Maria and Manuel he said in Portuguese,

'Can I introduce you both to Helena Stratton, the owner of the Quinta das Laranjeiras.'

In turn they both said Olá (hello) and Maria speaking in Portuguese asked if Helena had had a good night's sleep.

Helena smiled, this was it, the time had come for her to try out her pretty rusty Portuguese, she had learnt the language from her mum and granddad, but she had hardly used it all since Granddad Silva had died. In California she hadn't much call for it, and whilst she had been practicing at home, using a web site she had found, she knew she was out of practice. She breathed in, looked at them, and shaking Maria's hand first spoke directly to her.

'Bom dia e obrigada, eu dormi muito bem, e foi muito gentil da sua parte me deixar a caixa de frio' this loosely

46

translated to 'good morning, I slept very well, and it was very kind of you to leave me the cool box.'

All three of them looked at her with no small measure of surprise. Marco Gonçalves looked impressed and said, 'You speak Portuguese, I didn't know that, this is going to be a great help to you.'

For some reason, this innocent and generally reassuring remark galvanized Helena who continued speaking in Portuguese.

'Senhor Gonçalves I may be English, but my great grandfather was Portuguese, and he was taught English only as a second language. My grandfather was brought up speaking both languages, mainly because his father preferred to speak in his native tongue. My mum was also taught to speak Portuguese as a child, having bi-lingual mother and grandfather meant I too was taught Portuguese.'

Helena realised she sounded a little priggish, and gave them a small smile before continuing more softly.

'Though I confess, that I only ever expected it would come in useful if I came here on holiday. The fact I am here today in totally different circumstances is taking some getting used to.'

The three people in the hall were watching her with a high degree of interest but they said nothing, so Helena continued addressing her solicitor.

'When we discovered the solicitors address in the letter from granddad da Silva; well we simply had no idea at all. Apparently, mum never ever discussed my granddads letter with my dad. As I am sure you can all imagine, my mum's death has been a terrible shock for my father and I, and now that I am here, I am hoping that you will be able to shed some light on all of this for me.'

Marco, seemed to be thinking how best to reply to this decidedly emotional response from Helena, but in the end decided to simply say,

'I would be pleased if you would consider calling me Marco. We are going to be dealing with each for some time, and if we can be less formal, I think it will help us both on this journey.'

Helena let out a long breath, which she hadn't realised she had been holding in, then she thanked him and said in that case her name was Helena, and she would be pleased if he, and Maria and Manuel called her that.

Marco then spoke in rapid Portuguese to Maria and Manuel, they handed him a large set of keys and then they both disappeared down the right-hand side of the stairs on the ground floor.

'I hope you don't mind but I have asked them to make us some coffee. Maria has brought the necessary ingredients with her, she will also service your bedroom.'

Helena who was not prepared for the later part of the statement, looked aghast, and quickly said that it wasn't necessary for her to clean the bedroom, as she would do that herself.'

At this comment Marco's smile deepened, showing a row of straight white teeth, and he proceeded to shake his head.

'Did I say something funny?' she queried

He responded, but gently.

'Well yes actually, it does seem that I have a lot of information to give you, before you can fully understand what you have inherited.'

Briefly smiling back at him Helena instinctively felt that she could trust this personable man, and she motioned around the hall.

'Okay then, it seems there is no time like the present, shall we find somewhere to sit?'

Rummaging in his briefcase Marco said,
'I have a plan of the house, and I think that the second door over there on the left leads into the drawing room, let's see if these keys are labelled.'
He sorted through the tags on the enormous bunch of keys in front of him, after only a few moments he said triumphantly
'I think this maybe it, shall we try?'
Walking towards the door he indicated, Marco then passed the keys to Helena.
'I really think it should be you who does this. It has been over forty years since anyone from the da Silva family saw these rooms, and it's only fitting you should be the first to do so, go ahead please.'
Helena took the bunch of keys, they were much heavier than she had expected, and consequently they nearly ended up on the floor!
She noted that her hands were trembling a little, but she didn't know if it was with anticipation of what was behind the door, or because she had just received yet another bolt of electricity as Marco had passed her the keys. With unsteady fingers she put the key into the lock and tried to turn it. Nothing happened, so she tried again, but it quickly became clear to her that whatever strength she possessed was going to be insufficient to turn the lock, which perhaps hadn't been opened in almost five decades. Marco stepped forward, and after first looking for confirmation from her said. 'Let me try, it may be very stiff.'
As he put his hand on the large and ornate key, their hands brushed together once again, and Helena felt another unexpected tingle surge through her skin. Marco looked at her questioningly, but immediately turned back to the door and continued to try to undo it unfortunately, it would not budge for him either.

'Clearly I am not as strong as I thought!'

'Perhaps it's the wrong key? It may have been wrongly labelled.'

Helena replied, but Marco who had continued trying shook his head.

'I don't think so, it fits in the mechanism, but I think it may be seized up.' Helena replied without thinking.

'I wonder if we have any WD40 anywhere?' Marco looked at her before asking her

'What is WD40?

'It's a sort of oil spray workmen use to loosen or lubricate mechanical objects, you know like secateurs that have seized.'

Then Helena realised how English that response was, and she gave a nervous laugh.

Marco merely said

'Perhaps Manuel has some in his workshop, let me go and ask.'

Whilst he was gone Helena, stretched her arms, her neck muscles were a bit knotted and she thought that she must be holding herself in tension. Relax she said to herself, it will all be okay just go with the flow.

A few minutes later Marco was back along with Manuel who was carrying a small pot of rather black grease, following a quick exchange in Portuguese, Marco said,

'No WD40 I am afraid, but this is what Manuel uses for greasing parts of the Quinta's garden machinery, let us give it a go.'

Manuel put some of the black grease onto the locking mechanism of the key, before inserting it into the lock.

'This may take a little time' Manuel said Marco, 'Maria has made coffee you can take it in the kitchen, it's the door at the back of the hall on the right-hand side.'

Marco nodded his head and turning to Helena said

Let's go, perhaps I can fill you in on a few things whilst we wait.'

With that Marco and Helena walked in the direction he had indicated, once there, Maria placed on what appeared to be a recently cleaned wooden kitchen table, some coffee, along with a plate of Portuguese custard tarts called Pasteis de Nata. They took seats opposite each other at one end of the table. The kitchen was quite dark, despite the two windows that over looked part of the garden. Helena thought this had something to do with the dark wooden furniture and woodwork. It was quite a large room dominated by the black range, which was placed against the rear wall, it looked as if it was at least as old as the house itself.

Marco watched as Helena poured the coffee into the two cups, she was most definitely not what he was expecting. For one thing she was beautiful even without makeup. Her air of sadness and vulnerability had unexpectedly and somewhat disconcertingly brought out something protective inside and this shocked him. She seemed to him to be totally out of her comfort zone, but he also detected something else, a hint of passion or perhaps a hidden strength, either way he looked directly at her before saying.

'Helena, just how much or little do you know about your great-great grandparents?'

'I know absolutely nothing at all,' she replied shaking her head.

'Obviously, I know that they existed, in the same way we all know that we had ancestors we never met, and having found granddads letter I now know both of their names, but that is the sum of it. To be honest the first tangible knowledge about them came from your firm, after my solicitor had contacted the solicitors named on the note in granddads letter to mum. My father for instance, had no idea that granddad Silva had left mum anything else other than his house in Princethorpe. He thinks she didn't mention it because she couldn't see how any property or land we may have had here in Portugal would have had much value, after all granddads letter is more than a little vague. We can only assume that after reading it she placed it in her keepsake box and forgot all about it. It remained so, until we subsequently found it. You have read it of course.'

Marco nodded in assent, whilst Helena thought to herself that she could recite it from memory.

My darling Sofia,

If you are reading this then I want you to be happy for me, because at long last I am sitting holding hands once again with your mother, whilst looking down on you, William and beautiful Helena. In writing this letter I don't mean to cause you any additional pain but there is a family story - a mystery if you like - which you might want to pursue at some point, it concerns the Portuguese side of my family.

You already know that apart from my mum and dad, I had known virtually nothing about my ancestors. I must have had grandparents but regrettably my parents never spoke of them much. I do know that my father and my grandmother left Portugal for America in 1913, when he was only a small child. My father never really knew his own father, he thought he saw him last when he was about 5 or 6, but I gained the impression he wasn't sure. In tragic and difficult circumstances, he said he lost contact with his mother who was also called Sofia in about 1922/23.

Before I left Pennsylvania to come to England my father gave me the enclosed. It is just the name of a solicitor his mother gave to him, and his parent's names, which are different (I have the feeling that perhaps they were not married) and their approximate birthdates. He told me that his mother had said to him more than once that she had inherited from her grandmother an old village house and some rough land nearby. I think he thought I might want to pursue it, England being much closer to Portugal than to America. I imagine any land is likely to be of little value, and I have never bothered with it. I regret a little not doing so. It is after all my only link with my Portuguese heritage. So my darling Sofia, I leave the solicitors address with you, follow it up if you want. If you don't want to then perhaps darling Helena will be the one to do so. Teaching her Portuguese was a joy for me and perhaps in doing so I have fulfilled part of my duty to that heritage, maybe it would be fitting if it fell to her, a child of this travel mad generation to find out if there is anything behind the story.

Be happy, and don't grieve for me,

Amo and beijinhos (love and kisses)
Dad.

Marco had already seen both pieces of paper, as Elizabeth had emailed copies to his Lisbon office a couple of months ago. The scrap of paper was old, and dated 1918, and it had just the name and address of a solicitor in Maçao, on one side and the name of Luis's mother and father on the other. Helena looked up at him and said

'I assume my great grandfather had given this note to my grandfather just before he and my grandmother emigrated to the UK.'

June 1918
Your parent's names are
Sofia de Jesus Silva born in Vinha Velha, in the
Conselho of Maçao about 1882 and Rafael Alencar,
born about 1866
Nunes solicitors, Rui Velha, Maçao.

Reflecting on what had unfolded ever since Elizabeth had contacted Nunes solicitors, always filled Helena with a sense of what might have been, if earlier generations in her family had pursued it. She knew of course that, 'what if's' are just that, 'what if's' and now it had fallen to her to unravel the story. In truth she was still reeling from its impact. It was just at that moment that she looked up and could both see and feel Marco studying her with concern, but also something else, which she could not identify.
'So' she said looking at him over her coffee, which was surprisingly good, 'What can you tell me?'
'I think the best place is to start at the beginning, from what we know now it's an interesting story. A love story if you will, one in which, passion, duty and ultimately personal pain were much in evidence. This house was

lived in last in1972. That was the year your great-great grandmother Sofia da Jesus Silva died. She lived here for two periods in her life. Firstly, from its original date of construction in 1905, until 1913 when she and Luis left Portugal for America. We found a ship's manifest that shows a Sofia da Jesus Silva and a Luis da Jesus Silva aged 8 travelling on the SS Roma bound for Providence, Rhode Island in 1913. We know she was not at the Quinta in 1914, so I think we can be pretty sure it is they. You will of course have gathered that Sofia and Rafael were not married.'

Helena digested this bit of information for a few moments before replying

'I think Dad and I had guessed that they were not married, so it confirms that, but raises so many more questions.'

'Indeed, it does, but before we delve into that, shall we explore the second period?'

Helena nodded in assent and he continued.

'Sofia on hearing of Rafael's death, in a copy of a Portuguese newspaper her employers had regularly sent over, made the decision to return to Portugal. Obtaining a berth from New York in early 1925. By this time Luis would have been a young man of nearly 21, who we know from Sofia, had some years before moved to Pennsylvania to undertake an indentured apprenticeship as a carpenter with a gentleman and master carpenter, Abel Moorcroft. The next bit is guesswork on our part, as we have no proof it was the same family, but it appears Luis married Eleanor Moorcroft who was probably Abel's daughter. We think they must have married sometime around 1923/4.

We believe Sofia originally intended to return to America, but clearly she didn't, because in late 1925 she was once again resident here in the Quinta das Laranjeiras.'

Helena lifted her head, and shook her hair from her face and said, 'Presumably you can explain that turn of events?'

Marco went on

'Some yes, but regrettably not all, it's a complicated story and we will have to show you documents, some of which are in the Alencar family archive in Porto. I hope your prepared for some travel Helena?'

Nothing about this journey had the capacity to surprise Helena anymore, and so her mind was mulling over these new bits of news when Manuel came into the kitchen and told them that he had managed to free up the seized lock, and stood waiting for them to follow him back.

Helena looked up at this man she had only just met, and who was clearly waiting for her to move, but she was torn between staying, and continuing with Sofia's story, or bolting for the drawing room, so she didn't move. In the end the decision was taken out of her hands, as Marco in response to Manuel's news, stood up and said, 'Shall we?'

They put down their respective coffee cups, and followed Manuel out, walking side by side. They stopped just a few feet outside the door that would give them entrance to the drawing room. With her tummy fluttering she turned the key in the lock and pushed, much to her surprise the large door swung quietly open. At first, she couldn't see anything. The room was totally dark. Gradually as her eyes adjusted to the dimness within, she could make out vague outlines of furniture and other objects but that was all. But Manuel with a torch in hand had already moved ahead of them, and a few moments later they heard the unmistakable sound of metal being drawn against wood, and suddenly morning light entered the room. Manuel had debarred the internal shutters that covered one of the now exposed full height wooden framed glass doors, he then moved onto the remaining shuttered pair.

Helena whose eyes were now adjusting to the light, saw immediately that every piece of furniture in the room, and the objects on the walls, were covered by what looked like ancient and yellowing dust cloths. Close by her side she heard Marco draw in a deep breath, her own body had become so rooted to the floor, that when she heard metal on wood for a second time it made her jump.

She turned in the direction of the noise, just in time to see the shutters opening; but this time instead of light simply filling the room, she saw individual rays of the sun stream in, as outside the sun had at last, broken through the clouds.

In the sun's rays danced millions of individual motes of dust, they seemed to fizz and swirl around as though they had just been released from a deep sleep. They moved as if in a hurry to experience the daylight before it disappeared, apparently anxious to bathe in its bright and warm light.

'That is so beautiful' she said out loud continuing to watch the vortex of dust rise and fall.

'It's probably the first time those shutters have been opened in a very long time' Marco remarked.

'And this dust is even older, we should probably open the doors.'

Manuel, searched for the keys, but when he tried to open them they would not budge.

'More grease is required' he said pulling on the handles.

'Perhaps we should call in a proper locksmith to do this as I expect we will have the same problem with other doors and I wouldn't want to break anything. Shall I give Lionel a call, he is best suited to do this I think?'

Marco nodded in agreement, and Manuel went off to call him, at the same time Helena thought who is Lionel? But she absently replied,

'That sounds like a sensible idea.'

In the meantime, she had turned 180 degrees, and was now closing in on the marble fireplace in the middle of the wall, on the extreme right-side. On either side of the fireplace were what appeared to be matching half-moon tables, and above them were two beautiful wall sconces, made in metal in the shape of a small bouquet of flowers. They were inundated with old spider's webs and they hadn't been wired in, obviously they were designed to take candles only. Over the fireplace covered by a heavy brocade bed cover or maybe it was an old curtain, reposed what Helena thought might be a large frame probably containing a painting of some size. Somewhere deep inside she felt a visceral thrill, the hairs on the back of her neck rose, this physical reaction was followed by an urgent desire to uncover it.

Inexplicably she felt it was important, it's proximity was affecting her physically, her legs felt as though they were pinned to the ground, and her heart was beating a little faster than it should have been. Instinctively she knew it would be a painting of one of her ancestors, but which one? She felt quite odd; it was as though the painting itself was talking to her albeit silently, telling her that it wanted to see daylight very desperately.

But it was obvious even to her that to reach the top of the material would require a tall pair of stepladders, or maybe even a ladder or two. How long she had stood rooted to that spot, contemplating the options for uncovering it, she wasn't sure, however she was woken from her reverie when she heard Marco calling to her.

'Helena, I have found something here, that I think you most definitely will want to see.'

Turning around from her position contemplating the shrouded frame above the fireplace, Helena noticed that one side of a pair of double doors in the left-hand wall of the drawing room had been opened. Manuel, unbeknown to her had returned, and he and Marco were both beckoning her forward. With a great deal of reluctance, she left the fireside, mentally promising the painting she would be back very shortly with the means to free it from its covers.

To approach the double doors, she had to weave her way through the still shrouded furniture that barred the way; both men were just inside the room standing on the left-hand side. As she entered she found herself in a square, perfectly formed library and study. All the walls were wood panelled, and curiously everything in the room was uncovered, making the contrast between it and the drawing room immense. Manuel had already debarred the shutters on the only window in the room, which was west facing and over looked the driveway. Late morning sunlight spilled into the room bouncing of the glass in the bookcases, which were full of leather bound books. The bookcases lined the full width of the south wall, and the majority of the north wall apart from the single door that presumable led back to the main hall. Particles of dust as in the drawing room, danced and swirled in the intermittent rays of sunlight, only to fade from view a few seconds later, as the sun withdrew its penetrating rays. In front of the window, was a handsome and very finely made desk, its carved legs with adjoining c shaped stretchers, was surmounted by two draws on top of which was a fine walnut desk. In front of the desk was a charming cream painted chair, its padded oval back and ample round seat were covered in a cream silk material depicting exotic birds and flowers in what had once been wonderfully jewelled colours. Placed to the rear of the desk was a crystal inkstand, on which lay a very dusty, but obviously gold fountain pen. A glance at the inkwell told her that any ink that had been inside must be long since dried up. In front of the inkstand was a large cream handsomely tooled leather-bound blotter, with its aged and now faded cream blotting paper, and adverts dating back probably to the 1930's. Reclining on the blotter was a second fountain pen, this time black, but with a fine gold top, though this one was ready for use; its gold nib open to the air, with its top simply lying next to it. The fountain pen was set to one side as if the owner had just left the room in the middle of a writing a letter, and would be back shortly to continue to finish it.

Helena noticed that on the right side of the desk was a cream leather paper holder, which contained several sheets of fine quality writing paper, now bent double as if drunk. On top of the blotting paper lay a single sheet placed slightly on an angle.

Helena took in the scene, the single sheet lay exactly at the same angle she preferred when she wrote, and maybe her great-great grandmother had also written on a slight angle too. Helena was disappointed to see that the single sheet was devoid of writing. It was only then that she noticed Marco held in his hands two items, one a single piece of used blotting paper, and in the other some pages of the same writing paper but on which writing could be clearly discerned.

Helena automatically stretched out her hand to take the papers from his proffered hand, saying at the same time, 'What do you have there?'

'I believe it's the start of a letter written by your great-great grandmother Sofia to her son Luis, however it looks like it wasn't finished. I noticed a small piece of the writing paper tucked under the top sheet of the blotting paper, and so I had a look.

It's dated March 1972, which I know was just shortly before she died.'

Helena felt her heart catch, whilst her legs once more felt like jelly, in fact her whole body seemed to be vibrating as she came closer and took the pages from him. Marco pointed to the silk chair and she sat down gratefully, but also rather heavily, causing more dust to rise and gyrate around her. Then she took a deep breath and started to read.

March 1972

My darling Luis,

It has been so very-very long, since I saw you. I have lost count of the times during the last fifty years, when I would have given up everything I own, just to know you were alive and well. There has never been a day when I didn't think about you, and wonder what you might be doing and what you might have become. I fervently hope you married and somewhere in the world I, and your father have grandchildren, and even great grandchildren. That would have been such a joy to me.

I am sorry about my sentimentality, but I am a very old woman, and I feel all my ninety years, and as my life draws to a close I have a deep yearning to set out our story so that you can understand more about your family, should your whereabouts ever be discovered.

I continued to write to you at the address in Pennsylvania until I finally reconciled myself to the distressing fact that you were not receiving my letters. I was frantic with worry, and I guessed that something serious must have happened to prevent

61

you from writing to me. Not knowing what you were doing was like having an open wound, which never healed, but I hoped and prayed that someday I would hear from you again. Sadly, I never did, and I feel that pain acutely every day of my life, more so as I have grown old. However, I still have hope and in case you or your descendants are found this is the hidden truth behind the Quinta das Laranjeiras, it's our story.

In the spring of 1925, some twelve years after we left Portugal, I learned, of the death of your father Rafael. As you can imagine this was news that distressed me greatly. In coming to America I had abandoned a precious and lost life, then my contact with you our only son had been broken, and now my precious love was dead. I felt numb and so alone, I asked God what had I done to deserve such pain and loss, but I received no answer, so I endured.

When I heard the news about Rafael, I spoke to my employer and asked for some time to travel back to the place of my birth, so I could pay my respects. My employers were good Portuguese people, who were very understanding, and they agreed that the two eldest of their children, could do without their governess for a few weeks. So very soon I was on a ship bound for Lisbon. Before I left, even though I hadn't heard from you for three years, I wrote once more and told you this. My investigations since proved of course that you never received this, or any of the letters I had written since 1922.

We had such bad luck darling; I have learnt that my letter of July 1922 telling you of my employers move from Brooklyn to Manhattan, was probably never received by you because it arrived after the awful fire in May that swept away the area you lived in. If you survived the fire and wrote to me subsequently, at my employer's old address, I in turn never received them, so each of us was completely unaware of the changing events in each other's lives

In 1925 I returned to the land of our births, to pay my respects at your father's grave. I think I went back to feel if possible a connection with him one last time, and I fully expected to be returning to New York shortly thereafter.

Except, that was not what fate or God had in store for me. Whilst I stood my lonely vigil at your father's tomb, I was overcome by the strongest feeling that he was urging me to return to the Quinta, the place where for some time we had been happiest. I could not shake the feeling off, the more I thought it fanciful, the stronger the compulsion was. If I am truthful, I was not at all sure I wanted to make this journey. It would be exceedingly painful for me to return to the Quinta, and even more so if I returned and saw members of his new family living there. I also doubted they would be happy to be reminded of his years of indiscretion if they saw me. But the compulsion was so strong I had no choice, and the next day I began the long journey, but in some trepidation. Two days later I arrived in the early afternoon, as I approached the Quinta the familiar smell of pines, and oranges infiltrated my senses. I was overcome by such strong emotions, experiencing such happy and exceedingly painful memories that I almost turned away. But I didn't, I couldn't until I had seen it. The first of many surprises on that day was that as I approached the Quinta it seemed to me to be unoccupied. This was strange because although the main gates were open, the shutters on the windows were all firmly closed. Indeed, it looked more than a bit neglected. I gazed at the front of the house for some minutes, as memory after memory assailed me. I walked round the outside of the house and into the garden, where you used to play; I didn't go to the lake.. The Quinta seemed a little uncared for but not so much as an empty house should have been. I retraced my steps and eventually sat down on the seat under the orange tree in the driveway. I was surprised to feel peculiarly at peace, as this was an emotion that I wasn't expecting. I prayed, and then whilst I was contemplating the still lovely lines of the house, the front door suddenly opened

63

and a gentleman who I did not know came down the steps and walked towards me. Without any preamble, he asked very kindly given I was a stranger to him, if I knew the Quinta. Having acknowledged I used to know it very well indeed, he proceeded to ask me how. I felt no shame as I told him very simply that it was built for me. He then asked me my name, so I told him that my name was Sofia de Jesus Silva and I was the mother of the son of Rafael Alencar de Mascarenhas Silva Brás Noronho e Alencar. To my great surprise his face lit up with a broad smile and he said 'If you can prove that Senhora, then I have some very good news for you.'

News, that truly astounded me. The gentleman you see was your father's solicitor, and whilst sitting down beside me in the shade of the orange tree, he gently and slowly advised me that I had been left the Quinta in Rafael's will, along with an annuity for my lifetime, and a capital sum had been settled on you his acknowledged and only son Luis. Even today I find it amazingly serendipitous that he was present in the house at all that day. Though the strong feeling that I had experienced at your father's graveside, that your father wanted me to visit here I could not easily put to one side. Senhor Gonçalves went on to tell me that he was on one of his bi-annual visits. His firm were obliged by the terms of your fathers will to send a solicitor twice per year to check the state of the house, until I was located, or it was proved that I had died, and your father had no other living heirs. He told me they had placed advertisements in several newspapers searching for me without any luck.

So, my darling son, my life was transformed once again. I found that I could live here in the Quinta after all because your father had wanted me too. In 1926 I instructed an inquiry agent from New York to try to trace you, giving him the address of the Master craftsman you were apprenticed too in Pennsylvania. After some weeks he wrote and told me that his searches had been in vain. He had discovered that in 1922 there had been a serious fire in the vicinity in which you

worked and lived. This fire destroyed the workshop and home of your employer.
Many people lost their lives that night including members of the Master
Carpenter's own family. Those that survived had lost everything, and the whole
community was effectively dispersed. He could find no trace of you or your
employer's family, it appeared they had simply vanished and their whereabouts was
unknown.

This was devastating news, had you been killed, or were you saved to start a new
life? It wasn't until this point I realized you would not have received any of my
letters. Even if you had tried to contact me in Brooklyn, you would not have found
me. I can only imagine what you must have thought if my letters were sent back
unopened. What an unhappy set of circumstances. All I was left with was the
uncertain prospect that that you could be dead and buried, or as I hoped were
living elsewhere starting again. Fate seemed to have cruelly separated us, just as my
fortunes and yours had taken a turn for the better.

I tried many more times over the years, but always my enquiries failed, but I knew
as only a mother knows that you were alive. And even after my death I hope this
letter finds you. I shall in my Will instruct agents once again to try to locate you one
last time, but now it is late, the sun is dropping behind the orange tree, which has
grown large since I planted it. In truth I am feeling more than a little out of sorts
tonight, there is much more to tell you of course, why I felt we had to leave, and of
what happened between me and your father. I will do that tomorrow, and then
hopefully you will more fully understand the circumstances why I felt we had to
leave Portugal.

Helena put the pages down, tears that had been
gathering as she read, now stung her eyes, and fell on to
her cheeks, she tried rather unsuccessfully to brush them

away with the back of her hand. Finally, she gained enough control to say to no one.

'This is so sad, I feel devastated for her, I wonder why she never completed it, and I wonder why is it still here?' As she said this, questions were racing around her head at the revelations in Sofia's letter, and she didn't know which one to seek an answer to first. Only then did she realise she had spoken in English, and Manuel who had heard her, but didn't understand what she had said nevertheless realised she was upset, and he patted her lightly on her shoulder, however, before she could say anymore, Marco with a prescience that must have come from regularly dealing with clients in distress, looked at her and very gently said,

'Sofia was, as I understand it hospitalised for the last few days of her life, she had suffered a massive heart attack. As I found these under this sheet of blotting paper, I think it's likely that the attack occurred before she had time to return to the library to complete it.' Waiting a few minutes before continuing so she could absorb the information, he continued,

'The fact, they were almost entirely covered by the blotting paper, probably means no one saw them when they came to lock up the house. Nothing in here is covered, which is a little unusual as well. I think the house has its own story to tell, and, I am beginning to think that parts of this house may have been covered and locked up for some years prior to her death. Not surprising perhaps, given the size of the house.

When Sofia died, the remaining parts were locked up in haste, and I think we can surmise that no one checked in here. Certainly, her Will never instructed us to search for Luis a further time.'

Helena looked at him questioningly.

'So, you think it has lain here unfinished and unseen for more than four decades?'

'I would think that highly likely yes,' he murmured.

'Do you want to read it?

'If you don't mind I think I will it may add to our knowledge, Sofia was largely solitary, and whilst we know quite a lot about her, everything we learn adds more richness to her story. My father told me that even our yearly visits to see her and deal with the estate were often fleeting. Sofia was interested to know how her investments were doing other than that she had little to say to us most of the time. Her relationship with my grandfather was very strong, but with my father it became, well, more business-like.'

As he took the offered pages from her, Marco turned and spoke to Manuel.

'Manuel could Maria make some more tea or coffee, and do you have any brandy or port anywhere as I think Miss Stratton has had a shock.'

Manuel excited by the double doors, and went to find his wife.

Helena continued sitting in the chair, her elbow was upright on the desk, and her chin was resting on her right hand, but her mind was grappling with all that she had learned from reading the half-finished letter. She was rather glad that her father would be joining her here at the Quinta in a couple of days' time, she desperately needed someone to talk to, who could help her make sense of these continuing, unexpected and frustrating events.

A few minutes later Marco looked up from the pages and said.

'This does explain a few gaps in our knowledge. I think in the early years of her return here much of what she shared with my grandfather her then solicitors were perhaps not as fully documented as would be today. As I

67

said their relationship was more informal, and the 1920's were a difficult time here in Portugal. People kept themselves to themselves, especially out here in the countryside. I have gained the impression from my father that Sofia was quite secretive, perhaps she never felt totally secure here, despite the Will being very clear.' Helena nodded thoughtfully,

'I wonder why Luis and Eleanor never tried to find Sofia after the fire? They clearly survived and went on to have my grandfather.'

'We don't know that they didn't try, perhaps they did; but if your grandfather didn't know about it, or perhaps didn't communicate to your mother, then I guess it's a question that is likely to remain unanswered forever.'

'It could be he didn't know of course. My grandfather I mean. He wasn't secretive, so I am sure when my mum found the letter after his death, she probably thought it was a trifle odd, just like we did. I think we can infer from the letter that he never mentioned it to her whilst he was alive. Dad and I have talked about this endlessly, and all we can come up with is, that in the aftermath of his death, having to handle his effects, she simply put it to one side. Like me, she must have thought she would have been pursuing a small and potentially abandoned house. She couldn't have had any idea as to the extent of the legacy, or surely she would have pursued it earlier?' Helena said this rather sadly.

'They were different times, and presumably your mother had her own life to pursue, you and your father to look after, perhaps she thought she didn't have the time or energy to be chasing a phantasm.

Marco replied, before asking her if she wanted some air. Helena shook herself.

'No, no thank you but I do need something to take my mind off this for a while. I want to take the cover of the

picture above the fireplace in the drawing room, do you think we could ask Manuel if he might help me?'
Marco looked at her, and wiping a bit of dust from his hands on a handkerchief he pulled from his pocket replied,
'Certainly, you employ him after all.'
Helena gave him a puzzled look, before saying to him.
'I do? I had no idea.'
She gave him a wan smile.
'I'm sorry, I assumed you had just asked them to help out, was that on the list of things we were going to discuss today?'
Marco pointed to his briefcase.
'Yes it was, and there are many other points we will need to discuss, but the majority will now have to wait until Monday, I am afraid I must leave shortly, we have a family wedding this afternoon, and I must pick up Isabel by two o'clock.'
Helena felt a stab of regret and checked her watch.
'Oh dear, I had completely lost track of time, it's the weekend and I guess you don't normally work on a Saturday. My apologies, please don't feel the need to stay, we can catch up on Monday.'
But to Marco, Helena looked dejected by his statement.
Helena, even as she spoke the words, knew it wasn't what she wanted. In fact, she desperately wanted to get some handle on what she had inherited, but she also knew it would be unfair to press for him to stay.
Marco though sensed her disappointment; he looked at his own watch, and seemed to make a decision, before saying much to his own surprise and hers.
'Listen I can spare another hour or so, and still make it. That should be enough time for me to give you some basic facts, do you want to stay in here or return to the

kitchen? I am sure I could find another chair if you prefer to remain here?'

Helena gave him a grateful look.

'No, let's go to the kitchen, then I can ask Manuel to look for a ladder, and we can drink the coffee Maria is making.'

Inside she felt better knowing he wasn't leaving just yet, and that she may be able to gain some sort of handle on the Quinta, and the financial situation. Together, they made their way through to the kitchen, and in her slightly rusty Portuguese Helena asked Manuel if he knew where there were step ladders high enough to for them to be used to uncover the painting above the fireplace.

'Yes, I will fetch them.'

He turned and then disappeared through a door at the rear of the kitchen next to a large and old cabinet, on which was displayed dusty plates, dishes and kitchen paraphernalia.

Maria who had been busy cleaning the dresser, stopped when they entered and brought them the coffee, but apologized and admitted they didn't have any alcohol other than wine on the premises.

'It doesn't matter, I am okay now, the coffee will be more than enough thank you Maria, oh and would you mind awfully looking to see if there is a second bedroom that my dad could use when he arrives on Tuesday, I am more than happy to help with any cleaning required to make it habitable?'

With a smile, and a swift nod of her head, Maria accepted the challenge, and also left, leaving the two of them together.

'So' said Helena, 'I suppose it would be best to understand the arrangement with Manuel and Maria, you said they worked for me, so what are their roles?'

'As a couple they are retained by us as the executors of Sofia's estate mainly in the capacity as caretakers. They ensure the gardens around the house; the land, the olive and fruit groves are kept in a reasonable clean condition to comply with the fire regulations. Currently the estate does not harvest what is grown here, we on the estates behalf sell the rights to harvest the crops to local producers. In turn the local producers maintain the trees etc. Manuel liaises with them to ensure compliance, and in addition to keeping a watch on the land, they also report any problems they see with the exterior of house. They are actually very good and tend to let us know quite quickly which allows us to make repairs in good time. What they are paid is, I think reasonable for this caretaking responsibility. As part of their remuneration, they have one of the number of small houses in the grounds, rent and repair free, and an annual retainer of six thousand euros. This money is deducted from the estate annually as per Sofia's wishes; she always had a couple to help out. It is a modest income by British standards, but they have the use of half an acre of land around their house, and so they grow their own vegetables, and keep chickens and a couple of goats.'

Helena was contemplating this arrangement, when Marco as if reading her thoughts went on,

'I imagine they are anxious to know if they will still be needed, but I don't think you need to make any decisions for a while yet.'

Replying more to his last comment than any other, Helena said,

'I fully understand, but I wouldn't want them to fret unnecessarily. Do you think perhaps you could let them know that they are not to worry, I can't see me doing anything in the next few months or so to affect the status quo as far as they are concerned.'

She paused, 'I think my Portuguese is perhaps at the moment insufficient for conveying this to them.'

Marco with some relief showing on his face replied, 'Of course, I can, but from what I have heard so far, your grasp of our language is pretty good, maybe the accent is a bit odd but if you decide to stay here that will improve quickly.'

He gave her an encouraging smile, and noticed that her shoulders relaxed a little.

He had been surprised when he first saw Helena, standing on the top of the steps, he had a picture in his mind of the woman he thought had inherited this sizeable estate, but Helena was nothing like it. She seemed to him to be quite fragile, uncertain, even overwhelmed by it. He knew, from his conversations with Elizabeth Briggs, that Helena and her father had no idea at all about the Quinta. Indeed, Elizabeth had been at pains to point out that they were both still in considerable shock at having lost their Sofia so young, and these latest revelations whilst providing a welcome distraction, had nonetheless compounded their sense of loss. Marco could understand that, Elizabeth had told him quite a lot about Helena and William, so he knew that Helena had taken a sabbatical from her job in America, to help care for her mum during her terminal illness, and support her dad. He also knew, as Elizabeth had mentioned it in passing, that Helena's long-term partner had unceremoniously split up with her only a matter of weeks ago, thereby ending a five-year plus relationship.

Marco knew Helena must be intelligent, but he wondered how she was going to react to the news about the size of her inheritance. He found somewhat inexplicably that he was worried for her. She seemed a little delicate, wandering round with her arms wrapped around her chest, with her flashing green eyes that reflected the colour of her jumper. He wanted to encourage her as much as he could, and he had to admit to himself that he found her surprisingly attractive, and that was definitely something he hadn't expected. His own life was currently complicated enough on several fronts. Work was becoming increasingly difficult, and on top of this he was uncomfortable with the fact that Isabel felt more for him than he could reciprocate. Even now he wasn't sure how that had happened, as he believed he had always behaved towards her like she was an old friend, and nothing more. Well, perhaps this afternoon he should try, if the opportunity arose, to gently make clear his feelings for her didn't include love, let alone marriage. He hoped it wouldn't make Mondays meeting with Helena awkward, as this had nothing to do with her.

He realised that a silence had descended, and quickly he roused himself to concentrate on the job in hand. With what he hoped was an encouraging smile on his face he turned to Helena and said,

'Perhaps a brief overview of the extent of the Quinta, and the financial position may be useful next, it will help you put into perspective what you have inherited. Also, it may help your thinking, about what you might want to do. Firstly though, you should know that we have made an appointment at the bank for you on Monday morning, where you can open your own accounts. Until this is done we can't transfer any of the funds from the existing accounts. Isabel Raposa, the local manager of the Montepio Bank, is going to meet you at ten o'clock. I, or one of my senior staff can join you as well if you wish. There are other banks of course but currently the Quinta's three accounts are held with Montepio, so it would be seamless to do the transfer, but it is up to you.'

Helena thanked him, and said she was happy to be guided by him, and then accepted his offer to have someone with her; she figured that having someone to support her through these necessary transactions would be helpful. She couldn't help but think a lot was going to happen very fast, and once again she wished that her dad was here to lean on; she would phone him this evening and thought cheered her somewhat, so trying to sound positive she turned to Marco,

'Okay so hit me with the details, I promise I will try to take is all in.'

He reached inside his briefcase and took out two folders.

'This one is for you, please read it at your leisure, and after we have visited the bank on Monday, I can answer any queries you may have.'

Helena smiled to herself, so he was intending to come to the bank on Monday, rather than send a member of staff, inside her a little bubble of happiness welled up at this knowledge.

'That would be really great, I am sure to have many questions for you.' Marco nodded.

'Perhaps we should start with the basic facts about the Quinta and then move on to the financial side.'

Helena nodded in assent, and Marco continued

'The highlights are that the Quinta das Laranjeiras has grown quite large over the years. Your great-great grandmother invested in more land, and so now there is a total of 34 hectares. Several crops are grown, but by far the largest part of the land is given over to olive production. In total there are 22 hectares of Olive trees, of the Picual specie these are good for making azeite or what you would call olive oil. There are about two acres of cerejas (cherry) orchards, and just over 2 hectares of vines. Many of these vines are very old, there are about 6500 vines made up of .6 of a hectare of Cabernet Sauvignon, .9 of a hectare is Tourega Nacional and the remaining .5 is Petit Verdoux.'

On hearing this Helena was surprised, she knew of the grape varietals, and her immediate thought was that they should make good wines; she noted that for a later discussion.

Marco continued,

'There are approximately 700 fruit trees, including plums, pears, apples, figs, oranges, lemons almonds, apricots, and peaches. Also, there is a about a hectare of cork oaks, 3 hectares of eucalyptus, and some lovely specimens of centenarian olive trees. In addition, there is an acre of vegetable garden and various areas of ornamental gardens and a small lake around the house. There is a small dam the source of water is drawn up from deep underground sources as well as the run off from the local river.'

Marco then paused to give these facts time to sink in. Helena looked very confused and more than a little surprised, so he said

'It's all set out inside the folder, so you can read more at your own pace' Helena nodded vaguely but didn't speak so he continued

'Lastly of course there is the Quinta itself, quite a lot of outbuildings and six small houses dotted around the estate. Apart from the one Manuel and Maria use the remainder are empty but in a reasonable condition. In truth, they are very old and don't have modern facilities, a bit like the Quinta itself, which needs a great deal of modernisation!'

At last Helena found her voice and resorting back to English said in a shocked voice,

'I don't know what to say; I originally thought I had inherited an old house and a few acres of land, this is, well this is a different kettle of fish. How am I going to manage all of this?'

Marco, gave her a look which was a cross between amusement and fascination before saying in a quiet voice,

'If it proves too much for you, you could always sell up.'
Helena looked at him horrified,

'No, actually I couldn't do that, I am not a quitter, at least not until I know what I am letting myself in for, and decide its beyond me, however knowing about the vines intrigues me, so some food for thought.'

Marco was encouraged, so she did have some fight in her, and that might be all she needed.

'Good. Okay that's the bare bones of the estate itself, as I said the detail is in the folder, and my advice is to get on a horse and go and see it all. It's a great way of getting some perspective.'

'But' Helena squeaked 'I don't have a horse, and anyway I haven't ridden since I was 15!'

'Oh, didn't I mention the stable block? There are two horses, and a couple of donkeys, these are yours too. Hugo Coelho looks after them on his land, but you could always bring them back here, I am sure he will have equipment you can use.'

He was nearly laughing now, as he saw the confusion writ large on her face.

'Is there anything else you have forgotten, like I own a gold mine or four hundred hens?'

'No Miss Stratton, no gold mine but there must be chickens somewhere, I just don't have the number, would you like me to go and count them?'

On hearing this Helena let out a peal of slightly hysterical laughter, and had the good grace to look sheepish.

'I'm being ridiculous aren't I. I am so sorry, but it is such a lot to take in, I feel completely overwhelmed.'

'Do you want to leave the finances for another day, when you have your head around the estate?'

'Tempting as that is, no, I don't think so. I might as well have it all. I am not going to sleep tonight anyway so do your worst.'

'Well if you're sure, let me give you the financial basics, bearing in mind Isabel Raposa will go through all of it in great detail on Monday.

Helena suddenly said, is Isabel Raposa related to you? If Marco was surprised by this sudden change of direction, he didn't show it, and simply said,

'No, but she is an old friend, it is her I am picking up to take the wedding.'

Helena nodded, and felt a prick of something remarkably like jealousy, which she acknowledged was ridiculous as she had only met him a few hours ago, and he was her solicitor, she fought off the irrational thought, by asking him to go on.

Marco, then took from his briefcase a second folder, and opened it at the first page before continuing.

'The Quinta has three accounts, the first is the business account, all the income and debts of the Quinta are paid into or out of it. This is the account that pays Manuel and Maria's salary, as well as repairs to the buildings, the grounds and boundaries. As of yesterday, this account held two million, one hundred and fifty-six thousand euros.'

Helena looked at him in complete astonishment on hearing this, but she did not have the chance to say anything, because Marco went on,

'The second account contains Sofia's private funds, it's basically made up of the total of the unspent funds from her annuity, plus interest, it also includes any income from her own investments. Since she died, of course no new funds have been received apart from the annual interest from our investments on her behalf, but it has been well invested and continues to grow. At any one time fifty per cent of this account has been invested in government bonds, in line with the terms of her will. Again, as of yesterday this account held approximately one million and six hundred and sixty-seven thousand, this year's interest from the investments won't be received until end of December.

Helena's jaw dropped.

'Wait a minute.'

She shook her head, and pushed her hand through her curls. 'Just give me time to compute.' Marco watched her intently.

'Are you telling me that I inherit nearly 3.8 million pounds?'

Marco, looked up from his spreadsheet, and rubbed the bridge of his nose.

'Well actually no you don't,' and noting the confusion on Helena's face, went on quickly to clarify,

'Firstly, its Euros not British pounds, and secondly we have not yet discussed the third and final account shall I continue?'

He said this with a hint of amusement playing on his face. Helena still reeling from his last disclosure swallowed hard and nodded her assent. Marco looked down at his spread sheet.

'Lastly, the third account is the sum of the initial capital plus it's accumulated interest that was set aside for Sofia's son Luis. All the capital has been invested since Rafael died. This money was held in a slightly complicated Trust. Complicated, because under the terms of Rafael's will, this money was left solely for the use of Luis, or his direct descendants. When Sofia was told of the provisions for this part of Rafael's estate, she worked quickly to ensure that he or his direct descendants well into the future could still claim it. At the time she herself had no idea where he was, and in turn the Alencar solicitors were in the dark about this fact. Sofia felt it necessary to negotiate an agreement with the Alencar's, which set out what would happen to the legacy, if Luis himself never claimed it. The agreement that resulted was a work of pure genius on her part, and the Alencar's of course agreed because they assumed that Luis would come forward in her lifetime. I don't believe they thought they would still be dealing with the de Silva's beyond her lifetime.

So, the agreement was drawn up and signed, it set out, that if in her lifetime Luis or no direct descendant of his came forward to claim it, the sum held in Trust would fifty years and one day after her death revert to the Alencar family. This seemed to her to be a good compromise. Giving sufficient time for any direct family to come forward and if not, it would be returned to the family of her beloved Rafael. This arrangement is specifically expressed under the terms of Sofia's will. Clearly, you are the only living direct descendent and you will have claimed the inheritance within the fifty years and one-day time restriction. The Alencar family has managed the Trust fund since that time, on his and his heir's behalf; hence they have been meticulous in investing it. As of the end of March this Trust had a value of seven million six hundred and twenty-one thousand euros.'

Helena felt all the blood drain from her face. She stared at Marco as if he was the bearer of bad tidings. She felt cold all over, and an involuntary shiver ran the length of her body. She looked at Marco's impassive face.

'You're not joking, are you?' she stammered out, in a barely a squeak. She swallowed hard, her throat felt like it had dried up.

'You're seriously telling me I have inherited over eleven million pounds?

'No,' he said with the hint of a smile on his face.

'I remind you again, that the inheritance is in euros not pounds, so at the current exchange rate of 1.20 euros to the GBP that's about 9.5 million pounds.'

He smiled as he said it though.

'Congratulations Miss Stratton it is a fine inheritance, but should you decide to continue with the Quinta. I think that a large amount of what you have inherited will need to be invested in her, if she is to become a modern house as well as a profitable business concern. So you may want to reconsider at your leisure whether you remain or sell up.'

Sitting in the cold kitchen with its old-fashioned range, wooden table and ancient fittings, it was easy to see what he meant, but Helena already knew that in less than 24 hours the Quinta had begun to get under her skin, and she wasn't sure she could walk away from it so easily. Quickly she asked him.

'Do you know what the current value of the Quinta and its land is?

'That is a very interesting question, to be honest it's worth what anyone is prepared to pay for it. Our economy has been severely hit by the global downturn so it's difficult to say with accuracy. However, we know that generally property prices are severely depressed, so our current book value of 3.9 million euros is likely to be much higher than its actual market value. As you have already seen the Quinta requires a lot of modernization, and farms are not necessarily what the market wants currently.'

It seemed to Helena, that in asking this specific question Marco's demeanour had changed, had he become a little more formal, and perhaps less friendly, or was that just her imagination? He went on

'You could put it up for sale to test its current value, of course, is this what you would like us to do?'

Helena prickled and in a voice more strident than she meant said

'Absolutely not, I was just trying to get my head round the extent of it, both in monetary and land terms. It seems I have inherited over eleven million euros in bank accounts, hectares of productive land, and a Quinta worth millions of pounds. It's a hell of a lot to take in when only two months ago all I owned was an old mini car, and a savings account with a few thousand pounds in it. I think it's essential to speak to my dad, he has a sensible head on him, and as you say I need to digest what you have told me. I also should have some idea of what I would want to do with the place, if I were to keep it. I guess the vineyards must yield about ten thousand litres of wine per year, but as for olive oil I have no idea.'

Marco, who had visibly relaxed on hearing Helena's response, reminded her.

'Currently the Quinta does not produce either oil or wine, so I have no idea of the production figures. You would have to talk to other specialists about that, but I can put you in touch with some if you want, and the current contractors would also be able to give you some details of current production levels, if you asked.'

Helena however, knew about wine production. This was what she and Tom were doing in California, managing a boutique vineyard for the De Brett family. Yes, she knew about viticulture, and how could olive oil be so different? Ideas began to form in her mind. One step at a time she told herself, one step at a time.

She got up from the kitchen chair, and checked her watch before reluctantly thanking Marco for his time and patience.

'I need some fresh air let me walk you to your car.'

Marco packed his folder into his brief case, and told her that he would give her back the letter from Sofia to Luis on Monday, when he met her at the bank if that was okay with her.'

'Yes of course it is, I look forward to seeing you then.' she replied moving towards the door.

'Just one more thing Helena, we took the liberty of withdrawing five thousand euros from the Quinta's business account on Friday, in case you needed any ready cash.'

He took out of his briefcase a grey envelope and handed it to her. She couldn't recall ever handling this amount of money, and it felt very odd, she wanted to throw it up in the air and see what it looked like, but she also realised that would be very silly, and not at all business like. Marco who had been watching her closely said.

'On Monday, once the accounts are transferred you can access as much or as little as you like, but in the meantime my father thought though you may need to agree some works before then and of course here in Portugal you might need to pay deposits in advance. He suggested speaking to Senhor Vitor Martins, a local builder who should be able to give you a well-priced quote on what it would take to get the house up to modern standards for instance, I have his number here.'

He handed her a small piece of paper with a number on it.

'About 7 pm is a good time to get hold of him before he drinks too many red wines in café central.'

He gave her a small wink, and she smiled.

'Thank you for that, please tell your father I am grateful for his help, and I will give Senhor Martins a call sometime later.'

They walked in silence to the front doors, and down the steps, where they shook hands, and again Helena felt a small frisson of something strange, like a tingle from an electric shock, and she was sure he had felt it too. Marco let go of her hand and was just about to get into his car, when he hesitated and pulled out his wallet from his trouser pocket, after looking inside he took out a small card and wrote something on the reverse side before offering it to her.

'My personal mobile number is on the back, if you need to speak to me please do call me on this number.'

Helena took the card from his hand, being careful not to make contact with his hand, but looked at him with gratitude spreading through her face.

'Thank you for this, I really appreciate it and I promise not to use it unless I have too.'

He acknowledged her, before getting in the car and winding down the window,

'Manuel and Maria will help you all they can, and in Vila de Rei there is a nice Churrasqueira, they do great BBQ chicken, goodbye then until Monday.'

Helena, said to him 'Enjoy the wedding.'

And with that the engine started, and the car disappeared down the drive. Helena stood watching it go, before turning around and re-entering the house.

Back inside the hall, Helena was unsure what she should do next. As she was debating this, Manuel entered and seeing her in two minds wandered up to her, and his slightly singsong voice said.

'My cousin Lionel should be here in a couple of hours, and he will be able to assess the situation with respect to the door locks, but he might not come, sometimes he is a little unreliable.'

He then made a gesture with his thumb pointing it towards his mouth a couple of times, seemingly a sign that indicated that he had a tendency to drink too much. Helena thanked him for his efforts before replying with 'Vamos ver', which in English means 'we are going to see' before continuing with,

'Manuel did you manage to find some ladders?'

Manuel nodded vigorously.

'Yes Menina.' Helena smiled at his use of this word, whose literal translation was 'girl'. However, she knew it was a term often used by older people to address a younger woman in polite and friendly terms. Her grandfather had called her mother and her by this term, and he told her that, her parents could call a woman of sixty Menina! She smiled at his automatic use of the term, but said.

'Please call me Helena' she said to him. 'I prefer it.'

'Okay, Menina, I mean Helena, I have put them in the drawing room.'

'Can you help me then, that is, if you have time, I want to take the covers of the portrait.'

'Of course. It's not a problem for me,' he replied.

'But I will fetch Maria as well, as we will need to move a few things out of the way, so we can have better access.'

As he left to fetch Maria, Helena noticed he limped a little, and made a mental note to ask if this was a just current problem or an old injury.

After remaining in the hall for only a few minutes, Manuel and Maria returned, and all three of them entered the drawing room. It seemed to Helena, that they were all a little uncomfortable. She really didn't know how to treat them, and it seems they were a little wary of her. Maria was still wearing her pinafore just as she had when Helena first met her, she had a couple of cobwebs in her hair and on the back of her sleeve. Helena tried to lighten the mood and pointing to them said

'I guess by the eccentric covering of cobwebs a bedroom for my dad has been found?'

'Yes Menina, perhaps when we have finished here you can come and see, it needs a bit of a deep clean, but I think it could be a lovely room.'

'Fantastic. Once I have done this shall we go and look together?'

Helena gave her a smile of friendship and reassurance, as she turned once again to face the fireplace.

Maria nodded, then silence resumed. It seemed that both Manuel and Maria were obviously waiting for her to make some sort of move. Helena, whose sensitivity to those around her was something of a legend, turned to Manuel, and asked him how he thought it best to proceed. His chest swelled a little, and he was clearly pleased she had sought his opinion, and he proceeded to tell her what he thought. Having listened to what he said, and appearing to give it consideration she agreed.

'Okay Manuel, when your ready shall we see what we have under here?'

Manuel manoeuvred the ladder until it leaned against the wall over the centre of the painting.

'First, I need to see how this cover has been fixed, and then we can decide how to remove it.'

He stepped on the first rung and made his way up to a level on the ladders where he could view the top of the frame.

'It is draped down the back a little way, and it feels quite heavy. We may need two of us one on either side to remove the cloth so that we do it without causing problems. I will fetch another ladder, I am pretty sure there is second one in the barn out the back.' He climbed down, muttering

'I won't be long!'

As he hurried out of the room. The ladies could hear his footsteps echo on the solid floor of the hall. Helena who had now turned to face Maria said,

'Maria, how long have you and Manuel worked here at the Quinta?'

'Twenty-two years, we took over from Manuel's father, when he broke his hip. Silly old fool fell out of an olive tree he was pruning in the garden, and then he couldn't move. Unfortunately for him, he wasn't found for several hours because he lived here alone. Once he came back from the hospital it was obvious that he couldn't continue his duties here. Manuel and I had only just married and Senhor Gonçalves asked us if we would like the job and the living, we were over the moon. To have my own house what a stroke of luck, even if Manuel's dad lived with us until he died!'

'I am sorry to hear that.'

Maria gave a shrug of her shoulders before replying,

'It was a long time ago and he was an old rogue. He loved nothing more than being waited on hand and foot. He used to sit out there under the old orange tree, drink red wine, and smoke his filthy rollups with a variety of other old folk who turned up to have chat, and then he would demand lunch for all!

Quite a character was Rui, right until the day he died. At his funeral, many people said he had led a charmed life, perhaps they were right I wouldn't have minded eight years sitting under that tree being indulged by my daughter in law!'

Helena laughed, as Maria had said this in an affectionate way, and it was obvious to her that despite him being an old rogue, she had liked the old man a lot. Helena was about to ask about how Manuel acquired his limp, but before she could continue the conversation, the sound of Manuel coming through the hall with a ladder stopped her. He had been gone quite a few minutes, and the reason for that now became clear. He entered the drawing room followed by an older man who he introduced to Helena as his cousin Lionel.

'Lionel helped me with the ladder, it was difficult to extricate, and better still he has offered his help with removing the cloth, before he takes a look at the locks.'

Helena went over to him and shook his hand and said she was pleased to meet him, and that it was good of him to offer to help, to which he responded with a nod, the hint of alcohol on his breath was more than masked by the strong smell of garlic and cigarette smoke.

Quickly returning to Maria's side, Helena thought maybe he was a man of few words, but when she was alongside her, Maria whispered.

'Not good, he is just nosey, he drinks too much red wine, and helping out is just a good excuse to have a look around, and delay starting work!'

Helena just about managed to stifle a laugh remembering what Marco had told her about not being able to have secrets here, and it seemed to her that she was perhaps the new object of local attention and gossip.

With crossed arms and looking quite stern Maria, joined by Helena watched as the two men positioned the ladders either side of the portraits frame. Climbing up to a level where they could reach the cloth on either side they took hold of the cloth and very gently tugged at it. Clouds of dust started to rise from the old cloth and eddy around, Lionel began to cough immediately, and then he began to sneeze, as the effects of forty or more years of accumulated dust began to have an effect. It was quite funny really, Helena and Maria tried to stifle laughs but the comical sight of Lionel on a ladder trying to stop sneezing just made matters worse! After a few minutes the two guys came down the ladders and went outside, into the fresh air, to allow the sneezing to stop, Maria, went and fetched bottles of water, whilst the dust subsided. Ten minutes later with handkerchiefs tied around their noses and mouths, and looking more like robbers than workers, they continued. Pulling the cloth gently upwards just released more waves of dust, filling the air and swirling around in the rays of the sun. More vigorous tugging then commenced and a few minutes later the cloth was freed. As it fell, a fresh burst of dust was released, which was sent roiling around the immediate vicinity. Followed shortly afterwards by a final tsunami of dust, as the cloth itself landed partly on the floor and partly on the marble hearth of the fireplace with dust erupting like ash from a volcano. Lionel started to cough once more, and Helena who had covered her mouth sneezed, but slowly very slowly the dust began to subside and what was revealed was not what any of them had expected.

Helena's first reaction was one of mild disappointment, it wasn't the front view of the portrait that she was expecting. Instead it was the back of a large and old canvas.

Manuel turning to Lionel, who by now had his coughing reasonably under control, limited himself to saying,
'We will need to bring it down, so we can turn it around, but I think it is going to be too heavy for the two of us on our own. We need a couple of people underneath it to secure it as we pass it down.'
In her eagerness to see the picture Helena suggested that perhaps she and Maria could help. Manuel shook his head and looked at her.
'I think we needed a couple of young strong men; this is heavy, and if we don't secure it properly and it is dropped both the frame and the picture might be damaged.'
Clearly Helena who didn't want to do anything that might cause damage reluctantly nodded in agreement.
'So Manuel, where are we going to find two fit and healthy young men?'
Surprisingly it was Lionel who, in a voice deep and crusty responded.
'I will call a couple of cousin's, I am sure they would be willing to help this evening after they have finished work.'
Helena was surprised at the sound of his voice, which was almost the exact opposite of the man himself. Lionel was tallish but stick thin, and she had imagined his voice would be high and reedy, instead, he had a deep bass tonal quality, and she wondered, rather irrationally, if he could sing.
Manuel in response to Lionel's offer merely waggled his head, and that was that. It seemed to Helena that she was going to have to wait a little longer to see who was in the painting. She was thoroughly intrigued to know why the painting itself had been turned to face the wall, it was as if her great-great grandmother Sofia didn't want to see it.
Slowly, both Lionel and Manuel descended the ladders, and chatted for a few moments, then Lionel pulled out his

mobile phone, and went outside to make a call to the two 'cousins'. Once the call was made, he and Manuel proceeded to look at the locks on the drawing room exterior doors.

Maria, asked Helena if she was hungry, her stomach answered for her by rumbling in agreement, so they made their way to the kitchen. Once inside Maria produced from a cool box, a couple of cheeses, a loaf of bread, dish of olives, a bottle of dark green olive oil inside of which was half a dozen garlic cloves, and some plump ripe tomatoes. They sat down and helped themselves to the food, chewing contentedly in silence. The bread was soft and the cheeses tangy, the garlicky olive oil was surprisingly strong and pungent, and very fruity. After a while Helena thanked her for the lunch, which Maria then explained was really 'lanchar' or afternoon tea given it was nearly fifteen minutes past four. Maria covered up the food that remained, before asking Helena if she wanted to see the bedroom she had chosen for her dad. 'Yes, let's do that,' Helena replied with a great deal of enthusiasm. If she couldn't see the picture perhaps looking in a new room would be some consolation. Leaving the kitchen, they crossed the hall and proceeded up the stairs. Maria walked ahead passing Helena's bedroom and entering the last room on the left.

This room was actually much larger than the one Helena had slept in last night, and it was also furnished somewhat differently. It had two large windows on one side and a third facing forward. Immediately she realized it must be partly be over the drawing room and the library below. Maria had managed to open the shutters and the room was very light and airy, the afternoon sun bathed the room in soft golden light.

'This will do very well Maria, dad will love it, we will need to buy a new mattress and bed linen, and can we get these by Tuesday?'

'I will call Senhor Zé on Monday and make the order, I am sure he can obtain one even if he has to fetch it from the central warehouse. I will give the room a good clean on Monday.'

Whilst in the room, Helena had a 'light bulb' moment, subconsciously she must have been giving some thought to all the work that was going to be required if she was going to live here, because she suddenly realised that most of it would be highly specialized requiring professional input. This would not only be disruptive, but it would inevitably cause a lot of mess. Even though she had been here less than twenty-four hours, her previous decision to live here while any work carried on around her, now seemed at best ridiculous at worst completely mad. In reality the size of the house and its needs were on a scale she could not have imagined. She wondered to herself if there was another alternative?

'Maria, I understand that there are other properties on the estate are any of them habitable?'

Maria shook her head 'I don't think so, apart from ours none have electricity, or bathrooms, they have not been occupied for many years.'

At hearing these words Helena's heart sank a little, still she mused it can't be that difficult to make one small house habitable quickly, she had the money now, so she resolved to ask Manuel to recommend to her a good but rapid builder. Then she remembered what Marco had told her about Senhor Martins. As she thought of this the idea of renting a house came into mind, perhaps there were houses for rent nearby? It might be good for her to pursue this as an option, she would check that out too tomorrow. But for now, she kept her ideas to herself.

91

After her musings about alternative accommodation, Helena was deliberating whether to walk around the remainder of the house, or to venture out into the grounds in the immediate vicinity. Her desire to enjoy the journey, vied with her impatience to see everything at once, but this inevitable tug of war ended today with a win for her sensible side. Reminded, as she was that if she did, she would be reverting to childhood, and behaving like an over excited child who couldn't wait until Christmas morning.

Helena, remembered fondly the Christmas's of her childhood when, having woken up at some ungodly hour of the morning and realising it was Christmas day, she would run down the stairs and on opening the door to the living room would see the huge pile of presents under the Christmas tree.

It was always a real tree, with large red baubles, gold tinsel and twinkling fairy lights, and the room would smell of pine. On the mantle shelf she would first check if Santa had eaten the mince pie as well as taken the carrot for Rudolf. Back then she had loved the thrill of tearing off the wrapping paper, which at the time seemed more interesting than really appreciating the presents inside! With those reminiscence's in mind she steeled herself not to release her inner child by rushing into each room, after all, these 'presents' had been here for more than nine or ten decades and they would still be here tomorrow and the day after and the day after that.

Holding that thought she found Maria and Manuel and let them know that she was going to look around outside. Manuel offered to accompany her, but she said she would be fine on her own, and would he mind fetching her when Lionel's two cousins arrived. With Manuel having agreed, Helena walked out of the still sticking front door, and wandered slowly up the drive towards the entrance gates. From a short distance away, she could see that the gates themselves. Last night these were open, and hidden from her view. Now she could see them clearly, they appeared to be made of cast or wrought iron which though she couldn't tell. For a pair of entrance gates, they were quite marvellous, even beautiful, very ornate, and once again in the art nouveau style. The metal work must have once been painted the same green as the House, but time and the weather had turned most of it black and rusty. On either side high white stanchions anchored the hinges, which themselves blended seamlessly and gracefully into the curved walls which levelled out at a height of about three metres. These walls stretched away into the distance on either side. Helena turned around to face the house, which was now about one hundred or so metres away. The driveway leading up to the house was bordered by alternating orange and olive trees. She breathed deeply and picked up hints of pine, orange blossom and something else she couldn't define. The overarching canopy of branches provided cool shade for anyone walking down the driveway. Ahead of her on the left-hand side about twenty-five metres further on, and set back a little was a semi-circular cut away. One very old and large orange tree formed the backdrop of the half circle, sticking out from the grass were the corroded remains of two cast iron garden seats. As she approached she could see that they were large enough to comfortably seat a couple of people each.

Rust covered most of the cast iron frames and the wooden slatted seats had long since rotted away. The branches spreading out from the ancient trunk provided a protective and shady cover for those who must have sat here on a hot summers day. She immediately thought of Rui and his cronies, drinking red wine and calling Maria to bring lunch, she smiled at the thought. It was very peaceful here, the orange trees were coming into flower, and the smell of orange blossom was fleetingly caught on the wind, and here and there cascades of small white flowers were much in evidence.

Was this where her great-great grandmother had sat that day when she returned? It must be she thought and then Helena wondered, and not for the first time why the house was called, A Quinta das Laranjeiras (The Orange Farm) perhaps this old and venerable tree had something to do with it. Smiling to herself, she placed her hand on its gnarled bark, there and then she decided that one of her first acts would be to ensure that these seats would be repaired if possible and replaced in the same position she had found them. This thought was hotly followed by a second, she desperately needed to get a small notebook and a pencil to carry around with her, so she could remember all the promises she was making to herself! With that happy thought in mind she continued to move forward, noting that the trees all looked healthy, and they provided a lovely approach to the front of the main house especially right now with the orange blossom in evidence on many but not all of the trees. Coming to a halt about fifty metres from the front of the house, the trees curved gently outwards in a half circle before stopping all together as they came up against the white painted boundary walls. Helena studied the houses front façade, in the centre were the double height doors the top of which were hidden under a veranda that covered the entire front face of the house, before making a 90 degree turn down both sides of the house. Two sets of windows echoed each other on either side of the main doors, the two windows nearest the doors were about a metre and or so wide, and a couple of metres high. These windows had metal frames split into two parts. The uppermost twenty per cent was filled in with pale green glass. The remainder of the window was one piece of solid clear glass simple in design. The two outer windows were marginally taller and wider, but with the same pale green upper fixed section. The only difference was that whilst these also had a fixed pale green glass panel, the clear glass part was made up of twin opening lights. As Helena looked at the house the window on the far-left hand would, she realized, be the one they had un-shuttered in the library. Its opposite number still shuttered was one of the presents she had yet to unwrap. The thought made her fingers tingle with anticipation in exactly the same way as seeing a present had always done when she was a child.

The veranda was not exceptionally wide, may be two and a half metres, its supporting structure was probably made from cast iron, topped with leaded panels for the roof. The roofs circular supporting stanchions were braced on their upper parts by sinuous and seemingly delicate cast iron mouldings in the art nouveau style. It was all very elegant, the veranda framework had traces here and there of its once pale green paint, obviously done to match the glass in the top of the windows. She imagined when newly painted it would have matched the glorious effect of the gates. Now of course it was in need of some not inconsiderable tender loving care.

The upper floor consisted of five windows, once more they mirrored those down below apart from the central one, which was located above the entrance doors below. This window was actually a double set of doors, and they opened onto what was a small Juliette balcony. Here once again the ornate surrounding balustrade was made from the same cast iron mouldings as the bracings on the veranda. The doors were beautifully made and inset with glass, and topped at the highest point by twin moons made from opaque glass. Higher still, were two small windows close to the eaves, which Helena assumed must be set in the attic. In contrast to those below these were circular and bifurcated half the glass seemed to be clear and the other a shade of darker green. They looked a little odd, and she wondered if they had been added much later, perhaps when storage space was required in the house, and because there were no windows originally two had been hurriedly created. Helena mulled over this incongruity, and wished she had access to the notebook she promised herself, so she could jot down a note to self to identify the door that led to the attic space.

She also wished she had thought to bring a hat, the truth was that the sun was quite strong, and she was beginning to feel the effects on her neck and shoulders. She made yet another mental note to herself that she needed to buy a hat. To remove herself from the suns heat, Helena walked up the steps into the shade of the veranda, and turned left walking to the end of the front of the house. From here a two-metre high yellow privet hedge stretched away stopping only when it reached the perimeter wall, enclosing this, the left side of the garden. Turning right, she continued under the veranda until she came to the second double doors that led from the drawing room. One of these now stood open, and she could hear the sound of metal on metal coming from the other. Lionel who was on his knees peering at the lock was making some progress it seemed. Stopping in front of the open doors she looked out at ground level over what at some time must have been a wonderful formal garden. Now sadly neglected, the only hint of its former glory came from the still cleared pathways. Inside the incomplete parterres the planting had gone, with just the odd old and spindly rosebush surviving as evidence. It must have once been a lovely space, over on the right-hand side she could see a small wicket gate set into far-right wall, this presumably gave entrance to the yard and barns at the rear of the house.

Directly in in front, and centrally situated, was a wide opening that transected the garden wall giving a glimpse of the view beyond. Intrigued Helena made her way towards it passing the empty weed filled parterres, as she came closer to the opening she could see what would soon be, a flower filled covered walkway. For about twenty-five metres a cast iron framework in a similar design to the veranda supported a number of very old wisterias, whose flowers were just beginning to form. In a couple of weeks, the whole of the framework would be dripping with flower spikes. The pathway was made from crushed stone, which had become almost solid from years of being walked on. Helena lingered underneath the still maturing wisteria's coolness, ambling slowly toward its end point. Here she emerged into a large area of lawn, which to her surprise wrapped around either side of the Wisteria walkway for some tens of metres. About fifty metres in front there was a sizeable body of water, too large to be called a pond but too small to be called a lake, beyond which the land gently dipped away down to the valley floor some distance away before rising up again on the other side. From this vantage point she could make out a village on upper flanks of the far side. Its tiny white houses and terracotta roofs sprinkled themselves upon the uppermost part of the valley side spreading out across the top. The bell tower of the local church could be clearly seen rising above the houses, marking its position in the heart of the village.

The view was lovely, a variety of trees filled the valley, with just the occasional glimpse of a red roofed white house, dotted here and there. Helena made yet another mental note to herself to ask what the village was called, and once again rued the fact that she didn't have a notepad.

Jutting out into the small lake was what looked like the remains of a wooden pontoon, from her vantage point it looked seriously old, and unsafe. Helena was forcibly struck by the thought that whilst the fabric of the house had been maintained, other parts had been sadly neglected, she supposed that because it was a wooden structure that wasn't in use it had been allowed to fall into ruin. She imagined that the Trustees, not knowing if the descendants would ever claim the house had decided to do the minimum to ensure boundaries remained intact and the house was kept wind and water tight. Perhaps, Marco had been right when he said that if she chose to make her home here, a good proportion of the money she had inherited would be needed to restore the place, and then maintain it. The small lake was perhaps signalling to her that it too was in need of some repairs, certainly its rickety half missing wooden pontoon had seen better days.

Looking down at her watch Helena was shocked to find she had been outside for nearly two hours, her throat was dry, and she needed a large glass of water. Dinner was also something she needed to consider, hadn't Marco mentioned a Churrasqueira in Vila de Rei? Surely that was open on a Saturday evening, and so she turned around and retraced her steps back to the house.

As it transpired dinner was the one thing she didn't have to worry about. On entering the house, Maria announced that she had made Ensopdo de Borrego (a lamb stew) and that she was welcome to eat with them at about out eight o'clock. Helena who loved lamb hot pot, quickly thanked her and said as long as it was no trouble she would be happy to join them. Maria's reaction to Helena's acceptance of her invitation was to give a broad smile. Helena imagined that Maria was pleased she was happy to try her cooking.

Just then, Helena's thoughts were interrupted by what sounded like a badly misfiring engine, which then stopped abruptly. She heard car doors slammed shut and Manuel talking rapidly. Leaving Maria in the kitchen she entered the hallway, just in time to see two young men of no more than twenty-five years of age enter through the front door, following Manuel. Manuel called Lionel, who emerged from the drawing room.

Lionel greeted the men, before saying in his rich bass voice

'Menina Stratton these are my young cousins, Carlos and Antonio, they have come to help with the picture.'

Helena, moved forward and shook both their hands as she said

'Hello, it's a pleasure to meet you, and thank you both for coming to lend a hand'

Carlos, the taller of the two, replied in English,

'Hi, it's nice to meet you too, I speak a little English if we need it.'

Then before she had chance to reply, Antonio, also spoke

'Me too, nice to meet you Menina, welcome to Ameixeira.'

If they were expecting Helena to be surprised by the fact they both spoke a little English then they got their wish as she was genuinely taken aback, and it showed clearly on her face. Composing herself she said,

'Thanks, it's helpful to know,' smiling at them both whilst continuing in English.

'If we get stuck we can use it, but actually I prefer to keep speaking Portuguese it's the only way for me to regain my proficiency.'

Antonio, a tubby young man with a mop of quite long brown hair, nodded.

'Certo' which basically means 'of course', and the conversation continued in Portuguese.

Lionel with a little twinkle in his dark grey eyes that Helena hadn't noticed before said

'Okay, let's go and see if we can turn this picture around, so we can all see what has been covered up.'

As one they all marched in the direction of the drawing room, Lionel, who seemed to have taken charge of the proceedings was leading the way, when they arrived in front of the fireplace he addressed the other three men.

'Carlos, I think its best if you go up the left ladder, I will do the other one, and Antonio and Manuel can support the picture from below.'

Heads bobbed in agreement, and Carlos and Lionel ascended the ladders. Maria joined Helena and they watched proceedings from just behind the large still shrouded sofa, so as not to be in the way.

Lionel asked Carlos if he was ready to lift.

'Yes boss' he said rather cheekily to the older man, before

together they both took hold of each side and lifted it upwards, they had to go up quite a way, before the hanging wires were released from the two picture supports.

'This is quite heavy boys' he said, 'if you're ready down there we are going to lower it now.'

Both Manuel and Antonio nodded in unison, and slowly the bottom of the picture frame was lowered into their waiting hands.

As soon as the two men below had a firm grip on the frame, they descended the ladder step by step, to allow the guys below to lower the frame a little more each time, and in this fashion bit by bit they eventually placed the frame on the wooden floor.

Helena exhaled, she hadn't realized she had been holding her breath all the time the painting was lowered to the ground.

'Phew, well done everyone it looks heavy.'

All four men acknowledge that it was, with varying degrees of emphasis, sweat beaded Lionel's forehead and they all seemed relieved it was on the ground.

Helena whose growing impatience to see what was underneath the cover, quickly said

'Well guys shall we turn it around and see what we have?'

Manuel who had turned to face Maria, grimaced and then said

'Maria, before we move it, can you put the dust cloth on the floor in front of us, so we don't scratch the floor, or the frame.'

Maria moved swiftly to do as her husband requested, and Helena followed her, between them they placed the cloth doubled over on the floor in front of the picture, and then coughing slightly from the dust they backed away. Then looking directly at the guys, Lionel said

'We lift after three okay?'

Once again, the three heads all bobbed in agreement.

'One, two, three,' and they lifted the painting six inches of the floor before beginning to swing the painting round.

A few shuffles of feet later the painting was facing the right way, resting on the dust cloth and Helena and everyone else could see it in all its detail. Carlos and Lionel held it upright whilst Helena looked for the first time on what she instinctively knew were her great-great grandparents, and their son Luis. Silence fell on the room as they all gazed at the picture. Then, as if some unknown force had suddenly loosened their tongues everyone tried to speak at the same time.

Helena though was stuck for words and the babble surrounding her seemed to fade and become distant white noise. The subjects of the painting mesmerized her. Immediately she noticed that the three figures in the foreground of the painting were quite informally posed. To her, it looked like someone had just happened along and had taken a quick snapshot just at the right moment. The gentleman was standing up but leaning his right shoulder against the bark of a very old orange tree. Two or three metres above him was the bottom of the tree's canopy and numerous oranges from dark green to a fully ripe bright orange could be seen. Just to his left-hand side and slightly in front of him, was a double seat on which was sitting a quite beautiful young woman. Her green eyes were softly focused on a sleeping child of about two or three years of age, whose hands were guarding a spinning top. The child was lying on a large woven cloth onto which other toys also lay close by. Her pale green dress contrasted sharply with the dark green leaves of the orange tree. Her long loosely flowing hair was the colour of honeyed caramel, into which a sprig of orange blossom looked like it had just been placed. Far into the background was part of the Quinta itself, clearly newly constructed, and radiating an air of congratulatory self-importance. The painting was quite charming and competent, but she doubted it was professionally painted. Rather it seemed to Helena that the painting was done as a bit of a fun. Too many of the fine details were not quite executed correctly. Even the perspective didn't look quite right, but it was a charming painting. Helena came closer and leaned down to see if she could see the artists signature, and there in the bottom right hand corner it was just possible to make out the signature 'Celeste de Jesus Silva 1907' unhappily the painting was in quite a poor condition, it was very dirty with visible crackling of the paint.

Helena stood up, and was suddenly aware that the room was now silent.

'What do you think of the painting Menina Stratton?' said Carlos.

'It's…. charming, I guess it must be of my great-great grandparents and their son Luis my great grandfather, I can't see who else it would be, and it's dated 1907 and signed Celeste da Silva, I imagine she was a relative of Sofia?' Helena continued to stare at the picture, Carlos interrupted her thoughts.

'It is nice, but it badly needs a clean, I imagine it has hung in here for many decades, with the presence of wood smoke from the fires and the smoke from all these candles. It is quite dried and cracked in places, and it would look much brighter for being restored, though it's no Picasso!'

Contemplating Carlos's comments, Helena agreed 'Your right of course but I like it. Maybe it was turned to the wall in an attempt to preserve it? But there is no point re-hanging it in this state, I need to get it to a conservator, the frame looks pretty dull as well.' Whilst the chatter continued amongst the others Carlos warming to the task said quietly.

'I know of one in Coimbra, my old university professor's wife is a conservator, she has worked on some quite famous paintings, I could ask him if she is interested if you wanted me too. It wouldn't be cheap though.'

Without thinking Helena responded.

'Cost isn't an issue, this is probably the only image I will ever have of them, it's the first tangible link with my past and it has to be restored even if the painting itself isn't a Picasso!'

Turning and addressing Carlos.

'Carlos if you really don't mind calling them, would you please? I would be grateful.'

'Of course not, I will try him on Monday, and let you know what he says, do you have a mobile number I can reach you on?'

Helena gave him the number, which he added to his mobile contacts whilst she waited. Meanwhile the other three manoeuvred the painting so they could stand it up against the wall, Manuel went to cover it up with the cloth they had taken down, but before he could complete the action Helena said to him.

'No Manuel please don't cover it up, I prefer to see it, it's been covered up too long and it can't get any more damaged than it is now.'

Nodding his agreement Manuel put down the cloth.

Lionel, who in the meantime had been looking at his watch, indicated that it was time he went home, Helena, looked at her own watch and couldn't believe it was nearly 7.30 in the evening.

Lionel, having packed up his tools, ushered Carlos and Antonio towards the door, then he said goodnight before telling Manuel he would be back on Monday morning to continue with his work on freeing up the locks, if the Senhora wanted him too. Helena on hearing this immediately said

'Yes, yes please Lionel it would be great if you're free.'

Speaking directly to Carlos and Antonio she shook both their hands.

'I am grateful for your help with the picture if you tell Lionel what I owe you both, I can give the money to him to pass to you on Monday.'

Carlos shook his head. 'There is no need for that, we were happy to help, and I have always wanted to see inside the house so it's quid pro quo!' Antonio meanwhile with a quick eye to future business glanced at Helena. 'If you need any help with the electrics me and my dad can help, just ask Lionel to contact us, and we can come and quote you.'

'They are good electricians' said Lionel whilst Manuel nodded in agreement.

'I went to school with Ramiro,'

And as if it was a further endorsement of his professional character he went on,

'I am Antonio's godfather, so I can say they do good work.'

Helena smiled inwardly at this blatant attempt to secure his friends good reputation. 'Thanks for that, I will bear it in mind, my dad will be here on Tuesday and that is his line of work, so I want to talk to him about first.'

'No problem, you know how to contact us.' said Antonio

'Goodnight Menina, have a good weekend' said Lionel, and with that they all departed through the front door.

Helena felt exhausted, whilst she knew she hadn't done any physical work today, her brain was reaching overload, filled up to overflowing by what she had heard and experienced during the last ten hours or so. Suddenly she felt quite overwhelmed and if the truth were known a little tearful, she wished desperately that she had someone here with her, to share these experiences, which had been so much were more intense than she had expected. Perhaps she should have let her dad come with her, he had offered, but she had said to him that she wanted to sort out the accommodation first, and she had quite liked the idea of doing this on her own, but now she wished she had agreed.

Shaking her head at her own stubbornness, it was a few minutes before she noticed that Manuel and Maria had quietly disappeared, and she was alone in the darkening drawing room, with its covered furniture, and the painting of her ancestors. She sat herself on the edge of one of the old covered chairs, with dust once again rising all around her, coughing again, she resolved that tomorrow she would take the covers off and throw them out. Her brain was quite frazzled. Today had been a day of remarkable revelations. Everything was on a much larger scale than she had thought possible. How could she be a multi-millionaire, with a grand if albeit faded manor house, with thirty-four hectares of land? What on earth happened to separate her great-great grandparents, and why did Luis and Sofia lose touch? Glancing at the painting, they all seemed so happy and content, what could have led Sofia to want to turn this happy scene to face the wall? Was it simply an act of protection or something more prosaic? So many questions, and so many mysteries, she was sure she wouldn't sleep tonight, and that thought made her feel sick, as she would be alone in the house. Maria interrupted her reverie.

'Menina, dinner is nearly ready, you have about ten minutes if you want to quickly wash your hands.'

Helena, who hadn't even heard her come into the room, jumped at the sound of her voice, so lost in her own thoughts as she was.

'Yes good idea, I won't be long, thank you.'

Getting up from the sofa Helena took a last look around the room, before crossing the hall and going into the downstairs cloakroom, where she washed her hands and face, before returning to the hall where she bumped into Maria,

'I really hope I am not causing you any trouble Maria, its very kind of you to share your dinner with me.'

106

Maria looked on the face of her new boss with apprehension, before putting her arm in Helena's and gently leading her to the kitchen.

'Come on, I think you could do with a glass of wine, I found some in the cellar, it looks pretty old but it's probably ok, and you look to me like it would do you good! As for dinner I always make too much anyway and it's nice to have someone else to cook for other than Manuel.'

As they entered the old kitchen, something smelt great, on the table was a large brown casserole dish, a further dish containing some cabbage and carrots, a loaf of bread, some olives, and three plates. She sat down gratefully in the same seat she had used at lunchtime, Manuel opened the wine filled his glass, and then drank the complete glass down with some gusto.

'Pretty good, better than my homemade anyway.'

He then filled Helena and Maria's glasses in turn, before refilling his own, and raising it in the air.

'Saude a Nossa' he said, the Portuguese for good health, when they had all clinked glasses, Maria took the lid of the casserole dish, and the smell was even more divine, Helena's mouth watered in anticipation. Whilst Maria served the lamb stew into large bowls, Helena tasted the wine, it was not just good but fantastic, and she picked up the bottle but could hardly read the label.

'Mm this is good' she mumbled, 'Are there many bottles in the cellar?'

'Yes of course many, but it's pretty horrible down there, dust, cobwebs, and it needs a good clean like the rest of the house and I am sure I heard mice, or maybe rats.'

As a person with a dislike of anything that was small and furry, Helena gave an involuntary shudder which made Manuel laugh, Maria passed a bowl to Helena, and invited her to help herself to vegetables, as she did so she made a mental note to herself to check the cellar tomorrow, she was intrigued by what the cellar might contain. Helena put the first forkful of the lamb into her mouth, she hadn't realised just how hungry she was, she savoured its taste before exclaiming to them.

'Oh my, this is good Maria, it's so tender, what's this in the bottom it's delicious'

'Bread, it soaks up the cooking juices'

'Bread, just bread?'

'Yes, nice fresh crusty bread, we put it in the bottom of the casserole dish, and when the meat is nearly cooked, we transfer it from the saucepan, to the casserole dish along with the potatoes and leave it to cook for a further half hour or so, well until the meat is cooked.'

'I must learn how to cook this, it's just divine.'

During the next hour they ate the casserole, drank the bottle of wine, and opened a second, and finished off with some fresh fruit. Helena learned a little bit about Manuel and Maria, and they told her about the local area. She was very surprised to discover that she may have an elderly relative from Sofia's side of the family living in Cováo . Manuel told her that she was called Maria do Carmo, and must be close to eighty now, she was a widow, but had children and grandchildren. As near as Helena could make out, she was a direct descendant of Sofia's brother, which would make her a distant cousin several times removed. This was exciting and unexpected news, she hoped that she may have known the middle-aged Sofia when she herself was a child or young woman. Yet another item for her non-existent notepad, she must go and see her and find out what she knew of Sofia if anything at all.

Over dinner Maria and Manuel offered to stay in the house until her father arrived, Helena felt the knot in her stomach free itself, and she accepted readily the offer and told them that she was profoundly grateful, it was after all a large house and unfamiliar. Whilst she was not exactly frightened about being here alone, she admitted to herself that knowing other people were in the house provide a nice layer of comfort. At nine thirty and feeling a bit drowsy, Helena picked up the hurricane lamp, and bid them both good night saying, it had been a long day, and she needed to call her father. Maria, said in about five minutes she would bring up some hot water to wash with, and that she had already put the hot water bottle in the bed. Once more Helena mellow from the glasses of wine, thanked them again for all their help before making her way through the hall up the stairs. A few minutes later Maria arrived her torch creating shadows and magnifying the shapes of the furniture, the jug of water she placed on the console table, before checking that Helena had everything she needed. At the door Maria said she hoped she would sleep well, and then wished her goodnight. The hurricane lamp was already lit, casting a soft glow over part of the room. As Helena moved over to the chair by the window which, over looked the almost empty parterres, she contemplated what they must have looked and smelt like in their prime, full of roses, and other plants. Her eyes now adjusted to the light, fell on the opening in the walled garden that gave access to the now darkened Wisteria pergola beyond, and as she did so she speculated about where the gates were. When she had walked through earlier today, she had noticed the very large iron hinges, from which gates should have been hanging. Perhaps they had been deliberately taken down, and were now stored somewhere. After considering this for a few minutes, she gave up and decided to ring her dad. Picking up the mobile she saw that there was a text message in her inbox, clicking on the icon to open it, she was more than a little surprised, and secretly pleased to see it was from Marco, her heart gave an uncharacteristic little flutter, as she read his message.

```
Helena, I hope your day has been
interesting and not too overwhelming, and
that the two M's have looked after you. I
sincerely hope you sleep well, until
Monday. Marco
```

What an unexpected but pleasant surprise, she pictured him suited at the wedding, and enjoying a nice glass of red wine surrounded by a large family. So very different from her own small family, and probably for the first time in her life, she regretted not having siblings. Reality she knew sometimes has a habit of intruding when you least expect it, and it did so now, as she contemplated the fact that her only known family consisted of just her and her lovely dad. Maybe, here in Ameixeira there was a chance she might find some more, so she shook her shoulders, as if by doing so she could rid herself of all her gloomy thoughts, and then she dialled her dads home number. William, answered the phone quite quickly, and Helena guessed that he had probably carried the handset into the sitting room and had placed it on the side table near his chair. Helena speedily apologized to him for the lateness of the call, which he brushed away, before she went on to briefly fill him in on all that had happened in the last twenty-four hours. Half way through her call, she realized that the phone was nearly out of charge, and with no electricity in the house she couldn't do anything about it. Making the umpteenth, mental note of the day 'to self' must ask Maria if she could charge it for her at her home. Helena finished the call with her dad quickly telling him about the lack of charge, and that she would see him on Tuesday. The absurdity of having to ask someone if

110

they would charge her mobile, on the day she found out that she was a multi-millionaire, was not lost on her. However, the upshot was that she had no effective means of communication, and she smiled to herself such was the bizarreness of life. Tomorrow she also needed to find an Internet café, so she could use her I pad, and check her emails.

Laying on the bed she reflected on her Dad's reaction to today's revelations, his initial shock was short lived, and within a few minutes he was completely rational and very calm. He was pleased for her but said she didn't have to rush into anything and in fact it would be good to take her time. Helena didn't share with him the fact that already she felt that the Quinta was getting under her skin, in case he thought her a little mad.

However, for her part she couldn't deny that she felt a huge wave of relief at being able to share the news Marco had given to her, it was a weight of her mind. Her father it turned out was cool about it, almost too cool, perhaps like her the reality would kick in later. Whilst washing before getting into bed Helena realized that she really could do with a shower, perhaps she should book them both in a hotel until she could resolve the little plan that was forming in her mind, after all it was one thing her living like this, but it really wasn't fair to subject her dad to it too. Once more Helena, made a further mental note 'to herself' to view the cottages tomorrow as soon as Manuel was able to show her where they were.

When Helena woke up the next morning, the sun was streaming through the window, and a quick look told her that it promised to be sunny and warm Sunday. Picking up her watch she saw it was eight forty, and she had slept well, perhaps due to the delayed effects of the journey, and the three glasses of red wine consumed with dinner the evening before. Very good wine indeed, and she remembered her note to peruse what else the cellar contained.

The house was very quiet, and she wondered if the two M's were in or not. They hadn't said they were going out, but it was a Sunday perhaps they had gone to church? Eager to explore Helena got out of bed had a quick strip wash, brushed her teeth, once more with water and resolved that today she would drive to a supermarket. Once down stairs she headed for the kitchen, where a note lay in the middle of the table.

Helena,

We have gone to Cováo , the Church service starts at 9.30. This Sunday there is a market in the square so if you need to buy some things it might be useful for you to drive down. We may also be able to introduce you to Maria do Carmo, and if you come we can introduce you to Vitor Martins the builder. It is also possible to get breakfast in café central, we will be there after church. We don't work on Sunday.

Regards

Maria.

Senhor Martins, she had told Marco that she was going to call him last night but had forgotten. Still it seemed there was a good chance that he would be in Cováo today, she picked up her fleece and left via the kitchen door, as the front door was still sticking. Helena locked up behind her, then hoisted her canvas bag over her left shoulder and walked around to the car.

The car was parked in a shady spot and this morning it was covered by a film of dew, even though it was promising to be a lovely day. As Helena drove out from the driveway to the Quinta, she appreciated for the first time in daylight that she would see the rest of the village of Ameixeira. The night she drove in had given her the impression it was a hamlet really but maybe it was larger than she thought, now she would get a better glimpse. After a hundred metres or so she passed on the left what must have been the house the two M's (as she now thought of them) it was a small pretty white washed building on two levels, with a small barn to the right-hand side. The land to the left of the house had been worked and rows of vegetables stood in neat lines, and a few chickens could be heard. Five or six hundred metres further on the rough track came to an angled T-junction. Here the road was finished in quite old tarmacadam, on the left-hand side, there were a couple of small houses which looked unoccupied and next to them were a couple of ruins of what had probably once been houses too. The road continued sloping downhill and she could see the outlines of a couple of other properties, but from her position it wasn't obvious if they were occupied or not. Helena resisted the temptation to turn left and to go and see, and instead turned right. Shortly after, she came to a point where the road split into two, which probably constituted the central part of the hamlet, she knew the way out was to take the left fork whereas the smaller right-hand fork led to a few more properties. Taking the left fork she passed in front of a house whose exterior was in good condition, but the shutters were closed, and it had the appearance of being unoccupied. This white washed house was bounded on both sides by the two forks in the road, she drove slowly forward and at the end of the house separated by only five metres or so, there was a smaller white washed building, not large enough to be a house, but it was well cared for, maybe it was some sort of storage building. A further twenty metres on just as the road curved to the left, she saw a driveway to her right that sloped very gently upwards. On either side it was bounded by low white washed walls, inside of which were pretty gardens with lawns and flower filled borders. She was immediately transported back to England with its traditional cottage gardens, so this was not what she would have expected in a small hamlet in Portugal, it piqued her interest. She slowed down, and observed that at the rear of the driveway ran the very small road which, had forked to the right. Behind this narrow road was what to her looked like a newish single-story house, which stretched both to the left and right. It looked pristine with its bright white painted façade and deep blue window and door reveals. A recessed porch held two large terracotta pots from which Bougainvillea's grew. The external grey shutters to the windows were open, and Helena, concluded that the house was lived in. A tall white painted barn next to the garden on the left of the driveway as she was looking at it, obscured the rest of the house, which disappeared behind it, so without getting out and walking around she couldn't tell how far it went to the left. Taking her foot of the brake, Helena moved forward quite slowly, the road continued to curve to the left and once beyond the barn she noticed on the same side of the road as the single-story house, there appeared to be two more houses joined together. Both were old, and one was two storied, the taller house appeared to be in better condition than the other. In front of them were a couple of ramshackle farm buildings, which looked like they were about to fall down. Beyond these stood a further house whose roof had collapsed. Continuing to accelerate, she passed a further two houses on the road that led to Vinha Velha these whilst intact, nonetheless gave her the overwhelming impression of being unoccupied, the land in front of them was hugely overgrown and she could make out a few olive trees which seemed to be covered in brambles. The village it would seem had few occupants. She drove on slowly, until she arrived at the junction with the main road, which was flanked on either side by a couple of derelict houses, across the road was the sign that pronounced the village of Vinha Velha. This was another small village straddling both sides of the road, and once again the mixture of old houses, and ruins made her think that maybe this central part of Portugal was certainly depopulated and maybe impoverished. As she drove, she passed three or four villages displaying similar characteristics, before Cováo rose up in front of her in the near distance. The village was perched on a hill, at the highest point, looking down on the village was a very large and splendid white cross. Its prominence was such that she guessed it could be seen from some distance all around. Just before she entered the built-up part of the village, a choice of two roads were available, the main road curved to the right sweeping in front of the village which lay to the left of it, whilst a turn to the left led directly up the hill to the village. Understanding that this had been the road she had used on Friday night albeit in the opposite direction, she turned left and proceeded to drive up the hill that she believed would lead her to the village square, and café central. However unlike on Friday night when this road was disconcertingly empty, this morning all along the left-hand side of the road was were a series of parked cars, with only a couple of spaces free. Parking her mini in one of them, she picked up her canvas bag from the passenger seat and exited the car, locking it before strolling up the hill, where she emerged as expected into the square and saw the café she had entered on the Friday night.

On reaching the square she glanced all around taking it all in. On her immediate left and almost opposite the café were steps leading up to a large flat area, then to the left there was yet a further set of steps, which led to the doors of a modest but fairly modern church. On the right was the large willow tree, she had noted on Friday evening. The square in stark contrast to Friday night was now thronged with people. Many older men were sitting on the low walls talking in groups, and people were entering or emerging from the café. Few women were about, and Helena guessed that they were still in the church, from which she could hear the singing of a hymn. As she walked towards the entrance to the café, she became aware that she was the object of some interest. Pushing her bag higher up on her shoulder she approached the café, and as she did so she heard someone call her, she turned towards the voice and recognised Carlos, one of the young men who had helped with the picture yesterday.

'Good morning, are you going into the café, or buying some things from the market.'

'Hi Carlos,' she replied. 'Both, the market doesn't close yet does it?'

'No, it starts to shut down about 12.30 when everyone goes home for lunch.'

'That's good, then I have plenty of time, it's pretty busy isn't it, is it always like this on a Sunday?'

'Most Sundays yes, but there are more people about today because of the market, so it's busier than normal, it only happens once a month. People come in from the outlying villages, were you heading for the café?'
'Yes, I was, I need breakfast.'
Do you want me to introduce you to a few people? Or would you prefer to introduce yourself?'
'If you wouldn't mind that would be great, I must admit I feel a little self-conscious, are all the women in church?'
'Yes, in about fifteen minutes they will all come out and the men will be dutifully waiting outside, and the café will appear to be empty.' He said this with an amused and wry smile playing on his face.
'The ladies know their husbands have been in the café drinking wine, but they turn a blind eye.'
Helena smiled at this subterfuge, and said
'Can I buy you a coffee, or something else?'
'I will take a coffee with you and a small glass of red wine, my mum and sister will join me soon, and I can introduce you to them. My sister is a primary school teacher, and she speaks good English.'
They walked the last few metres into the café, which was full of men, small glasses of wine and coffee cups littered most of the tables, and despite the no smoking sign, the air was thick with the smell of tobacco. Helena noted the shiny bright orange painted walls, and over the door by the exit sign a piece of the plaster that met the ceiling had clearly fallen out, and now contrasted sharply with the pink paint on ceiling which she hadn't taken in on Friday. A harried looking woman whom Helena recognized as the smiley person who she had spoken to on Friday was collecting up the glasses and cups as fast as she could. Once at the bar, Helena ordered from the gentleman who was behind the counter.

117

'Good morning, two coffees, and a glass of red wine, and a ham and cheese roll please, Senhor.'

'Certainly Menina' came the reply 'I will bring them over.'

Carlos and Helena made their way to one of the tables that had just been cleared by the lady, who on seeing me, also wished me good morning

'I see you found your way to the Quinta then.'

'Yes, I did thanks to you. As you said it was quite easy, though perhaps it would have been easier if the Sat Nav had recognized the village, I was so glad you were still open.'

'You were lucky, normally we would have been closed, but it was the Pirez twin's birthdays, so we had a few more customers than usual.'

Carlos at that point said

'Alice, this is Helena Stratton'

'Pleased to meet you formally, if I can help in any way please ask'

Helena who instinctively liked this woman gave her a smile.

'It's nice to meet you too and please call me Helena, and I know it's a bit cheeky, but the Quinta doesn't have electricity, and my mobile is nearly out of charge, would you mind me plugging it in somewhere?'

Alice who didn't seem at all put out by Helena's request picked up her hand and pushed it forward.

'Pass it to me and I will do it for you.'

Helena pulled out the phone its charger and the adaptor, and handed them over.

'Thank you very much I really appreciate it.'

Alice smiled

'It's no problem,' before she disappeared off behind the counter and plugged it in.

Just then the coffees and breakfast arrived, and Carlos said, 'Thanks Antonio, this is Helena Stratton the new owner of the Quinta das Laranjeiras.'
Antonio nodded at her and held out his broad hand. 'Welcome to the area, we hope to see you in here from time to time, and don't worry if you're the object of some attention today, the people here are just curious!'
When he had left them, Carlos told her Antonio was the owner of the café and Alice was his wife, they had worked in France for some years, before returning and opening the café fifteen years ago. Alice is the fount of all knowledge locally it comes from being in the centre of village life.'
Helena noted that information as she settled back into the chair and drank the warm coffee and munched away on her breakfast. Ten minutes later she heard the sound of church bells, Carlos said the service was over, and immediately most of the men left the café, and ventured out into the morning sunshine, leaving the café deserted! Alice and Antonio quickly came out from behind the counter and used the lull to hurriedly clear up the cups and glasses that remained. Within a short space of time, families started to enter the café, many people greeting each other with kisses on both cheeks and hugs. Helena sat back taking in the lovely hum that was invading the interior of the little café, realising as she did so that despite the half empty villages this was a close and friendly community.
She turned to glance at the notice board, which was adorned by posters advertising a variety of things, from the dates of a number of forthcoming Festas, a Fado evening in Tomar, firewood for sale and even a car. One notice caught her attention, as it was advertising a holiday let in a village called Valhascoso, an idea formed

119

in her mind, so looking back to Carlos she asked him where it was.

'About 8 kilometres from here in the direction of Macao, it's on the other side of the valley from you'

'So not too far then from Ameixeira.'

'No not really about a fifteen-minute drive' glancing towards the door he stood up.

'Ah here is my mum,' and he went to greet her.

A woman whose age was difficult to ascertain came towards their table, arm in arm with a much younger woman. Carlos's mum could have been fifty, but looked older, dark hair flecked with grey poked out from her black headscarf, but above all she had the face of someone who was very sad. Helena immediately wanted to envelope her in a hug but knew that might be considered impolite. Noting that she was dressed entirely in black, she figured she was in deep mourning, she had seen women dressed like this in Greece. In contrast her daughter, was tall, dark haired with lovely features, and she was dressed in a pair of black jeans, a pink blouse, with pink wedge sandals.

Carlos who had stood up, as they came towards the table said

'Mum, Louisa, come and meet Helena Stratton who owns the Quinta in Ameixeira. Helena this is my mum Maria and my sister Louisa.'

'I am very pleased to meet you.' Helena said in her rusty Portuguese.

Carlos's mum replied that she was pleased to meet her and kissed her on both cheeks before sitting down rather heavily as if she was carrying the weight of the world on her shoulders. Louisa stayed standing up and shook Helena's hand before asking her mum if she wanted coffee.

120

'Let me get those.' Helena said getting up and going to the counter, Louisa followed her and after the order had been placed, they agreed as it was busy they should wait for the coffees, whilst waiting Louisa said in an interested and soft voice.

'Are you really going to live in that old house? It's been empty for years.'

Surprised as she was by the directness of the question, she hesitated a moment.

'Yes actually I think I am. It needs a lot of work of course, so it may be many months before I can move in.'

'Will you stay in a hotel or rent a house here then, or just leave someone in charge whilst you're back in England?'

Helena liked Louisa's directness and realised that she had asked an interesting question, and it was one that she needed to give some considered thought to, but in the event, she replied,

'At the moment I am not sure, maybe a mixture of both, I think I would like to stay close by during the renovations, but that depends if I can find a house to rent. I am not that keen on long stays in hotels, you get fat!

Louisa grinned, 'I know what you mean, it's too easy to eat big breakfasts, and then because you have to eat out every night fast food can become the norm, not that there is a burger bar within thirty kilometres of here!'

Alice who had been busy at the coffee machine, turned gave them their order on a small tray, and they worked their way back through the throng of people to join Maria and Carlos. Helena had wanted to ask Louisa about her dad, but she decided against it, because if as she thought was the case, her mum was a widow, maybe now wasn't the time to bring it up.

Instead the conversation turned to the people who lived in Cováo and the villages that came under the freguesia (parish council) consequently they pointed out a few

121

people to her, such as the Priest, and a couple who lived in Vinha Velha. Apparently, no one in the café today was from Ameixeira, but Carlos told her that normally there would be. Occasionally someone came over to speak the family and Helena was casually introduced as the estrangeiro (foreigner) who had come to take over the Quinta in Ameixeira. Where possible Helena made it known that her great-great grandparents were Portuguese and at least one of them came from this area. But she needn't have bothered, it seemed that everyone knew who she was, and that normally led to a warm response and many people nodded wisely and kissed her cheeks like she was there long-lost relative. In between all of these interventions, Louisa told Helena that she worked in the primary school in the larger village of Vila de Rei, but at the moment like Carlos, she was living at home with her mum.

Carlos, who had left the table to talk to some other people, was one of only one of a handful of young people she had seen, and she remarked on it to Louisa and her mum. Louisa told her how the young people left to pursue careers and jobs in the larger cities, and over time this had de-populated the villages, and many schools had closed. Many of the houses, were still in family ownership, but no one wanted to live in them, so they were simply falling into ruin. It was, said Louisa largely because of no one having the money or the inclination to repair them. It was a sad truth that the younger generations, no longer wanted to pursue the subsistence agricultural lifestyle of their parents and grandparents. Looking around at the people in the café Helena could perhaps see why, hard work had etched hard lines on their faces, even so there was evidence that many people also appeared to be living to quite a good age. Helena noted that Maria, had hardly spoken during these conversations, she seemed content to just sit still and drink her coffee, her eyes were generally lowered, and she emanated an aura of incredible sadness. Helena thought that maybe all this family happiness around her just reminded her of what she had lost, and apart from getting up to greet relatives, Maria didn't actually participate in the running conversation at all. Helena, could understand that, her dad she knew still had that look of sadness, maybe if they met a shared sense of loss might mean that they would be able to console each other. She made yet another mental note to ensure they met at some point.

Twenty minutes later Carlos came to say they should be going, and Louisa and her mum said goodbye with more kisses and left. Before they did so Helena had already extended an invitation to Louisa to visit the Quinta the following week, perhaps early one evening if she had time, and she should bring her mum too. Helena had passed over the number for her mobile which Louisa punched directly into her own, whilst saying she would call Helena to arrange something. Buoyed up by this potential friendship Helena glanced about the café. It was thinning out now as some families made their way home to lunch. As the people in the café dispersed, Helena noticed Maria who she hadn't seen come in, she was sitting in the far corner with a group of ladies, all of whom gave her a wave which she returned. She had only been here two days and already she had met three Maria's, if, as she thought it was going to prove a common name it was going to be difficult to separate out one from the other!

Feeling content with the contacts she had made so far, she decided to seek Alice's help, so when she approached to clear the cups, she asked,

'Alice, I could do with some assistance. Might you have some free time later to help me with a couple of things.' Alice though clearly harried, smiled.

'Of course, can you give me twenty minutes or so, it will have gone quiet by then.'

During the discussion that followed they agreed that Helena would pop out and look around and buy a few things from the market, and that she would return in about half an hour, leaving plenty of time for Alice to tidy up before she sat down. Alice went back to clearing up, and Helena hoisted her canvas bag over her shoulder and emerged from the darkened café into dappled spring sunlight. As she looked around she saw a shady spot and went to sit on the low wall beneath it. From this vantage point she noticed a number of doors were open onto the street, and she observed people enter and then emerge minutes later with shopping bags, she was intrigued. One of these just happened to be in her line of sight, and very close to café central. It had a slightly tatty plain brown door the bottom three or so inches being decayed in places, this was propped open, revealing a dark interior and she could make nothing out from where she was sitting. She was fascinated. Getting down from the wall, she crossed the road, made for the door and peered inside. To her astonishment she saw that it was a shop selling a range of household items. Down the left-hand side were buckets, mops, fly swatters, and other equipment she couldn't identify. As she took the single step inside the doorway, on her immediate right was a sturdy wooden screen of about two metres in height. From where the screen ended, a long wooden and very old counter extended down the entire length of the shop. The wooden screen seemed to be acting as a protection from the elements. She could see that in the middle of the counter about half way down there was a hatch that would allow access to and from behind the counter into the shop area. The hatch was propped up with a metal catch, the sort you saw in pubs back home. From where she stood there didn't appear to be anyone behind the counter, so she inched further inside, as she passed the wooden screen, and peered behind it, she saw the top half of a small elderly man; round framed black glasses were perched precariously on the end of his nose, his bald head was shiny, and his lips were pursed in concentration. He was sitting on a wooden stool, and she hadn't seen him because he was half hidden by the wooden screen, and half behind the counter. A newspaper lay on the counter top in front of him, and clearly his pursed lips were caused by something he was reading. As she took a few steps further in, over the top of his glasses he looked up and glanced at her. The looked at each other, Helena noted that was wearing an old navy-blue jumper with holes in the sleeves, and the front of his jumper was stained with what she took to be spots of food. Helena said good morning.

'Bom dia Menina, posso ajudar? (Good morning young woman, can I help you?')

Responding to his question Helena nodded.

'Yes please, do you sell toothpaste,' he nodded his head, turned behind him and opened a draw, and pulled out from within a single tube of Signal toothpaste which he placed on the counter, before looking up at Helena with eyes full of curiosity. Helena said

'Thank you very much.' He said,

'Mais alguma coisa' ('Can I get you anything else?')

'Well no, not today but I see you sell a range of goods, I think I am going to need some of these very soon.'

'I sell a good many things, and not everything is on display so if you don't see it, please ask as I may have it.'

Helena took a few moments to look around the small shop, hanging from the ceiling were buckets, saucepans, hand brushes, watering cans and mop buckets, and some more items that she did not recognize. There were brooms of all varieties leaning lazily on the walls many covered in cobwebs, some with sturdy wooden handles, others with plastic handles in a variety of colours, more the type you would use indoors. Behind the counter, she could see washing up liquid, alongside packets of nails, knives, forks, spoons, Tide washing powder, bleach, and she could swear she smelt moth balls, it was like stepping back in time. Whilst she was occupied looking around, an elderly lady with white hair and wearing her Sunday best clothes came in and said good morning to the shopkeeper, she also bid Helena good morning, before turning back to the shopkeeper and asking if he had yeast. This time, he stood up and opened a draw underneath the counter, and pulled out some dark parchment paper, then he also brought out from under the counter a small tub with a green lid, as he opened it, the fragrant smell of fresh yeast assailed the shop. From the tub, he took a small bloc of fresh yeast and neatly folded it into the parchment, before putting the lid back on the tub.

'One and a half euros please,' he said to her and she opened her purse and slowly counted out sufficient coins, before bidding them both a good day and she left. Helena then asked if he had hand soap, another turn to the rear, and another draw opened, and out came three bars of soap, he then opened another draw and brought out a Palmolive brand liquid soap. Helena chose the bar of soap with a bee and a lemon on. The shopkeeper then wrapped both items in brown paper and placed them in a bag and passed them to Helena, who promptly paid, before saying goodbye. Once outside she was struck by

126

how old fashioned the shop was, apart from in period dramas or comedy's like 'Open All Hours' on television she hadn't ever been in a shop like this at home. Smiling to herself she then wandered around the small market, and brought some salad items, a loaf of bread and a large round cheese which was made from a mixture of milk from cows, sheep and goats, it was called Tres Igrejas (three churches) which made her grin once more. The lady selling it was keen to persuade her to buy the largest one, and as it was only eight and half euros Helena readily agreed. It was quite pleasant in the sun, so she wandered from stall to stall, on one there were a variety of small cakes and biscuits, all very brown, and unadorned by the icing that she was used to seeing in the UK. Across the square was another set of buildings and one had an open door, once again there was no signage to indicate what might be being sold inside. So she entered and found it was a small food store. On her left-hand side were a few crates with vegetables and fruit inside, these looked to Helena as if they were almost beyond their best and quite different to the bright highly laid out displays in English supermarkets. On the right-hand side were several shelves stacked with tinned, and packet products. Then a disembodied voice said.

'Come in, come in, what can I do for you Menina Stratton?'

'Hello?' Helena replied, looking around to see where the voice was coming from.

'Where are you, and how do you know who I am?'

'We all know who you are Menina Stratton.'

Replied a voice both bright and surprisingly deep. A few moments passed, then the owner of the disembodied voice arose from behind an ancient cooler cabinet and straightened up. Surprisingly she was no more than four feet ten inches tall. A sprightly older woman with dyed

127

auburn hair, who's roots showed steel grey, stepped out from behind an old fashioned cold counter.

'The plug socket is a little old and every now and then it just stops working, it needs throwing out really but what can you do. She shrugged her shoulders, and then said, 'Just so you know my name is Dona Lourdes, my husband Vincente is somewhere nearby I think. He might be fetching chicken feed for someone, we keep all that next-door, but like all the men though, as soon as he can he disappears, and goes to the café with his friends. If you ever can't find him that's where he will be! So what can I get you?'

Her tone conveyed to Helena the impression of mock chastisement, rather than true suffering, giving Helena the impression she wasn't cross at all. Helena gave her a knowing and conspiratorial smile,

'Actually, I don't need anything at the moment, I am just trying to get a sense of what is available locally.'

Dona Lourdes shrugged her shoulders again before quickly saying

'It's no problem, we don't carry as much as we did, most people prefer to go to one of the many supermarkets in Abrantes these days, but some of the old people don't have transport so we stock the basics.'

Listening to this rather resigned and matter of fact response, Helena look around a little more closely. Clearly, the shop had seen better days, but it was easy to see that even with the limited stock on display, it was probably a lifesaver for people who couldn't get to the towns. The result of her observations was that she now felt a little guilty that she didn't need anything, she had the sudden thought that she probably needed to support the shop so that it could remain in business. So pushing aside the plastic flaps that did little to prevent the cold air escaping from the archaic cold cabinet, she looked inside. After a few seconds she picked up some local Iberico ham, and from the shelves near the till a couple of tins of tuna with ring pulls. A tetra pack of orange juice, and a packet of tissues completed her purchases.

Dona Lourdes, gave her a grateful look, before packing everything into a plastic bag, and asking,

'Have you met Maria do Carmo yet?'

Helena, shook her head, 'No not yet, I expect that I will over the next few days or weeks, I think she may be related to me, but I am not sure, I understand that de Silva is quite a common surname.'

'Yes, it is a common name, but my dear it is true that Maria is part of your family, through the marriage of her grandmother with the son of your twice great grandmothers brother. Your cousins though generations apart. Maria lives in Cováo now, in the house of her husband's parents, she has been here since her husband died three years ago. The house is a bit rundown.'

Helena thought she had said this almost as an afterthought, but she wasn't entirely sure.

'Does she have other family close by?'

'Unfortunately no her daughter died in 2003 in a car accident in Lisbon. Her youngest son lives and works in Germany, he visits at Christmas and Easter.' Her two grandchildren live in Lisbon, I last saw them eighteen months ago.'

'That's tragic for her and the family, but interesting news for me, as it sounds like I have more of a family than I thought possible.'

'Yes Menina Stratton, you have Portuguese relatives, I am sure they are looking forward to meeting you.'

She said this in an odd sort of way, but Helena didn't probe, it was time for her to be getting back to the café. Helena bade her goodbye, left the shop and retraced her steps back to the Café. The square was now much quieter. Many of the traders were starting to pack up, whilst some older people were making various last-minute purchases, but in general the hub-hub of a couple of hours ago had subsided.

Back inside the café, a few men still stood around chatting and drinking the small glasses of wine, which seemed to be the standard size served. Alice saw Helena enter and when she sat down she gestured that she would be over soon. Five minutes later Alice came over with two cups of coffee on a tray, and obviously tired sat down rather heavily. Helena said

'You look like have had a busy morning, do you close up shortly?'

'Yes, we have been a bit rushed off our feet, our son normally helps on Sunday, but he isn't around this weekend. Sunday's are our busiest time really,' then she sighed with a degree of relief. 'But we close around one o'clock, until four pm when we re-open, Monday were closed so it's something to look forward too.'

'I must remember that, for the future.' said Helena giving her what she hoped was a supportive look. Alice continued,

'Well we have about half an hour now, so what is it I can do for you?'

'Carlos said you're the local font of knowledge, so if you could help me with some general local facts that would be great, though firstly do you happen to know if there are any properties for rent locally? I think I may need a house with at least two bedrooms for about three or four months? Preferably with Wi-Fi.'

Alice thought for a few moments, she knew of several of course, but she had figured out that Helena would probably want a modern home, with modern facilities, and these were few and far between in this lovcality.

130

'There are two that I know of which would be suitable, but I think they will already have bookings right through the summer that is from around mid-June until early October, and I doubt that they will have Wi-Fi, but I could check for you if you like, to be honest most of the property for rent locally wouldn't suit you at all, but I am happy to ask around if you would like.'

'If it's no trouble that would be fantastic. I've decided that work on the Quinta is going to cause a lot of mess, and so it's probably best if Dad and I do not try to live in it at the same time. A rental house would be better than stopping in a hotel, and I prefer to be close to keep an eye on things.'

'Yes, I understand, it wouldn't be very nice living and sleeping in a building site! I remember when we had some small works done, I got really annoyed with the dust.' she replied. Helena nodded vigorously,

'Talking of works, I really need to speak to a few good builders and plumbers and quickly, the sooner I can get them in to give me a quote the better, are their people that you would be comfortable recommending?' Alice looked around, and then lowered her voice a little,

'Well Joao Gonçalves is very good, as is Vitor Martins though he comes with something of a reputation, but if you can get over that well…'

Alice saw Helena's look of surprise and interest, and she went on quickly to say,

'Don't worry he is a good builder, but at some time or another he has upset everyone in the vicinity, but it always blows over, it's just a bit uncomfortable when it happens. People take sides. Personally, I think he is as he is, because he is a little man, they always seem to have something to prove don't they!'

131

Helena stifled a laugh at that, and thought he must be quite a character. Even Alice had the good grace to laugh as well before continuing.

'He is a bit of a card, and he was in here earlier, but he has gone now, I can get him to call you if you want. Joao is also very good but a bit more expensive, but certainly I would ask them both to quote. They will know several plumbers, and there is always Jesus Alfonso Dias, he is local and very well thought of. Though I am not sure if he could handle a big job too easily, he only has one hand, and this affects his speed, so if you wanted things fixing in a hurry, best to consider someone else, though I am sure he could do with the work.'

Helena, thought of how these were hardly good recommendations, and so she couldn't help it, she put on her most serious face and said to Alice,

'So Alice you're recommending a one-handed plumber and a small and generally disliked builder.' The look on Alice's face was a picture of horror, and Helena laughed. Alice then realised she was joking with her and quickly joined in, soon the rest of the café were looking at them as if they were mad! Alice leant forward and whispered, 'It does sound ridiculous when you say it like that doesn't it.'

Then they both laughed some more, and the remaining locals stared even more at them. Alice seemed unperturbed though, and lent forward conspiratorially, 'Don't worry about that lot, they probably think we are talking about them, and it won't hurt them to be the object of female laughter!'

Looking round the room, Helena found bringing hers under control quite hard, but eventually they both managed to stop - just about.

'Everyone seems quite friendly.'

Helena said it more as a statement than anything else, and Alice nodded.

'Is there anything else I can help you with?' Alice said looking at me.

'One thing I wondered if you knew Maria do Carmo?'

'Of course.'

'Do you think at some point you could introduce me to her, I understand that she is related to me.'

'Yes, I can, in fact this Wednesday is a good day, as she often pops in on her way back from the doctors. Maria sees the nurse once per month to have her blood pressure checked, if you come in about four o'clock that's probably a good time. I'll just go and get your phone it should be well charged by now.'

When Alice she came back to the table, Helena gave her the number of her mobile and said,

'Please do call me if you have any news about the houses, or if you think of any other tradesmen, and thank you so much for your help.'

Helena then stood up to leave, just as she was doing so a middle-aged couple walked in, they greeted Alice with hugs and kisses, and asked how she was. Helena could tell by their accent that they were not Portuguese, thought she wasn't exactly sure what nationality they were. He was a shade over 6-foot-tall, square jawed, with a good physique, and in his younger days she thought he would have been considered handsome. His hair was a now cut close to his head, in what she recognized was a no 2 buzz cut, which only emphasized the broad square jaw line. In contrast his wife was only about five feet, with bright blue eyes and mid length curly blonde hair. Possessed of a shapely and full figure and still pretty features, she was dressed in a long pair of white linen trousers and a beautiful blue loose top. Little and large sprung into her mind, but hand in hand they seemed very well suited to each other. One of those increasingly rare couples that just 'fitted' together.

Alice, who was still addressing them then said,

'Jane and Henry come and meet Helena, she has just inherited the Quinta das Laranjeiras in Ameixeira you will be neighbours.'

to Helena she simply said.

'Jane and Henry are English.'

Helena was completely flummoxed by this news, and she sat back down just in time for Jane to lean over and kiss her on the cheeks before saying in Portuguese,
'It's nice to meet you, we knew you had arrived, the gossip gets passed around quickly here, we would have probably popped in tomorrow to say hello.'
Helena said Hi back and Henry introduced himself, before asking Alice if it was too late for coffee's and a glass of Vinho do Porto.
Obviously, it wasn't, so Alice went off to fetch the drinks, and they both sat down next to her on table.
Helena, then spoke in English asking them if they wanted to continue in Portuguese.
'No, let's stick to our native tongue our Portuguese is improving but we have some way to go.' Jane said with a droll smile to Henry before adding.
'Yours is much better I am so jealous.'
'Well, it's probably a bit easier for me as I learnt when I was a child, my granddad and my mum both spoke Portuguese and, so I was learning it from the time I could speak. To be fair I am a bit rusty myself, but it is coming back slowly.' And she gave them a wry smile.
Henry, filled the hiatus in the conversation.
'So Helena, when did you arrive and what are you going to do with the Quinta? Or is it too early to say?'
Jane interjected.
'Don't pester her fish, she has only just arrived, but it's a lovely building we have often admired it, from the outside obviously, I am a real fan of art nouveau design, I bet it's beautiful inside.' Helena shook her head.
'It's been trapped in a time warp for a very long time, and it's going to require major renovations as well as

modernisation before it is fit to live in. Though from what I have seen so far it could be beautiful once more.'

'It is a shame we won't be here to see it, we are off to Australia on Wednesday, for a long holiday staying with our son and daughter in law, and our two young grandchildren, but I would have loved to watch its transformation.'

'Did I hear Alice say you lived in Ameixeira, is it by any chance the white house with the blue window surrounds?'

'Yep, that's the one.' Henry confirmed.

'We have been living here for over seven years since we took early retirement. We extended the house about eighteen months ago, it has lovely views over the valley to Cardigos. I imagine the view is not dissimilar than the one from the rear of your Quinta.'

Alice who had now returned, and had finished setting down the newly ordered drinks, said to Helena.

'I will call you if I get any information about the rentals, I am off now, someone has to cook lunch. It was nice to meet you.'

She gave all three of them a hug and the usual kisses on both cheeks, before finally turning to Henry and Jane and saying

'Have a fabulous time in Australia, enjoy the family time, and give them my regards.'

Jane and Henry thanked Alice and said they would see her in September, meanwhile as Alice exited through the back of the bar, Jane turned to Helena and asked,

'Are you here on your own Helena?'

'I am, but only until Tuesday. Then my dad is coming for a while. I must pick him up from Lisbon Airport at three o'clock. But before then I have to find us somewhere to stay, I had hoped we could stay in the house, but the truth is it isn't suitable for us to live in really.'

'Oh what a shame, is it in a poor state inside?'

136

'Well… yes and no is probably the best answer. Obviously, it has not been lived in for over forty years, however, the Trust has maintained the structure well, so its sound. Really the main problem is there is no electricity in the house, and the plumbing is rudimentary, I have a downstairs working loo but little else, and the fixtures and fittings that were left inside are pretty decayed.'

Lifting up her arm and mock smelling underneath she continued

'I haven't had a shower since I left England on Thursday. I probably am as smelly as a rotten cheese! That's the reason why I was asking Alice about local rental possibilities. It doesn't sound too promising though, it seems the two that are local, may already be booked up for the summer. If I can't find a rental we will have to use a nearby hotel, but it's not ideal.'

Henry looked meaningfully at Jane before saying to Helena,

'How long do you think you will need the rental?'

'Probably three months maybe four, it's difficult to tell until I get some quotes, but I will be a bit surprised if we hadn't got the house in a fit state to live in, at least in part by the end of the summer.'

Jane returned Henry a conspiratorial look before saying.

'How would you like to rent our house, if of course it's suitable for you?'

Helena was so surprised by this offer that her mouth opened, but no words came out, she looked like a gold fish that's gasping for air, and it must have showed because Jane touched her on the forearm.

'Seriously Helena you will catch flies with your mouth open like that,' and then she chuckled.

'Listen, we are serious. We are way for four months and it's better for the house to be lived in rather than shut up.

137

Obviously, we would have to ask you to look after the plants etc.; but it's not an onerous duty.'

Helena still hadn't spoken, she could see them looking at her waiting for a response. So as she often did she said the first thing that came into her head.

'Tell me do you have Wi-Fi?'

A smiling Henry answered in all seriousness.

'Yes, and BBC1, BBC2, BBC4, ITV, and channel 4.'

Helena seemed to come back to herself at that point.

'I am so sorry, you must think me awfully rude, and you have only just met me. Offering me your house to rent has rather taken me by surprise!'

'Well, given that we are off Wednesday morning, and you have your dad coming on Tuesday, it seems neither of us has a lot of time to waste. So if we are going to do this we must sort it quickly, and in anyway it's in my nature to be decisive, isn't it Fish' said Jane chuckling again.

Henry interrupted.

'Why don't we finish up here and you can come and look around the house, then if you like it you can think about it overnight and tell us tomorrow.'

Helena was grinning from ear to ear.

'Are you really sure?'

'We wouldn't have offered if we weren't sure.'

'Well that would be brilliant, if it's no trouble.'

'Honestly Helena it's no trouble, in fact why don't you stay for lunch. I expect you're not sorted for today.' said Jane picking up her bag and standing up.

'Let's go, there is no time like the present, and the café is about to close anyway.' she looked over to where Antonio was wiping down the bar.

'Bye Antonio see you in September.' He waved goodbye and they exited into the square that was now almost empty of people and cars. Henry pointed out his car to

Helena and then asked her where hers was parked.
Helena pointed to where her car was parked.
'Fine, I'll turn around and pass you, then you can follow
us back, and just pull up on the drive.'
Within a few minutes Helena was in her car following
them back to Ameixeira, and she couldn't believe her
luck. Driving along behind Henry, she suddenly brought
herself up short: was she rushing things? After all she
hadn't decided to do up the house, or had she?
Somewhere deep inside she knew the answer to that
question. But brushing it aside for now, she concluded
that in any case she needed to be here for some time to
resolve the estates future either way. So whatever she
ultimately decided to do she would still need a base to
work from, and if Henry and Jane's house was suitable,
and she was almost certain it would be, then she would
take it any way.
Ten minutes later Helena was out of the car and crossing
the small road she had noted earlier that morning. From
this vantage point it was possible to see that their house
was much longer than she could determine from the
road. It went away to the left and stopped as it met
another house that jutted out its whole width to the side
and in front of it. Helena assumed this house was one of
the two houses she could see from the road.
Henry unlocked the door and said in a slightly self-
mocking voice
'Welcome to South Fork.'
Helena was about to follow them in when she stopped.
'Why South Fork?'
Jane gave an easy laugh.
'It's a joke really, and not of our doing, you can blame the
nickname on friends of ours, Barbara and Bernard. When
they first visited, they joked that it was like South Fork

from Dallas, and you know how it is sometimes these things just stick, and it's so outlandish it's funny!'

Once through the door, Helena found herself in a decent sized rectangular hall, with four doors leading off it, the one to the right was open.

'Come through to the kitchen Helena, and I can give you a tour, Fish can you put the kettle on I am dying for a cup of tea.'

Having surmised that the honorific 'Fish' was a nickname they used for each other, Helena thought it was quite sweet, recollecting with a pang of sadness that her dad always called her mum Pidge; she had always assumed that it was short for pigeon but now with a shock she realized that she didn't know, she would check that out with her dad next week

Henry went over to a large modern stainless-steel range, and put a gas ring on, over which he settled an old fashioned styled cream kettle.

The kitchen was contemporary, large and dual purpose. At the opposite end to where they had entered, was a modern glass faced log burner built into a full height chimneybreast. The wood burner itself was raised above the floor by about two feet, and underneath was an opening stacked with a neat pile of logs. To its right was a stylish TV, facing the Fire was a comfy three-seater sofa, and against the back wall a good sized wooden dining table and six leather chairs. The spacious and contemporary kitchen took up the remainder, and by far the largest part of this room. The gleaming sleek no handled white kitchen units, were laid out in a L shape that started to the right of the kitchen door and ran along the front wall, the last one ending just behind the Sofa. The double sink was placed underneath one of the two windows in the room. But what dominated the room was a considerable sized island unit. The island unit was topped by a beautiful white work surface that was flecked with what looked like tiny pieces of multi coloured glass. Above this island unit was a long lighting unit containing three clear glass dropping lights, minimalist in design, but striking nonetheless. Almost every wall was covered in paintings, and Helena was particularly taken with a couple of very large paintings one of a goat and one of a goose. Henry noticed her interest and said

'The goat is called Charles and the goose is Bill, they are by Paul James, we have a third a cow called Adrian, he is currently on sabbatical at Jane's sister's!

'They are fantastic, such characterful faces.'

'They are, that's a feature of his work, we wish they were original oils, they would be worth a lot of money, but unhappily they are only limited-edition prints. But I should not complain as we have a few original works from lesser-known artists. In the past we liked to go to final year art student shows, you can pick up some nice work, and who knows in future we could own a superstar's work'.

As he said this he was smiling mischievously.

Jane who had been unlocking the doors and listening to the exchange interjected,

'Let's go and have a look outside and then we can have a cup of tea.'

With that she ushered Helena out of the large double doors, and through the fly screen doors, they emerged under a large veranda, to the right side was an informal seating area, with two three seater outdoor sofas, and two chairs arranged in a square, in the centre of which was a low glass topped coffee table, with an interesting phallic shaped succulent on it. Jane noticed Helena's stare, and said

'Yes, it does doesn't it, but I kid you not, when we were given it, it was already that shape, if somewhat smaller, but it is growing well, so we use it as a talking point!' Helena, giggled and said,

'I bet it turns a few heads.

Before she turned her own to the left-hand side where she could immediately see two separate eating areas both with large tables and eight chairs, a BBQ, plus a swimming pool. But the most impressive sight was the view, the lovely gardens slopped gently downwards, before the valley dropped away and returned upwards again to a village on the other side. It was almost but not quite the same view, she had seen when standing by the lake in the Quinta.

Jane who had been watching her take in the view came up to her and quietly said,

'It was that view that sold us the house, well that and the pool!'

'It is quite beautiful.' Helena said wistfully as they walked out from under the veranda pulling down their sunglasses as they did so. They then walked towards the pool, passing one dining area under the veranda, then on the right steps that led down to the terraced gardens. A little further on the pool opened out in front of them, its water sparkling in the sun, it looked like just the place to be on a hot day.

'The pool isn't heated, so it's a bit chilly at the moment, but it gets up to about 28 degrees from about July. We like having a quick dip in and out right now, it's too cool to linger very long, but I find it wonderful and refreshing. All of our sun beds are stored away, but we have six or so.' said Jane as though warming to her task as a putative rental agent!

Helena gazed over a formal rose garden, with its rose bushes and rosemary plants, in the centre of which was an old Olive tree, beyond that was another square of planted garden containing lemon trees, bordered by lavender bushes. Beyond this square, was a further large patch of land on which nothing was planted.

'What do you do with that' she asked

'Normally it's our small vegetable patch, but of course, as we are not here this summer, nothing has been planted. You could plant some if you have time. Nothing is nicer than picking and cooking your own produce.'

They continued wandering around the well-kept gardens, passing through a gap in the hedge to a set of steps that led down to a terrace below which was full of olive trees. As they were returning from the far side of the olive grove Henry called to say the tea was ready.

They ambled back towards the steps, and made their way to the seating area. Helena was struck by how quiet it was, the only sounds were those of the birds chattering, and insects humming in the nearby bushes.

Helena sat down gratefully, Henry passed her a cup of tea, and she took her first sip and sighed with pleasure, it was the first she had had since leaving England. Jane meanwhile had produced a plate of lavender shortbreads which she offered around. Helena picked one and took a bite, she thought it was totally delicious, and a soft but crumbly texture with just a hint of lavender. As if by agreement no one spoke; instead they lingered over the first few sips of the tea, and savouring the satisfying taste of the shortbread. Helena who had continued glancing around, began noticing the little things that she had missed during the walk. She settled further back into the comfortable sofa and put her feet up on one of the poufs. She felt slightly drowsy, and let herself relax back into the plump and soft cushions. Despite being under the veranda and out of the direct glare of the sun, she still had on her sunglasses, she put her tea down on the side table, and closed her eyes savouring the warmth of the day and the comfortable surroundings….

Helena woke up with a start, all she could hear was the sound of Cicadas, she must have fallen to sleep, and was now totally embarrassed, even mortified. Opening her eyes, she took off her sunglasses and straightened up, and thought, oh my god how can I have done that, Jane and Henry must be horrified. She shook herself, and got up from the sofa. The teacup that had been by her side was nowhere to be seen, nor could she see her hosts. Then from inside the kitchen she heard soft music, as well as the unmistakeable sounds of food being prepared, she opened the fly screen and went into the kitchen. But before she could begin to utter the apology that was on her lips, Jane said,

'Ah your awake, did you have a good nap? I moved your cup, so would you like another?'

"Jane, I am so sorry that was totally unforgivable of me, how long have I been sleeping.'

'Only about fifty minutes, you looked so peaceful we just relieved you of your cup and sneaked away. But now your awake you can help me with the last of these vegetables, then I've taken the liberty of putting a couple of towels in the bathroom, you said you hadn't been able to shower, so why don't you go and take advantage of the facilities? There is a hairdryer and brushes if you need them in the wicker box by the dressing table in the first spare bedroom. Afterwards I can show you around the rest of the casa.'

'That's so kind, if you're sure, I'd love too.'

'Of course, I'm sure, I wouldn't have offered if I wasn't.' Jane gave Helena a broad smile before continuing.

'I have a daughter a bit older than you, you remind me of her a bit, I would like to think that if the circumstances were reversed, your parents would have helped her. By the way there are lots of toiletries so please use whatever you need.'

Jane put her hand on Helena's arm and gave it a little squeeze, then after they had polished off the vegetables, Jane showed her to the spare bathroom, and left her to it. Returning to the kitchen to continue the preparations for lunch.

Twenty minutes later Helena emerged, and smiling at Jane said.

'Jane thank you, I am so grateful for the use of the bathroom. I feel a tad human once more. I used a squirt of the deodorant that was in the bathroom cabinet as well, I hope that was okay?'

'No problem, when we have guests they always leave what they don't use, so there is always a large selection of toiletries in that bathroom.'

Henry came in, and he didn't mention Helena's falling to sleep instead he said he was going to make more tea.

'You two go and do the tour, and when you're finished this will be ready.' said Henry smiling at Helena, and giving Jane a kiss on the cheek.

'Ok then, let's go, we will start in here.' Jane led Helena to a door on the left-hand side of the wood burner.

'This is the master bedroom.' They both went inside, where immediately on the right-hand side was a walk-in wardrobe, and on the left a freestanding mirror fronted wardrobe. Beyond the wall that acted as the left-hand side of the walk-in wardrobe was a very large bed. On the wall opposite the bed was a black lacquered modern chest of draws, and matching dressing table. Next to those was a freestanding roll top bath that was fitted into the far corner of the room on an angle. Helena who was taking it all in, thought it charming. Overhead in the centre of the area containing the bed, was a traditional style eight arm crystal chandelier, against the modern furniture it should have looked odd, but it fitted in well. On the right-hand side a wall jutted out to three quarters of the bedrooms width, and beyond the roll top bath, hidden behind the wall was a double sized walk in shower with two overhead shower heads, a bidet, loo and two matching sinks but at different heights.

'Oh gosh, this is lovely space.' Helena exclaimed. 'A gorgeous room.'

'Well I don't know about that, but it suits us, we put the chandelier up in here, because it was a piece I used to have in the kitchen of our house in England and I wanted it up somewhere. Originally, I thought I would put it in the kitchen but then I thought this space was calling out for something, it also helps the roll top bath blend with the modern furnishings.'

'Well it does work, it's fabulous' said Helena as they left the room and crossed the kitchen, into the hallway.

'In here is the pantry which I couldn't do without! Next door is a loo and washroom.'

Passing through the forth door in the hall, the door immediately on the right led into a large utility room, with an American style fridge freezer, washing machine and tumble dryer, granite worktops over more white units. The passageway doglegged left, before going straight on, and immediately against the left-hand wall was a large very old metal wine rack, maybe five-foot-high by six feet long. It was almost full. Further down the corridor Jane pointed out the bedroom and bathroom next door.

Helena nodded, these were the two rooms she had just vacated; the bedroom was medium sized, with all the normal furniture, simply decorated and with full-length muslin nets covering the windows. The bathroom, was a good size with, as she discovered a powerful overhead walk in shower, along with two sinks, loo and bidet.

146

The room beyond was a further bedroom, Helena thought it slightly larger than the first in which she had dried her hair, and this room came with a door opening directly onto the veranda in front of the swimming pool.

Lastly, they went through a door at the end of the corridor, emerging into the most stylish and contemporary living room Helena had seen for some time. It was like something you would see and read about in Homes and Gardens magazine.

It was an almost square room, and they had entered it on the extreme left-hand side of what was the rooms rear wall. The wall on their left-hand side contained two windows and on the right-hand side were a set of double doors and a single window. On the back wall running from the right-hand side of the door to a meter from the end of the right-hand wall, was a magnificent very modern dual-purpose shelving system. Mostly this was filled with books, but every now and then one of the alcoves had in it a piece of modern glass.

The predominant colours in the room were shades of lavender, purple and sage green.

'The sofa is gorgeous it looks very comfy.' Helena said to Jane

'We brought them with us from the UK, it's a Ligne Roset.'

'I love the colour.'

'They make great contemporary furniture, but this design is a few years old now, but you can still buy it it's a classic.

A glass-topped coffee table was placed in front of the sofa on which sat the most extraordinary piece of glass Helena

had ever seen. The Television sat on top of a chocolate brown sideboard. In one corner was a Bang and Olufsen upright six space CD player, a wonderful contemporary piece of design and Helena felt a stab of envy. Ever since she had seen one of these in a house of one of her friends from University, she had wanted one. The thought struck her that now of course now she could buy ten if she wanted, and she decided that she would buy at least a couple! The walls supported some lovely pieces of artwork, they all looked original, and she noted the Australian influence in the one or two pieces of aboriginal art. However, on the wall between the two front facing windows was something she had never seen before. It was a large one-and-a-half-meter square, wall hanging made from wool woven in a geometric pattern over a wooden frame. The overall impression was that it its base colour was purple but interwoven with orange, yellow, red, blues and white used to separate the individual blocks of colour. It was truly remarkable. Jane saw her taking it in, and came over to stand beside her.

'That was a piece we commissioned from a local Portuguese artist called Joao Videira, it's made from Arraiolos wool. We choose the colours, and just left him to interpret what we wanted. It's fabulous isn't it.'

'Wow, it's not just fabulous but unique, how did you find out about him.'

'It was serendipitous really, three years ago we went on a short trip to Évora, and stayed in a little boutique hotel, in our room a smaller version of this was being used as a bed head. All over the hotel were pieces of his work, like the cube over there.'

Jane pointed to a cube Helena hadn't noticed before, it was the same geometric design in a lattice worked over a square steel frame, you could see through it, but it was all in black.

'Gosh that's lovely too.' she said.

'There's more just look over there.'

Jane said, pointing to a further piece partly hidden by a contemporary freestanding log burner shaped like a wigwam, with a split central opening.

Behind it, leaning in the corner was a perfectly round tyre shaped structure, except it was completely covered by different colours of wool.

'You can probably guess that underneath the wool is a tyre, clever isn't it. Joao is very talented and doesn't live too far from here. Maybe you could commission some pieces from him yourself?

Helena nodded,

'He definitely is, and I most definitely will once the rooms are ready, I really like this room though it's fantastic, so contemporary and you have such lovely things, are you really sure you want to rent it out.'

'Yes of course, were cool about it honestly, we have house swapped a couple of times and I find people very respectful, and though we won't be swapping with you, I don't get the impression you're going to have time for wild parties!'

They were just about to leave when Henry came in and said tea was almost ready, Jane turned to Helena.

'Why don't you take your time, have another look around and when you are ready join us on the veranda.'

Helena thought it was perfect, more than perfect it was stylish, large and with the bonus of a pool. She already knew she didn't need to wait and think about it overnight, she was going to take them up on their generous offer now, in case they changed their minds! Helena directly followed them to the outdoor seating area, and sat down. Henry poured the tea, before saying

'So what do you think, is it any good for you?'

'Listen, it's perfect, and I don't need to think about it, if you're willing to rent it to me until you return then I will take it with pleasure. I promise to look after it, and water the pot plants.'

'Fantastic,' Henry said, 'it looks like we have an agreement in principle, though of course you don't know the rent yet!'

'Don't tease her Fish, honestly men can be a pain.'

Henry rolled his eyes at his wife, before turning to Helena.

'Well we thought if it's ok with you, 1500 euros per calendar month to include all the utilities etc.'

Helena, simply said

'Are you sure? That sounds more than reasonable for all that is here. You could get that for a week!'

'It's good for us.' said Jane 'in many ways its better the house is lived in. There are a few jobs that will need doing though. Like the maintenance and weekly cleaning of the pool that's if you want to use it of course!'

'Oh yes I will' replied Helena.

'In that case it might be best to send Manuel round to learn how to do it, perhaps you can add it to the caretaking duties he has at the Quinta. If he drops in tomorrow morning Henry can show him where the controls are as well as demonstrate how to do it. We can also show him where the stop cocks are and the electric circuit board, in case the power goes off.'

They continued chatting for some time about other areas of the house that would need attention. Helena took it all in, apparently the gardens automatic watering system, would need turning on two weeks after the last rainfall, which normally occurred by the end of May at the latest. Henry had already organised for the land around the olive grove to be turned over to reduce he spring growth. So a guy called Casimiro who Manuel knew, would turn up at some point in June to do this.

Jane kept popping in and out of the kitchen seeing to lunch which smelt fabulous. On the veranda, Henry and Helena chatted amiably about what brought them to Portugal and this area. Henry never asked Helena about the circumstances under which she had inherited the Quinta, but over a fabulous traditional Sunday lunch of Roast Pork, she volunteered the basics to them. Jane was captivated, and Helena could tell that she liked a mystery. Later in the afternoon, after a few glasses of wine, Helena asked if they could come and have a look round the house before they went. She had already decided that Jane had good taste and that it might be interesting to get her take on the house. Jane was only too happy to agree. They agreed to meet up the next day at about 3pm. Around six o'clock, Helena indicated she should be making her way back to the Quinta. She wished them both a nice evening, truthfully saying she was looking forward to seeing them tomorrow, and hearing what they thought of the Quinta.

Helena, waved goodbye to them, and set off for home contemplating on her good fortune, she realised that she felt more relaxed and happy than she had for some time. Her whole day had been fabulous, and though it was only her third day here, she felt that she could be part of this community quite easily. Today everyone had been friendly, and she felt very much at ease here. Jane and Henry were so empathetic, she reflected on her good fortune at meeting them, and felt that in getting to know them in the future they may become quite good friends. Although they were nearer her dads age than her own, they were good fun, in one way, she thought, it was a shame they were not going to be around, on the other hand she did get to stay in their lovely house right on the Quinta's doorstep.

On arriving back, she parked the car and walked to the rear of the house and into the back hallway, which led directly into the kitchen. The two M's were not about; they were probably spending Sunday in their own home. Helena looked around the kitchen, noting the two doors. One she knew went into the entrance hall, the other she hadn't yet opened. Despite the house being empty, and the light beginning to fade, her curios nature got the better of her, so she headed toward the door and opened it. Once open she saw it was a large storage area, possibly a former pantry. The stone floors, were dark, and the shelves rose up one after another continuing all the way up to the ceiling. In the floor at one end was a large metal ring in what was obviously a trap door. Helena wondered if this led down to the cellar, but if it was then it seemed odd, for one thing people would be carrying bottles in and out of it, no, it didn't feel right, but it clearly led down to something below the room. She put her hand on the solid ring, but it didn't give easily, and then she thought it probably wasn't wise to lift it up whilst she was in the house alone, after all what would happen if she fell in, or the trapdoor shut itself! She gave an involuntary shudder, and looked up and around the pantry, a window high up provided a reasonable amount of light, though it was pretty dirty, and covered in cobwebs. The pantry had many shelves on which stood bottles and jars with indeterminate fillings, placed here long ago, and subsequently unused. Disconcertingly she could hear scurrying noises and realized that mice or maybe something larger was also perusing the shelves, and that was sufficient for her to make a hasty retreat back into the kitchen; which was when she noticed the cool box on the dresser. On top of it was a note from Maria to say she had left it for her, and they would be back later that evening. Looking inside she could see a couple of filled rolls, a bottle of orange juice and a small cake like those she had seen earlier in the market. Helena had of course brought some provisions herself in the market, which Jane had put in her fridge whilst she was there. Helena now put these inside the cool box, more for protection from any roaming rodents, than for keeping them cool. The kitchen itself was not exactly cold, but it wasn't warm either, the antique range, was not lit today, so the temperature in here was lower than it had been the day before. Helena supposed that she could light it, but to do that she would first have to find where the logs and matches were, and she realised that she should have found out.

Shrugging that off, she ventured out into the hall, and not for the first time felt that little tingle of anticipation, there were three doors on the left-hand side and she wondered if they were now unlocked. The first that she tried wouldn't budge, neither would the second, the third however yielded to her touch. Lionel must have managed to undo this one yesterday she thought. The door came open quite easily, and she stood in the doorway, waiting for her eyes to adjust to the lack of light. Slowly items came into focus, she could make out a pair of heavy draped curtains, covering a shuttered window on her right-hand side. She moved towards them, and the curtains let out a lot of dust as she brushed by them in order to remove the bar that she could see was holding the shutters closed, exactly as in the other downstairs rooms. With a degree of force, she managed to force up the metal bar that held the shutters pressed against the window. However, even when released the shutters they remained closed. So she pulled on the ornate metal handles that were attached, and this allowed the wooden shutters to fold backwards albeit with a bit of a squeak. Once done, she turned around and was a little surprised to find she was in a bedroom whose proportions mirrored those of the Library on the opposite side of the house. In here everything was uncovered. The bed was a large double with metal foot and head boards made from wrought iron. Lots of ancient pillows covered in what was once a creamy coloured satin were piled up against the bed head, and the bed covers were pulled back from the bed just like they would be if someone had just got out of bed. It made her shudder. The two bedside tables covered in a thick layer of thick dust were fairly elegant made from wood apart from a four-inch wrought iron upper, to the rear and sides, which she assumed was to prevent items being inadvertently pushed off. On both bedside tables were matching ornate wrought iron candleholders which would take three candles. In both the candles were burnt down to stubs. Additionally, on the left-hand side was a book, lying rear side uppermost. She picked it up and turned it over. Its title was Livro do Desassossego. (The book of Disquiet) by Fernando Pessoa. Helena didn't know the book or the author, it was clearly quite old, and so she placed it back down. Next to it was a silver backed gilded hairbrush, of the sort you would see lying on the dressing table in a stately home. On the right was a small box of matches, a green fluted bottle and a glass.

On the opposite side from the window was a large tall boy, in the corner a gilded chair similar in style to that in the library, and on the wall next to the door was a very pretty marble topped dressing table. The dressing table contained the rest of the dressing set in the same gilded silver as that of the brush, which was all sitting on a moulded pale green glass tray. Two more candle holders sat on either side of a wooden frame containing a single central mirror flanked by two smaller side ones. Everything was covered in layers of dust; everywhere there were cobwebs many of which contained the desiccated remains of long dead insects. Helena used a pillow of the bed to brush the cobwebs out of the way, so she could see what the dressing table might contain. Whilst she waited for the cobwebs and dust to settle she looked around the rest of the room, which had been painted a soft shade of lemon yellow. About a foot from the ceiling was a hand painted fresco of vine leaves, flowers and grapes that ran around the whole room. As in her bedroom upstairs the paint had faded, but she imagined not as much as it would have done had the room not lain in darkness for nearly half a century. For some reason that she found difficult to explain she felt excited. She pulled out the small padded stool from under the dressing table, brushed off the dust lying on the top, before checking its structure. It seemed sturdy enough, so she sat down, but not for the first time in this house she found herself enveloped in clouds of fine dust. As dust died down she saw the dressing table contained three draws, so she pulled on the handle for the left-hand drawer. Inside remarkably dust free, were a couple of pillboxes, an old bible, and an over-elaborate mother of pearl page marker. She then opened the middle and largest draw, inside lay several pairs of silk gloves, and underneath these was a beautiful shawl. Helena pulled it out, it was as light as a feather and silky smooth, and it was adorned by beautiful birds, plants and flowers, and was edged in red silk tassels. Its condition was remarkable, as were the gloves and the remaining shawls she found underneath. The gloves were too small for her hands, but she placed the pretty shawl around her shoulders and looked in the dusty mirror. It looked great and she decided to take it upstairs with her, musing that perhaps she might use it one day. Realising that these items must have belonged to her great-great grandmother Sofia, she brought the shawl up to her nose and breathed in, but could detect nothing but the musty smell that remains when clothes have been unworn for some time. With that smell in her nose, she put down the shawl and opened the third draw, and looked down at its contents. In here was a small lavender pouch, the lavender long since having lost its smell, under which was a lace edged handkerchief, which seemed to be covering something. Helena carefully lifted out the folded-up handkerchief, and placed it on her lap. As she did so, her heart started to do crazy things, she could hear it beating more rapidly than it should have been doing, a ripple of excitement coursed through her and she with a great effort she willed herself to calm down. A minute or so later and with a calmness that belied her physical state, she unfolded the sides of the handkerchief and revealed a bundle of envelopes, bound with a blue ribbon.

Chapter 9: Revelations

The envelopes were thick and expensive, off white in colour, and adorned with dark blue copperplate writing. Helena freed the ribbon that had been loosely tied in a bow, revealing eight small square envelopes. Everyone was addressed to Sofia de Silva, Quinta das Laranjeiras, Ameixeira. They were clearly old, and it seemed they had been handled many times. For although the quality of the envelopes was exceptionally good, over handling had caused parts to split, and some pieces were missing. Helena examined everyone, and discovered that on the reverse side was a crest, and on the reverse side of each envelope was written:

Count Rafael Alencar,
Palacio De Carvalho,
Oporto 3689-231

Helena, asked herself if this the writing of her great-great grandfather? It was a beautiful copper plate, bold strokes, written with firmness. She picked up the envelope that was first in the pile, and looked inside for the letter. Disappointment flooded through her. It was empty, she quickly searched the remainder, all of them were empty, apart from the final one which contained a small piece of parchment on which was drawn a large orange tree, at the foot of which laying on the ground, was a small bunch of forget-me-knots tied with a blue ribbon.
Helena stared at the small sketch, wondering what on earth this was supposed to represent, and where were the letters that were presumably the contents? Why would Sofia have kept the envelopes separately from the letters? Surely the contents would have been precious.

Did she wrap them up as carefully as the envelopes and put them somewhere else? It was odd, but she felt that the letters must be here somewhere, so she embarked on a frantic double-check of all three draws, emptying everything onto the bed, but this exercise revealed nothing. The bedside cupboards came in for the same treatment but once again to no avail. Once she had embarked on this she couldn't stop, so the Tallboy was next. Opening the top drawer, she was disappointed to see it was sparsely filled with only couple of silk purses, and several pairs of glasses.

Every draw was emptied, but like the others they contained mostly underwear, stockings, night shifts and in one several more pairs of gloves. However, there was no trace of letters or anything else other than the normal accoutrements of daily living. Yet, Helena was sure they must be here; in the bedroom that Sofia must have used towards the end of her life. Or if not here, perhaps in a special place that Sofia used for her precious items. Like a zealous detective she awkwardly pulled every draw from its frame and checked underneath and the back, but still nothing was found. In her desperation even the covers of the bed were pulled off and shook thoroughly, the only reward for this activity was clouds of dust and a fit of sneezing. All the cushions and pillowcases came in for the same attention, but all to no avail, wherever the letters had gone to, they did not appear to be in this room. Sitting down heavily on the edge of the now messed up bed, shadows began to play on the walls, it was becoming dark, the sun was quickly disappearing below the horizon, and shortly it would be nightfall. After picking up the envelopes, shawl, handkerchief and ribbon, she closed the window shutters, but didn't bar them. Then before closing the door, she gave a fleeting look around the fast darkening room before making her way upstairs. Once inside her room, she lit the hurricane lamp, and sat down, feeling very deflated. Logically where would a woman presumably feeling sentimental put her most precious possessions? Her mum had put hers in her keepsake box, she wondered if Sofia had had something similar? Without electricity wandering around a dark and largely unknown house was almost impossible, and searching with only a hurricane lamp conjured up an image of Florence Nightingale walking down shadowy corridors, and she laughed inwardly at the ridiculousness of it.

However, the frustration was getting to her, the house had many secrets and she wanted to discover them. She remembered rather uncomfortably how, as a child in the lead up to Christmas, with the anticipation of Santa Claus and his big red sack full of presents, she had similar feelings of frustration, why wasn't it Christmas tomorrow! Still she wasn't a child anymore.

Gazing out of the open bedroom window, the trees in the near distance were bent slightly over, the wind had suddenly picked up, leaves rustled as they caressed those closest to them, and a few stars speckled the sky. Helena closed the window, and moved to the bed, the silence enveloped her, propping herself up into a half lying half sitting position with the cushions, her eyes closed automatically, as she willed a solution to come to her.

Twenty minutes later, footsteps on the stairs, announced that Maria was approaching her bedroom. Getting off the bed to open the door, before Maria, torch in hand could knock. Maria was carrying a large thermos and a small pail of clean water and a hot water bottle. As the door opened and she came in she said,

'I thought you might need this in the morning, the thermos contains boiling water to add to the cold.'

'Thank you, Maria that is kind, of you, if you have five minutes I have a couple of things to tell you.'

Despite the shadows thrown by the hurricane lamps glow, Helena thought she saw a momentary flicker of concern on Maria's face.

'Yes Helena?'

'Please don't look so worried, it's nothing serious.'

'I made up my mind yesterday that it would be ridiculous to try and stay in the house whilst serious work is being carried out at the same time. This afternoon, Senhor and Senhora Clarke a couple I met in café central, offered to rent their house to me. I presume you know them?'

'We do they are very nice.'

'When I was introduced to them today, they told me that on Wednesday they were leaving for Australia for four months, and they offered me the rental of their home. That's where I have been this afternoon. It's perfect and so close I can keep an eye on things here during the day, but be comfortable at home.'

'That is good news for you. I know they generally go away every year, so what luck! Does that mean you don't need the room for your father cleaning?'

'Yes, it does. Henry and Jane are going to stay the night in Lisbon on Tuesday, in fact I am going to drive them to the hotel, before picking up my dad from the airport. After tomorrow, you can sleep in your own home once more.'

'Does that mean you're going to stay then?' Maria questioned.

Grinning as she looked at Maria she said.

'It looks like it, doesn't it! I am very much going to need yours, and Manuel's help, in putting the team together to make the renovations happen, and then to manage the estate afterwards.'

Impulsively Helena gave her a hug, which Maria returned, before saying to her. 'I know you're going to be happy here, and we will do all we can to help, do you mind if I go and tell Manuel, he has been worried that you wouldn't need us, that you would bring in people from the City.'

'Has he? Oh dear, I am sorry about that, the truth is I want, if I can, to use local people wherever possible. After all, if I am going to live in this community it would be good if others could benefit from the Quinta as well. Perhaps you can help tomorrow with names and recommendations?'

'Of course we can, and thank you, I am so happy, I hope you sleep well, see you in the morning then.'

Maria left, and Helena felt something that had been long dormant, it was a spark of hope, and it wasn't the prospect of being a millionaire that had caused it. Far from it instead it was the thought of being part of a community, in a house which already felt like home. This was it, she had, with that conversation, publicly committed to the Quinta and tomorrow she had to start the journey. Sitting back down on the bed, it seemed that the house had heard it too, and was stretching itself in happiness, as from nowhere came an orchestra of different sounds from all over the house! Helena couldn't wait for her dad to feel this too, he so deserved to feel some joy, and she just knew that her mum would have wanted them to be here and happy too.

An hour or so later, having got undressed and into bed, she began to read her book, sometime later and full of contentment, she fell into a dreamless sleep.

The next morning, a horn woke her up once more, it was being pressed down and held several times, she reached over and glanced at her watch, 8.35, about the same time as on Saturday. It was a noisy mystery, and she resolved to find out what was causing it, the minute she saw Maria.

161

It seemed that her decision making of the previous evening had netted dividends, as this morning everything appeared brighter. Arriving in the kitchen, Maria was nowhere to be seen, however Manuel was sitting at the table, on seeing Helena he quickly asked what should he do today. Despite not being prepared for his question, she responded with.

'Do you mind keeping an eye on Lionel when he arrives, and as far as possible please continue with your normal routine. But if you get chance, can you contact Antonio's father and ask him if he could meet with me on Wednesday morning to talk about the electrics. Also, could you call Senhor Vitor Martins, and see if he could come around at eight-tomorrow morning?'

'Of course, consider it done, anything else Menina?'

'Please, I would prefer it if you called me Helena.'

'No Menina, I can't do that you're my boss, it would be right.' Then he smiled impishly before saying,

'Well at least not for a few weeks anyway.'

Helena chortled at this before commenting,

'When you're ready then, you decide.'

'Yes Menina, I will.'

Maria, now returned to the kitchen with a tray on which was a flask of coffee some slices of fresh bread, butter and a Kilner jar of some orange coloured jam. Helena, spread the butter on the wonderfully fresh bread, before opening the Kilner jar, the fragrance that escaped from it was wonderful. Maria and Helena could smell vanilla and both of them took a spoonful out of the jar. It was a vibrant, deeply squishy apricot conserve, with strips of vanilla pod inside. Spreading a good spoonful on the bread Helena sank her teeth into it. After savouring it for a few moments she said that it was absolutely the most delicious conserve she had ever eaten.

'Maria this is wonderful, did you make it.'

'No Menina, it's not my strong point, Senhora Clarke dropped it in at my house this morning, saying she thought you might like it for breakfast with fresh bread.' Helena talking with her mouth half full, mumbled that the bread was great too, and asked Maria where it came from. Maria looked at her with a slightly puzzled frown on her brow.

'The baker of course, didn't you hear him?'
Helena gave a shake on her head, then suddenly, the penny dropped.

'Do you mean that hooting on the horn I heard earlier is the baker?'

'Yes, he comes every day, apart from Sunday.'

'Well I can't say I like being woken up by the horn, but if he delivers bread like this, then I can live with it!' Grinning from ear to ear Helena continued to slather apricot conserve on top of the next piece on top of the plate. She was quiet for a few moments, chewing contentedly, before glancing across the table at Maria.

'Maria.'

'Yes Menina.'

'Do you know any local women who might like to help us clear the house? I would pay them for their time, oh and yesterday I met Carlos's sister Louisa and their mum, so I was going to ask Louisa, if her mum would like to help she seems so incredibly sad, I thought it might get her out of the house, do you think that a good idea?'

'Yes Menina, that is a very good idea, Maria hasn't been herself since her husband died eighteen months ago. I am sure Maria would benefit from getting out of the house. You know that Louisa went back to live at home, because she was so worried about her.'
She said, a little sadly.

'No, I didn't know that, that must have been an anxious time for her. I have Louisa's mobile number I will give her

163

a call, and see what she thinks. Anyway, do you think you could find two or three more?'

'Well I could call Dona Lourdes, or Alice, they would be able to give me some names. When do you want them?'

'I was thinking that we should probably start emptying rooms next week, but first I need to know where we can store stuff.'

'No problem, you have lots of out buildings, but we will need boxes etc., and probably a skip or two for stuff you don't want to keep.'

'Could you do that for me Maria whilst I am out? I have to go to the bank, in Abrantes this morning and open some accounts.'

'Yes Menina, but they are going to want to know how much you're going to offer to pay them, and how is it that they are going to get here, many won't have transport.'

'Mm I hadn't thought of that, I suppose we can hire a couple of taxis? As for pay rates I have no idea what's reasonable, here do you?'

'I guess five or six euros per hour plus free lunch would do it!'

'Okay, then let's go with that, we don't know how long we will need them, but let's say a maximum of a couple of weeks from ten am until 3 pm. Oh, and they don't have to work every day if it suits them to only a few days per week.'

A short while later Helena phoned Louisa, and left a message on her answerphone, she then washed and changed into her one and only black suit, picked up her bright red suede Jimmy Choo shoes, and was ready to drive to her appointment with Senhora Gonçalves. The trusty sat-nav behaved well, and at just after nine-fifty she arrived outside the branch of Montepio.

Helena noted that Marco's car was already parked, and at the thought of seeing him again the frisson she had felt on Saturday returned. Applying a little light lipstick, she took off her driving shoes, and put on her Jimmy Choo's, before picking up her briefcase, which though looking the part only contained her handbag, passport, and the files Marco had given her. Punctuality had always been important to her, so with three minutes to spare, she was at the counter, indicating that she had an appointment with the manager at ten o'clock.

Almost immediately, a frosted glass door on the customer side of the counter opened, and a tall, slender young woman came out to greet her.

'Miss Stratton, it's a pleasure to meet you, won't you please come in Marco is already here.'

Isabel Gonçalves, was of mid height, dark haired, attractive, and was wearing a navy-blue dress, and white high heeled sandals. Her toe and fingernails were painted a deep cherry red, to match her lipstick. She gave the impression that she didn't need to try very hard to be glamorous, she was wearing just the right amount of makeup, and her perfume was a light floral. Once inside the room, Helena was offered coffee or iced water before being shown to one seat of a pair. Senhora Gonçalves moved to the other side of the desk, before saying in Portuguese,

'Marco, has just gone to the bathroom, he should be here shortly, how was your journey, did you find us alright?'

'Yes, my trusty sat-nav got me here with ten minutes to spare.'

'That's good, I imagine it can be a bit disconcerting when you're not used to our roads, our signage is at best, poor, and at worst atrocious! Marco told me that your sat-nav didn't recognize Ameixeira on Friday night, so it was just as well the Café was open.'

Isabel said this half smiling as if trying to keep the conversation light and flowing.

'Yes, it was, otherwise I would have had to have slept in the car, which would have been a tad uncomfortable.'

The phone on her desk rang at that moment, and after a quick exchange of words, she quickly apologized, saying she had to pop out for a few seconds to check something, but she wouldn't be long.

The office they were in, wasn't large, or very opulent, apart from the desk and chairs, there was a sideboard complete with lamp and a tray for files, an upright coat stand, and a pot plant that had seen better days. It was minimal, and fitted the ethos of the bank, which was owned by the people who used it, as she had found out from Jane who also banked with them.

Then the door opened, instead of the manager returning Helena heard the soft but lyrical voice of Marco speaking in English

'Miss Stratton it's nice to see you again, I trust you have been well?'

Helena stood up and smiled, before presenting her hand for the expected handshake. Marco took it in both hands, and then unexpectedly lent down to give her a kiss on both cheeks. Just as he was doing so Isabel Gonçalves entered the room, and she gave him a puzzled look before resuming her best professional voice, and addressing Helena said,

'I am sorry about that, but an old and valued customer wanted a quick word, I hope I have not kept you both waiting too long.'

It was Helena who was smiling at Marco, that replied.

'No, far from it Marco, only arrived a second or so before you.'

On hearing this Marco sat in the seat next to hers, and picked up his briefcase, opened it, and then turned and looked directly at Helena, without meeting Isabel's gaze.

'Helena, I just need to go through a couple of formalities, firstly do you mind confirming for the record that are you happy to have me present during this conversation, and if you are, and would like me to advise you on any aspects please just ask, otherwise I will let Isabel take you through the accounts.'

'Yes of course, I am perfectly happy with your being present, and you can be sure that if I don't understand anything I will speak up.'

'Thank you, are you happy with that confirmation Isabel?' Isabel whose attention had been on Helena now turned to Marco and said,

'Yes perfectly, thank you Marco, so shall we get down to business?'

The next hour passed in a blur, Isabel explained the accounts, the charges and the service they would provide before asking,

'So would you like me to open new accounts for you in your name?

Helena nodded in agreement, and they then spent some time, going through the formalities associated with setting up of the Quinta's accounts, plus a personal account for herself.

Marco signed over the monies from the business and Sofia's personal accounts, and eventually they were finished. Helena was officially a millionaire.

Her heart was beating a little fast, but for a young woman the overwhelming sensation that she felt was one of great responsibility, tempered by a sense of being on a great adventure, both of which were threatening to overwhelm her.

Helena stood up, thanked Isabel for her help and said she was looking forward to having a long and fruitful relationship with Montepio. As she turned to leave, Marco said,

'Helena, do you have ten minutes, I just wanted to catch up with you about the Alencar Trust.'

'Yes of course, I will wait outside for you.'

'I will only be a few minutes.' He said smiling at her.

Walking out of the bank, she passed a number of posters of bright yellow sunflowers urging people to save, or open accounts, Helena had to admit that they were a more inviting marketing tool, than some of the British banking equivalents. Outside the sun was shining in a blue sky, and it felt like it was going to be a warm day.

Leaning against the car door, she closed her eyes, and turned her face to the sun and soaked up the early morning rays, as she heard the cars streaming by on the adjacent road.

'Hello again,' said Marco whose silent approach hadn't reached her ears through the sounds on the road.

'Hi' she replied.

'Do you have time for a coffee? There is a little café just five minutes' walk up the road.'

'I do yes, I don't need to be back in a hurry, though perhaps I should be as there is so much to do, and actually I would like your opinion on a couple of things.'

'Ok, it is this way.'

They walked slowly up the road, and Helena filled Marco in on her good luck with the house in Ameixeira, telling him that she had resolved to clear the house in preparation for the renovations.

Once at the café Marco ordered, and they sat down at a little table in the corner of the room. It was busy, people popped in and out on a regular basis, ordering a quick espresso, or a pastry to take away.

'So you have decided to stay already?'

Helena returned his gaze his eyes were smiling, and although today he was dressed in a suit and tie, he still managed to look pretty cool.

168

'Yes, it looks like I have, well at least I have told the two M's that I am staying and have galvanised their help to organize some trades to give me quotes.'

'I can help with that if you like, there are some good people around who would be only to delighted to provide a orçamento (quote).'

'Thanks for the offer I appreciate it, but no thanks. I visited Cováo yesterday, and I got a real sense of how fragile this small community is. Without local shops elderly people without transport are isolated. So for me, it will be important that the Quinta does its bit to enable the community to survive. Wherever possible I'm going to use local trades employing local people. I understand that might mean progress is not so fast, but the house has stood empty for so long another few months won't make any difference.'

Marco listened to this passionate statement and thought that she looked lovely when fired up; it must be something to do with the red glints in her hair and those soft green eyes, he was conscious that he was observing her with a mixture of admiration and something else he couldn't put his finger on, but before he had chance to nail it down, she spoke,

'Does that sound a bit soft to you?'

'No not at all, I find that I admire that type of thinking and approach, perhaps I've been living in a big City too long.' He sipped his coffee. Helena took advantage of the lull in the proceedings to also drink her coffee and eat some of the cake. She looked up and saw that Marco was studying her quite intently, it made her blush and to hide it, she said.

'Dad arrives tomorrow, and I am sure he will be able to help, his Portuguese is bit basic, well very basic really, so that will be interesting for us, still I have a feeling it will do him good to be here and to have something useful to do.'

'How old is he?

'Young really 57, he stopped working a year ago, when mum became ill and he has never gone back, he was an electrical engineer. Now of course he doesn't have to return to the world of work unless he wants too. The reality is I need him here to support me, so I guess that's a form of work as well.'

She gave him a slight smile, and as she did so she wondered what his kiss might be like, his lips looked so soft and inviting. Then she shook herself and returned to business.

You wanted to talk to me about the Alencar Trust?'

'Yes. I did. In order to be able to transfer this to you, there are certain formalities that we need to go through, they are not difficult, but we need to pick a day to visit the Alencar family solicitors in Porto. What remains of the Alencar family have asked if you would be willing to meet with them, I imagine they are somewhat interested in you as a member of the family they never expected to know. Carolina, the eldest surviving Alencar is not a direct descendant of Rafael, Luis was his only child of course, Carolina is descended from Rafael's younger sister Isabella, I have spoken to her at some length and she is looking forward to meeting with you. Also, they have kindly agreed you can have access to the family archive, where I gather there are letters you might want to see.'

'Wow that's fantastic, I meant to tell you that yesterday I found a number of old envelopes tied together all addressed to Sofia, and on the back, was Rafael's name. Unfortunately, the envelopes were all empty apart from one which curiously contained a small piece of parchment, on which was drawn an old orange tree, with a bunch of forget-me knots at the base of it. I am hoping that we find the letters somewhere else.'

'A bit of a mystery then, I imagine the house has plenty of them, I've never really explored it, or the grounds. One of my staff used to do the annual check.'

'You're welcome to visit, come for the day if you have time, in the meantime when do you suggest we visit Porto?'

'I think maybe it will have to be the end of next week, as my diary is pretty full at the moment. Let me make the arrangements and I will then confirm with you. I hope we will be able to meet with the Solicitors and visit Carolina on the same day, but if that's not possible we may have to stay overnight in Porto.'

'I don't think that that would be a problem, I would quite like to see Porto anyway. Just let me know when.'

Marco looked at his watch

'I must be going I need to be in the Lisbon office early this afternoon.'

Without thinking twice, Helena said,

'Are you going to be there tomorrow?'

'I am as a matter of fact, why?'

'Jane and Henry, the couple who have rented me their house, are spending the night in Lisbon before flying on Wednesday. I offered to drop them off at the Hotel Avenida Palace for one o clock. My dad is not due to arrive until 3pm, and so won't emerge from the terminal building until 3.30 or so, so I have a couple of hours to kill. If you're not tied up could we do lunch? I am sure we can find things to talk about that would mean it's a working lunch for us both.'

'The Avenida Palace, that's a great hotel, lucky people. I tell you what, why don't I meet you there and we can walk to a little restaurant I know not too far away. If we have the light lunch option, we can ensure your away in time to pick up your father.'

'Great, and thank you. I suppose I had better be going too, otherwise nothing is going to get done today.'

As soon as they reached the car park, Helena gave Marco the two kisses on the cheek that she had come to realize was the normal greeting or departing etiquette. She was surprised to feel that his skin against her lips was smooth like silk, and once more she felt the same tingle she had experienced in the Quinta and she was pretty sure he had too.

They said a final goodbye until the next day. Marco started his car and drove away, and Helena was just about to start hers too, when she glanced up at the bank, and noticed Isabel standing at the window of what must be her office, she idly wondered if she had been there long.

The drive back to Ameixeira, was slow, which allowed plenty of time for her to mull over her newly acquired wealth, and what she was going to do with it. Apart from the money that her Granddad had left her, that enabled the completion of her PhD, in relative comfort compared to other students; Helena had never had money of any significance. Not frivolous by nature, she enjoyed nice holidays, and a good bottle of wine, and over the years she had acquired a small but modest collection of wine, but in the main she had saved for what she wanted. Now of course everything was changed. The Quinta though had to be made to pay its way she had to become a businesswoman and an entrepreneur and quickly.

During the time at the bank, Helena had agreed to continue to invest in the same stocks and shares as previously, and after she had outlined her basic plans for restoring the Quintal, she had placed half a million euros in a new account for its restoration and transformation, it would need more than this of course but it was a start. This account was to be used primarily to cover the work

172

in the house, restoring the gardens and modernizing at least two if not three of the cottages in the grounds. Soon she would have to give some thought to the future for the products the Quinta produced, but at least for this year, as contracts for the grapes and olive oil had already been let there was no immediate rush to resolve this.

However, half a million euros was a lot of money, and already with her earmarked spending, the initial inheritance was reduced. Of course, soon she would have the more substantial monetary inheritance from her great-grandfather but until this was in the bank she thought it ought to be prudent.

Plans to restore some of the cottages was a first step towards making the Quintal pay its way, using the assets to bring in income by renting them as holiday lets. Helena hoped that the water quality of the lake might also be good enough for guests to be able to swim in it, which would be a nice bonus. Failing that she could build a communal swimming pool, after all she might not want too much extraneous noise near the house!

Last night whilst she lay in bed all sorts of ideas for the rentals came into her head, perhaps each cottage could have a cottage garden, planted with vegetables they could pick and use whilst staying there. Obviously, she would have to employ a gardener or two to keep these stocked and producing, but she would need one anyway for her own gardens. Though her biggest idea and one she knew she could do was producing their own wine and label. Helena already had the vines, she had the know-how, and a boutique winery might also be an attraction for guests. Perhaps they could bottle part of each year's production and label them with the guest's names for them to take away.

As the thoughts flowed thick and fast, each plan had seemed more extravagant than the one before, reigning in her imagination was necessary, and she told herself to stick to the basics. First of those was the acquisition of a permanent estate manager and more urgently a fixed term project manager. The issue was where could one of these be found locally? Perhaps Louisa as a local graduate knew where she could look for one.

Arriving back at the Quinta just in time for lunch at 12.30, she noted that the two M's were already seated and waiting in the kitchen. Maria had made a lovely tuna salad, and had opened another bottle of the wine from the cellar. Helena put her briefcase down, and said she was going to change. Ten minutes later dressed in a pair of linen trousers and a floral blue top, she sat down in her usual chair.

'Maria, can you show me the cellar this afternoon?'

'Yes Menina after lunch, but first eat, you must be hungry.'

Helena wasn't actually hungry at all, but the salad was light, and she tucked in.

'Maria do you drive?'

'Yes of course.'

'If I gave you a list would you mind going shopping for me later, as I needed provisions for the house.'

'Ah Menina I would if we had a car, as it is I have to use my brother's car when I go shopping. Manuel has his motor bike, but I don't use it unless I have too, and it would be no good for the supermarket anyway.'

'Oh I see, well you could use mine but its right-hand drive, would that be a problem?'

'No I don't think so, but you will need to show me the controls.'

As she drank her wine, Helena pondered on the future means of transport or, as at the moment, the lack of it, she clearly needed to buy a reasonable sized run around. Something that could be used by anyone working here when needed. Making a mental note to see to this at the end of the week, she glanced up to see Manuel looking at her longingly. Suddenly she knew what to do about it. Recognising that buying a vehicle of any sort was likely to be a big deal around here, she spent some minutes trying to look as though she was thinking hard. Fifteen minutes later she turned to Manuel who was sitting down chewing on some bread, and said,

'Manuel, are you very busy tomorrow?'

'Well I have things to do but nothing that won't wait a day, why Menina?'

'How would you and Maria like to go and buy the Quinta's first all-purpose run-around vehicle?'

Helena studied him, and was gratified to see him lean back and nearly fall of his chair, once steadied, he looked at her, his face full of uncertainty before saying.

'You want me? To go and buy a new car for the Quintal suitable for business use?'

Helena smiled at the enthusiasm that was written all over his face,

'Yes, I think so, after all you know the garages, and what type of vehicle we need around here, and both of you will be driving it quite a bit. Though I think we will need something rugged, four-wheel drive, with capacity for at least four people and ample space for carrying stuff. Perhaps even a tow bar for a trailer?'

Manuel's face was displaying a grin from ear to ear, he had the look of a man who had just had one of his wishes granted.

'Yes Menina, yes I know where the garages are.'

As she was looking at him, his facial features changed again, he tapped his nose, and looked as if he was carefully weighing up the pros and cons before speaking, he then said,

175

'But I don't think we need to buy a brand new one, we are going to be using it for mainly business reasons, so perhaps one a couple of years old, but with low mileage, will be sufficient.'

'Well if that's what you think I am happy to take your advice, we don't want to have any problems with it though, it needs to be reliable. I imagine we should be able to buy one for thirty thousand euros don't you think?'

Manuel was clearly beside himself, he looked as if he had just won the lottery. Helena who had sat back in the chair to observe his reactions and those of Maria, who had been listening intently to the exchange, said,

'I will speak to the bank this afternoon, then once you have decided on the vehicle, we can call the bank and they will transfer the money to the showroom directly. It will need to be insured for any authorized driver, so that will have to be sorted by the garage as well. I understand we are insured with Allianz so perhaps you can call them.'

'Yes Menina, we will go and look tomorrow, I will make sure I choose a good car for us.'

With that he scraped back his chair and left the kitchen, Helena thought to herself, that as he left, his chest was a little broader and his stance a tad taller, and his limp less noticeable. Once he had been gone a few minutes, Helena turned to Maria and asked

'Maria, do you mind if I ask you about Manuel's limp? How did he do it and does it cause him any problems.'

Maria, looked at her, a hint of concern flitting across her face.

'He had polio as a child, so he has pretty much always limped, sometimes it seems more pronounced than at other times. You know, when he was younger he was badly bullied, and even now he is very conscious about it. He told me once that he was always worried he wouldn't

176

be able to get a job as no one would employ him, and it took him an age to ask me out. In general girls didn't want to go out with someone who limped, even if he was good looking.'

'The world can be a cruel place Maria, but he is happy now, isn't he?'

'Yes, this job has given him a degree of pride, if not status, he is a kind man, and a good worker, and unfortunately that can't be said for all men here in central Portugal.'

Helena smiled at her.

'I have no doubt he is, it seems to me that both of you are kind and good people, so let's see if we can do something about improving his status then,' Helena said winking at her.

'Perhaps when people see him driving around in a new vehicle with the Quintals logo on it they will raise an eyebrow! Maybe I can give him a title that send signals to the community he is a trusted member of my team. I will give it some thought.'

'Oh Menina, he would be so proud, and I confess it will be nice to go to church on Sunday in a car rather than on the back of the motor bike!'

They both laughed at that, and Helena gave her a hug, which Maria returned with a tear in her eye.

Once lunch was over, Helena ventured back into the drawing room, she had agreed with Maria earlier, that they were going to remove the covers from the furniture to see what lay underneath. Henry and Jane would pop in some time later, and at any moment she expected to see Lionel arrive. Going upstairs, for a band for her hair, she decided to change into some older clothes, she put her hair up, which she then covered with an old hat, she had found in Sofia's wardrobe, a floppy straw number which fitted her well. Twenty minutes later, she and Maria had

177

unfastened both pairs of doors, and opened them wide, then in earnest they began to pull the covers off.

Sadly, many covers disintegrated in their hands, and the air became full of fine dust, they stopped frequently to allow it to disperse or settle, and whilst waiting they took the opportunity to sit on the uppermost step of the steps leading down to the garden and the parterres.

'I would have liked to have seen this when it was first planted, it must have been beautiful' Helena said to Maria.

'I guess it would have been lovely, though it would have taken some years before its full effect could have been appreciated. Maybe there exists planting plans from when the Quinta was built, they might give you some idea about what plants were used in it?'

Helena nodded, why hadn't she thought of that.

'Yes, of course, there are bound to be some somewhere, maybe in the Alencar family archives, or perhaps even in the library here?'

'Well perhaps when we have finished in here, we can check the draws in the library or even the shelves themselves.'

A few minutes later with the dust having settled a little bit, they got up to return to the task, it was sometime later when they heard a car on the driveway.

'Jane and Henry must be here.'

Helena said excusing herself and making her way to the front door. However, it wasn't them. Instead a small, slight man emerged from a battered grey van. The van was devoid of signage, but even to an untrained eye, it shouted out that its owner was a builder.

'Menina Stratton? Hello, my names Vitor Martins. Manuel phoned me this morning, and said you wanted to consult with me.'

'Ah Senhor, I am pleased to meet you, but I wasn't expecting you until Wednesday.'

'Well, I was in the area anyway so thought I would call in, do you have time now?'

Senhor Martins looked at Helena as if he wanted to eat her, it was a slightly uncomfortable and definitely lecherous look, but she remembered what several people had told her, and she gave him a small smile.

'Well I suppose so, I am a bit dirty though, and if you could wait inside a few minutes I will just go and fetch Manuel, in case we have any problems with translation.'

However, within a second of her uttering the last word, Manuel appeared in the hallway as if by magic, turning around Helena saw Maria winking at her. Then Manuel said,

'Ah Vitor, you've arrived early I see.'

'Well you know how it is, I was passing and thought why wait until Wednesday, as long as Menina Stratton has time, I have time'

Helena, looked down at him and said firmly

'I have time.' before turning to Manuel and saying

'Manuel will you come with us, as you know the house and grounds better than me.'

'Of course, Menina' said Manuel sounding decidedly officious.

Helena pointed the way towards the drawing room

'Why don't we go through to the drawing room, we can sit down if you don't mind the dust and I can talk you through the basics, then perhaps you and Manuel can walk around together, I am sure you won't need me.'

They found seats in the dusty drawing room, and Helena explained to Senhor Martins that she wanted a quote for quite a lot of work.

'Senhor Martins, the house has been well looked after structurally, therefore I am not envisaging any major

179

problems with the roof or the structure of the walls. However, we have no electrical wiring, and the plumbing needs replacing. All of this will have a major impact on the existing walls, and floors. I envisage that the original plasterwork will have to come off, to give the plumber and electrician access as I want everything hidden in the walls, not surface mounted. Then of course, everything will need re-plastering in lime render. Where there are wooden floors I want them keeping where possible and repairing like for like, and if, as in the Library there is wooden panelling I want that carefully removing and replacing when the work has been completed. I will ensure the plumber and electrician's work with you to make everything go as smoothly as possible. I need a number of new bathrooms, and preferably en-suites in about four bedrooms. Though as yet I need your advice on which rooms are best suited for this. Lastly, I need a new extension for an enlarged kitchen, preferable built on to the back of the existing Quinta, with glass walls so we can take advantage of the views beyond. I need a summerhouse in the grounds by the lake, and the pontoon on the lake is unsafe. Pathways require some care as well. There are cottages in the ground that need refurbishing to include modern facilities. Do you think you can handle this amount of work?'

Senhor Martins swallowed, and his enthusiasm for such a large contract was barely disguised.

'I am almost positive I can, as long as you don't expect me to start work tomorrow.'

'Of course not, next week will be fine.'

Helena looked at him without batting an eyelid, but eventually she couldn't contain her own pomposity any longer, and she laughed out loud, quickly followed by Manuel and Maria, a few seconds later Senhor Martins also began to chuckle.

180

'Your joking with me Menina, its unkind.'
Though she noticed that he seemed relieved, that she
was not as severe as she had first appeared to him.
Softening her tone, she went on.
'No Senhor, I am not joking about the amount of work,
only about the start date. I imagine I have left many
things out, and I am going to rely on your knowledge to
give me a quote that covers everything, I am open to
suggestions as well. My father will be here from
tomorrow, he is an engineer by profession and he will no
doubt take a keen interest in your views.'
Helena turned to Manuel.
Manuel perhaps you could show Senhor Martins around,
once your back I am sure we can find a bottle of wine to
have a drink together. Turning then to Senhor Martins,
she said,
'Obviously, I imagine you will need to come back several
times in order to scope the job, if you need access to the
estate please call Manuel he is my Estate Supervisor,
and he can be here to assist you. In all things he has my
confidence.'
Manuel who had sat listening to Helena speaking, nearly
choked on his coffee, but then did well to hide his
surprise at his new title. Helena thought that his chest
puffed out a little and Maria smiled and mouthed, 'Thank
you.'
'How long do you think it will be until you can give us the
quote? I don't want to rush you of course, but equally I do
need to get on, as it's the 3rd of the month today, do you
think you might have it by the close of the month?'
'Certainly, I can give you the quote for the house by then,
it may take longer to give you the quotes for the other
parts. I take it the house is the priority?'
'It is, though I would like work on one of the cottages to
go on in parallel, so that in September, when Senhor and

181

Senhora Clarke come back I can move into it, whilst work continues. As you go around can you decide which cottage would be best to convert, I need two bedrooms both en-suite, a lounge and a kitchen with a utility. That must be ready within four months.'

'Okay Menina, I better get going, I will call back in before I go, come on then Manuel time to give me the tour.'

With that they both left the room, Maria went over to Helena and gave her an unexpected hug, when she had finished she looked at Maria and said

'I suppose he is my Estate Supervisor, you must be my housekeeper, and as I have just changed your job descriptions, you both deserve pay rises, don't you think?

'Menina, do you really mean that? Me a housekeeper, are you sure?'

'I am sure Maria. Someone needs to look after the legions of women that will be cleaning up here.' She smiled at that.

'I will talk to Manuel about the pay, and I prefer to still pay you as a couple. There is one thing though I will need to employ an Estate Manager, and a Project Manager, so Manuel will have someone else giving him direction as well. I hope he won't mind that?'

Maria looked at her with a wry smile on her face.

'Manuel is sensible, he will understand that you need special expertise, and he knows his own limits he will be cool and supportive. You've already made him a happy man. When he knows we are going to get a pay rise I am sure he will be over the moon, I think you have just secured a loyal employee for as long as you want him.'

'Well an employee yes, but I hope a friend too, and please call me Helena!'

'Yes Menina, I mean Helena, I think you have, god bless you.'

Chapter 10: Cellars and Secret's

The crunch on the gravel was becoming ever louder and, emerging from the side veranda and walking around to the front, Helena was just in time to see her temporary landlords approaching the house. They waved at her, and she waved back

'Hi Helena, I hope were not too early?'

'No, actually its good timing, the builder has just arrived, and Manuel is taking him around freeing me up.'

Giving them both quick kisses and Jane a hug, Helena gestured with her arm in a large arc,

'Where do you want to start!'

'Oh, inside please, we have seen the outside a few times haven't we Fish.'

Henry nodded

'Yes, it is a lovely building, and the iron work on the veranda is amazing, art nouveau I guess.'

'Yes, I think so too.'

Stepping forward Helena turned to face the house.

'Shall we go inside? Though I warn you that many of these rooms are in exactly the same state as they were forty years ago. Some of them, even I haven't yet seen, because the locks are seized. It's also pretty dusty everywhere.'

'That's good I don't have to worry about making a mess then.'

Jane chipped in.

'No, I don't think that's going to be an issue, you're more likely to go home muckier than when you entered!'

Once inside the hallway, they gravitated to the already open double doors that led to the drawing room, crossing through the hall before going inside.

Jane was entranced, she looked everywhere, and then her eyes fell on the painting.

'Helena, this is gorgeous, I know this is going to be a beautiful and really elegant room.'

'I hope so, Maria and I have made a small start in here, removing the dust covers, so we can see what we have, at some point we will need to decide what furniture we keep, and which is going.'

Whilst Helena was speaking, Jane had made her way to the doors overlooking the garden, and was staring outside. Henry meanwhile had walked over the painting. Seeing him casting an appreciative eye over it, Helena joined him.

'That, we took down from over the fireplace, it's my great-great grandparents and their son Luis. It seems to have been painted under the old orange tree half way up the drive.'

Jane moved over to join them, and looked at the painting.

'It's lovely, what a beautiful woman, is it Sofia?'

'Yes, it's Sofia, my mum had the same name, she was beautiful too.' said Helena, with a hint of sadness entering her voice, knowing that her mum, was never going to see this.

'My dad is going to be surprised at the likeness.'

Henry who had been quietly studying it, said

'You think it was painted by the old orange tree in the drive?

'Yes, I think so, the setting looks about right.'

'I agree about the setting, but I don't see how it can have been the same tree. I understand that a few do live to quite an age, but no more than ninety to hundred years, so if it was the same tree it would be nearly two hundred years old now. The tree in the drive doesn't look two hundred years old!' Helena frowned.

'Your right of course, maybe I got a little carried romantically if you know what I mean. It can't possibly be the same tree but the tree in the drive is old now, so it must have been planted a long time ago'
Henry nodded and turned to Helena nodding.
'I agree, perhaps something happened to the original tree, and another was planted in its place?'
'That sounds perfectly plausible, it's a nice thought that we can see the same setting now as they did a hundred years or more ago, don't you think?'
'Yes, it is, and looking around this room it's likely that you're seeing it today much as it would have been then, if the other rooms are the same, you have a mini time capsule on your hands, you could open it as a museum!'
Jane who, through out this conversation had been wandering around the room, as Henry and Helena were talking, now turned towards them and said.
'The furniture in this room is gorgeous, it's all period, you have got to keep it all! Ok some of it needs reupholstering, the mice have made their homes in some pieces, but it's all from the art nouveau period, just like the styling outside. Just look at this sideboard the marquetry is beautiful.'
'Have you looked inside it, Helena?'
'No not yet, why do you want to?'
'Ooh yes please'
Jane who was just about to pull on the door handles, stopped when Henry said firmly
'No, you don't Jane Cheryl Clarke, we will never get out of this room if you do, and we don't have the luxury of time! You will have to let Helena do that, come on we need to see more of the house.'
With a degree of reluctance, Jane agreed and followed Helena, who had pointed in the direction of the Library.
Maria then arrived with tea, she greeted them both

185

warmly before handing over mugs, and thanking Jane for the tea bags. For the next hour or so all four wandered around hugging their mugs, whilst visiting all the rooms that were open apart from Sofia's bedroom. Helena who was really enjoying sharing the house's treasures with them then ventured.

'Just one last room to go, it's across the hall, I am sure this is the room Sofia must have been using as a bedroom before she died. Interestingly, in the dressing table I found some very old envelopes addressed to Sofia.'

Jane answered questioningly.

'Envelopes you say, letters as well?'

'Unhappily not, just the envelopes they were tied with a pale blue ribbon, and carefully wrapped up in a lace edged linen handkerchief.'

'How enigmatic, I take it you looked for the letters?'

As they passed through the door and entered the untidy room, Helena responded to her with

'I have had a good look around, that's why the room looks a mess, but I didn't find anything.'

Jane turned to her husband.

'Henry, do you think there maybe secret draws in the furniture?'

'Mm, there might be, but you would have to be quite patient in trying to find them, sometimes draws can have false bottoms or backs.'

Helena looked at them both quizzically.

'Secret draws Henry what do you mean?'

Henry replied.

'In the past safes were not that common, so furniture often contained the odd secret draw into which precious papers were placed for safe keeping.'

'Go on then, spill the beans how do you know about this.'

'Well I am not an expert, but some years ago I did a short course on 18th and 19th century furniture, at the Hemswell Antique Centre. At the time I was very interested in antiques, because we had recently brought an old Georgian House, and we wanted to buy appropriate furniture. Obviously buying Georgian antiques was generally beyond our means but there was a Georgian revival in the late 19th and early 20th century so reproduction pieces could be obtained at reasonable prices.'

'A man of hidden talents is my husband' said Jane proudly. Helena was quite intrigued by this possibility, it made sense to her, after all the letters had to be somewhere, she turned to Henry and asked,

'But how would I know if there were secret compartments?'

'Ah well that's the problem of course, if the furniture was well made, many people wouldn't notice the subtle differences in width, height or length. As for where the catches are that would release the secret compartments, well it is simply a case of trial and error.'

'Well, I've learnt something new today, and I'll look at the draws again at some point, perhaps I might be able to detect any differences, now I know they might exist!'

Jane who had been looking around, suddenly said

'Where is the wardrobe? Sofia must have had a wardrobe, where would her clothes be otherwise?'

'Good point' Helena replied

'When I looked in here for the first time yesterday, I didn't give a thought to the fact that there wasn't one in here. But your right, she must have had one, and I can't see any evidence in here of one having been moved; the floor is a pretty uniform colour.'

Henry who was approaching the painted wooden wall panels next to the Tallboy, said

187

'Maybe there is a door behind one of these panels.'
With that all four of them moved in unison towards the wall.

'But how would a panel open?'

'In all the films I have ever seen they simply press the wall and the door is revealed!'

Jane said this a bit tongue in cheek, before Henry looking at them said,

'I think Jane is right, shall I try Helena, I am a bit taller than the rest of you, if there is a door in here, the release catch might be at any height.'

All three of them nodded in assent, and watched absorbed as Henry felt along the right-hand edge of the painted wooden panels in the wall, after a few minutes and half way down the upper panel, they heard a click, and the panel opened.

'Wowzer, we found something' said Jane.

Henry put his fingers behind the panel and a hidden door opened. They peered inside, it was dark, and it took a few moments to adjust to the light levels. In front of them was a short corridor, maybe three metres in length that ended with a door at the rear. Maria said she would fetch a torch, so they waited, once she came back they passed it to Henry who went ahead, and turned the door handle, it was a little stiff, but it yielded to his turn, and he found himself in a bathroom. Natural light was coming in from a long window high up on the far wall, below which was a large bath, surrounded by wooden panelling. A beautifully sink with green patterning and a matching toilet were also placed on the far wall. The right-hand sidewall was a bank of eight doors, consisting of four half-height doors, laid out side by side, two on the floor to waist height, and the other two on top from waist height to the ceiling. Next to them were two sets of full-length doors. Once they were all inside, and had had a moment to look around,

188

their astonishment was apparent. Jane walked towards the doors and said to Helena

'Do you mind if I open one?'

'No, of course not, go ahead let's see what's inside.'

Jane opened the bottom pair of two doors on the extreme left, revealing a number of deep shelves, one of which contained what looked like a stack of linen sheets, on the next were towels of various shades of blue.

'This cupboard seems to contain household linen.' She then opened the pair on the top. These contained a range of folded up clothes.

'Look at these' Jane said beckoning them forward

Inside were shelves covered in a faded silk fabric, on top of which lay folded men's shirts, and what appeared to be quite old-fashioned men's underwear.

Helena pulled some out, she thought the clothing was very old, vintage maybe, did these belong to her great-great grandfathers?

'What do you think' she said turning to Jane who was at her elbow.

'I guess this stuff is Edwardian, look at the collars. It was probably made close to a hundred years ago.'

Jane lifted a shirt from the top of the stack, and shook it out. It was in remarkably good condition, although now a faded cream rather than perhaps it original white, but with only an odd hole here and there created by a moth.'

'Shall we try this one?' Henry said from somewhere behind us.

Helena nodded, and Henry pulled open the doors; inside instead of shelves there was a hanging rail, from which shrouded outfits hung.

'Bingo!'

'Bingo indeed, I think we have found Sofia's wardrobe.'

Henry stepped back, and Helena looked inside, she brushed her hand across the clothes that hung there, before reaching in and taking out one of the shrouded hangers. Whipping off the ancient cotton covering she found the most beautiful pale pink silk dress.

'This is gorgeous, it looks couture and very old, maybe 1900's.'

The sleeves were short, puffy and covered with lace, it had a quite low neckline, and the bodice was embellished in lace, and from just under the bust came a thick band of dark pink silk from under which the floor length skirt emerged. Apart from the centre panel of the skirt, which was plain, the remainder was covered in an outer layer of beautiful pale pink lace, matching the bodice and sleeves.

Jane who had continued to check what was inside the other covers, said

'It looks like there are half a dozen or more dresses here, what a find.' To which Henry replied

'Well, it's a good place to check for any other hidden draws or panels, so good hunting Helena, but we must be off still got lots to do before you pick us up in the morning.'

'Do we have to go, I am just thrilled by all of this.'

Jane bemoaned looking pleadingly at him.

Henry replied with a look at Helena.

'You really can't take her anywhere, she would be here until its dark if she had her own way.'

Then turning and putting his hand firmly on his wife's back he steered her towards the door,

'If you want to go to Australia we have to go, we still have things to do!' he said breaking into a smile.

'Okay Fish, your right I suppose, but Helena you have to keep me updated on your finds, remember I expect an email every now and then.'

They all trooped out of the bathroom, Helena passed the pink dress to Maria, who had offered to re-wrap it and hang it back up, Henry who was in the hall waited until both Maria and Helena had closed the bedroom door. 'Ok Helena we will see you tomorrow then about 10.45, I can give you the keys once I've locked up. Oh, and Manuel popped round this morning, so he knows how to clean the pool for you. We have moved a lot of our own personal possessions into the small spare bedroom, so they shouldn't be in your way.'

'Thank you both very much, it's a real godsend, and I appreciate it a lot.' Helena walked with them to the front door, they all said goodbye and she watched them disappear down the drive. Noticing as they did that they stopped a few moments to look at the Orange Tree. Maria and Helena then went into the kitchen, where sitting down, they both drank a glass of water, from the bottle in the middle of the table. Maria who had been unusually quiet in Sofia's bedroom said.

'This house is a puzzle. I had no idea that there was a bathroom off that bedroom. But then I suppose, I've only been in the house a few times when small bits of work have had to be undertaken, and even then, I have only been in a couple of rooms. To be honest I found the house quite unnerving, though now you're here it seems okay, odd isn't it.'

'It is I agree, and I wonder how many more secrets it has to share with us?'

'Maria do Carmo might be able to shed some light on it, she must have visited here, and maybe her parents passed to her some information.

'Well, it's funny you should say that, as I have arranged with Alice to meet Maria in the Cafe on Wednesday afternoon, so perhaps then I will find out.'

They finished drinking their water, and within ten minutes were back in the drawing room, carefully pulling more covers of the paintings and furniture. Helena reflected to herself that Jane was right about the upholstery, much of it was either mouse or moth eaten, and she doubted what could be saved, but if the frames were ok, perhaps they could be re-covered. Helena made yet another mental note to ask Carlos about it, perhaps his professors wife might know someone who specializes in fabrics. Much of the furniture though was in really good condition and she was beginning to think that maybe these rooms had been closed up for a much longer period than forty years. An hour or so later, with everything now uncovered, voices could be heard from the veranda. Manuel was returning with Senhor Martins, Helena and Maria waited on the steps, for them.

'Well Menina, what a perfectly lovely building you have, I hope you have deep pockets though, it is going to cost quite a bit to get the house up to date, whilst conserving much of what exists at the same time. I have had a quick look at the cottages as well. I will need to comeback with one of my men, to do some measuring of them and the house. Do you know who you might be going to use for plumbing and electrics?'

'No Senhor Martins, not yet. Is it a problem?'

'In truth it would be better to know who I might be working with, as depending on who it is the quote might be higher or lower. But I will give you a ball park figure by the end of next week, and as soon as you know who you are going to instruct I can firm up the price by the end of the month. Obviously, I can supply both trades, and give you an inclusive price if you prefer?' Helena had been warned to expect this by Marco, so she politely replied.

'That's a kind offer, but I want to use a variety of local people as far as possible, I am seeing Ramiro Agosto and his son Antonio about the electrics this week, and I have a contact for a plumber too. I expect to be able to tell you by the middle of the month, as long as they can quote quickly. You should also know I am asking for quotes from other builders.'

'Of course Menina, but you know I am the best, I have many testimonials, the casa of Senhor and Senhora Clarke I built that eight years ago. It is a good house, you have been in it. I am also cheap but good quality.'

He said this without a trace of humility, he clearly believed in himself Helena thought, and that can't be a bad thing.

'Senhor, I do not doubt that you are a good builder, your reputation goes before you, and I expect you know that; but my father would be unhappy with me if I obtained only one quote. So do your best, visit as often as you like to make sure the quote is inclusive, because I want a fixed price. Now shall we have a glass of wine?'

As if on cue Maria appeared with a carafe of red wine, clearly not the one we had been drinking from our cellar though. Manuel poured and we all drank to each other's health, ten minutes later Senhor Martins said he must be going indicating he had a lot to do, but he would be back tomorrow with one of his men to measure up more precisely. Once he had gone, Manuel told Helena that as they were walking around, Senhor Antonio tried to find out if any other builders were being asked to quote. Manuel said he told him that he had only been asked to call him, but he had heard me talking to Senhor Gonçalves about others!

Helena wasn't surprised by this, she had given it quite a lot of thought, as Marco had already endorsed his work she had resolved not to call in another builder; it seemed as though this would be a waste of her time, and more importantly the other builder's time, as no one was going to quote as low as Senhor Martins would. But now she resolved to call in a builder from outside the immediate vicinity as well, but only to quote for the cottages and the

193

extension, maybe a little competition would be a good thing after all. As she explained all this to Manuel and Maria, they suggested a builder from Maçao, and Helena asked Manuel to go ahead and call him, and get him to come over and quote for the cottages and the extension. As it was now late afternoon, Maria said she was going home to begin preparations for dinner, so Helena decided to check with Lionel which rooms were now open. Walking back through the hall, she called Lionel, a muffled voice came from upstairs, and a few seconds later Lionel was hanging over the bannister rail.

'Yes Menina, what can I do for you?'

'Hi Lionel, two things please, firstly which rooms down here are now open? and secondly do you have the phone number for the plumber, who is disabled?'

'All the rooms off the Hall are now open, but inside the sitting room, I am having problems with the windows to the far side. As for the plumber, yes, I have his number, do you want me to call him?

'Do you mind?'

No Menina, I know him it's probably easier, besides he can be a little reserved.'

'In that case if you don't mind, it might be better if you call him. Could you ask him if he can come and see me sometime on Thursday or Friday?'

'Of course, I will call him tonight.'

'Thanks Lionel, oh and isn't it time you went home?'

'Shortly, just working on a particularly difficult lock, I may have to force this one, unless you know a burglar!'

'Me know a burglar, maybe,' she grinned 'But not here! What seems to be the problem.'

'Come up and see.'

Once at the top of the stairs she saw Lionel turn into the end bedroom that faced the rear of the building. Once inside though she found herself in an inner hall that contained two doors. One, immediately on the right was already open and clearly led to a bedroom, however the one on the left was shut, this door was made very simply, and it had no embellishments and curiously no handle, just a lock.

Lionel was kneeling beside the door; beside him on the floor were the full set of the Quinta's keys marked with the rooms names or numbers, however Lionel informed her that as yet, he hadn't found one that fitted the lock. Helena turned to Lionel.

'It's quite a small lock, so are we looking for a simple key?'

'Not totally sure, all the keys here are quite elaborate, I have tried all the ones I know don't belong to another door, but they simply don't fit, and I have a feeling we are not going to find one, anywhere in the house. I have a lot of keys at home, I will bring some I think might work and try them tomorrow, but if they don't work, we will have to force it.'

Having given it a quick once over Helena pronounced, 'Let's hope we don't have to do that, I don't really want to lose anything of significance, though as you say it's a really quite plain door, is this the door to the attic space do you think?'

'I think so, it's not uncommon to have access to an attic space from an inner hallway.'

'We will need access to it when the work starts, so it has to be undone at some point, okay then let's leave it until tomorrow and see how you get on then.'

Helena left Lionel packing away his tools, and she retraced her steps back down stairs. On impulse she decided that if Maria had returned, she would ask her to show her the cellar, before darkness set in.

Within a few minutes, Maria entered the kitchen and agreed to show her the way to the cellar. They took the first door on the right in the inner hall, which led to the old laundry room, once inside Helena saw that as well as the old laundry facilities, it contained a staircase clearly going down. They had picked up torches, descended the staircase, where a further door led to the under croft. Maria unlocked the door, and they stepped inside, it took a little while for their eyes to become adjusted to the light levels, but slowly, and with the aid of a torch Helena saw that they were in quite a large space. Against one wall were a number of barrels of different sizes. On the other side was a run of metal wine racks. At one end of these was a cage, with yet another small run of wine racks inside. The cage was made from iron bars in a simple design, though it went from floor to ceiling. They reminded Helena of the customs and excise sheds she was used to seeing, where wine and spirits were held prior to release after tax and duty had been paid.

'Do you have a key for this lock Maria?'

'No Menina I don't.'

Helena thought to herself, if they have a locked cage, there might be some real treasures in here. She walked away from the cage, and with the aid of her torch surveyed the racking. It was quite old, metal and she thought it might be French. Pulling out a bottle from the middle of the rack at about shoulder height, she tried to brush of the dust, but she couldn't make out the label.

'How many bottles do you think are here Maria'

'A lot, but just exactly how many I have no idea, I only came in here for the first time the other day.'

'I wonder how old the oldest bottle is? Let's take this one back upstairs and see if I can read the label.'

As they turned to go, Helena suddenly said,

'Maria where in here is the wine we are drinking, with dinner?'

'Just here by the door, I don't really like coming down here, so I just grabbed that which was nearest, I hope that was okay?'

'It's fine Mariia, so on our way out let's pick a couple more for dinner!'

Helena heard Maria pluck a couple of bottles from the rack nearest the door, whilst she plucked another one from the rack at the other end of the cellar. Helena wondered if the cage held the vintner's records, they must be somewhere. They would need to look for a key or get Lionel to force the lock. It would be very interesting to check the stock inside, it must be quite old, and it could be that she was sitting on some gems. Going past Maria, she waited at the top of the stairs for her to lock the cellar door, before saying.

'Maria, does the trapdoor in the pantry drop down into the cellar?'

'No Menina, that door used to give access to the coal and logs for the range and fires. But the wooden ladder has long since disappeared. I expect in more recent times it wasn't used, as there is a wood store just out the back of the kitchen. If you look on the outside of the house there is a small set of double wooden doors, that is the external hatch.'

'I see I should go and look tomorrow.'

Making their way back into the kitchen Helena put her two bottles on the table, she was just going to find a cloth to carefully wipe them, when her mobile rang, it was Louisa.

'Hi Louisa, lovely to hear from you.'

'Helena, I am pleased to catch you, I spoke to my mum like you asked, and after a little persuasion I think I have managed to get her to agree to come and help.'

'Oh that's great news we will need all the help we can get.'

'Well it is good news apart from the fact that she says she doesn't want paying, she is just happy to help.'

'Mm okay, well I am sure I can find some way to pay her in kind, we can put our heads together about that can't we?'

'Yes of course, anyway she said just let her know when you need her, and she will come. Oh by the way I can't come on Wednesday, the head has called an early evening meeting, do you know there are times when I wish I wasn't a teacher!'

'I suppose all jobs have their down sides, talking of which, which I wasn't, I wondered if you could help me with something. I have decided to stay here and restore the house, I can't possibly oversee this, as well as work out the Estates future strategy, so I need to employ a couple of managers. First, I need to employ a short-term project manager, who can oversee all the works, liaise with the trades and plan in the schedules its possibly a role for six months. Then within the next couple of months or so, I will need a permanent Estate Manager. I wondered, as a recent graduate, if you knew of anyone with skills in these areas, preferably someone local.'

'That's great news Helena, and yes as it happens, I do know someone who would be good for the short-term role, and I could give some thought to the permanent role over the next few days.'

'You do? That's fabulous, because I know I don't have the capacity to do it all. Besides I need to concentrate on the Quintals future. So can you put me in touch with them?'

'You already know them, its Carlos of course'

'Carlos, you mean your brother?'

'Yes of course! He completed a degree in business and economics, three years ago, then decided to spend a further year studying design, mainly because the jobs market was so depressed, and of course dad had become unwell. So he didn't want to move away from home, like many of his fellow students. Obviously, he has no substantial management experience, but he has enthusiasm!'

Helena was unsure.

'Louisa it's a good thought, can you let me think about it overnight, but to be honest I was really hoping for someone who could hit the ground running, and it sounds like Carlos might need support.' Louisa looked crestfallen.

'Oh dear, I haven't explained myself very well have I. Carlos has loads of practical planning experience, he used to help out in the company my dad managed in Serta. It was a large commercial building company with contracts all over Portugal. At first, he worked some of his summers labouring on building sites, but then before he went to University, he took a gap year and spent a whole year working with them, he assisted the planning co-ordinator. Every summer whilst at University, he worked his summers in the offices. They wanted him to work for them when he graduated, but dad was ill, and it was too far. He knows the building game and he has the project skills. Would you just talk to him?' Louisa looked at Helena her eyes pleading for her to say something positive. Then she continued.

'He has given up so much since dad became ill, and now he won't leave home whilst mum is so sad.'

Helena felt guilty at hearing this from someone she hardly knew, this community and its people were really getting under her skin, and deep inside she hoped something positive might come from this. She put her hand on Louisa's arm.

'Don't worry, I will talk to him if you think he would be interested. Why don't you ask him to call me as soon as he can? And I am glad you explained all of that, and I wouldn't normally pry, but do you mind telling me what happened to your dad. It's not because I am nosy, it's mainly so I don't put my foot in it with your mum.'

'He died of throat cancer. He became poorly just over four years ago, it was gradual at first, and he had a cough that just wouldn't go away. He smoked of course, so he thought that it was just a smoker's cough, after all nearly all men here smoke and coughs are common. After about a year, mum persuaded him to go to see the doctor, eventually he was diagnosed and began treatment. Dad, well he continued to work for some time. The company was very good about it, he went part time for a while before he had to stop. We, and he, knew it was terminal, but mum just couldn't accept it, ultimately of course there was nothing else the doctors could do. He died nearly two years ago, and mum still hasn't got over it. Carlos used to smoke too, but he stopped the day dad was diagnosed.'

'I am so sorry Louisa, and thank you for telling me, I can empathise so much with you all, my mum died of cancer too, only seven months ago, I loved her like crazy, but I am only here because of her death, so maybe this is meant to be.'

Louisa and Helena talked for a little longer, Helena reflected that it was good to talk with someone who had a shared experience, and she thought that Louisa felt it too. Before they hung up she agreed that Carlos would bring his mum up on Thursday, and he would call before then to arrange for the two of them to meet.'

Helena sat on the chair for a few minutes thinking about the conversation she had just had, it would be fantastic if Carlos had the skills she needed, as he might be able to start straight away. The fact that he spoke good English would be a bonus; because her dad was bound to want

200

to be involved someway, and she didn't want to have to spend all of her time translating that would be a poor use of her time. Louisa said she would call him quickly, so with luck and a fair wind perhaps they could meet quickly to discuss the role.

Helena then shifted her attention to the two bottles of wine she had left on the table, she looked around for a damp cloth. On the sink was a cloth Maria had left on the side, Helena ran it under the tap, and then wrung it out tightly, before gently wiping the label on the bottles. The first label was a little fragile, but she managed to make out the name Periquita. Excitement rose inside her like a bubble, she knew this brand, it was a famous wine from the Douro, and made by the Fonseca family, and it was probably one of the oldest Portuguese wine brands, still going. Though Fonseca was probably better known in England for its Port wine.

Wow, Helena thought to herself, I wonder how much of this wine was in the cellar and which vintages. This bottle seemed to indicate it was bottled in 1956, but she wasn't entirely sure. The second bottle's label was a little less fragile it was from the Tapada de Chaves winery, a wine from the upper part of the Alentejo. This particular bottle was the 1962 vintage. The contrast with the bottles they had been drinking couldn't have been greater, these were recent, with modern labelling, the red was a Vila Jardim, Escolha from the Quinta Vale do Armo, and these two bottles said 2014. Helena could understand the old wines in the cellar, Sofia had clearly brought these whilst she was alive, but the modern wines constituted a mystery, how and why were they here? So she made another mental note to ask Marco about them.

Dinner when it came was a wonderful rabbit casserole, and it was delicious, eating rabbit was a first for Helena,

but she vowed it wouldn't be her last, after that came a
nice fresh fruit salad.

During dinner she talked with Manuel about how she saw
his new role, casually dropping in that she was giving
them a pay rise with immediate effect. He was excited,
and told her that he was going to buy Maria a new sofa.
Helena smiled at his enthusiasm for something that back
home she wouldn't have given much thought too.

Manuel of course was keen to talk about cars, and he did
so, he told them both that he had narrowed it down, and
would be going back tomorrow to give them a test drive.
Helena gave him 1000 euros, to secure the vehicle until
she could transfer the money from the bank. He counted
the money out and then said he would write a receipt.

'That's really not necessary Manuel, I trust you just make
sure you buy a good car.'

Helena was almost sure she saw a tear form at the
corner of his eye, so she quickly changed the subject.
Outside the sky was now a deep black, Maria had lit the
hurricane lamps some time ago, and as they finished
their coffee, she asked Helena if she wanted some hot
water for a wash. Conscious that she was going to Lisbon
the following day, she agreed, before saying to Maria,
'Would you mind me using the bathroom in your cottage
tomorrow morning to have a quick shower?' Maria
hesitated before saying

'Of course, we don't mind it's no problem at all, but its
perhaps not what your used too it's pretty basic.'

'Maria as long as the shower works that's fine with me if
you're okay with it, and when I get back from the airport
with dad we will move into the South Fork, and you can
go back home.

'Yes, it will be good to be in my own bed, but it has felt
like a little adventure the last few days.'

'I reckon there is going to be a lot more of those Maria, have you had any luck with finding some ladies for the clearing out?'

'Not yet, I've put a call or two out, and I am very hopeful by Friday we will have a little band of workers, some will come to be nosy of course, but many will be pleased to be working.'

'Let's see if we can make it more fun than work then, because if we do they will come back another time. Oh and by the way, Louisa told me that her mum is coming to help, I think she will be here on Thursday, though she doesn't want to be paid.'

'Excellent! It will do her good to be out of the house, and having something else to think about.'

Helena's mobile phone rang at that moment, and she saw that it was a number she didn't know, so speaking Portuguese she answered

'Hello, Helena here.'

'Hi Helena, it's Carlos. Louisa has just got hold of me and told me your looking for a project manager, well I am definitely more than interested, though Louisa said you might be looking for someone with more experience, and if you are then it's no problem, I can understand that.'

Helena detected something more than just hope in his voice, so she simply said,

'Why don't we meet Carlos, I can tell you what I want, and you can tell me how your skills might fit with it. I am afraid I don't have anything so formal as a job description, but I can give you a broad outline of what I think the job will entail, and you do understand its only for about six months?'

'Yes, I do, Louisa made that clear to me, so when can we meet?'

203

His enthusiasm was unfortunately for Helena rather infectious, and she knew how he felt at the opportunity of having a new job, so she said

'Where are you now?'

'At home.'

'Well, if you're free why don't we meet in Café Central in half an hour?'

'Really? I mean of course, certainly, if you're sure, well I will see you then, and thank you.'

'No need to thank me I haven't done anything yet.'

'No of course not, I mean thanks for agreeing to meet me, see you soon.'

As she clicked off her phone she caught Maria and Manuel looking at her with faint half hidden smiles. Helena flung her arms in the air.

'I know I know, I am a bit impulsive but it's dark and I have nothing else to do tonight!

A quick wash and fifteen minutes later she was back in the car and on the road to Cováo , she noticed that streetlights started in Ameixeira, but they didn't extend down the unmade part of the road to the Quinta. Clearly some negotiations would have to be made with the electricity supply company if the Quinta was to connect to the local supply. Perhaps then the street lighting could be extended to the end of the drive.

As she passed through the villages, she thought how pretty they looked at night. All around she could see lights twinkling in small ribbons in the distance along the valley road, on arriving in Cováo, she headed straight for the café and parked outside. Carlos though was sitting on the wall on the opposite side. Helena went over to him and said,

'Hello Carlos, shall we go in?'

However, Carlos surprised her.

'Helena, do you mind if we stay outside? Helena was puzzled, but replied,
'if you want, but why?'
'Well, to be honest the café is busy, and if we go in everyone will be able to tell we are talking about a job, the chances are they will all be listening. If you decide not to offer me the job, everyone will know, it will be embarrassing for me.'
'I see, I hadn't thought of that, no problem we can talk here,
but what will people think if they see us talking outside!'
Carlos had the good grace to colour up, until Helena told him she was joking, so they then went and sat down on a bench under the old Wisteria.
Over the next hour Helena outlined the plans to him much as she had done with Senhor Martins the builder, before explaining that she wanted to be able to concentrate on the Quintals future, which meant she wouldn't have time for managing the refurbishments. Helena was also clear that her dad would be here and that he was likely to want to help in some way but as yet this was unresolved, but it might impact on the role. Helena ran through each of the various elements of the project and then asked him how he thought he might proceed to map it all out. Carlos, set about doing so with some enthusiasm, convincing her that he had the planning skills necessary to both set out the schedule of works, and subsequently project manage it.
To Helena what came across well was that he understood the delicate nature of the role, in as much as he needed to liaise with the trades, and build confidence with them, whilst holding them to account both individually and collectively. One of the things that clinched it for her was that it was patently obvious that he had worked on building sites, so he had seen first-hand,

some of the factors that might introduce delays, or cause friction amongst the various specialists. Helena knew that being able to spot these difficulties early, and getting a quick resolution would be crucial to keeping to the time scale.

She was, in truth, more than a little worried about giving him this sort of responsibility at his age, but then she asked herself what would she have done if someone had offered her the same sort of responsibility at the same age. After answering that question positively, her answer was a no brainer. He would learn on the job, and as she herself had found out often the best lessons are taught this way. In her head she knew she was taking a risk. However, she reasoned that it was a calculated one, and if it didn't work out then it would be her problem to deal with it at the time, but in her heart, she felt it was going to work out okay. She was observing him closely as they sat under the Wisteria, in the dark, with the temperature dropping quickly, she had asked him about his plans for the future. He haltingly told her all about them, then his father had died, and everything had come to a stop. He had had such high aspirations, and at twenty-five his whole life still lay before him, suddenly he stopped talking.

'Helena, sorry am I boring you with all of this and it's not relevant to the job is it.'

'No, you're not boring me at all, listening to your hopes, brought back some happy memories for me.'

Helena, knew right there and then that she was going to offer him the job, she felt she could work with him, and more importantly that he would do a good job; yes, he was young, but he was brimming over with confidence and enthusiasm and she felt that both were necessary requirements for success. Helena, leant forward put her hand on his forearm and said

'So Carlos, would a salary of say 20,000 euros per annum be okay for you and when can you start?'
Carlos blinked, in the dark Helena could make out his Adams apple moving up and down as he fought to control himself.
'Caramba, do you mean you're really offering me the job,'
'I think that's what I just said.'
'Wow, I don't know what to say, 20,000euros per year that's a lot of money.'
'Well I guess you're going to earn it, and its only for six months as you know. So, do you accept it?'
'Yes of course Menina, I mean Helena, or should I call you Menina again now that I am going to work for you, wow I am so confused!'
'Helena will be fine Carlos, but I am not a push over, I have high standards and expect the same from those who are going to be working with me. Not to put too finer point on it, I expect you to work a five-day week, standard hours 8am until 6 pm, but with a two-hour break for lunch, but if things require it then we work within reason until the issue is resolved.'
'Of course, I wouldn't do anything other, it's just brilliant for me if you're sure, when do you want me to start?'
'As soon as you can, what are your current commitments?'
'I am labouring for a guy in Sertã, but its casual, I am sure I can be freed up by the end of the week, next week at the latest.'
'In that case let's make a start on the Monday. We need to get you a laptop, so you can use it remotely with a 4G card, at least until we get some electricity and telephones and wi-fi on site. I am setting aside the kitchen in the Quinta as the temporary office in the first instance.
My idea is to use one of the barns at the back as an office, but it will need some work first. So that's your first

207

task really, it's going to be a little while before the quotes come in and we decide on who we are going to use, so you will have time to sort the office out first. Manuel tells me the smaller of the two barns out the back would be suitable, it just needs clearing out and fitting up. If we don't have electricity quickly then we will have to use a generator, and of course we need wi-fi as soon as possible.'

'No problem, I can come and have a look at the barn over the weekend, once I can see what space there is it will give me a better idea what we can fit in. How many people do we need to accommodate?'

'Four initially, oh by the way we will have a vehicle you can use by then as well, Manuel is sorting one out this week.'

'I do have a car, it used to be my dad's, but it's good to know there is one I can use if I need to.'

'Right then Carlos, can I buy you a glass of wine to celebrate your new job, because I don't know about you, but I am parched, and cold.'

'Do you mind if I just call my mum and Louisa first they are waiting at home for me.'

'Go ahead, why don't you ask them to come down and celebrate with us?'

Carlos made the call, and shortly after they saw Louisa and her mum Maria walking down the street, they came towards them and congratulated Carlos, with hugs and kisses, before all four of them crossed the road, and went inside the café. Although there were few people inside now, they all went quiet when Helena walked in. She immediately understood Carlos's reservations, it might not have been the best place to conduct a job interview! Alice, smiling as usual, bade them a good evening, though she looked surprised to see them, greeting them warmly before asking what they would like. Once the order was placed Helena took the opportunity to tell her the good news about Henry and Jane offering to rent her their house. Helena shouldn't have been surprised to hear she already knew, but she was, and when Alice told Helena she knew about Manuel and Marias new roles too, Helena threw her hands up in the air and laughed. Clearly news of every variety travels as fast as Marco had indicated to her it would.

'Well then' Helena said to her,

'You can't possibly know this piece of news, so can I be the first person to introduce you to my new project manager Carlos.'

Alice, needed no encouragement, and she simply flew from the back of the counter and gave him a bear hug, and that seemed to be the cue for everyone present to congratulate him to. His mum looked on with pride and she smiled, and Louisa gave Helena a big enveloping hug.Half an hour later, whilst they were all still celebrating in the café Manuel entered, so he was given the good news too. For the next half an hour, Carlos and Manuel talked about the barn and ended up agreeing they would meet up on Saturday to think through how best to transform it into a working office as swiftly as they could. Louisa's mum Maria, was a little more talkative, and Helena made a special point of telling how pleased she was to hear that she had offered to help. But finally, the impromptu party broke up, everyone wished each other a good night, and Carlos walked with Helena to her car.

'I promise I won't let you down Helena, thank you for giving me the chance, my dad would be proud.'

He kissed her on both cheeks and then walked off catching up with his mum and sister. Helena watched them go, before getting in her car, and driving off down the now deserted streets back home.

Helena woke early the next morning, she dressed and went down to the kitchen where Maria and Manuel were already sitting drinking coffee. It was a slightly overcast day, and it threatened rain, so when Maria gave her the key to their house she also gave her an umbrella. Looking out from the back door, on a morning in which clouds had gathered, Helena walked quickly down the drive. Whilst she was gone, Maria and Manuel returned to the subject of last night's revelations. Maria said to Manuel,

'Do you think everything is going to be alright?'

'Oh yes, Helena may not have years of experience, but she knows what she is doing, and she is intelligent, I don't think we could have wished for more. Carlos of course is still young, but he hasn't worked all those years with his father without learning a thing or two. Helena has given him an opportunity to prove himself and getting that around here…. well it was never going to happen was it, Carlos has much to be grateful for I think.'

'I hope Maria will benefit too, she has been in deep mourning too long, and its time she came back to reality, she is only 53, far too young. I know it will be difficult, but she has made a start, thanks to Helena.'

'I have a feeling that Helena is going to provide a real boost locally, she seems to have picked up quickly how the land lies, but we will still have to help her.'

'We will Manuel, we will. I like her a lot and I am looking forward to meeting her father, I hope he picks up the language quickly though, or Helena will be worn out just translating!'

'What do you think she will want to do with the Quintal?'

'More than we do now that's for sure. She has been to university and as she told us she has spent the last five

210

years running a winery in the USA, I expect she might want to produce wine rather than continue to supply the Fernandes family.'

'The olive groves too?'

'Well why not?'

'We could be in for quite some change then, I wonder if that will be a good thing?'

'I think it will be, this Quinta has been neglected for too long, and I believe only good can come out of it being renewed, of course we will have to wait and see. But at least for now, we don't have to worry about having no home, you're getting a new sofa, and we have a pay rise, it's a pretty good start.'

Unbeknown to them both Helena had returned whilst they were in mid-conversation. As she heard them say her own name she had stopped from pushing open the door, she hadn't meant to listen in, but what she heard made her smile. Whilst she knew that she didn't need their approval, she was pleased to hear it, and it gave her a nice glow inside. These were good people, and they had said that they were going to help her; well she didn't doubt that over the next couple of years she would need their help and goodwill, and that of others too, so it was gratifying to know she had made a good start. She backed out of the door, and then made a point of coming back in noisily, and half an hour later she was back in the kitchen drinking coffee and eating a croissant.

Manuel confirmed to Helena that this morning he was off to Abrantes to test drive three vehicles. A Toyota Land Cruiser, a Land Rover Discovery and a Mitsubishi Outlander, he was like an eager salesman, reeling off the specifications, pros and cons, and making her aware that in terms of price they were all roughly the same. Manuel asked if she had a preference, which she hadn't, and then he said two were dark green and one was a wine red. Did she mind the colour, at which point Helena stood up, put her hands up in front of her!

'Manuel, I don't know one end of a vehicle from another, it's one area I've never been much interested in. Whichever you choose will do, I trust you to make the right choice, whatever the colour.'

Maria smiled rather indulgently,

'Manuel is taking me with him, so I can go and look at sofas. Ours is twenty years old, I am so looking forward to choosing a new one.'

'That's great Maria, I wish you a good choosing.'

After they had left, Helena tidied up the bedroom, put her dirty washing in a plastic sack, ready for the washer in South Fork. Helena found that she had slipped into referring to the house by its nickname, courtesy of Jane and Henry's friends Barbara and Bernard who first coined the term. For her it was easier than referring to it as Henry and Jane's house, having packed her case, she left the room. On top of the landing and glancing all around she reflected on the fact that the next time she slept here the house would be finished. A tremor of excitement coursed through body as she contemplated this; but was also determined that she and her dad were, first and foremost, going to really enjoy the journey too, as how often does a thirty-three-year-old English woman get the opportunity to remodel and refurbish an Estate like this. On that exciting thought, she picked up the case ran down the stairs and out of the house through the front doors. Her car was covered in raindrops, although the drizzle had now stopped, and the clouds were beginning to break up, inside the car, she placed her suitcase and washing, and drove the short distance to her home for the next four months 'South Fork.'

Once there, she picked up her things and walked to the front door and rang the bell.

'Come in come in,' said Jane. 'We are nearly ready aren't we Fish, why don't you drop your suitcase in your bedroom Helena?'

Helena felt slightly odd to hear Jane her say her bedroom, but she did as she was asked, and placed her suitcase on the floor by the walk-in wardrobe, as she did so Jane called out.

'I've changed the bed for you, and made the bed up in the furthest bedroom for your dad. The fridge is clean and empty, apart from milk, and some jars of jam. The freezer contains a few bits and pieces, so feel free to use them, nothing is more than a month old, and it's a shame to waste it.'

'Your both being very generous, I don't know what to say.'

'Don't be daft, were the ones who get to spend a night in a luxury hotel in Lisbon for nothing, I am really looking forward to it it's a great way to start our trip.' she then turned to her husband and said,

'Fish, where are the passports?'

'I put them in your handbag like always.'

Henry retorted from somewhere down the corridor.

'Don't panic already we haven't left the house yet.'

Helena grinned, before turning to Jane.

'By the way, I have already transferred the four months' rent to your account, plus a little extra for you to treat your family to a nice lunch on me, one day.'

'You sweetie, you needn't have done either of those things, but thanks on both accounts, I will drink a toast to your health with a nice bottle of chilled champagne, so Cheers!'

Henry who had been somewhere down the corridor, now walked into the kitchen, he was carrying a large file.

'Hi Helena, I thought this might be useful for you, it's the guide we made when we did the house swap, it has a lot of basic stuff in, like where the stop cock is, etc. the other thing is we do occasionally get power cuts, Ameixeira along with Perogoncalves are on a branch at the end of the substation line and sometimes it takes a little longer for us to be reconnected. Last year we had no power for most of one the day, if that happens I suggest you don't open the freezers. Candles are in the pantry and the hob is gas, so you can still boil water and cook.'

'Interesting, thanks I will remember that, are you both good to go?'

'Yes all done, if you give me your car keys I will put the suitcases in the boot and car.'

Henry busied himself doing that, whilst Jane told me she would expect email updates, and that if I had any problems just to call, we both moved towards the door. Jane gave me a bunch of keys to the house and said I should lock up!

Having locked up the house, and checked the door, Jane squashed herself in the back of the mini, next to one of the suitcases and they set off for Lisbon. They chatted as the scenery around them changed as they passed through. Helena remarked that she was amazed by how little traffic was on the motorways. Henry replied,

'It is fantastic, isn't it, I now detest driving in the UK, it's just one big traffic jam, but here I have fallen in love with driving once again, it's a pure pleasure. Obviously, the cities are busy, but a lot of European funding came to Portugal for road building, and now the main trunk roads are excellent, and ridiculously quiet.'

Helena saw that he was right they came across no appreciable traffic until they were on the outskirts of Lisbon itself.

'Shall I put the sat-nav on Helena as I have no idea where the hotel is.'

'Good idea Fish,' said Jane. 'The one-way system is a little difficult to understand, I remember the first time we stayed here, we could see the hotel we wanted, but couldn't find the right way to access it, Henry got really mad didn't you darling!'

'No I didn't', I was just frustrated, it should have been easy.'

So they put the sat-nav on in the hope it would guide them us to the hotel, unhappily it seemed that the sat nav was a little out of date, but after a couple of wrong turns, and toots of horns eventually they arrived.

Helena parked the car in the hotels underground car park, and they all got out, a porter came to pick up the suitcases, and he showed them into the lobby. Helena had already told them that she was meeting her solicitor in the lobby, before going out for lunch at a local restaurant. After Jane and Henry had booked in and were ready to be taken to their room she kissed them both goodbye and wished them a fabulous holiday, and promised to keep in touch. As they were whisked away she secretly smiled hoping they liked the suite and the champagne, she had booked as a surprise. Helena shivered pleasantly, because she really got a kick out of giving people surprises, and this should be a good one. Their openness and hospitality to someone they had only just met was amazing, and she knew that they would become good friends once they returned from Australia, and they had more time to get to know each other. Helena glanced at the clock in the lobby, she had about ten minutes to wait until Marco arrived, so she wandered towards the squashy sofa's set out in the large public guest area. Sitting down she picked up a magazine from the coffee table, and had only just began to read it, when she heard a voice from behind her say,

'Hello Helena.'

Helena turned slightly, and her breath caught in her throat, Marco was dressed in a casual pair of dark blue trousers, a loose-fitting pale blue linen shirt, and a pair of Birkenstock's. From her seat the aftershave he was wearing smelt divine, his black/blue curly hair nestled casually on his collar. Helena stood up, and thought he looked like a young Sasha Distell but with a Portuguese rather than French accent, and his eyes were looking into hers as he said,

'If you are ready we should go, the table is booked for 12.40, so we can get you to the airport in time to pick up your father.'

Shaking herself from her contemplation of his eyes, she moved towards him and shook his outstretched hand, the now familiar tingling went up her arm, she kissed him on both cheeks, and once more I marvelled at how soft his skin was. As soon as she pulled back from him she said 'Yes of course, let's go.'

As they walked towards the hotel door, which the concierge opened, Helena suddenly felt a little dowdy, she hadn't of course brought her whole wardrobe to Portugal, but even so she realised her clothes were not quite as chic as perhaps she had once thought they were. She made a mental note that it was time to invest in some new clothes. Marco might have been reading her thoughts.

'There are some lovely clothes shops in this district, worth taking a note of in case you decide to go on a shopping spree. You look very nice by the way.'

'You don't look too bad yourself.' She said whilst glancing up at him. 'Quite casual, I expected you to be in a suit, straight from the office.'

'Normally I would have been, but my late morning meeting was cancelled, and I had already booked the afternoon off, so I was able to get home and change. The restaurant is such that both suit and casual are the norm, obviously not jeans or shorts, but this is acceptable.' He said pointing to his own clothes.

Helena was so glad she had opted for her wide legged white linen culottes, matched with a slightly flared red smocked top, and kitten heeled red Jimmy Choo sandals. These being her one indulgence as Helena just loved shoes.

Strolling the short distance to the restaurant, they arrived outside a discreet entrance with a sign indicating 'A Sierra'. Marco opened the door to let Helena through.

Once inside, she was taken aback by the modernity of the interior, which was in sharp contrast to the external building.

Clean crisp lines, large modern glass chandeliers, white leather sofas, and waiting staff, dressed in black and white, with long black crisp aprons, stopping below the knees.

A smart young woman, greeted them immediately.

'It's nice to see you again Senhor Gonçalves, your table is this way.'

They followed the elegant young woman to a table on the roof terrace, it was tucked away in a corner, surrounded by potted palms.

'Joaquin will be with you shortly; can I get either of you an aperitif?"

Declining because she knew she had to drive, Helena asked for a sparkling water with a slice of lemon, Marco asked for the same. A few minutes later a young man placed the drinks on the table, and handed them both menus.

Marco, studied the menu, for a few minutes, then clearly having decided, put the menu down.

'Would you like a glass of wine or champagne with your lunch Helena, I guess we can have one.'

'Yes please I'd love a nice chilled Vinho Verde.'
she replied as she was still perusing the menu. A few
minutes later she looked up at Marco,
'Do you have a recommendation for lunch?'
'Mm several but if you want something light I would go
with a Salad Niçoise, not very Portuguese I know, but
they do a good version here, and it's not too heavy. We
can always have a lovely pudding afterwards if we have
time.'
Joaquin returned, but Helena declined the salad, ordering
instead a rib eye steak, and salad. Marco seemed
surprised by her choice, but then ordered the same.
They then both went to speak at the same time, Helena
laughed.
'You first,' Marco said.
'I was going to ask you something that has been puzzling
me.'
'Ok no problem, go ahead.'
'Well, I know the name of the solicitors on the scrap of
paper that was passed down from Sofia to Luis and
ended up with my mum, wasn't your company, but at the
time she gave the solicitors name to Luis she couldn't
have known she was going to inherit the Quinta could
she, so what was it she thought Luis might want to
contact the solicitors about?
'Aah, yes I can see that might appear odd to you, the
answer though is quite simple really.
'Sofia's parents were from families who had their own
businesses, Sofia's father was a blacksmith and in those
days, this was a good business he was a man of means
in the village he came from. Moreover, her mother was
the daughter of a Miller, they were proud people, and the
marriage meant the couple were reasonably well off.
Sofia was one of three children, her older brother was
expected to inherit the Black Smiths business, and the

218

younger brother the Mill. As a girl Sofia wasn't going to be left out though, and when she was 15 she inherited the house of her maternal grandparents, and some associated land. Had Sofia married a local man no doubt she would have lived in the house, the ruins of which still exist. Unfortunately, in the late 1960's it was largely destroyed by a severe wild fire, which destroyed a number of the local villages.

In short Sofia always knew she had property here in Portugal, and this was house that Luis would inherit.'

'But how did your firm get involved?'

'When Rafael died, our firm was the one charged with managing the estate, until we found Sofia, or her whereabouts was made known to us. On the day my great grandfather came across her when she visited the Quinta, they forged a strong working relationship, so she continued the arrangement and we became her solicitors. One of the first tasks she had for us, was to make contact with her old family solicitors and ensure, by any means, that if any of her descendants contacted them they should immediately inform us of course. They were paid a small annual retainer for simply doing that. When you contacted them, they simply phoned and passed your name on to us.'

'So what happened to the original house and land, do I still own that?'

'No. When she inherited the Quinta, she passed on the house and land to her nephew. When he married he moved in, and gave it to his daughter Maria do Carmo da Silva, when she married Jorge Nunes. They unfortunately would have lost everything when the fire destroyed the house.'

'That is awful, didn't they have any insurance?'

'No, the reality is, it wasn't, and still isn't, normal practice to insure these very old houses, wildfires are frequent,

219

and many people couldn't afford the insurance premiums then or even now.'

'So what did they do?'

'I have no idea, I guess they moved into another family property, probably on his side of the family.'

'Maria do Carmo da Silva Nunes is still alive you know!'

'Is she, I didn't know that but then we never had any dealings with anyone other than Sofia.'

'She is close to eighty years old now, I am meeting her next week, I am sure she will have some knowledge of Sofia, I hope so anyway.'

Just then, Joaquin arrived with lunch, for a few minutes, they sat in silence as they ate, Helena remarked that her Vinho Verde was delicious. Every now and then she sneaked a quick look at Marco, who was clearly enjoying his steak. When they had finished, he asked if any more questions had sprung to mind.

'Not questions as such, I am interested in the Alencar family, I feel they are more remote, yet Rafael Alencar was my great-great grandfather, what if anything can you tell me about them?'

He nodded.

'A historically powerful titled family, in 1910 when Portugal declared itself a Republic, titles were disbanded, and the old nobility titles ceased to be anything other than an honorific, as a family though they were still reasonably wealthy. Today, they have less money, compared to those times. During the 1910's and 1920's they had invested heavily in the US Stock market, consequently in the Wall Street crash of 1929 their investments nosedived, and over the next ten years or so. those losses increased as the market failed to regain its former strength. The Alencar's ended up selling a lot of the family property and silver. Rafael married aged 44 in 1910, but the marriage failed to produce heirs, and he divorced in 1918, he ended spending the remainder of his life quietly in his house in Porto.

Rafael had a sister and a younger brother, so when he died in 1925, the younger brother Alfonso inherited the now defunct honorific title and the property. He married and had two children, both girls. When we visit Carolina, she will be able to give you more information and of course they have already agreed to give you access to any relevant Alencar papers.'

'I am looking forward to that, and to meeting Carolina, do we have a date yet?

'I am sorry but not yet, my diary is pretty full, and we need a couple of days, I hope we can go towards the end of the month, unless you want to go on your own?

Helena was tempted but then thought it would be much better to go with Marco, so she said she didn't mind waiting as she had a lot to do in the next few weeks. Though she didn't have too of course, she nonetheless brought Marco up to speed on progress so far, he was seemed to be quite impressed.

'Do you envisage spending a lot more money?' Helena nodded absently.

'If you do we need some advance notice to move it out from its invested funds.'

'I doubt we will need any more for some time, firstly I have to come up with a plan for the Quinta, it has to be able to pay its way, and I have a couple of ideas, but they need fleshing out. But I know I can't do it all on my own; I need an estate manager, and some specialist advice so that's got to be one of my first priorities.'

'Obviously Helena it goes without saying if you need any help, we are happy to assist, and on a personal level I would be pleased to help if I can.'

As Marco spoke Helena glanced at her watch, it was nearly three pm, she looked up.

221

'Where has the time gone? I am sorry, but I have to go, or I won't be in the terminal building when my dad arrives.'

Marco smiled, pushing his hair back from his face.

'You have plenty of time, if we leave now you will be there with fifteen minutes to spare.'

An argument followed, over who was going to pay the bill, in the end Marco said he would allow Helena to pay it only if she joined him for dinner one evening where he paid. Helena felt her tummy flutter, and quickly agreed, and too soon they were back at the hotel car park. Once in the car park they said goodbye with the usual kisses, and Helena walked the few metres to her car with a little spring in her step, and on top of that Marco had said he would call her. Helena got in her overly warm car, put on the air conditioning and then tapped into the sat-nav the airports address, and got ready to drive off, as she did so she noticed Marco hadn't moved to get into his car, he waved, and she waved back before he did so.

Twenty minutes later having parked in the airport car park, she followed the signs to arrivals. The airport wasn't massive, but there were lots of people waiting by the exit doors, many had flowers in their hands, she assumed this was another local custom. Helena just loved airports, the joy on the faces of people who hadn't seen each other perhaps for weeks or years was infectious. As she waited for her father to show himself she watched a number of joyful reunions, and one in particular brought a tear to her eye; an elderly man accompanied by a middle-aged couple, came out of the terminal doors, and an elderly woman slowly made her way up the ramp followed by a substantial family. When they met the two-elderly people embraced as if they were never going to let each other go. Helena heard the family chatter and worked out that they were a brother and sister, and this was their first meeting for nearly thirty years since the brother had emigrated to Brazil. A mum with two small children couldn't contain her happiness when her husband came out of the doors, her two children running up the ramp both shouting Pai, Pai, the Portuguese word for dad, before throwing themselves into his open arms.

Some moments later Helena's father emerged, he looked round for his daughter amongst the sea of faces. Helena frantically waved her arms trying to make herself seen above the large crowds, when he saw he waved back her before marching resolutely down the ramp towards her. She had missed him, and she gave him a big hug, before she linked her arm through his, and they weaved their way through the crowd heading towards the car park.

'Good journey dad?'

'Yes love, no problem, I like this travelling business class, a man could get used to it!'

Helena had brought his ticket for him, and the use of British Airways business class lounge meant he could relax, rather than wait around in a crowded airport.

'Well I think I can afford to send you back the same way when you have had enough of Portugal.'

Squeezing her arm Helena's dad asked,

'So my daughter has become a millionaire, how does it feel?' Helena rolled her eyes.

'To be honest dad, it hasn't sunk in properly yet, though I do know I have inherited a great responsibility, not only in the Quintal, but with the local people too. It's not too dramatic to say that I feel a weight of expectation, as you will see there is a lot to do, and I need to make sure the money is spent wisely, or it will get eaten up quite quickly. Basically, we need to make the Quintal pay its way, more than it does now.'

'You've already decided not to sell up then? You know what I mean take the money and run?'

223

'I don't know how best to describe this dad, but I couldn't even if I wanted to, the house its bewitched me, my history is here, and I can feel it. The house has secrets it wants me to uncover.'

Her father looked at her as if she was losing her marbles, so she quickly said,

'Yes, I know, it sounds mad to me sometimes, but you just wait until you go there, I can't believe you will be immune to the vibe.'

'Well in that case we better go and have look at this manor house of yours which, it seems, has got under your skin so quickly.'

The drive home was pleasant, the sun had broken out from the clouds, and William enjoyed the countryside as it flashed by. They drove home chatting about all sorts, Helena told him about her employing Carlos, and giving Manuel and Maria new roles. He laughed when she told him about Manuel's reaction to being asked to buy a car for use on the estate, and that she had an electrician coming tomorrow to see what needed doing, and that she hoped he would be the one to go around with him.

'Of course love, I want to be useful, and that is something I can do to help. What about plumbers?'

'Haven't got to that yet dad, I gather there is an excellent local plumber who lost an arm three years ago, he is very proud and whilst he continues to work, he isn't as speedy as he used to be. I have to have someone who can keep up with the other trades, but I would like to use him some capacity.'

'Maybe he could take a supervisory or a quality control role, or sub contract plumbers to work under him. Why don't you let me have a chat with him, I can ask Carlos to translate, then it would be man to man thing, and if he is proud I am sure we can find the right words to keep his pride intact.'

'Oh would you dad, that would be fabulous, it's going to be such a boon having you here.'

As they approached Cováo, Helena began to point out local places, Senhor Zé's all-purpose shop, the church, Dona Lourdes grocery shop, Senhor Antonio's iron mongers that strangely sold fresh yeast, as well as buckets, brushes, various sizes of nails and other assorted bits and pieces and of course café central.

'Do you want a coffee dad, or shall we come another day?'

'I'm a bit tired to be honest love could we do it another day.'

'Okay no problem I am coming back tomorrow afternoon if you prefer to come then or whenever you want.'

William nodded his assent, saying,

'Let's see shall we, right now I could do with a nice shower and a lie down.'

As they approached Ameixeira, Helena glanced at the clock on the dashboard it said 5.45, she thought to herself that they had made quite good time and as she pulled up the drive to South Fork she realised she felt a little tired herself.

'Come on then dad, let's get your case out of the boot and get inside. As she approached the door, William said, 'So this is to be home for a few months then, well it looks lovely.'

'It is quite lovely, and I am very lucky to have been offered it, dad welcome to 'South Fork.''

'South Fork?'

'Well, it's a funny story I'll tell you later over a cup of tea.'

Once inside, she opened the shutters, showed her dad around and put his case in his room, and pointed out the bathroom. In the kitchen on the island unit was a box of groceries and a note from Maria. In which she said she hoped that these would help until they could go to the supermarket, and that I would find a cold cooked chicken in the fridge, along with a one pot veal casserole that just needed heating up. Helena said to her dad, that Maria had supplied dinner, and getting out the casserole, she put it in the oven, managing to figure out the controls without any problem. Then the kettle was put on the stove, and Helena went to her room, and opened her case. She couldn't find the washing sack, so wandered to the utility where the washing had been washed and dried and was now ready for ironing. It was clear Maria was taking her housekeeping role very seriously.

From the utility, she heard the first faint whistles of the kettle, returning to the kitchen she turned it off when it reached its crescendo, and made the tea. Beyond the kitchen, she could hear the shower running, and knew that her dad would be out shortly. Opening the doors to the veranda she took the tea outside to the far terrace, which was still in sunshine. Sitting on the swing seat, the view from here in a straight line must have led to the Quinta, but you couldn't see at all it from where she was. It made her feel all warm inside to know it was just beyond view, and patiently waiting for her return.

The fly screen door opened, and Helena called to her father,

'I am over here dad, tea is ready.'

Her father moved out from under the veranda and stood still, he simply looked at the view down and over the valley to Cardigos, Helena could tell he was taking it all in. She watched as his head sometimes moving left, sometimes right, soaked up all the atmosphere. Slowly, he made his way towards the swing seat, admiring the gardens planting, the swimming pool and finally the rose garden.

'What a beautiful spot Helena, the view is to die for.'

'Yes, it is isn't it, Jane told me it was the view and the pool that sold the house to her, and I can see why. The Quinta has a similar view but from a bit further round. The Quinta is straight in front of you as the crow flies.'

'Well if it has a similar view to this, then I can't wait to see it love.'

'We could walk round after tea if you want to, but it will be dark soon, so you won't be able to see much of the inside.'

'Can't say I am not excited to see it, but I think your right, probably best to wait until tomorrow morning, then I can see it all.'

In comparative silence they sat drinking tea and listening to the birds, and buzzing of the insects, very occasionally chatting. Finally, William turned to Helena and said,

'You know love, I still find it difficult to understand why your mum never said anything about all of this. Do you think she had any idea of the scale of Sofia's legacy?'

'The answer to that is most certainly no.

Marco, I mean Senhor Gonçalves my solicitor, explained to me today what was covered by the note that Sofia gave to Luis, and which Luis in turn gave to Granddad. Obviously, in the end that note led me to the Quinta, but the original note and solicitors address, had nothing to do with the Quinta at all; because when Sofia wrote the note she was referring to a house she had inherited from her maternal grandmother. That house was a modest village house with some land, somewhere near here. If you think about it at the time she penned it in 1918, Rafael was still alive, but also she had no idea he was going to leave her the Quinta, let alone a capital sum for his son Luis or his descendants.'

'I see, then how was the link made?'

'Quite easily really pop, you see after Sofia returned and discovered she had been left the Quinta and everything

227

that went with it; she also grasped that having lost contact with Luis in America, there was, if he still had the note, an outside chance that Luis might one day try to contact the family's solicitors about the house his mum had inherited. It was a long shot, but it was the only shot she had. So, she took the prudent step of asking Marco Gonçalves grandfather to contact the firm named in the original note, in effect her families' old solicitors in Maçao. Between them it was agreed, with an annual retainer sealing the deal, that should anyone make contact with the solicitors in Maçao, they would inform Marco's grandfathers solicitors immediately, the story behind it is a bit more complicated than that, but the rest they say is history. Once Elizabeth made contact with them, they contacted Marco's firm and they picked it up from there. The original house and land referred to in the note from Luis, Sofia gave to her great nephew. What is astonishing, is that apparently, she tried numerous times to find Luis, using detectives and newspaper adverts, but all to no avail, and in the end, it was that long shot that worked, talk about serendipity.'

'Well I am a believer in fate, so perhaps you were the one destined to be here, and maybe your mum realised that. Where is Sofia buried?

'Good question dad, I have no idea. I suppose it would be too much to wish that she was united with Rafael one last time and buried with him. Much more likely she was buried locally, Marco will know, and so might Maria do Carmo, and I am seeing her tomorrow.'

'It seems to me that mysteries still exist then, not least of which is why Sofia left here for America?'

'I assume it was something to do with Rafael getting married, but as nothing in this has been straightforward, it could be something else entirely of course.'

During the rest of the evening, Helena, showed her dad round the rest of South Fork, and whilst sitting in the lounge drinking a glass of port, she brought him up to speed on the finding of the old envelopes, the secret bathroom, with its cupboards full of old clothes, and the mystery of the wine in the cellar.

By nine thirty her dad was yawning, and said if she didn't mind he was going to get an early night, ready for the mornings adventure. Some twenty minutes later they were both in their respective bedrooms fast asleep.

The sound of singing coming from the kitchen, woke
Helena, she listened for a few seconds, her dad was
belting out Granada at the top of his voice. She loved to
hear him sing, for many years he had been a member of
the local Amateur Operatic Society, and he had a super
voice. So she lay in the large and very comfortable bed,
listening to him, smiling to herself, this was the first time
she had heard him sing since her mum had died. When
he stopped, it was her cue to get up, so she popped on a
dressing gown, and wandered out to the kitchen.
'Morning Pop, I heard you revelling in the spirit of the
Mediterranean, even if it's the wrong country, though I
suppose to be fair Granada isn't so far from here.'
Her father broke into a smile.
'Morning love, for some reason today seemed the right
day for a song, and as I don't really know any Portuguese
classics, 'Granada' seemed a good substitute.' As he
moved towards the teapot he said, 'Do you want a cup of
tea, there is some fresh in the pot.' Helena nodded 'Mm
yes please.'
Strolling toward the island unit, Helena picked up the mug
of tea her dad had just poured, and gave him a kiss on
the cheek, and peered out of the window.
'It looks like it's going to be a nice sunny day.'
'I think so love, though there is a bit of a nip in the air
outside. By the way I love the bedroom, and that door out
on to the veranda means I can come and go without
disturbing you. So this morning I stretched my legs,
before making the tea.'
'Good for you, but I think your legs will be well stretched
by the end of the day. I have the feeling it's going to be
busy, I can't wait to see your face when you see the

Quinta. I know you've seen the photos, but they don't do it justice at all.'

'Well then what are we waiting for, let's get dressed, grab a bite of toast and vamos!'

'I see some Portuguese has rubbed off on you then?' said Helena vamos being translated as "let us go"

'I am beginning to think I may have picked up a bit here and there.' Her dad said chuckling to himself.

'Perhaps so Pop, perhaps so, vamos ver!' she replied, and laughing they moved off in different directions to get dressed and ready for the day. Fifteen minutes later a couple of slices of toast having been washed down with some fresh orange juice that Maria had left for them, they locked the door to South Fork, and walked out of the village and down towards the Quinta das Laranjeiras. This was the first time Helena had walked to the Quinta, so for both of them it was the chance to see things from a new perspective. Passing a well-presented house on their right, they continued walking until they reached the T junction in the road. From there they glimpsed a few other buildings in the village, mostly ruins, but one or two which looked like they might be inhabited. Approaching the T junction, they could see an older woman emerge from the house on the far right she was carrying a full to the brim washing basket. Helena waved and said good morning.

In return she put down the washing basket and came towards them. Helena speaking in her best Portuguese said,

'Hello Senhora, my name is Helena Stratton, and this is my father, we are pleased to meet you.'

The woman, was dressed in a zip fronted and armless tunic, quite pinafore like, underneath which Helena could see part of an old red cardigan, and black ankle length leggings. Her shoes were well worn, covered in mud and

231

dust, with odd laces. She was about 4 feet nine inches tall, with tight curly grey black hair, framing a round freckly face, sitting on quite a stout body. On her nose a pair of glasses, with dark red frames perched precariously.

'Good morning, my name is Maria-Elena, are you the new owners of the Quinta?'

Helena explained that they were, and that we were staying in Henry and Jane's house whilst the renovations were carried out.

At this disclosure, she seemed to bristle a little, Helena though continued as if she hadn't noticed and asked, 'Were you aware of this Senhora?'

'No, I spoke to them a week ago, but they didn't say anything then.'

Helena gained the impression that it was the fact, that she didn't know about it was what had upset her.

'Yes, they off to Australia for four months, and we came to an arrangement, it was all very last minute and only agreed on Monday to be precise, they probably didn't have time to tell you.'

Helena explained this as diplomatically as possible which seemed to mollify her a little, as she loosened her lips which previously made her look like she had been sucking on a lemon.

'Well I do hope you will come and have a look at some point, in fact I have asked Maria to find me some ladies to help clean the place out, its paid work of course, so if you have time and fancy helping out, just let her know.'

'Not sure about that, the work I mean Gilberto doesn't like it if I don't have his dinner ready, though I guess we would both like to see inside the old place again. My mum used to do a little cleaning for Dona Sofia, maybe fifty years ago, I visited with her a few times when I was a girl. Gilberto never has seen inside.'

'Well your both welcome anytime, the builders won't get going for a few weeks, and we would be pleased to show you around sometime.'

She turned to her dad who had been politely waiting by her side and said,

'Let's go.'

and turning to Maria Elena she said

Goodbye Senhora'

Her new neighbour replied

'Goodbye.'

but didn't move, and they could both feel her eyes watching them.

'Has she gone Pop?'

Her dad knelt down and pretended to tie a shoelace, and was able to look behind him.

'Yes, but only just, she seems a little strange.'

'I imagine she thinks we are strange too, let's give her the benefit of the doubt, it may simply be that she was put out about not knowing about our renting South Fork. Funny though they never mentioned her at all, perhaps they don't get on.'

They continued walking down the lane, until they could see the gate, which had already been opened by Manuel.

'Impressive,' said William as they walked through them, Helena pointed out the cutaway where the orange tree was and the old broken seats. She had already told him about the painting, and the fact that these trees must have been replacements for those in the original painting. As they passed the cut away the Quinta came into full view and Helena's dad stopped and gazed at it.

'Oh love, your mum would have loved this, it's just beautiful.'

Helena linked her arm in his, and saw the moistness in the corner of his eye and she gently squeezed his forearm with her other hand, after a short while she tapped him on the arm and said

'You know Pop, I think she would have adored it too, so it's our job to make sure that we do it justice, and make it something that both Sofia's would be proud off, if you're ready shall we go in?'

Her father bent his head down and gave her a kiss on the cheek, then he straightened up.

'Come on then let's do this.'

Arm in arm they went up the steps, Helena turned the handle that opened the door. Once inside, William contemplated the spacious hall, with its beautiful doors, and staircase leading up to the first floor. Helena led him into the drawing room, and immediately took him to the painting, her dad looked at it for some time before passing comment.

'I can see the likeness, your mum looked like her great grandmother, you on the other hand have something of your great-great grandfather in you.'

'Do I Pop?'

'Yes, you do, it's all around the eyes, but unfortunately for you, I am afraid the rest you get from me!' he joked.

As they were studying the dirty painting, Manuel and Maria came in, and Helena quickly introduced them to her dad.

'Pop this is Maria the housekeeper, and her husband Manuel our Estate Supervisor.'

William said hello, and that he was pleased to meet them. Helena translated, and they said they were pleased to meet him too. Manuel though was very excited, and more than anything else he wanted to tell me about the car, so we all sat down whilst he explained he wanted, subject to my final say so to purchase a Toyota Land Cruiser.

'Ok Manuel if you're sure about it, then go ahead, how much is it?' 'Twenty-eight thousand euros, I managed to get it quite cheaply, she is not quite two years old and has a two-year warranty as well as low mileage too. The salesman told me it was a bit of a bargain, as it had been returned because the family who owned it, couldn't afford the repayments.'

'Oh that is depressing, I feel so sorry for them, and I would rather not have known that.'

Manuel looking directly at her declared,

'I suppose it's not a nice thought, but if it wasn't us it would be someone else.' Before going on to ask her if he could pick it up later.

'Fine, I will call the bank and ask them to move the money. By the way I don't suppose you know anything else about the family who had to give the car back?'

'No not really, the salesman said he thought he may have lost his job or something like that.'

'That's heart-breaking, is unemployment high here?'

'Yes, and its rising and its worse of course among the young, the economic down turn is being felt all over the place.'

'Manuel, this afternoon when you go to pick it up, will you ask if they are happy to share with you anything about the family who had to give it up.'

Looking a bit puzzled Manuel wiped his brow.

'Okay Menina.' He said as he turned and left the room. Helena and her father returned their focus back to the drawing room, before Helena showed him around the Library, she had already filled him in on Sofia's half written letter. William gazed around and then picked up a pen from the desk, playing with it between his fingers.

'So have you looked elsewhere in here for the other part?'

'No Pop I haven't, because I don't think she ever wrote it, but I suppose there might be more secrets in here for us to discover, I haven't had an opportunity yet to look around. I am hoping that when the ladies come to help with emptying out the house, we may come across more papers.'

'Who is organising that for you then, Maria?'

'Yes Maria, but tomorrow, the mother of Carlos is coming down to have a look around, and she has offered to help for free. Both Carlos and Louisa hope coming here will help her recover from her husband's death, by giving her something to focus on outside her home.'

'Oh dear love, what happened?'

Helena proceeded to fill him in, and said is a shame you don't speak more Portuguese, I think the pair of you would have a lot in common.

'Perhaps, but sometimes you don't need words, just kind actions.'

'True very true Pop.' Helena gave his arm a squeeze. Just then she heard wheels on the gravel drive, they both looked out of the window in time to see a small white van pull up. Helena recognised Antonio as soon as he got out of the car, and the older guy must be his dad Ramiro, turning to her dad Helena said, that these were the electricians, and that she wanted him to take an interest in this if he didn't mind.

'I'd be happy to love, give me something to do.'

'If you get stuck with the language Antonio speaks some English so just ask him to translate, but I expect if you're talking about electrics it will all make sense, just remember, a socket is a tomada, wire is fio a plug is a ficha, for plurals just add a s so plugs become fichas. Oh and electricity is electricidade, once you remember that it should be a piece of cake for a man of your intelligence!'

'Thanks for the vote of confidence love, let's see then.'

Helena went to the front door and invited them both in. Antonio introduced her to his dad, and she in turn introduced them to her dad, explaining that he was an electrical engineer, and that he would accompany them as we walked around.

Antonio's dad was the opposite of his son, tall and very thin much like a string bean, he wore a blue overall, and carried a notebook. His hair was sandy coloured, and his eyes were a deep blue, his moustache was almost gingery, and on his nose sat a pair of half-moon glasses. Helena explained that the house was not connected to the mains, and that this would need managing first, before going on to explain that all the trades, builders, plumbers and electricians would be required to work with each other, their individual plans would need submitting so that they could be incorporated into the main project plan that Carlos would manage. He will be responsible for sorting out any difficulties, and co-ordinating the work schedules. Helena added that in parallel to the main house, a small cottage in the grounds needed also to be finished by the end of August. Antonio, who had listened carefully interjected.

'Carlos has already explained much of this to me, and it's not a problem, we can fit in. The biggest issue for us will be in scoping with you what you want in terms of sockets, wall lights and ceiling lights, as well as in the kitchen the appliance sockets. Electrics for any boilers etc. We can work with almost any builder or plumber.'

Ramiro who had been quite quiet until then joined in the conversation.

'Will the builder be removing all the existing plaster, or wall coverings?'

'Yes, it's pretty old and cracked, so in most places it will go, in the library and other rooms that have wooden panelling these will all be removed and replaced when the first fix has been done.'

'O Ramiro' said William addressing him for the first time.

'Are you able to sign off the electrical wiring that will be done here or do you need to get in a specialist like they do in some countries.'

Antonio translated and then O Ramiro said

'No Senhor Stratton, I can sign it off, I have the correct qualifications I can show you the certificate if you like.'

William seemed to understand what he said and nodded his head, before saying,

'No, that won't be necessary I was merely thinking about making an allowance for this in the plan. Now what ampage are we working on here, and what type of electrical distribution board do you use?' With Antonio translating and the three of them descending into detail, Helena decided it was time for her to back out, so she left them to walk around, but reminded them about the small barn which we would be using as an office, which would also need immediate attention once they had an electricity supply on the site.

She wandered into the kitchen where Maria was stretching up and pulling out crockery from the huge wall cupboards.

'I thought I might as well wash all of these and pack them up, since we are not going to need them, and the builders might want to use the space for storage'

'Good idea, I'll give you a hand.'

They worked away chatting occasionally for half an hour when Helena suddenly remembered that she hadn't seen Lionel since Monday.

'Maria, where is Lionel?'

'Ah Lionel. Well he can't come back until this afternoon, he already had a job planned in this week and he needed to do it, he didn't want to say anything in case you thought him unreliable and got someone else in.'

'Silly man, he didn't have to worry about that, I understand people can't just drop everything for me. When do you expect him back?'
'He said he hoped to be here by three pm.'
'Why don't you call him and say there is no rush, the work here is his, and explain that I understand he has pre-commitments.'
'Okay I will go and call him now.'
Maria dried her hands on her apron, pushed back her hair with the back of her hand and then went outside to make the call, I could hear her speaking rapidly in Portuguese, and within a few minutes she was back.
'Lionel said thank you, he will still try to get here today if he finishes quickly, as he wants to sort the door to the attic for you.'
'That's good of him, I am interested to know what's up there. You know those two windows at the front, don't seem to have been put in when the house was built, I think they are a later edition. Given the amount of external storage I can't quite see why Sofia felt it necessary to convert the attic space. What do you think Maria?'
'I really have no idea, but now you have said it, the style of the windows isn't right, round instead of rectangular, and they do spoil the lines of the house.'
'Your right you know, I hadn't thought of it that way before, but they do spoil the front of the house, maybe I will have them taken out.'
For the next half an hour they worked solidly moving out all the kitchen paraphernalia, and emptying the pantry of its old jars, plates and serving dishes. Whilst they were doing all of this they heard the three men, walking around and discussing various items or points of view.
Helena even heard her dad, chipping in in a stilted Portuguese about "plug points low down" and even at

239

one point she heard him saying "two on either side of the bed", so he had remembered some things after all.

A quarter of an hour later, they came into the kitchen to discuss what was wanted in here. She described to them her plans for building on a kitchen extension on the back of this room, creating a large open plan kitchen with glass walls, and a veranda beyond. In general Helenaindicated plug points for the new appliances, that there would be a central island unit with hob, two ovens etc, plus on the current back wall an oil-fired range cooker probably an Aga, for the winter. Helena indicated that they should quote for that and if she wanted more it could be added later. Ramiro then addressing William said they were off into the grounds, to look at the barns and houses, William with his hands in his pockets seemingly searching for a handkerchief, told them to go ahead, as he was dying for a cup of tea.

Maria who had listened to the whole exchange, said softly,

'Perhaps we should all have a quick break, sit down everyone and

I'll put the kettle on.'

After she had done that, Maria pulled out from the cupboard a couple of teapots and coffee pots, matching milk jugs and sugar bowls and a couple of dozen or so brightly coloured mugs.

'I brought these yesterday in "Casa Espaço", I thought with all the people that are going to be working here over the next few months we ought to have a stock,' Maria joked.

'Brilliant Maria, what a good idea, I assume you have the bill?'

'Yes Helena I have the bill, but not for the biscuits, they are my treat this time,' she smiled brightly.

Everyone sat down and chatted, whilst the tea mashed, and the coffee was poured, the biscuits were delicious, and Helena had to stop herself eating more than was good for her, though she noticed the same didn't apply to Ramiro or her dad!

After tea was finished, the guys went out into the grounds, and Maria washed up, once that was completed she looked over at Helen.

'So what shall we do now Helena? I've finished in here, but there is still a lot of rooms which are now unlocked but which we haven't yet explored.'

'That's true enough' said Helena smiling to herself as she had been unable to resist the temptation to peep in all of them as Lionel managed to unlock them, but that's all she had done. Her immediate thought was to nose around in the sitting room, where there were tall fitted cupboards on either side of the fire, and a large sideboard, but the thought of Sofia's bedroom and the letters that might be hidden there proved an irresistible pull.

'Come on Maria, let's go explore Sofia's bedroom, then the walk-in cupboards in her bathroom, I feel sure there is more to discover, than we found the other day. We have an hour until lunchtime.'

'Okay that sounds like a plan,' said Maria who had a way of making each task sound like one she was going to enjoy.

'Just let me get some bin bags, and a broom, from the pantry.'

Once she had them in her hand, they trooped off to the bedroom. The bedroom was in darkness, so Maria quickly went and opened the shutter on the window: soft light flooded into the room, both women looked around, all was just as they had left it, the hidden door that opened onto the small corridor was ajar, and beyond that the door to the bathroom was closed. Maria, ever practical, said

'Shall we start by stripping the bed, and seeing what that reveals?'

Helena nodded, and the work began, the quilted blue satin topper, was almost intact, apart from a few holes, which Helena hoped had been made by moths rather than mice. Nonetheless having shook it soundly and found nothing hidden, they then bundled into a bin bag, and were showered in dust for their efforts. Next came a couple of woollen blankets, definitely moth ridden, which also went into the bin bag. A white cotton top sheet with now yellowing lace work edging was next, this though was in good condition, Helena was looking at the detail of the lace.

'What do you think Maria can we save this, it's pretty and seems quite old.'

Maria took the sheet from her and perused it. 'Maybe, we can try anyway, let's put it in a separate bag.'

They tackled the mini mountain of cushions next, two large bolsters, two pillows and then three square previously plump cushions. All of them were covered in mismatched covers. Firstly, they moved the very dusty cushions out of the way, plopping them into another black bin bag, before taking off the faded pillow case covers. Nothing was inside them the pillows themselves were covered in faded pale blue and white striped ticking. Helena gave them a good pummelling to check nothing had been hidden inside, before saying to Maria,

'I think these are well past their best, we should put them on a bonfire!'

Maria however couldn't reply as Helena's violent pummelling had caused so much dust to rise, that she was having difficulty stopping the coughing which had started a few seconds earlier. Helena went to the window and tried to open it but to no avail, so they both backed away into the hall to wait for the dust to subside, as by now they were both spluttering, coughing and sneezing. After a few minutes Helena managed to say,

'I am sorry Maria, I've made us both cough, I'll fetch some water.'

She went to the kitchen and came back with a couple of bottles of water, which they began to drink gratefully as they sat on the stairs.

'Well I guess I had better not do that to the bolsters,' Helena said grinning at Maria.

'Perhaps not, if you want to maybe you should do it outside!'

'Agreed.'

With that Helena got up and went to check on the room, the dust had subsided now.

'I think it's safe to enter now, shall we carry on?'

Maria got up, and followed her back into the room, she put her bottle down on the bedside cabinet, and then went to take the cover off the bolster nearest to her, whilst Helena was gingerly tackling the other one. Once the pillowcases were off it was clear to them that nothing was hidden inside, so they were also dispatched to the bin bag. The bolsters they put outside in the hall.

'Okay then the bottom sheet next,' Maria said.

They picked up the sheet at the corners, and pulled backwards. A little dust rose, and they quickly bundled the thin sheet into the bin bag too. A blanket lay on top of the mattress, and this too was pulled off exposing a very old and quite badly stained mattress. It was sagging in parts, badly stained and pretty much all of its original pale blue cover was now a dirty off white.

They both looked at it a little sadly, thinking of the proud woman who had last slept here just before she died. Helena said sadly,

'I wonder why Sofia didn't buy a new mattress, this one must be from the 1950's, maybe even older.'

Maria turning to Helena with an apologetic half glance said,

'Come on let's get it off it doesn't look heavy at all, we should be able to manage this without male help, and we can take it into the hall, and let them move it from there.'

'Good idea, but I can't see any hand holds, so it may be a bit unwieldy'

'Okay Maria, after three we will pick it up from the headboard end, one, to, three.'

They both heaved it up, before realising they hadn't decided what the next move was going to be, unfortunately Helena pushed it towards Maria, who became off balance, and in order to stop herself from falling, let go of her corner of the mattress, which then dropped down knocking over her water bottle, the water from which ran all over the bedside table. Helena quickly pulled the mattress back and let it drop back on the bed. Maria who had steadied herself on the wall, regained her balance, and picked up the water bottle, but the majority of the water had by now already spilt out, and was dripping off the top of the bedside.

Grabbing a couple of the old pillowcases from the bin bag, Helena tried to soak up the water.

Then she started to laugh, and Maria followed suit, before they both sat on the bed and waited for the laughter to stop. Once Helena had regained a modicum of control she moved to the bedside table, and mopped up the remaining water, as best she could. She picked up the table and dried down the sides, before moving to the back, whilst in the process of doing so Helena thought she heard a small sound.

"Did you hear that Maria?'

'Yes, definitely something but I am not sure what.'

Helena turned the bedside table round, and looked at the back but couldn't detect anything out of the ordinary. Moving around to the front, she opened the drawer, pulled it out and checked all around but that seemed normal too.

'Mm I am sure I heard something.'

she said with a puzzled look on her face. Then she peered into the cavity where the drawer had been, nothing looked amiss, so she gingerly put her hand inside and felt around but all she could feel was smooth wood, no holes or hidden drawers. At this point Helena was beginning to think she had been mistaken, when Maria turned to her and said,

'Let's turn it upside down.'

Picking it up by its elegant legs they turned it upside down and put it on the mattress, using one of the old pillow cases they wiped away all the cobwebs from underneath, and there in front of them was a small projecting lip of wood. They both looked at each other, and without saying anything Maria went to fetch the other bedside cabinet, and turned this upside down too. But no protruding lip was to be seen. Helena turned her attention back to the slightly damp cabinet, which she turned the right way up, and noticed a small piece of round metal protruding out from the centre of a flower that formed part of the raised metal fretwork, whose purpose was to stop items falling off the top. Helena pushed the round piece of metal back in to the flower, and the edge of the lip receded. She pressed in the same place again and the metal popped out and the lip reappeared. They looked at each other Maria's face was surprised but expectant, as Helena bent over and pulled on the lip of wood. Once she pulled on it she found herself staring at a slim line hidden draw, along the top of which was a locking plate made of what she thought was brass. The whole draw must have

245

fitted into a compartment that was about half the width of the cabinet itself. The drawer though, was empty.

Helena immediately turned her attention to the other bedside cabinet, and pressed on the central part of the flower, nothing happened, she tried several times, still nothing. She turned the cabinet upside down to examine it, and hope flared they were identical.

'I am sure there is a drawer in here', but it's stuck and I can't see how to free it, I wish Lionel was here he might have the tools to help us,' said Helena.

Maria who was also excited by the prospect of a secret draw said in reply,

'I'll call him and see if he is still coming, shall I?'

'Good idea, I might break the thing otherwise, which could cause more of a problem.'

Two minutes later Maria was back.

'He is coming and will arrive in about fifteen minutes, but it means he won't be able to come back later today, is that okay?'

Helena who was flushed, and could hardly contain her rising excitement said to Maria,

'No problem, this is so exciting I just hope that it's not empty too.'

They made their way back into the kitchen with both bedside tables, and waited for Lionel to arrive. Whilst they were waiting William, Ramiro and Antonio came in, looking with some curiosity at the two upturned tables. Helena explained what they had found, and they all started to talk at the same time, before as if by mutual consent they all settled down to wait as well. The wait was short lived, as ten minutes later Lionel came in through the kitchen door.

Maria explained what the problem was, and everyone watched as Lionel firstly experimented with the first bedside, pushing in and out the central part of the flower.

No one was entirely sure what he was looking or listening for, but he clearly did. He then moved to the second bedside cabinet and pressed the centre of the flower just as we had done, with the same result as nothing happened. Lionel then pulled out his small tin of tools, and after a few seconds selected a very fine needle like hooked probe. This he inserted around the central part of the flower looking for a weakness or a gap, he then fetched his can of oil and placed a few drops of oil all around the centre of the flower.

Everyone in the room was focused on him, and when he looked up he winked!

Next, he turned to the bottom of the cabinet, and probed around in the place where in the first cabinet the lip of the drawer appeared. He then turned and said,

'I believe the mechanism at this end is rusted up, it may be at some point in the past something has been spilt and not properly cleaned up. I might have to force the wood apart, if I can't get the flower mechanism to operate properly, but we need to give it some minutes for the oil to penetrate and see if that works.'

Maria who hated to be idle said to no one in particular that she would put the kettle on, whilst they waited, and she immediately busied herself making coffee. The rest of the group mused on what, if anything, could be in the draw.

William said he thought it was likely to be empty like the other one, Helena of course was hoping for the letters that had once been inside the envelopes, she and Maria had found in the dressing table. Lionel who had lifted the cabinet up to his ear a few times eventually pronounced, 'There is something in here, I can hear a very slight but soft sound when I shake it, but it doesn't sound like paper.'

247

He tried the flower a few more times but to no avail, so he asked if it was ok to force the lock, being careful to say he hoped he wouldn't do too much damage to the cabinet itself. Helena swiftly   agreed, and so Lionel picked up a long thin hooked end metal file, which he inserted slowly just right of where the locking plate would be. Slowly he jiggled the file both forward and backward as well as left and right, but still the draw remained shut. He then changed the file for a slightly thicker but still slim metal saw, once this was inserted he began to saw at an upward angle at whatever was engaged in the locking plate. Not many seconds later he was through, he pulled out the saw, reinserted the hooked metal file and pulled it towards him, the drawer faltered and came free. He pulled it completely out from its compartment and a small flat brown leather drawstring pouch, fell onto the table. They all stared at it, then as if by common consent Helena picked it up, and felt it. The leather was old and cracked, but inside she could feel it contained a metal key, she pulled on the drawstring, which disintegrated into several hardened pieces, she then tipped the pouch's contents onto the table. Two keys landed with a metallic clang; one was small approximately two and a half centimetres long, quite ornate and shined like burnished gold, the second was larger maybe four centimetres and a simple design in dull grey metal, with an open bow.

Helena could feel the five pair of eyes completely focussed on her, she picked up the smaller of the two keys turned it over in her fingers, before passing it to her dad.

'What do you think this key might be used for Pop?' Meanwhile Maria who had put her fingers inside the pouch, as if feeling for something, now turned the pouch inside out, and shook it, but nothing else was inside.

Lionel in the intervening time had picked up the larger key, and said to himself rather than anyone else.

'I wonder? Menina, I think this might be the key to the attic door'

'What makes you think so?'

'Intuition, nothing more really, it's a simple door key, and so far, the only door in the house we don't have a key for is the attic.'

'You could be right, maybe we can check it out later.' Helena was suddenly conscious that in uttering those words, she had deflated the atmosphere in the room, which just few seconds ago had been both expectant and excited. However, if this was the key to the attic, she wanted to explore it without an audience. When Lionel had tried to unlock the attic door previously, her sixth sense went into overdrive, and it had just started up again. No, despite the disappointment on the faces in the room, this was a job for her and her dad alone.

With that, her dad with a clear purpose to move the discussion onto other things, and popped both keys back in the pouch, he looked up and spoke to Helena.

'I think we have just about covered the Manor House Helena, these guys wanted a quick word with you before they go.'

Helena, was grateful to her dad for his intervention, but found it difficult to calm the pounding in her heart, and find a way to ensure when she spoke she sounded normal.

'Lionel, thank you for coming back to help us, I know you need to leave and return to your job for the day, shall we see you tomorrow then?'

'Yes Senhora I will be here at eight' with that Lionel picked up his tools and left via the kitchen lobby, as he did so Helena then turned and addressed herself to the two waiting electricians.

'Have you seen everything you needed to Antonio, Ramiro? My dad said you wanted to clarify a couple of things with me?'

'Thank you yes, we have seen more than sufficient for now, we may need to come back and verify the odd query, but we will speak to Carlos about access.'

'Great, it's no problem please come back as often as you like, if it helps with your quotation.'

Senhor Ramiro, with a grave face then looked directly at Helena before speaking,

'The only other concern is about our timetable, which you will understand is heavily dependent on the builder's timetable. Obviously, we can begin first fix electrics without having an electrical supply, but we will need the builders to have stripped the walls back in the house before we can begin. I have already told your father, that any delays once we begin may mean additional costs for you, because it may be impossible for us to find other work to do without notice. Should we be successful in gaining the work here, then we will need to block out at least two if not three months. I just wanted to be sure you understood the commitment on both sides.'

'I understand this Senhor, it's one of the reasons why we are employing a project manager, in these situations everyone becomes reliant on others. But you must not worry, once the quote and your work plans are accepted, we are committed to you, and it will be down to Carlos to make sure the job keeps moving along, with as little down time as possible. We could of course operate with a small degree of flexibility, to suit us both, I am sure we can work that out. In the meantime, I am looking forward receiving you quote for the house, and separately for the barns and cottages.'

Ramiro nodded, and shook Helena's and her father's hand, saying he would get the quote for the house to them by the end of the month at the latest.

Helena's dad showed them out, before returning to the kitchen,

'They seem good guys, and they clearly know what they're doing, they asked some intelligent questions, I feel confident that they can do the work, but I expect that's not what you're thinking about right now, is it? I bet your itching to try the key to the attic!'

'You read my mind, thanks for helping back their dad, it could have been a bit awkward otherwise, I really can't explain my reluctance, I just have a strange feeling about the attic space, and truthfully would rather look without an audience. Obviously, you and Maria are welcome, Manuel won't be back until later, so what do you say Maria, shall we go and see if Lionel is right?'

'Yes please, I like a mystery, and even if it's not the key to the attic, it must be a special key for something otherwise why hide it, along with the little gold one too.' Helena nodded.

'Well, I have a feeling that one is for a small box or case, it's very much like the ones that used to be used for jewellery boxes, or old-fashioned writing cases, and tea caddies.'

Taking a quick glance at her watch, she said,

'Well it's 12.30 now, shall we go and test Lionel's theory? Helena, led the way as all three of them left the kitchen, and quickly made their way up the stairs to the inner hallway, with the key in her hand, she looked at both of them, there was a slightly wild gleam in her eyes as she said,

'Here goes.'

Inserting the key in the lock she turned it twice clockwise, the key met some resistance, but then unlocked. She

then took hold of the key bow and pulled, it was a bit stiff.
She pulled again, and this time the door gave, opening
outwards. Despite the darkness they could see
straightaway that they faced a rickety open tread wooden
staircase whose first step was on their direct left, but
which immediately began a tight curve to the right before
rising steeply upwards and straightening out. On the
right-hand side was a wooden handrail, whilst on the left
was a wall, presumably of the bedroom next door.
William, was the first to speak.
'I think we will need torches, and I am not sure about the
quality of this wood, so if anyone is going up, I am going
first, and before you say anything Helena, I insist.'
He said this looking at her with an expression which said
don't argue with me young lady. Helena couldn't help but
smile at her over protective dad, but she said in a slightly
sulky voice,
'Okay, okay I will go and fetch the torches from the
kitchen, but don't you dare go up there without me or I
will be cross.'
William laughed out loud,
'You sound just like a petulant child, now be off with you
before I send you to bed without supper.'
Both of them laughed out loud, and Maria who hadn't
understood a word they had said because they had
reverted to English, looked at them both shook her head
and said,
'Acho que vocês dois estão loucos!' which translated to "I
think you two are mad!"
To which Helena replied 'Acho que tu s correto' or "I think
you are right."
After which Maria also laughed, and said she would fetch
he torches, to give us time to calm down. Meanwhile
William stood on the first step, and placed his hand on

the ones in front of him before giving them a test with his foot.

'They seem sturdier than they look.'

Maria returned with three torches, they turned them on and in a slow procession, William in front, Helena in the middle, and Maria bringing up the rear, they moved upward.

William's torch was shining upwards, and it was possible to make out that the steep steps did not go too far up, before opening out into the attic space quite quickly.

'Well I wasn't expecting this' said William, as he stepped up the last step and out onto the floor of the attic proper. Helena followed him and saw what he meant, in front of them was a large empty space, fully boarded out but completely empty. Cobwebs festooned the rafters, and thick dust covered the floor, in a couple of places chinks of light were evident, where a tile had slipped. Once Maria was up on the attic floor as well, they all shone their torches around. A few seconds later Maria said, 'I think that might be a door over there.'

Following the beam of her torch, their beams joined with hers, and with the light from the three shining on the place she had indicated they realised that it was indeed door. As they walked towards it William said,

'There is no door handle, but there is a keyhole, pass me the attic door key Helena.'

Helena passed it to him, and with Maria shining her torch beam on the keyhole, her dad inserted it in the lock, he turned the key twice and the door opened inwards.

William was the first to step over the threshold into what, at first glance, seemed to him to be a perfectly formed nursery, complete with large rocking horse. The purpose of the round attic windows now became apparent, as the room was bathed in a diffuse daylight, which somehow was managing to force its way through the decades of spider's webs and dust and grime which was covering them both inside and out.

'Wow.' William exclaimed. 'Isn't this nursery furniture, just look at that rocking horse.'

Helena, who had followed him in looked all around the space before replying,

'It looks more like a set from an old creepy movie to me.'

All three ventured a little further in, brushing away decades worth of spider's webs. Every surface was covered in dust. There were half used candles in wall sconces, and in the candle-holders on an old chest of drawers and other pieces of nursery furniture.

Maria was the first to react.

'Just give me a minute, before you go in any further,' she said, as she disappeared through the door, and they heard her clattering down the stairs, she returned just a few minutes later with two brooms to which she had tied the old pillowcases.

She passed one to Helena, and then proceeded to walk forward, brushing to left right and in front effectively clearing a path through the cobwebs. The remnants of which hung down snagging on their hair and clothes as they walked further into the room. Helena could see now that in fact it wasn't a room, but simply a space into which the contents of a former nursery had been placed.

Between them they managed to clear enough space for them all to see much more clearly the scene in front of

them. William spent a few moments pulling stray
cobwebs from both Helena and Maria's shoulders, before
he said,
'The furniture in here must be over a hundred years old.
Look at the crib it's beautifully made.'
He moved towards it and gave it a gentle push, it slowly
moved from side to side, making a creaking noise as if
protesting at being disturbed after a long sleep. Helena
had moved over towards the ornate wrought iron single
bed, on top of which was an open box of lead toy
soldiers, with its lid lying beside it. Next to it was a
wooden spinning top, Helena picked this up, and wiped
the dust and cobwebs from it, to no one in particular she
commented.
'I've seen this before. I think it is the same top as is in the
portrait downstairs.'
Maria, meanwhile had moved towards the crib, which had
now stopped swinging, and she turned the top dust cover
aside. It was empty of course, but the crib was perfectly
made, and the covers were beautifully made. The top
coverlet must once have been a deep rose pink, before
the passage of time and exposure to sunlight had faded it
to a washed-out version. Maria picked it up, dust swirled
in the warm air, and through it she could see that the
underneath was still a vibrant deep pink. The covers
below were made of a cream satin, and lying underneath
and to one side was a small wooden doll. The doll was
about six inches long; it had flaxen hair, and was dressed
up in baby clothes. Maria said
'Look at this Helena, don't you think it's a bit odd.'
Helena who was still holding the spinning top looked at
her,
'I am not sure what you mean Maria, it looks like a doll to
me.'

'Well yes, it is, that's the point. The whole of this crib is dressed as if it's occupant would be a girl. I thought Luis was an only child, if so why is there a crib predominantly dressed in pink?'

By now both Helena and her father had, in response to Marias' question, edged towards the crib. Helena took the doll from her, she turned it over in her hand, and then picked up the coverlet from the crib. William who prior to this had been about to open the drawers of a chest, said, 'Well perhaps in the past colours didn't mean anything, like they do now?'

'Could be dad, but I agree with Maria, a crib with pink coverlets suggests a girl, it's odd, let's keep looking.'

'William went back to the chest of draws, and Maria continued sweeping overhead with the broom, Helena herself moved towards a wardrobe made of similar wood to that used in the Library. She opened the central door, and inside found a number of outfit's suitable for a young boy, they were in reasonable condition considering their age.

'This wardrobe contains clothes for a young boy,'

Then from across the room William piped up.

'Whilst this,' he said pointing to the contents in the draw 'Seems to contain mainly baby's clothes.'

Maria, who had just finished sweeping cobwebs from in front of the two windows, put down the broom and joined him at the chest of drawers. She opened the second draw down, and having looked at the contents she shook her head slowly.

'If I'm not mistaken this drawer contains maternity clothes, this looks like a corset that in times past would have provided support for a pregnant woman. Whilst these pads of muslin are clearly for the period of lying in, I remember seeing some similar to these in my grans cupboard. My grandmother used to deliver babies, before we had doctors and midwives.'

Helena, still carrying a boy's shirt and pants, in a dark blue heavy cloth, came over to look at the corset.

'That looks monstrous, how can pregnant women wear corsets!'

'Most women of certain generations wore corsets, I remember my grans hanging on the line, ' said William blushing slightly.

'Though to be fair they didn't look as hard or as uncomfortable as this one.'

Maria who was still holding the corset in her arms said, 'Helena, maybe you will have to do a little research, but with this boning and the stays I can't see how it could be anything else, I agree it looks uncomfortable to wear though. But then times were different.'

William continued to delve into the draw, bringing out some bloomers, and long elaborate linen smocks, and heavy gauge white silk stockings.

'These are definitely look like maternity clothes, obviously from Sofia's pregnancy with Luis.' He then closed the draw and opened the third one down, which contained more baby clothes.

Maria looked at them, and started to shake her head, eventually she found her voice.

'I am certain these clothes are for a baby girl, but what is odd is that there are only baby clothes, nothing in this draw suggests a child older than maybe one or two.'

Helena, came closer and she began to pull out the tiny sets of clothes that were lying inside. Exquisite tiny dresses, with lacy collars, embroidered hems and long sleeves, immediately she saw that Maria was right, all the clothes were for a baby or a toddler at most, and they were soft pinks, or cream. Laying to one side of the second drawer were a small stack of tiny silk bonnets, these were all trimmed with pink, peach or a pale green. In the bottom of the drawer was a beautiful hand knitted cream shawl, whose edges were scalloped in a pale pink. Helena knew that a hundred years ago all babies whether they be boys or girls would wear dresses, she had seen pictures of the Royal Family, but she had to admit that the predominantly coloured bonnets seemed to suggest these were for a girl.

Her father who had moved out to make way for Helena, approached a large trunk which was at the end of the single bed, he opened the lid, exclaiming excitedly, 'This is a toy box, and the toys are definitely for an older child.' Bending down he picked out a wooden horse, and a cart, and a large wooden Noah's Ark, complete with animal figures, a ball, some more lead soldiers and some coloured pebbles, opaque glass marbles and a teddy bear.'

Helena shuddered, it was as if a ghost had just walked by her and stroked her arm, her father saw her shiver.

'Are you alright Helena?'

'Yes, I'm okay a ghost just walked over my grave that's all, I think we should go down, and wait until we have more help to search in here.'

'Okay love just give me a few more minutes, I will see if there is a box or case something that the little gold key would fit.'

William said this, as he began to move around the room shifting objects out of the way.

'Okay dad we will see you down stairs.'

Helena made her way through the door and headed on down stairs, Maria appeared reluctant to follow, but after a last look around she too left the attic rooms. Once down stairs, Helena sat down heavily on one of the kitchen chairs and starred into space a faraway look in her eyes.

'What's the matter Helena, you are quite pale, has something in the attic upset you.'

'Actually, yes it did rather,' Helena went on to explain the meaning of the British saying - a ghost walking over your grave.

Maria nodded, before putting her arm around Helena and in a prim and slightly mocking voice she said,

'You do know there is no such thing don't you.'

Helena glanced at her.

'Of course, I know it's silly, but why is all that stuff up there in the attic? And if your right that the baby clothes are for a girl, what the hell does that mean?'

'It means that someone, but not necessarily Sofia had a baby girl, and left her baby clothes here.'

'But what if it was Sofia, why is there no mention of a baby girl or a grown up one in her will? She only mentions Luis, and as Senhor Gonçalves has already confirmed only the two of them were on the ships passenger list that left Portugal for America in 1913.'

'Maybe the baby didn't survive, in those times many babies died in infancy.'

'I think I need a drink, do we have any wine open? Then I am going to call Marco.'

Ten minutes later Helena had a glass of red wine in one hand and her phone in the other, her dad was still up in the attic, and Maria had gone up to take him some water and she hadn't yet returned.

Helena dialled Marco's number. A polite receptionist, who said she would put her through, answered the phone.

'Hello Helena, this is a pleasant surprise, what can I do for you?'

Helena explained to him about the finds in the attic and the conclusion they were coming to. Marco didn't speak until she had finished.

'I will check our records, but personally I don't recall seeing anything about a second child, may be my father might know something, can you leave it with me for a few hours. I will see what I can find out and call you back this evening.'

They said goodbye, and Helena felt a little better, she was sure that he would find something to explain the baby clothes, for some reason they had unnerved her. Even so it wouldn't explain why the nursery furniture was now consigned to the attic and locked away. As she was mulling over the fact that maybe Sofia had another child, her dad entered the kitchen, there were cobwebs in his hair, and dust all over his trousers.

'What have you been doing dad, your filthy!'

'Well, I had a good look around, and moved most of the furniture, but I couldn't find a box or a case of any sort, but if the little gold key was in the same pouch as the large one then I am inclined to think the box, or whatever it is the key opens, will be in that attic.'

Helena shook her head.

'I am not so sure dad, but I can see the logic of why you would think so. But just because Sofia had them both together, doesn't necessarily mean anything. I've spoken to Marco, and he is going to check if they have anything in their files about a second child.'

'Good idea, were they involved originally, I mean from when the house was first built?'

'I don't know dad, but they have been Sofia's solicitors since she came back in 1925, before then they were responsible for checking on the house after Rafael's death, but before that I don't know.'

When Marco calls later I will check with him, why do you ask?'

'Well love I have been thinking, and it seems obvious to me that when the house was first built, and Sofia and

Rafael lived here they must have had domestic help. The house is too big, and if Rafael was a Count then, surely, he would have had people working for him. I mean what do we know about him? Did he live here with Sofia all the time, we don't believe they were married, so it's more likely that he came and went. If you think about it he lived, as I understand it in Porto, he was the head of a family and he had business interests to attend to. If that's right he couldn't have spent much time, here could he?'

'Do you know something dad, I have become so obsessed with Sofia's story that I haven't given any thought to their domestic arrangements during her first period of occupation. But supposing your right, and he didn't live here permanently, he wouldn't have left Sofia alone would he. So maybe your right, other people must have been here with her all the time. After all he built the house for her, he loved her, they had Luis, so he must have put arrangements in place for the house and is bills etc. Maybe the answer to these mysteries lies in the Alencar family papers that Marco has arranged for me to see.'

'Maybe, there is more to this than meets the eye if you think about it. Some questions come to the fore, how did they meet from what we know she was the daughter of a humble Blacksmith in the middle of the countryside. He, on the other hand was an unmarried man, sixteen years older than her with a title, lands near Porto, and the weight of family expectations on him.'

'Well Marco did say it was a love story. I am mad with myself though for not asking him more. I seem to have got wrapped up in the house and Sofia without bothering to understand how it all started.'

William smiled at his impetuous daughter.

'Don't be hard on yourself, you've only been here five days and it's natural to feel frustrated, I am positive we

261

will get to the bottom of it. Maybe Marco and his firm can tell us more later.'

'Let's hope so dad, in the meanwhile I have another potential line of enquiry to explore this afternoon, I am off to Covão to meet Maria do Carmo, who everyone tells me is a distant cousin who knew Sofia, maybe she knows things that can add to the story. But first I am rather hungry so shall we get back home and have some lunch?'

William replied,

'Sounds good to me, I could do with change of clothes as well.'

As he stared down at his dust and web covered outer garments.

At three o'clock Helena had lunched and changed. She picked up the bunch of flowers Maria had brought for her in Maçao the day before, her dad was having a cat nap on the sofa, so she crept quietly out of the house. When she arrived in Covão the square was bathed in silence, as she sat in the car, she felt as though she was the only living person in the village. As soon as she exited the car a couple of dogs began to bark and almost as from nowhere a couple of heads appeared.

Helena said good afternoon, and walked towards Café central, it too was deserted apart from Senhor Ramirez who was seated behind the counter, reading a newspaper, he glanced up to see who had entered the shop, saw Helena and said

'Boa tarde Menina' (Good afternoon young woman) Helena replied with the traditional response of Good afternoon, and asked him if everything was ok. Senhor Ramirez said all was fine, but looked quizzically at the flowers in her hand. Helena saw his expression so explained that she was here to meet Maria do Carmo, and the flowers were for her. They exchanged a few more pleasantries before Helena ordered a coffee, and went to sit down and wait.

Whilst she waited, she reflected on the last few days, she realised she really knew very little about her great-great grandparents. In reality, she had very few facts about them let alone any clues to their personal stories, the more she thought about it the more she appreciated that she needed to know. Not because it would unravel a century old mystery, but because this was family, and it was her history.

Resolving to be more questioning and less romantic about it in future, she glanced up to see an elderly, but still sprightly woman enter the café, on the arm of Alice. They walked slowly over to where Helena now stood, Alice said,

'Helena esta é sua prima Maria do Carmo.' In English this translated as Helena this is Maria do Carmo your cousin. Before turning to Maria and saying

'Maria esta é sua prima Helena jovem de Inglaterra.' (Maria this is young Helena your cousin from England.) The older woman looked at her for a few seconds, before taking off her glasses and using an old handkerchief, wiped her eyes. Helena, stepped forward, and found herself enveloped in a surprisingly strong hug, which she returned.

'Why don't the two of you sit down, I guess you have much to say to each other' said Alice, I will fetch a couple of glasses of Vinho do Porto.

Helena now took a few minutes to look at the face of her cousin, her white hair, was still thick, she had a strong square face, with a darkening line above top lip. Her face was marked with multiple age spots, her nose was thread veined, but now she had taken her glasses off her eyes were bright and alive.

'These are for you,' Helena said handing her the flowers she had brought.

The old lady took them and lifted them to her nose.

'They are beautiful, and the fragrance is lovely, and quite a surprise for me, thank you Helena, I can't remember the last time I was given flowers, it must have been many years ago.'

'Your very welcome, I didn't know what else to bring, but I like flowers, so I always think most women do.'

Maria do Carmo da Silva, Nunes, looked at her through her rheumy but still bright eyes.

'Here we use too many plastic flowers, because fresh ones don't last in the heat. Our cemetery is a field of flowers very nice from a distance, but they are all plastic, hardly a fresh one in sight. It will be same for me, remembrance in tacky plastic flowers.'

Helena didn't know what to say in response to that, so instead said

'My father is here with me as well, he wants to come and meet you at some point, obviously he is not a da Silva, that heritage is through my mum who sadly died last year.

Maria do Carmo, gave her a sad smile, saying.

'I am sorry for your loss, I would have liked to have known my cousin.'

Helena returned the smile and said.

'You know I think my mum would have loved to meet you too, but if you like I can tell you about my family, then if you have time, maybe you could tell me what you know of my great-great grandmother Sofia, who I am hoping you knew.'

Maria, put the flowers down on the table next door to the one they were sitting on, took off her jacket, glancing at Helena she said,

'I will tell you all I know, but I was relatively young when I knew her, and I am afraid I wasn't as inquisitive as I should have been. She was old and could be cantankerous, and sadly I was young and interested in other things, but I would love to know about your family.' Helena told her the story of her mum's illness and subsequent death last year. She told her about finding the letter in her mum's special keepsake box, which was written to her by her father, Helena's grandfather da Silva, and the accompanying note with the names of Luis parents and the solicitor in Maçao. She then explained how having contacted the solicitors, they passed her details to another set of solicitors in Coimbra; who told her she had inherited a house and land in Portugal from the estate of her great-great grandmother. Helena explained as carefully as she could what had happened next, and that she had no idea of the size of the inheritance until she arrived here. She told her that ever since arriving she had been further confused by some things she had found, and now she wanted to find out how her great-great grandparents met. What had happened to make Sofia leave Portugal, and why Rafael left her the Quinta. She didn't tell her about the baby clothes, but she did tell her about the keys they had found in the hidden draw.

Maria, who had sat silently though out the telling of the story so far, took off her glasses, and rubbed her eyes, before saying,

'I haven't set foot in the house for nearly fifty years, I have been trying to remember when I last saw Sofia, I think it must have been in 1970. You know that the house I lived for a number of years is the one Sofia inherited from her grandmother. She gave it to my dad just after my father married my mother. When I married Jorge and I took the house, and mum and dad lived with us until they both died.'

'Yes, I did know about the house, it's funny really because it must have been this house that my great grandfather thought he would have inherited had he come back to Portugal, because he never knew about the Quinta at all.'

Maria do Carmo, might be elderly but her mind was still pretty sharp, and whilst she sometimes went off on her own path, Helena was delighted that she seemed to have a good memory. Maria after a short pause continued.

'I was born in the 1930's, as a young child I came to the Quinta a lot because mum and dad worked here most days. Even when I went to school I would go at the weekends with them.'

Maria chuckled to herself, clearly remembering something funny from many years ago, she moved on to say,

'Tia (Aunty) Sofia used to live in just the one room, her bedroom was next door, and I used to like playing on the upstairs landing, but I had to do so quietly, or she would come out and ask me to go and play outside. I didn't mind that because I never liked the kitchen where mum was, which always seemed dark and scary. One time I was in the kitchen with my parents, when we heard Tia (aunty) Sofia scream, mum and dad ran into the sitting room, where they found Aunty standing on a chair, pointing to the curtains, screaming there was a snake. I ran outside, because I knew it wasn't alive, it was a toy one I had found in a barn the week before and had hidden behind the curtains. Once they realised it wasn't real and they had all calmed down they came looking for me, I got a good spanking that night, and was banned from the rooms upstairs. I don't know why as I found the snake in a chest in one of the barns, but aunty wouldn't listen. Another time I vividly remember, I went straight out into the garden, and for the first time saw that the door in the garden wall was open and because I was a small child I went through it, and saw the lake. Aunty Sofia was standing on the edge of it, holding something in her hands. She didn't hear me come running up, but when she did see me, she marched me straight back to the kitchen, she seemed very angry about something. I heard mum and her having an argument, and after that the door in the garden wall was locked. I always wanted to swim in the lake though, and when I was older I asked Aunty why I couldn't, I told her I could swim, but she just said no, the lake was off limit's, even to mum and dad.'

Helena who had been listening with interest at these tales said,

'Well the lake area is pretty derelict now, though I want to restore it, but I agree her behaviour was a bit strange, perhaps she didn't like water herself, some people can become quite paranoid.'

'I suppose that might be the reason.' said Maria do Carmo, though Helena could see in her face that she wasn't convinced, her cousin went on.

'Anyway, as I got older and went to school I visited only at the weekends, and when I left school I occasionally went with mum and dad on a Sunday to see Sofia and we would take her lunch. Even then in the early 1950's she was living on her own and spent most of her time in the sitting room. There were times when I thought she slept in there, because I could tell her clothes were very crumpled. Mum, I know used to try to get her to go out, but I don't think she ever did. Every Sunday mum and dad would heat water, so she could have a bath in her living room, eventually my dad persuaded her to have a bathroom installed, because it became too much for them to carry the hot water from the kitchen into the old bathtub, which was placed in front of her fire.'

'Do you know when the bathroom was installed?'

'I do actually, because it was the year I had started to go out with Jorge, and his father was the plumber who installed it, so it would be about 1954. My mum and dad were then in their late fifties, and they were not in the best of health. Maria do Carmo was quiet for a few minutes she seemed to be lost in thoughts of the past, but then she said,

'When Jorge and I got married in 1957, we took over mum and dads house, and stayed there until the fire destroyed the house in the 60's. I still own it of course but it's just a ruin, and I am not sure Elias will want it.'

Helena now noticed that Maria seemed to be a little tired, so she asked her if she wanted to go home, Helena could drive her back, when she was ready. However, somewhat surprisingly she said she was fine, but if Helena wanted to go back with her she could see some old family photographs.

For Helena, this was an unexpected bonus, so she jumped at the chance and together they walked the small distance to her home, which was on the edge of the village, and from the outside it appeared very old and quite small. From the front it Helena could see two windows flanking a single dull brown door.

Maria, put the key in the lock, and went inside. They entered directly into a small hall, off which to both left and the right were several doors very close together. Maria turned into the second one on the right, it was tiny, measuring no more than three metres by three metres, it had a small fireplace in one corner, and an ancient electric cooker stood next to the draining board leaning on a small stained ceramic sink. A tall very old Formica floor cupboard sat against one wall and in the centre, was a round table and chairs. There wasn't the room to swing the proverbial cat.

'I will put the kettle on and make some coffee, you just take a seat a minute' said Maria, who turned to the sink and began to fill up an old metal coffee pot, before standing it on a gas ring by the side of the electric stove. She then picked up a plastic orange jug, screwed off the lid and emptied the contents down the sink, before washing it out. From the smell it was the dregs of coffee. 'I use this thermos' she said, 'because it keeps the coffee warm and I can use it all day, it's a bit old like me but it still functions, just like me too.' she said with a chuckle. 'Now the coffee pot is on let me show you into the siting room, it's a bit more comfortable.'

Helena followed her out and across the narrow corridor into the room opposite. This was not much bigger than the kitchen, there was an old sideboard on which sat a number of photographs, a very old vinyl sofa in a hideous shade of antique yellow, which was adorned with white lacy seat backs, a seriously old television was on a shelf placed high up the wall. Maria pulled out a small wooden coffee table, from underneath it and said,

'Please sit-down Helena, I will get my box.'

Maria then went to the sideboard and brought out an old cardboard box, which she gently placed on the coffee table.

'Why don't you look at the photos on the sideboard, whilst I get the coffee.'

Helena didn't need asking twice, she stood up and moved to the sideboard. The pictures were not all old, there were a number of two young adults, and in one picture they were dressed as if they had just graduated from University. Both young men were good looking, tall and dark, and they were smiling as their caps along with countless others were being thrown into the air. Helena

269

smiled remembering her own graduation photos, these though were a little different, the gowns seemed to be pinned with many red ribbons. In one photo, on either side of the two young men were clearly proud mum and dad and Maria herself. She had picked this photo up, and was studying it when Maria came back in with a tray on which sat two pretty cups and saucers, a plate of biscuit's and the jug of coffee.

'Ah I see you have found Ricardo and Tomas, my grandsons, along with their mum Monica and my son Basilio. It was taken at their graduation in Coimbra in 2009, just a few weeks later Basilio died in a car crash.'

'Oh hell, Maria I am so sorry, I had no idea.'

'It was a sad day, I remember it well, but that is not for today, you didn't come to hear about Basilio, there will be time for that later.' She said it with a sad half-smile, and Helena gave her a hug.

'Tell me about my younger twin cousins then, where do they live and what do they do?'

'Lisbon…. I don't see much of them, you know how young people are, always too much to do.'

Helena wasn't sure whether to be pleased she had decided she was mature enough to be excluded from being young, or disappointed she didn't consider her young anymore! Maria was oblivious to her discomfort however, and went on

'They phone though every now and then, and Ricardo is going out with a nice girl. Tomas well Tomas is what they call 'gay' these days you know what I mean.'

Helena grinned at this revelation from a white haired elderly woman, and she did know what she meant, but what made her smile was that Maria said this so matter of factly, with no hint of embarrassment. Helena realised she was dealing with a quite an extraordinary woman.

270

'Ricardo is a civil engineer, and ambitious he works all over Portugal, and has just spent two years in Brazil working on the Olympic games complexes, it is where he met his young lady Veronica. Tomas is very kind he is the one on the right, he lives with a young man called Pieter, who I must say is very polite; he studied land and agricultural management before moving to Italy for four years. They lived on some sort of commune, you know like those we had in the 1960's, it aimed to be what is it they call it these days 'self-sufficient' yes that's it. Though living here in the countryside, we have always been pretty self-sufficient, so I am not sure why he had to go to Italy, he could have stayed here! Anyway, whilst he was there he met Pieter, and they came back here so they could find paid work and settle down. Pieter found a nice job in a bakery in Lisbon, but Tomas is struggling. Not having had a proper job for four years hasn't helped him of course.'

Helena took the lull in the conversation as an opportunity to say,

'I gather from Carlos that it's quite hard for young people here at the moment, so if you're a bit different it probably doesn't help. He sounds like quite a character though!'

Maria do Carmo smiled her eyes twinkling.

'He is that, the life and soul of any family gathering.'

They then sat down, and Maria poured some coffee. She opened the box and flicked through a number of photos before passing one to Helena.

'That is Sofia along with my mum and dad at my wedding.'

Helena studied the picture, it was black and white and quite grainy, Sofia was not at all as she had pictured her since seeing the painting. In the photo she was small, and a little thin, and was wearing a pale green dress, which almost reached the floor, more 1930's than 1950's.

271

The expression on her face was distant and sad, but then again, the wedding couple didn't exactly look happy either.

Maria piped up as if reading Helena's mind.

'We all looked miserable in those days, but you know we weren't at all. It was just that when you could afford photographs you were encouraged to look serious, even on wedding photographs.'

Helena reflected on all the old photos she had seen of her grandparents and concluded Maria was probably right, but even so she thought Sofia's expression hadn't needed to be pasted on, she was undoubtedly a very sad woman.

Maria spent the next half an hour pulling out the photos she thought Helena might be interested in, before saying to her,

'If you want to borrow them you can, perhaps your father might like to see them.'

'If you don't mind that would be great, thank you Maria.'

Helena was thinking that there might be some photos in the box which might help them with the mysteries surrounding the Quinta. Helena promised to return them in the next few days, but Maria with that twinkle in her eye said,

'No need to rush, please take your time, I am not going anywhere, just yet.'

Half an hour later, after listening to more reminiscences, Helena noticed Maria was beginning to tire, so she thanked her time, the coffee and loan of the photos.

'No need to thank me, you're my family now, so I hope we might see each other from time to time.'

'We will I am sure, anyway I am certain that you will want to see the Quinta again, so why don't we come and pick you up next week and you can visit.'

'Helena, you read my mind, I would like that. It has been many years since I was inside, perhaps I could go and see the lake too, thank you my dear, here is my phone number, just let me know the day before so I can make sure I am okay to come.'

Helena made her way to the front door clutching the box of photos, once on the threshold she turned and gave her Aunt a hug, which was returned with uncharacteristic strength for one so old.

Helena left saying she would call her next week, as she waved goodbye and walked back to the car she pondered all that she had learnt. Little by little she was learning more, but she was still very conscious of all the gaps that remained to be filled. She had learnt that Sofia's younger brother Tomas, never married as he died when he was a teenager when he fell from a cork oak tree he and a friend were climbing. He along with Sofia's parents were interred in the cemetery in Cováo along with Sofia's parents, but the burial plots had been reused several times since, so no headstone remained. Maria also said that Sofia wasn't buried there. There had been a memorial service, but she thought Sofia had been taken to Lisbon for cremation. Again Helena wondered if Marco could fill in this particular blank.

At the thought of him Helena smiled she was looking forward to speaking with him, and she was conscious that it was not just because he might be able to give her answers to some of the mysteries surrounding Sofia and Rafael.

Before she left Cováo, she called in at the small hardware store where she had brought toothpaste the Sunday before. She brought a selection of brooms, mops and buckets, dustpans and a variety of cleaning materials. Senhor Antonio seemed eager to help, and

Helena smiled and thought to herself that this might be his biggest sale for years!

He helped her put the purchases into the rear of her little car, which was suddenly cramped, and thanked her for her custom. She managed to squeeze in avoiding the broom handles, and then she drove slowly back to the South Fork, to pick up dad before they went back to the Quinta, primarily to see the new car, which she knew Manuel would be dying to show them. Because the car was full her dad walked down to the Quinta, and once he arrived they went out together with Manuel to see the new runabout in the drive. In reality it was virtually brand new, and in much better condition than Helena's eight-year-old mini cooper.

'What do you think Helena, isn't she lovely'
said Manuel as proud as punch.

Helena and her father made a play of walking round inspecting the car, touching imaginary chips, before looking in the engine bay, and finally sitting in the driver's seat and scrutinising the inside and dashboard. Helena then turned on the engine, and listened for a few minutes, before turning the engine off and getting out. She could see Manuel was getting worried, so she finally looked at him and said

'You made a good choice, well done. Is she nice to drive?'

Manuel seemed to let out a sigh of relief her dad slapped him on the back, and said well done too. Now with his chest puffed out a little with some pride, he said

'Yes Helena, it is a good car, very nice to drive you will see.'

Father and daughter smiled at each other, before William asked Manuel if he would take him for a spin. Within a couple of minutes they were off, Manuel at the wheel, he clearly needed no encouragement to drive the car again.

Maria and Helena laughed at the pair of them, before Helena asked.

'Maria do we have any help yet?'

'We do, I have five ladies lined up, because when they heard that Carlos mum was coming tomorrow, my phone didn't stop ringing, and they didn't want to wait until Monday, so Manuel will pick them up tomorrow and they will be here at ten.'

'Wow that's excellent news, do we have packaging material, and a place sorted to put the stuff' Maria beamed

'Of course, they delivered the boxes yesterday afternoon, and last night Manuel and Carlos cleaned out a large space in the big barn.'

'Manuel and Carlos?

'Yes, Carlos volunteered to help Manuel. It's a good sign isn't it'

'Do you think so Maria? Truthfully I am quite worried about the responsibility of it all.'

Maria glanced over at Helena and with a look that was quite motherly she laid her hand on her arm and declared

'You do know that your arrival is causing quite a stir locally, don't you? The renovation of the Quinta is big news, and I know your actions so far have already made you some friends, it's going to go well.'

'I hope so, I really do.'

Half an hour later, the Quinta had been locked up, the two M's had returned home, and William and Helena were back in South Fork.

The minced beef taken out of the freezer earlier, was to be transformed into a Bolognaise sauce, and so with Radio 2 courtesy of the Internet playing in the background, Helena and her dad chopped peppers as they chatted about various things. An hour later with

Spaghetti Bolognaise in dishes and a glass of wine in hand they sat down at the dining table to eat.

Because of an incident that occurred when Helena was a moody teenager, this family meal was always eaten in a large bowl at the kitchen table. Helena reminded her father of it, and they chuckled at the memory, they could laugh at it now, but at the time it was both excruciatingly embarrassing for Helena and very expensive for her parents. It happened when Helena was 16, she had returned home from school, to find her mum had left a spaghetti bolognaise for tea, she had had an urgent call into work, so Helena was to heat it up in the microwave and sort herself out. As her mum and dad were not around, and there was something on the television she wanted to watch, she plated her bolognaise up and decided to take it into the living room to eat it in front of the television. To this day Helena still had no idea how it actually happened, but as she walked towards the sofa, the spaghetti bolognaise was suddenly slipping of the plate, falling towards the pale cream carpet which had only been laid three weeks before. Have you ever tried to catch spaghetti bolognaise when it's falling, well don't bother because you can't!

Looking back, it always seemed to her as if it was happening in slow motion, the end result was horrendous. Strands of spaghetti went everywhere, the sauce seemed to travel to the distant corners of the room, and she was still trying to clean it up when mum came back in. Needless to say, Helena was grounded, and the carpet had to be replaced since the central bright orange stain would not come out, and despite replacing the carpet, they could smell bolognaise for months afterwards. William thought it was funny how incidents like these become funny family legends with the passage of time.

Once dinner was finished they filled the dishwasher, and adjourned to the living room, chatting about the mysteries of the attic and the baby clothes, amongst other things. At eight thirty Helena's mobile rang, and she saw it was Marco's number.

'Hi Marco, are you okay?'

'Hello Helena, I am fine thank you, sorry to call so late but it's been a busy day.'

'Hey, it's me who should be apologising for taking up your evening I am sure you have better things to do.'

Helena knew she was fishing but honestly, she couldn't help myself. Her father cocked an eyebrow, he knew his daughter very well.

Marco replied brightly.

'Well I am not busy this evening so it's no problem. Anyway unfortunately, I can't find anything in the files that mentions a second child. We only became the estate solicitors in 1924, before then it seems that the Alencar family solicitors in Porto dealt with the estate. So perhaps there will be something in the family papers.'

'Oh okay, I suppose I will have to wait until then. If you have time I have another question or two?'

'Yes, I am no hurry please go ahead.'

'Do you know where Sofia is buried?'

'Yes and no, I mean she wasn't buried but cremated in Lisbon, in accordance with her wishes, and her ashes were spread in two places, some on the lake in the Quinta, the rest under the orange tree in the drive.'

'What? You mean my lake my orange tree?'

'Yes, her will was very specific, I didn't tell you because I thought you might be disturbed by it.' Helena breathed out in a whoosh.

'Well it is unusual, but I suppose no more unusual than having your own burial ground on your land.'

'That's true, apparently there is a metal plaque under the orange tree in the drive, that sets out the dates, it has an inscription on it too.'

'I don't recall seeing that, but then again I haven't looked closely, do you know what the inscription says?'

'Sorry Helena no I don't I only began looking after the estate three years ago, and so much of the historical information I am not familiar with, I have to glean it from the files.'

Helena thought about this and then replied with

'That's understandable, I will just have to go and find it myself tomorrow. I wonder why she wanted her ashes spread on the lake, why not on the parterre or elsewhere on the land.'

'I suspect we may never know the answer to that, after all some people want their ashes spread in strange places, I gather the Nile in Luxor is a favourite spot with western tourists.'

Helena laughed at that but could see what he meant, places that represented something in your life could have a strong draw.

'Anything else I can help you with?' Said Marco.

'No. I don't think so, but I had a good chat with my cousin today, she may be eighty, but her brain is very sharp.'

'Was she able to help in any way.'

'Maria invited me to her house, where we looked through some old photos, one or two were of Sofia, and I now know a bit about my younger cousins, her grandchildren, who both live in Lisbon. Oh and she did tell me a few stories about things that happened when she was a child visiting the Quinta. But as she said she herself was young and so didn't really take a lot of interest in the life of her cantankerous older Aunt.'

'Well perhaps the Alencar family papers will yield more, I have managed to re work some of my appointments and

278

dad has offered to take over one or two of them for me, so if your free next Thursday and Friday we could go to Porto if you like.' Helena felt an unexpected flash of excitement and quickly responded.

'That would be fantastic, I'm sure dad will want to come with us too.'

'Well of course if your father wants to come too that would be no problem.' Marco replied, but Helena thought she detected a tinge of disappointment in his voice, and her tummy somersaulted. She looked at her dad's face which was now full of curiosity.

'Can you hold on a minute Marco my father is here let me ask him.'

Helena put her hand over the phone and spoke to her dad. Surprisingly her dad said no, he thought someone ought to be here to supervise the ladies, and I should go on my own, he had time to see Porto another day.

'Hi Marco, it seems not. Dad wants to remain here and supervise the work going on, so it will be just me.'

'Great, I will book us into a hotel, and pick you up at 9.30, in the meanwhile call if you need to speak to me.' he said all of this in a voice which was now much brighter.

'Okay, I shall look forward to it, see you next week then.' They said goodbye and Helena took a sip of her wine, contemplating what next week might bring. But mostly as she settled down she was aware that she was looking forward to spending some time alone with Marco, and what's more she was almost certain that he felt the same.

Helena and her dad chatted about what they might find, and at ten o'clock Helena said she was tired, and was off to bed.

Once she was lying down, even though she was tired, sleep didn't immediately come, her mind flitted from a detail that was eluding her, every time she tried to grasp it, it flew away, she was sure she had heard or perhaps gleaned something significant today, but it wouldn't come. Eventually she drifted off into a sleep which was punctuated by weird dreams in which she was helping out Hercule Poirot, solve a long-standing mystery, because Captain Hastings was unavoidably detained in the USA.

Thursday began with bright sunshine and blue skies, with just the odd fluffy cloud. The weather forecast was for a lovely spring day and a top temperature of 23 degrees. Helena and her father arrived at the Quinta at eight thirty precisely, so she could show her dad around a little more before the ladies arrived to begin cleaning out the rooms. Although William had walked around with the electricians Ramiro and Antonio, he hadn't really had an opportunity to take anything in, so they walked into the grounds, and Helena pointed out the Parterre, the overgrown gardens and the lake.

Stopping at the edge of the Lake each knew the other was thinking about Sofia's ashes being cast into it, many decades before. Perhaps it was wishful thinking on Helena's part, but she thought she detected her presence here, in a way the lake seemed to her a sadder place than when she had first seen it.

Her father who had soaked up all Helena's imparted information, piped up,

'I imagine that this was beautiful before it became so overgrown, it wouldn't take much to bring it back though.'

'Yes, that's what I thought Pop, I've asked the builder to quote for it', but the house is the main priority, it will have to wait a bit I'm afraid.'

'Well you could get someone else in to do this maybe a landscape gardener, the whole space needs refreshing.'

'Actually, that's a very good idea, perhaps you could speak to Carlos about it, he might have some contacts. But I don't want the lake drained, cleaned up yes, refreshed with more planting yes, but not drained, Sofia's essence is in there and I am not sure disturbing her would be a good idea!'

'That's a very sensitive approach love.'

'Well I wouldn't want her ghost waking me up at night, because she had been woken up from her deep and hopefully peaceful sleep!'

'Shall we go and see if we can find the plaque that Marco told us about? We have half an hour before the ladies turn up.'

They made their way around to the front of the house and wandered up to the cutaway where the broken seats were. Both of them were wearing old clothes, and they set too removing what remained of the wrought iron seats.

'I will get Manuel to come and pick these up, they need to be repaired, he said there is a guy he knows who can do the job, so he can use the runabout to take them to him.'

'The pattern on the back here matches that on the veranda,' her father said, 'these were not cheap to produce, love.'

'I guess not,

Helena replied as they were huffing and puffing in the effort o heave them to one side.

'On top of which they are heavy too.'

Manuel then came around the corner and walked up to where they both were straining with the frames. They chatted for a few minutes, before he went to fetch them a rake, once he arrived back, he helped them put them to one side, before saying he was off to pick up the ladies from Cováo.

William now used the rake, to clear the ground from behind where the seat had been, as he raked, she heard the distinctive sound of metal on metal, William put his rake aside.

'I've hit something!'

Using their hands, they scraped away the covering of leaves, and what seemed to be decades of orange debris, which revealed a metal plaque, about two feet long and eighteen inches wide. With some difficulty they pulled it upright, but even so they could scarcely make out what it said. Helena went to the house to get a bucket of water and a scrubbing brush, whilst her father tried to prop it up against the bole of the old orange tree.

Once Helena returned, they spent a few minutes dousing the plaque with water and scrubbing of years of ingrained mud.

Ten minutes later it was clean enough for them to properly see what was written on it. The plaque was made from what Helena thought was probably bronze, the uppermost part depicting a beautiful old and spreading orange tree, whose oranges dangled downwards as if ready to pluck. At the base of the orange tree was a small circlet of four forget-me-knots, underneath which the following was impressed from the mould.

In memory of my lost loves
I lay at our tree a ring of Forget-me Knots
One for my one and only love
One for my beloved son
One for me, and the star that never shone
Forever together at last

Sofia Da Silva 1882 – 1972 now at peace.

Helena translated it for her dad, both of them were staring at the written lines, so deep in our own thoughts, that they didn't hear Maria approach, until they heard her stifling a little cry. Maria murmured,

'That is so beautiful, where did you find it?'

Helena translated what Maria had said, but her dad who had already understood the gist of it, and had put his arm around Helena's shoulders, lifted his head and turned to Maria and said in English.

'It was here, just lying in the grass, it must have been placed here after Sofia died, it's been overgrown for many years, maybe when the seating gave way it knocked it down and it just got buried by vegetation.'

Helena translated for Maria, who nodded in agreement. Helena, who had been staring at the words pointed to the fifth line and said in both English and then Portuguese, 'What do you think that line means?'

No one replied. Helena turned to her dad and then to Maria and said to them in both languages,

'It means something, I know it does, I think it relates to the baby clothes in the attic nursery.'

Maria, nodded thoughtfully before agreeing with her.

'I think so as well Helena, but how?'

Helena's brain was now making synaptic linkages very quickly, and she suddenly said,

'I think you were right Maria, Sofia had a second child that died, that's what that line means, but where is she buried, and what was she called?'

As they were contemplating this, Manuel drew up with a car full of ladies. Reluctantly Helena said,

'We will have to come back to this, we have visitors, and we need to put them to work.'

Manuel parked the car, and all three of them trooped over to where emerging from the passenger seats came four ladies of indeterminate age. Maria was the first to arrive and she kissed each of them before turning to Helena and introducing them all.

'Helena, Senhor Stratton this is Rita, Virginia, Maria, and Albertina.'

Helena and her father shook hands with them all saying hello, and welcoming them to the house. Once inside Helena explained that Maria was in charge, and she was going to show them the ropes, and that she herself would be along shortly. As they were walking towards the front door, another car pulled up and Carlos got out, went to the other side of the car and let his mother out. Helena waved, and Carlos waved back, he and his mum spoke for a few moments and then he got back in the car and drove off. Whilst waiting for her to come over Helena quickly explained who it was to her dad, they waited for her to come over. She kissed Helena on both cheeks following which Helena introduced her to her dad, she shook hands with him, and her dad who had been practicing the phrase said in almost perfect Portuguese that he was sorry for her loss, and that he knew how difficult it was for her.

Helena smiled inwardly, she was proud of him learning that phrase and saying it so gently, Maria in turn said the same thing back. They each held their gaze for a few seconds and Helena saw that the two of them understood each other's sadness very well. Helena hoped that a mutual understanding of loss might lead to a blossoming friendship, time would tell. The three of them followed the ladies into the hall, where Maria was busy marshalling them into the drawing room. Some thirty minutes later they were still walking around the house, in a little gaggle peering into every room. Maria and Helena had agreed the day before that it was probably best to show them everywhere first, because if they didn't, the ladies might go wandering on their own and then they would never do any work!

At eleven o'clock they began, and by 12.30 a number of boxes had been packed away and labelled. Some item's that seemed to Helena to be beyond repair were placed out in the hall for removal. Over a light lunch in the kitchen, Helena and her father got to know the ladies a little more, and they all seemed in good spirits, even

Louisa's mum Maria was chatting a little. In the afternoon, half the ladies remained in the drawing room whilst half moved to the dining room, and by three pm, they had made more progress, and it was good to hear laughter in the house, even if some of it sounded just a tiny bit naughty.

Manuel came to fetch the ladies at three pm, and they all left promising to come back tomorrow. Carlos's mum said she would continue as he couldn't come back to fetch her until five thirty, but Helena offered to drive her home after they had had a cup of tea. The four of them sat drinking tea and munching on biscuit's, the two Maria's were chatting away in Portuguese, with William listening intently. Helena made the odd translation, but her dad seemed to understand quite a bit anyway. It was then time for her to whisk Maria back to Cováo, but just as they went out into the drive, Manuel came back, and he offered to take Maria home too, so Helena who was smiling to herself was let off the hook, knowing of course that Manuel was still enjoying the novelty of driving around in the new car.

Earlier that day, Lionel had told Helena that the plumber would be coming at 4.30, and asked if it might be helpful if he were to join them. Whilst they were waiting in the kitchen with William for the plumber to arrive, Maria and Helena worked out which rooms they would tackle tomorrow, and once they had agreed, Maria disappeared to look out some more boxes. Lionel joined them a few moments later, having spent the day working on the remaining locks, and although Helena didn't need Lionel for translating purposes, she thought maybe Senhor Dias might be more comfortable in talking with them if he had someone with him he knew. At 4.30 sharp they heard a car in the drive, and Lionel unbidden pointed to the front door.

'I will go and bring him in, meet you in the kitchen.'
A few minutes later Senhor Dias entered the kitchen, Helena was immediately struck by how young he was, for some reason she was expecting a middle aged or even elderly man. In reality he was no more than thirty-five, well-built and tanned, his face was open and kindly, with a thatch of dark hair. His left arm was shrouded inside a sleeve that ended at the elbow. Both William and Helena stood up as he entered walking around the table to greet him, Helena gave him what she hoped was a broad and welcoming smile.
'I am pleased to meet you Senhor, I have heard good things about your work,' before offering him her right hand to shake. He grasped it with a firm gentleness, and said he too was pleased to meet her. Next, he was introduced to her William, they too shook hands before everyone sat down. The next hour was spent explaining what was needed. Helena was up front about how this aspect of the work needed to keep up with the pace of the other trades. Once the explanation was finished Senhor Dias placed his right hand on the table, and said, "I am grateful for you considering me, but I am not sure that I will be able to help you.'
He lifted up his left arm, and waggled his stump about, before explaining that he doubted he could keep up with other trades, and as we could see unfortunately, he was no longer as able as he used to be.
'Over time, I have found some ways to limit the difficulties, but a one-handed plumber is never going to be able to work at the speed of a two handed one.' He said this with a degree of self-deprecating humour that was endearing.
Helena explained to him that she was keen to use local labour where possible, and that it would be good to have him on board in some capacity. William, who had listened

287

quietly, spoke to Helena to check that he had understood
what had been said; then intervened and asked him if he
had thought about employing other plumbers, whilst he
provide the supervisory and quality control skills. Helena
translated for him.

Senhor Dias's face could be read like a book, and William
and Helena could tell that he had never considered this.
William then leaned forward and looked directly into his
eyes whilst saying to Helena,

'Can you translate for me?'

Helena nodded and explained to Senhor Dias what her
father had asked her to do, then William said,

'Senhor when one has to face one's limitations, like you
have had to, it really doesn't have to lead to an automatic
diminution of the working life you had formerly led.
Somewhere along the road, new opportunities can and
do open up. For instance right now I don't see your
disability, instead I see an opportunity for you to do
something different with your skills. This job is going to
need several plumbers for some time, they need
managing, and you're a relatively young man who could
learn new skills, after all it's not your brain that is limiting
you! We would like you to think about it, and if your still
certain you only want to work alone, then perhaps we can
consider letting the contract for the cottages individually,
as they are not so time critical.'

Helena translated, and she could tell her father's words
had made some impression on him, because after a few
minutes of silence he responded.

'Senhora, Senhor thank you for thinking about me,
perhaps your right, and I do need to think differently
about how I can work in the future, my wife would
certainly agree with you. I have always liked the hands-
on element of the work, but the truth is since the accident
I don't get asked to quote for much these days. Some

288

people continue to ask me to do work for them, but it's small jobs, and they don't mind if I am slow, but it takes me longer, so my earning potential is lower. Maybe, just maybe, this could be the opportunity I need to look at this disability differently. I will discuss it with my wife, but how long have I got, when do you need to know?'

Helena replied

'Sooner rather than later, we have given the other tradesmen until the end of the month to quote, we can give you a little longer if necessary. If you need any help with scheduling then give our project manager Carlos a call, he will help you. Do you know Carlos Perreira?'

'I know him a little.'

'Well he starts work with us shortly, and he will be happy to help you put together your plan, all you need to do is find the plumbers and sub-contract them to you. Why don't you spend an hour or so walking round with Manuel and my dad and you can see the scale of the work. If you decide it's too much then please quote for the cottages. I do though need to know if you're going to quote and for what fairly quickly as I might need to source another plumber.'

Senhor Dias looked at Helena and her father with incredulity writ large on his face.

'Do you mean you haven't asked anyone else to quote, I mean haven't the Oliveiras family from Abrantes been knocking on your door yet?'

Helena smiled, before answering.

'No Senhor, only you, as for the Oliveiras whoever they are, no they haven't as yet. We want to use people who live in this community as far as possible, if we can't achieve this then we will widen the search.'

'Caramba, that is amazing, okay let me have a look around and I promise to let you know as soon as I can.'

289

With that the three of them left to begin the tour of the existing if rudimentary facilities.

Helena sat in the kitchen and wondered if she was being ridiculous. So far it looked like they would end up employing a one-handed plumber, a builder whose morals were questionable, electricians who sought to hedge their bets over costs, a locksmith who was nosey, a fairly untried and tested project manager, and an estate supervisor and housekeeper who were good and kind but inexperienced. Caramba indeed!

Helena though had thought about this situation differently. Yes, they might have to soak up some additional costs by way of a loss of overall efficiencies, but she believed that any goodwill generated might one day turn into gold dust. Moreover, she realised that she trusted these guys, and was sure they wouldn't knowingly let her down.

After a few moments of quiet reflection her thoughts returned to the plaque, Sofia had ordered this to be made before she died, that much was clear, but was it meant to be cryptic for those of us who followed? Manuel had brought it up to the house and it now lay in the Drawing Room. Rising from the chair, she headed in that direction, and Maria silently followed. Once there she stared at it a few moments, before speaking in a voice that seemed unnaturally loud in the still air.

'What do you think Maria? Am I reading too much into that line, or was there another child? If there was, what on earth happened to her.'

Maria looked at her before replying

'It is a mystery no doubt. It could be read both way's, maybe she meant that the relationship between her and Rafael was the star that never shone. But it could also refer to a lost child.'

There was a moment's silence before Helena almost inaudibly replied,
'That may account for it, she couldn't declare her love for him in a more profound way than this could she.' before repeating the line out loud.

'One for me, and the star that never shone'
Perhaps we will never know, just like we will probably never know what happened to Luis in the aftermath of the fire. But I hope we do find out, because I really want to know.'
Helena and Maria were silent for some time, Helena walked over to the doors that led onto the garden, and stared in the direction of the lake. A short while later Helena turned to Maria.
'Maria, I am going to walk back to South Fork, will you tell my father for me, I will leave the car here, so he can drive back. Do you mind locking up?'
'No problem Helena, I will tell him. We shall see you in the morning then?'
'Yes of course, there's a lot to do. But for now I need to think, and it's easier to do that back at the ranch.'
They kissed goodbye, Helena picked up her coat and bag and walked out into the late afternoon sunshine. She walked slowly up the drive, and stopped in front of the orange tree.
Where staring at it she said very quietly to herself,
'So Sofia, what did you mean? If you ask me I think you had a second child and that's your star that never shone, but what happened? Where do I need to look to find out?'
Helena looked down at the base of the tree, at the now gaping patch of earth where the plaque used to be, originally, she had thought that perhaps the plaque had once been upright, and that it had fallen down as the seats had decayed, leaving the iron frame to fall on it, but now she wasn't so sure. Was this orange tree significant?

291

And why the forget-me-knots? The self-same image as on the scrap of parchment paper she had found in one of the envelopes. If, as her dad had said, this orange tree couldn't be the one in the painting, when did Sofia plant this one, it looked to her to be as old as the one in the painting. Surely Rafael even after he had married in 1910, would never have asked her to move away, so what happened to make Sofia leave here?

Tomorrow, she would ask Manuel to clear all the ground around the base of this tree and see if they could confirm how and where the plaque was originally placed. The air had turned a little cooler now, it was nearly six o'clock and the spring heat was dissipating, as the evening wind began to blow. Helena walked back to South Fork and let herself in.

Helena, lay on the sofa, a mug of tea on the side table next to her and closed her eyes. She really wanted to clear her mind, so she could concentrate on the mysterious plaque, and what it might mean. But as hard as she tried she couldn't gain any clarity. Her mind simply refused to give her any insight, moreover and very annoyingly the lines kept looming up imprinting on the back of her eyeballs, and she just couldn't get beyond them. Overcome by a feeling that something awful must have happened, she searched for a chink of light or flash of wisdom that might give her the hand up she needed. Nothing came, so she decided to list what she knew and didn't know, to see if she could make any linkages. Having set these down in her notepad, the stand out question that she always kept coming back too was, what was the reason why Sofia and Luis left the Quinta in 1913?

Sofia knew of course, that Rafael had married in 1910, could this be the reason? Even as she thought it she knew that it couldn't be right, because why would they wait until three years after the marriage had taken place before leaving. Or did Rafael force them to leave? Helena doubted that too, because once again there was that three-year elapsed period, and of course he subsequently left the Quinta to her and recognised his son with the inheritance. Did Rafael know that she was leaving and taking his son with her? She couldn't be sure either way, she really had no idea about at all; perhaps the Alencar papers would be able shed some light on this. Obviously, Sofia must have been deeply unhappy about his marriage to another woman, but surely it couldn't have been a complete surprise to her, could it? Did she find out in 1913 that the marriage was happy,

293

and then decide to leave? She thought it might have been possible but then again deep inside to Helena it didn't ring true. Besides she had gained the impression from Sofia's unfinished letter that they had been very much in love, but then these were different times. They were from different social classes and the pressures on them, and on him in particular to conform to the social norms of the time, must have been enormous.

Helena reflected on the fact that he had conformed in his forties, however, she just didn't think her great-great grandfather would have married secretly, whilst continuing to have an affair with Sofia. No, that was not the reason why they left. Helena was becoming more convinced that Sofia had a second child, but was it Rafael's, or someone else's? If it was her great-great grandfathers did he know about it? His last Will did not recognise any other child; which might mean he didn't know of the existence of a further child, or maybe he had known, but subsequently knew the child had not survived. Either way could Rafael's knowledge or ignorance of the birth and death of a second child be the reason Sofia left? Helena sat bolt upright, this was it, the flash of insight she needed had just occurred, she could feel it vibrating from her finger-tips to her toes. Sofia's leaving the Quinta was somehow connected to this second child. Where to look now for confirmation was the next step, but unfortunately for her, she still had no idea at all. Tomorrow, she would revisit the nursery, and get all the ladies to look for small box to which the little gold key might fit. Manuel could clear around the orange tree, and see if there were any other clues, and she herself would speak to Marco and see if he could arrange for her to meet the Alencar's any earlier. Satisfied at last that she had a plan, Helena, got up went into the kitchen and began preparing dinner for herself and her father.

The following day, despite the hint of drizzle in the air, Helena's spirits couldn't be dampened, she felt positive, and within a short time she had set everything in motion. After Manuel had deposited the ladies in the hall, Helena showed them the key, gave them a vague idea of the type and size of box it might fit, and then sent them off to search every room for something that the key might fit. All four ladies along with Maria in charge of them, were enthralled by the mystery and set about the task with gusto. Manuel, meanwhile had already moved outside and had begun clearing the area around the orange tree. Marco had agreed to ring Carolina, and try to bring the date of the meeting forward, but he didn't hold out too much hope.

Helena, Louisa's mother Maria, (or Maria P as they now referred to her, to distinguish her from the other two Maria's currently in the house) and her father then went up into the attic space to search it thoroughly for clues. First, they had to clear away as many of the cobwebs as possible, and Maria P stood on a ladder and washed the inside of the round attic windows to bring in some more light. This took a little time, and it was an hour or so later before they began to tackle the chore. William had brought up several large packing boxes, and as they sorted through the items they packed. William immediately went towards the toy box, whilst Helena and Maria P tackled the chest of draws. It was sometime later when Maria P said,

'I don't think these clothes have been worn, they look new to me.'

'Do you think so, I am finding it difficult to tell, given their age and all of these moth holes.'

'Well, look at this, the label still has a price ticket attached to it.'

Helena took the proffered garment, and she saw wrapped around the delicate label a piece of white silk thread to which was attached a piece of card onto which was very small writing.

'Have you found any others like this?' Helena said to Maria P who replied.

'No actually I haven't, but it's a little odd, because the clothes in this draw I am guessing would fit a child of about one year to eighteen months old, and none of them seem to have been worn. Yet they are handmade and likely to have been expensive.'

'Perhaps your right' Helena said, 'what do you think of these?'

Passing across to Maria the bundle she had already sorted through. Maria P took them from her and said,

'I think these have been worn, they feel different'

'What age do you think they are for?'

'There isn't much difference in the size, so maybe nine months or so, but in those days clothes were always much longer so it is difficult to be certain' Maria P replied.

William who had been quietly sorting through the toy box, suddenly said,

'The toys in here are all for boys, not a doll, a teapot, or dress in sight.'

Helena drew in a deep breath before pronouncing,

'Well I suppose that makes sense, especially if a second child was born and it was a girl as these clothes suggest, she obviously didn't live long enough to be given any.'

Maria P sighed a little, before saying

'But isn't that a little odd, surely all babies, especially one born into a wealthy house would have had some things to play with, mine did and we didn't have much money to speak of. I wonder if there is a second toy box somewhere?'

William who had been listening to this exchange nodded,

'I agree it's odd, but if a box exists then it doesn't appear to be in here.'

Maria, smacked her forehead, before saying rather excitedly to

Helena

'Do you think the gold key could belong to such a box?'

Helena caught her breath, and replied cautiously,

'It might, but it's a small key and wouldn't it be too small for a toy box?

William spoke next turning around and addressing them both.

'Well, perhaps it wasn't immediately necessary to have purchased a toy box, if there was a second child maybe Sofia initially used another box for this purpose and then sadly when the child died they never needed a larger one. I remember when you were little we used the cardboard box the TV had come in for your toys, your mum painted it to look like a castle, and it worked a treat until you were two, and you jumped in it one day and split the sides!'

Helena smiled at the memory,

'I don't remember that dad,' she said.

'Well I do, and it was me who built you your next toy box from scratch.'

'Now that I do remember, I loved hiding in it, you could never find me.'

The both laughed, and Helena explained the gist of the conversation to Maria P, who smiled as well.

They continued for a further hour, but turned up nothing of significance, eventually Helena said, she was thirsty and hungry and that maybe they should go down for some lunch.

Lunch was an animated affair, and it was good to hear the house filled with chatter and the occasional laughter, the ladies were disappointed they hadn't yet turned up any boxes, but excited by the prospect they would later. William, listened with interest to the local gossip, and occasionally said something, but mostly he sat quietly next to Louisa's mother, and listened much as she did. Occasionally Louisa's mother said something to him, and he would nod.

After lunch, Manuel who had found nothing by the orange tree, asked Helena if she wanted to look for herself, and as the sun had now come out, she joined him in the fresh air.

Manuel wasn't sure what to make of Helena's interest in the orange tree, to him it was just a tree, old and gnarled. He liked Helena very much, and not just because she had given him a pay rise, a new job title and a car to use, but because she seemed to love the Quinta.

He knew she had yet to visit the lands that made up the vast majority of her estate, and though he was itching to drive her around, he realised that she had to get a plan for the house first. Helena had asked him, some days ago, if he had ever seen any plans for the house, or gardens anywhere, but he had hardly ever had cause to go inside the house, and even if he had he didn't have keys for all of the rooms. Perhaps he should mention that Sofia, according to his father, had once used the cottage next to the old olive mill, as a retreat. His father said he would drive her down there in the pony and trap, and she would spend hours just painting, drawing or watching the birds. He himself hadn't been inside that particular cottage for years, but like the other cottages they all contained a couple of the old wooden trunks or chests that the people used for blankets, grain and other valuables. He couldn't see why Sofia might have left anything in there, but his father had told him that she did go there often, so maybe he should say something, just to be on the safe side.

As they arrived by the orange tree, Manuel had decided he was going to tell her about Sofia's use of the mill cottage, but Helena got in first.

'So you didn't find anything unusual Manuel, nothing to indicate how the plaque was fitted here.'

'No, I couldn't find anything to suggest how it was originally mounted. What's funny though, is I don't ever remember seeing it, which implies it was lying down when I took over from my father. But you know, he used to sit in the seats under the tree all the time, so maybe it was just obscured from view? The sad thing is that the tree is quite old maybe nearly a hundred years old, you can see that the trunk is beginning to split, and it will only take a good strong wind or a lightning strike to bring it crashing down. We should probably take it down, so it can't fall and hurt someone now that the Quinta is to be occupied.'

'You're probably right, but it would be sad to see it go,' she said, Manuel replied.

'I can understand that, but wouldn't it be nice for you to plant a new tree in its place to mark your inheriting the Quinta, and its renewal, I am certain we could get one from the fruit garden that is quite mature.'

'Do you know Manuel that is a brilliant idea, it would be like keeping the continuity going, and we could have a small ceremony and put the plaque up next to it, along with the refurbished seats!'

Manuel smiled.

'Well the seats are going to be ready in a few weeks, so perhaps if we take the tree down next week, and make the space ready for the week after next. Do you want to come and choose the tree?'

'I would love to do that, and as I don't want anyone to be hurt, let's go ahead and sort this, and thanks Manuel.'

299

Manuel nodded in acknowledgement of her thanks, and then turned to go, he had only taken a few steps when he turned around took off his cap, and scratched his head. 'Helena, just one more thing whilst I think about it, I know you haven't had time yet to visit the estate yet, and I don't want to rush you, but it occurred to me this morning, that my father told me that Sofia used one of the cottages in the grounds as a sort of quiet retreat. Apparently, she used to go there to read, paint, draw and just relax. All the cottages have chests or trunks in, and whilst I find it difficult to believe that she would have left anything valuable in them, well you never know. Could the box your looking be in there, it's a long shot but...'

Helena, felt goose bumps on her arm, and the hair on the back of her neck stood on end. Turning to him she said, 'Can we go now Manuel?'

If he was surprised by this sudden interest in the old cottage and her request, he didn't show it. Instead he nodded his head.

'Yes of course, I will fetch the car, and find the keys. This cottage is by the Olive groves, so a little too far to walk.'

Helena waited in the drive-way, as Manuel went to find the keys and fetch the car, she felt a stab of apprehension, then a degree of doubt, before finally settling on the potential possibilities that might exist. In any case even if it proved a wild goose chase, it would be good to see a little of the estate, and get a feel for the size of the place.

Manuel pulled up and Helena got in and put her seat belt on. Manuel, who hadn't got his on quickly did so, and then they set off. After driving for a minute or so Manuel who had been driving over carefully care said to Helena 'The Olive groves are about a five-minute drive away, the cottage is set in the middle of one grove, we will have to walk from the road. Sofia used to use the horse and trap or ride there, it's easier than driving, you can access the tracks that lead from the house.'

'Maybe I should go and see the stables, mind you it has been a long while since I rode, or perhaps I should just buy a quad bike.'

Manuel nodded in approval.

'The horses are a bit old now, we use them to help transport stuff occasionally, and we have an old well down by the fruit groves, we still use the donkey to help draw water in very dry months. Pato, likes the outing and its good exercise for him.' Helena suddenly had a vivid picture in her mind of an old donkey going around and around whilst an old man drank red wine under an olive tree!

'I would like to see that, though I thought that many wells these days used pumps to get water?'

'Many do, but those in more remote places, where there is no electricity, still do it the old-fashioned way.'

The car turned off the main road, and entered an unmade track, either side was filled with olive trees. The trees looked a little bare and she commented on this to Manuel.

'Last year this grove was cut back, olive trees need to be pruned hard every now and then to encourage new growth. It's normally done at the same time as the olives are harvested, which was quite late last year, in mid-December. So they have yet to put on new growth.'

'I don't know much about olive trees, or oil production, Marco, I mean Senhor Gonçalves told me we sell our olives solely for olive oil production rather than for eating.'

'Yes that's right, the type of olives trees we have make good oil, but we do harvest a few kilos for ourselves and Maria prepares our own eating olives. Will you continue to do that?

301

'Do what? Oh, I see, you mean sell the olives for oil. It's a good question Manuel, and the honest answer is I don't know, I need to find out more about it, and see what alternatives there are.'

Just then Manuel slowed down and parked next to an iron gate.

'Here we are Menina.'

They both got out of the car, and with Manuel in front and Helena following they opened the gate and closed it behind them. Helena noticed that all around her were olive trees, laid out in parallel lines, the ground around them was stony and here and there covered in a light smattering of grass. In the warm wind she could smell pines even though she couldn't see any.

Suddenly Manuel who was walking some ten metres in front of her stopped and opened a second smaller wooden gate, inset into a low whitewashed wall, which led into a small grove of mixed fruit trees. In front and about sixty metres away was a small white washed cottage, with the signature terracotta roof tiles. As they approached Helena could see that the cottage needed repainting, in places the lime wash had worn through so that the render beneath was exposed. The terracotta tiles looked in a reasonable condition, although in some places stones were also visible on top of them.

Once they reached the cottage, it was possible to appreciate that it was almost square, single storey, the front elevation had a door in the middle flanked on either side by two windows, whose inside shutters were closed. To the right side of the cottage was a further small building, and next to it a tiny open fronted barn, which was half stacked with wood.

Manuel, who had been silent on the walk to the cottage, was hoping that the door would open easily. He had last been inside maybe six or seven years go to check the

roof, after a particularly fierce storm had dislodged a number of tiles in buildings all over the estate. He thought that Helena would be surprised by the inside, as Sofia had made it quite comfortable, although of course like the Quinta itself it hadn't been used for decades. He observed that Helena had walked over to the small building to the right, and was trying to open the door.
'It's locked, it's what we call an outside kitchen.'
'Okay, do you have the key?'
'Yes, just give me a minute to get this one undone first.'
Helena walked back from the kitchen building and watched whilst Manuel tried to open the door, suddenly it came free, and the door opened inwards. Dust flew up from the floor, spreading like pollen on an unknown breeze; they waited for it to die down. Manuel went in first, and opened the shutters on both windows. Light poured in and Helena found herself in an L shaped room, myriads of cobwebs hung from the ceiling, and she had to brush these away as she went further inside. On one side was a wrought iron daybed, complete with faded covers. A small sofa and a winged arm chair were placed facing an inset, and rather ornate fireplace, over which was a wooden beam, filled with assorted bits and pieces. On the back wall were a number of small framed paintings and drawings, of views of the estate, they were simple watercolours mostly now very faded, and with the odd pencil piece. A large metal studded wooden chest was placed on an angle in one corner, covered by a now disintegrating cloth. Two small round matching side tables, had oil lamps sitting on them, both partly filled. In the hearth were a few logs and a metal poker. In the back wall on the far-left hand side there was a single door. Helena made her way to the door and opened it. Inside was a small room, with a single window overlooking the rear of the olive grove, it was furnished with a single bed,

and a further small trunk. On top of the trunk sat a wooden tray, which contained a book and a leather pouch. Helena picked it up and could tell that inside she would find a pair of reading glasses. Manuel who was standing in the door frame said

'So that's where they are!'

Helena, blinked at him, he continued

'I lost those glasses a few years ago, I must have put them down when I came to check the roof, I remember taking them off to clean them, because of the dust, but then I must have put them down and forgotten to pick them up again!'

Helena felt deflated, she thought she had found something that her great-great grandmother had used, and very reluctantly she handed them over to Manuel, who opened the pouch and sighed.

'Yes these are mine, but I doubt they are any use now! Shall we check the trunk in the other room?'

Nodding her assent, they both backed into the main room, Manuel picked up the cloth that covered the Trunk, and it almost fell apart in his hands. He dropped it on the floor, where more powdery dust rose up around it, he looked at the metal hasp, and then pulled it free from its securing mechanism. It wasn't locked. He pushed the lid upwards, so they could see inside. One side seemed to be full of painting materials, on top of these lay a number of clean unused canvases, to one side was a basket into which had been placed a couple of jars, and a lot of brushes of different sizes. Manuel took out the canvasses, and placed them on the daybed, so he could get to the basket, which he also lifted out, underneath were several metal watercolour paint pallets', some cloths and a folded away artists easel. Manuel pulled them all out, which exposed a now off-white sheet, folded in two. Into which had been placed a number of completed paintings. Helena, bent over and picked the first ones up, they were all similar, and the composition made her heart race, and her fingers shake.

Here were several paintings of the orange tree in the drive, but clearly painted after long intervals, as in each one the orange tree was a different size. The one she had in her hand showed the tree at a good height and age; she turned the canvass over and on the reverse, handwritten in a spidery but strong black ink, were the words March 1953, the next one showed the tree not as large and again on the reverse was the date March 1943, the remaining three all had March dates, but for the years 1933, 1963 and curiously 1926. In all the paintings, the trees were in blossom, but also had dark green oranges hanging down from laden branches. Once in date order, each painting revealed how much the tree had grown in the intervening years. In the 1926 painting, the tree was small, and the two seats looked enormous at the side of it.

In none of the paintings could Helena see a plaque, but each of the paintings', contained four forget-me-knots laying at the base of the tree.

Manuel spoke very gently over her shoulder

'Do you think Sofia painted them?

Helena couldn't at that point mange to speak so she just nodded her head, all the paintings were the same size, about fifteen inches square. Finally finding her voice she said

'We need to take these back to the Quinta, let's wrap them back up in the sheet. I know that this tree means something special to Sofia, it's not just an ordinary orange tree. There is a mystery about it and I mean to get to the bottom of it.'

This time is was Manuel who nodded sagely, and gently wrapped the paintings back up. The trunk was now

305

empty, so if she had hoped the box would be in here she was disappointed. There was nowhere else in the room that she could see that might contain a box. However, in the back of her mind she couldn't let go of the thought of secret draws and hidden rooms like those she had already unearthed. With one more glance around the room, she returned to the bedroom and the trunk, Manuel was waiting for her, and when she came in he opened the trunk. At first glance it seemed to contain a stack of blankets.

'Let's get them all out Manuel.'

'I think we should check right to the bottom just in case.' Manuel began to lift them out one at a time, as they came out he passed them to Helena, who put them on the bed. Half way down, the blankets changed to quite thick eiderdowns, and as Manuel pulled the second one out and passed it to Helena, a small wooden box fell out onto the bed. In complete silence they both stared at it, deep down Helena hadn't really expected to find one, but here it was.

Manuel bent over and picked it up, mainly because Helena still had the majority of the eiderdown in her arms. The box had sides that were inlaid with light and dark woods, and in the centre of the top of the box was an orange tree, designed and inbuilt into the lid in tiny pieces of coloured glass. The box was approximately twenty-four centimetres long, fifteen centimetres wide and ten centimetres deep. It was beautifully made, and it had a small brass lock, it didn't appear to be very old, or at least if it was, its condition was perfect. Manuel passed it to her, and she took it from him as if she was being passed a piece of Faberge.

The lid was locked firmly down, but Helena knew that she had the key which would unlock it, that key was in the leather pouch on the bedside cabinet in her bedroom in South Fork.

Helena put the box on the bed, and looking at Manuel, whom she could tell was as excited as she was, she said, 'Let's continue, we are not at the bottom yet.'

Manuel bent to pick up the next item from the trunk, a now off-white sheet, he handed it to Helena, who shook it before putting it down on top of the eiderdown. Several more sheets followed, which revealed nothing more. Finally, the last sheet came out and underneath it was a large sheet of brown paper, the type used to wrap parcels. Manuel picked this up too, and was then surprised to see a further canvas. This canvas, in composition was the same as those they had found next door, but it was unpainted, and unfinished. Where today in the driveway stood an enormous orange tree, in this picture a very small and insignificant orange tree was positioned. The seats were missing, and only a single outline of a forget-me knot lay at its base. The charcoal strokes seemed shaky, and the canvas had a sad look about it.

Manuel turned it over, on the reverse they could both see written in charcoal was the date March 1913.

Helena didn't remember the drive back to South Fork, but once they arrived there, she quickly got out of the car, opened the front door and went in to retrieve the key from the old leather pouch. Then she and Manuel drove to the Quinta, where Maria, her father and Louisa's mum Maria were in the kitchen with the ladies who had been helping, they were clearly packing up to go home. Helena who had already put the box down in the library along with the paintings contained her growing excitement and frustration.

'Hello folks have you found anything interesting?'

Maria said no, but they had worked well and tomorrow they would be ready to tackle the sitting room and library. William asked if they wanted a drink, but Manuel said he would take the ladies home first, and have a drink when he came back.

After he had left, William turned to Helena and said where had they been for the past hour or so?

'Sorry dad, but Manuel remembered something his father had told him about Sofia using one of the cottages as a sort of private space. On a whim we decided to go and have a look. Helena then repeated this in Portuguese for the benefit of the two Maria's, who had been hanging on to Helena's every word even if they couldn't understand it. Maria then said

'What did you find?'

'How do you know we found anything?' Helena replied

At which point all three of them gave her knowing looks, as if to say, "come on we know you did."

Her father then spoke for them all when he said,

'I can see it in your face, it's flushed, and Manuel couldn't get the ladies home fast enough.

'Okay, we did come and see!'

Helena strode quickly towards the library, and went inside, followed by William and the two Maria's.

Once in the library, Helena showed them the canvasses and the small box. Everyone began to speak at the same time, but after a few seconds, William said,

'Are you going to open it then love?' Helena shook her head.

'Not until Manuel is here, after all he was the one who led me to it, so it's only fair he is here when we open it, what do you think of the paintings?'

Louisa's mum Maria who was holding one in her hand and studying it closely said,

'They are all the same but not the same if you know what I mean. Isn't it a view of the orange tree in the drive?'

Helena beamed at her.

'Yes, I think it is, each one was painted about ten years apart, so the orange tree is getting bigger in each one. I can't help but think that the tree is significant, or at least the space the tree occupies is. The plaque we found is enigmatic too, it's all connected I know it is. But how? That is the mystery.'

Helena said this with more than a hint of frustration in her voice.

William, who had been turning the box over in his hands, was the next to voice an opinion.

'This is a lovely box, beautifully made, I think it could be French or Italian, the glasswork is just magnificent.'

He passed it to Louisa's mum, who took it and stared at the inlaid glass orange tree.

'It's the same one, isn't it? or at least a depiction of a large and venerable tree.'

Helena who had moved to stand next to her as she turned the box around in her hands, whispered,

'It looks like it, I hope that inside it, we might find something that can help us with the mystery.'

For quite a few minutes, and one by one they all handled the box looking at it from all angles, but mostly just taking in the pretty glass mosaic. Helena who had begun to lay the paintings out on the desk in the order of the dates on the reverse side, including the unfinished one was straining to hear the approach of the car.

Whilst she was waiting she mulled over the paintings, clearly with but one exception 1926 they were painted every ten years after 1933, during the month of March, it had to be an anniversary, but an anniversary of what? The 1926 painting Sofia had done almost as soon as she returned to the Quinta, perhaps she did it then because of course she wasn't there in 1923.

That sort of made sense to Helena, if of course Sofia got back on track, painting again the March of 1933, 1943, 1953 and finally 1963. The March 1913 drawing was never completed, but it was the first one, and Sofia and Luis moved out just a few weeks later, is that why it was never finished? She didn't know, but she hazarded a guess that this might be the case. What was so important that she marked it in this extraordinary way, it was like she was documenting the growth of the tree, but there were thousands of trees on the estate, so why this tree? She was so lost in her thoughts that she was unaware that Manuel had returned, until her dad tapped her shoulder.

'Manuel is back, perhaps we can get this box open now and see what we have.'

Helena looked up, and saw four faces all trained on her. Maria P who at that point had been holding the box, handed it to her almost reverently.

Helena took the proffered box, and sat in the chair; she already had the key in her right hand, in preparation for this moment.

With the four pairs of eyes fixed firmly on her, she inserted the little golden coloured key into the brass lock. It fitted, she looked up at them all and gave them a nervous smile, before swallowing hard and then turning the key to the right, it turned easily. A click more felt than heard, told her the lock was now open; she took out the key and very gently lifted the lid.

Inside the box, which was lined with pale green velvet, Helena saw what she had hoped existed but never really expected to find. It was a diary, Sofia's diary, covered with cream leather, exactly like the blotter. Carefully, she picked it up, and lifted it out. Underneath was an envelope, it was clean and, so she passed the diary to Maria who was nearest to her, then she lifted out the envelope. The box she could then see was empty with only the velvet lining in view.

Helena opened the envelope. Inside she found three items, a letter from Rafael to Sofia, a single lock of dark hair, and a further smaller lock of lighter hair, which was exceedingly fine in texture. The letter was old and well thumbed, and as Helena read the letter an enormous lump came into her throat, and tears prickled at the corner of her eyes, its contents made her sad, but it did explain pretty much everything. Having read it herself, she then read it out loud to the four people whose eyes were now totally focussed on her. Once she had done so she told her dad the gist of its contents, as whilst he had listened to her read it, she wanted to make sure he understood.

17th June 1910

Darling Sofia,

I am a coward and certainly not a gentleman.

311

I don't know how to tell you this news, in a way that will make it any easier for you to bear, but two weeks ago I married. Not a marriage of my choosing, but one desperately needed by my family. Having to marry was difficult enough, but what is crueller is I can, no longer, be with you my love, not even in the seclusion of our beloved Quinta. It has been made plain to me that our relationship, which, was barely tolerated by my own family when I was a single man, will certainly not be tolerated by them now, even less would it be acceptable to the family of my new wife.

Please, please believe me when I say I too will find this difficult to bear. I can't describe to you the pain I feel knowing that I am never going to be able to be with you or our son ever again. It is cowardly I know to communicate this betrayal in a letter, having so recently spent those sublime six weeks with you. I confess I did know then that I was going to marry Christina, and because I so wanted to enjoy our last weeks, and you were so happy I couldn't find it in my heart to tell you, though I promised myself so many times that I would. The pressure for me to marry and produce a legitimate heir has been mounting, for some time, years in fact, but I couldn't do it. I have done so now, only because my father made it clear that our family fortunes depended on it, and that I, as his eldest son, could no longer afford to indulge in love, duty to the family had to come first. Christina my wife, is wealthy in her own right though her family is of the manufacturing class. I am ashamed to say that I married her for her fortune and she in return gained a title for her family.

So, my love it is done, I can never repair the damage this will do to you, and I can only hope that you will forgive me one day. Luis, I know is too young to understand, and it's better that he doesn't, as I cannot acknowledge him. You may remain in the Quinta, no one will turn you out I have already ensured this, but equally I have no right to expect you to remain alone, so should you choose to leave, then I have left monies with Julio Carreira, which I hope will support you should you decide to pursue a life for yourself and Luis. I have enclosed a lock of my hair, I wish I had one of yours. I love you and I will never stop loving you until the day I die.

My love forever,

Rafael.

By early evening Helena, had reread the letter and the diary more than a few times, and she had she surmised the enclosed dark lock of hair belonged to her great-great grandfather, and the fine hair was Annabela's, but she was still puzzled. The receipt of such a devastating letter could have explained why Sofia and Luis left, but not why they delayed leaving. In the end it was the reading of the diary that provided the answers, it filled in the blanks and provide a clear picture of the events leading up to her great-great grandmother leaving the Quinta for America. The diary covered a long period, and many of the entries explained the key moments in Sofia's life between January 1910, and March 1913. That same night Helena settled herself down to read key excerpts to her father, with a large glass of red wine to hand, she began to translate the contents out loud.

5th January 1910

Such good news today, Rafael has written to say he is coming to visit in April and he hopes he will be here for six weeks, not as long as I would like but I know he has his work. I must be patient, but it has been some months since, we saw him, and Christmas was lonely here without him, but I know he must be with his family. Luis loved his tin soldiers and has played with them endlessly.

17th March 1910

Not long to wait now. Rafael has written again and tells me he will be here on the 30th March. I am so excited, and we have been cleaning the Quinta's main rooms, for his visit. Our little cottage is also ready. Luis's is very happy and hopes that he will take him to fish again in the lake.

6th April 1910

Today Rafael went to look at the olive grove with Joao. I may be wrong, but he seems a little distant, I have asked him if there is a problem, but he says not, he is just a little tired. He is very solicitous and brought me a lovely locket, and tomorrow we are taking a picnic to the cottage for the afternoon. Luis is to go with Isabel to buy a new pair of trousers, so we will be on our own. He is the dearest and kindest of men.

17th April 1910

Yesterday was such a wonderful day. Rafael took Luis to fish in the lake, and they caught a large perch, which Joao grilled for them, down by the lake. Luis is becoming curious about Rafael, today I overheard him asking Isabel why he comes here. Isabel simply tells him he is the Master here, and as such he visit's occasionally. One day he will ask questions about where his father is, and I dread it. He is a clever little boy and sometimes I wonder if he guesses that Rafael is his father, it is so difficult for us both to hide our love, but he is getting older and we have to be more careful, using the cottage was a good idea, and I love our time alone there.

314

25th April 1910

*Joao and Isabel took Luis out for the day yesterday, and Rafael and I had
the house and grounds to ourselves, we made love under the old orange tree,
like we used to when we first met. He was so tender and gentle, not like the
week before when our passion was so all consuming it was spent quickly. If
the orange tree could speak, it would be able to tell some wonderful stories, I
though am glad it cannot! But it was so clever of Rafael to incorporate that
tree into the Quinta, it is so special to me, and I know it was where Luis
was conceived, though Rafael said I couldn't be sure because we made love
every day, and of course not always in the same place, even now I blush at
the thought. Those were such wonderful times, the anticipation I felt when
we met in secret under our tree…. Now of course things are different, our
love is still as strong, but we have to be careful, Rafael has his reputation of
course, and whilst mine is lost forever, people are civil to me because of him.*

3rd May 1910

*Rafael is being so considerate, he took us in his new motor car to buy some
presents for Luis, and insisted I had a new dress, it came from Paris, and
it's so beautiful. Luis loved the motorcar, and wanted to drive it of course he
particularly liked how the car started, he kept shouting at Joao to do the
turning, it was amusing. But I am sure something is wrong, I kept catching
Rafael looking at me and his face is sad, I don't understand it, I know he
has to leave next week, and that always makes us unhappy, but this is
deeper somehow. On Sunday I watched him caressing my brushes, as if, as
if, he might never see them again. Then unusually he spent two hours with
Luis on Wednesday, they played with his toy soldiers, and I heard them
laughing from the drawing room. They were playing on the landing and
stairs, and of course he let Luis win the battle, I saw him ruffle his hair,
and tell him he should always obey his mother in all things. Luis looked at
him, and said 'I always do Sir' to which Rafael replied, 'Well that's a
good boy, your father would be proud of you.'*

9th May 1910

Rafael left yesterday very early, he told me in bed the night before, that I needn't get up to see him off as he would be leaving before six o'clock. We made love twice, he seemed to be more passionate than ever, and afterwards he held me tightly and told me many times that he loved me and would always love me. He seemed a little melancholic, so I tried to cheer him up by saying it wouldn't be too long before he was back again and maybe we could visit the coast, as Luis loves the sea. He responded by kissing me tenderly, and stoking my hair, I was so tired I fell to sleep in his arms, and in the morning, he was gone.

25ᵗʰ June 1910
Today I received a letter from my love, it was heart breaking to read, and I am sure Rafael hated writing it. He told me that he is now a married man, and cannot see our son or me ever again. What I feared has come to pass, our love as strong as it is, pales against his duty to his family and his line. My darling, I knew that there was something wrong, you must have been in agony, all the time you were here, knowing that when you left you would never return. My love I can't cry, and I must not. I have to keep up appearances, as the housekeeper of the Quinta I still have a job to do. You say we can stay here, but it feels tainted now, even our Orange tree is sick, a storm last week has weakened the tree, and half of it is dying, I know how it feels, part of me has died too. If it were not for Luis…

2nd July 1910
My love, I am with child, I know it, but what am I to do?

3ʳᵈ August 1910
If you knew you would laugh at me, as just like with Luis, I am so sick in the morning I can hardly get out of bed, Luis keeps asking what is wrong with me, I will have to tell him before too long, the pregnancy will show soon. Isabel and Joao have been so kind keeping him occupied, and it is so so hot that I stay in the cool of my room, where I can be sick in private

7ᵗʰ September 1910

My love, the sickness is much less now, so today I told Luis he was going to have a baby brother or sister, in the new year, by my calculations sometime around the 6th January if everything goes to plan. The new life growing inside of me is an unexpected blessing. How I long to tell you, that you are going to be a father again, but I cannot, it would break your heart and one broken heart is enough. I find that I cannot be angry with you, I know you will not want to lie with her, much less be married to her, you're a good man doing your duty however onerous it is. Though I confess that I hate the thought of you making love to her, and at night when I am alone in bed and happen to think of it, I cannot stop myself from physically shaking. But I will get over it, and we will be happy, I have something precious of yours to care for now as well as Luis, even if you never know.

23rd November 1910
I am pretty large now my love, and the baby is very vigorous, another boy I think. I pick the diary up every week, but many times I can't think of what to put inside it, so I put it back down in the draw. I have heard nothing from you since you left in May, you must be suffering so in keeping your pledge.

24th December 1910
It is Christmas Eve, and if I could have my dearest wish it would be that you would come, but I know you cannot. I saw in the paper last week that you have been in Brazil for some months, and in the New Year will go to the United States of America. Your wife is not with you, and it is selfish I know, but I feel better knowing that, at least she is on her own this Christmas too. I am close to having your child; the contractions have been coming occasionally. The doctor came yesterday and said it would not be long now, how I wish you knew, my love.

9th January 1911
My dearest love, we have a daughter, and she is so beautiful and healthy, the doctor is very pleased with me. I am very tired, and I need to think of a name for her, I would love to know what you would call her, but of course

that cannot be, so the name can wait until later. You would be so amused, Luis thought she was a doll, and was so surprised when she opened her eyes and looked at him this morning, he stroked her face with his little finger. I have to stop now as Isabel has just knocked and told me the milk nurse is here, and the baby is very hungry.

15th April 1911
I have neglected the diary, but between Luis and Annabela, I have no time. I chose the name and I hope you approve my love. Annabela Elena Graça da Silva she is a good baby, but I confess that Luis is finding adjusting difficult, I fear he is a little jealous and I have to watch him carefully, last week he put a lizard in her cot. He says he put it in as a present, but I am not so sure. The weather is nice today, so he and I sat outside under our orange tree and played with his soldiers, whilst Annabela slept in the perambulator. Luis is nearly seven now, and has begun to ask where Senhor Rafael is. I have told him the truth, that you are in Brazil, and that we might never see you again, because your work is in Porto, and you have to manage your family's estates. But he says this is your estate too, so I have tried to explain as best I can to him, that this estate is small and does not require your attention now. I find that whilst I think of you all the time, the pain is less, more a dull ache, and my love I have to move on for the sake of the children, who will never know who their father is. My own family find my position difficult, and you know they have ever since I moved into the Quinta all those years ago. Our contact has been sporadic, all except my grandmother who came yesterday to see Annabela. I love her very much, and it is difficult for her I know, but last month she gave me her old family house, I have the cardeneta (deeds). It is empty and if I wanted to move into it I could, I have thought about it, but how would I manage financially? So, for now I stay here, but it's good to know I have something that is mine.

Helena read these entries, and marvelled at Sofia's strength, to be able to continue a normal life under these difficult circumstances. Now on her second glass of wine, she was skipping through many of the entries, as the entries were becoming more frequent.

She looked over to her dad and said

'It was as if she was using the diary as a surrogate for not being able to write to Rafael, maybe hoping that one day he might read it.'

'Yes love I think maybe she was.'

'Do you think he knew where she kept her precious items?'

'I don't know, but if the cottage was a special place for them then leaving the diary there was her best bet, ' said William before Helena continued on.

28ᵗʰ April 1911

Annabela was poorly today, and wouldn't take her milk, Luis was very naughty, so I had to punish him. It makes my heart break to see him so jealous of Annabela, I don't know what to do.

6ᵗʰ May 1911

Thank goodness Annabela is much better today, I took her for a walk in the perambulator, whilst Joao occupied Luis with fishing in the Lake. He is growing so big my love, and he looks more like you every day, no one could doubt his parentage.

5ᵗʰ July 1911

It is so hot, we have had two weeks of very warm weather, and Joao has decided to teach Luis to swim in the Lake. Joao and Isabel have been so good with him, he spends quite a lot of time with them both. I am worried he is attaching himself to Joao, but what can I do. He needs a strong male figure in his life now to teach him the sort of things boys need to know. And I am so tired, with caring for Annabela that I cannot find the will to separate them. Annabela is growing too and is quite strong, Isabel says she looks like me, but she has your eyes my darling, they are a shade of green so like yours.

6th October 1911

What a summer we have had, the land is parched, and many of the trees are looking decidedly droopy. The parterres are suffering too, the only person who seems to be happy with the heat is Luis. He can now swim, and spends many hours down at the lake. I have warned him to be careful, and told him very firmly that he is not allowed to go on his own, so Joao and Isabel have been run ragged with his requests. Annabela is crawling now, and I imagine it won't be very long until she is walking. She is very slight of build, with chestnut coloured hair, and a little dimple in her chin, she is a delightful and happy child, and even Luis is becoming more interested in her now she is moving around.

4th December 1911

We are getting ready for Christmas, though it still feels more like autumn, as the weather is very mild. Joao has cut a tree and is currently fixing it in the hall in the usual place. I read in the paper last week that you are considering of taking a commission in the Navy. I am not sure what to make of that my love, other than you must be so unhappy you are choosing another life. I am sure your wife can't be too pleased about that, and I see no announcements about an heir, this must be disappointing for you. Europe seems very unsettled, and I hope that a conflict can be avoided.

1st January 1912

It is a New Year, and for us here at the Quinta, it is one starting with some sadness. Our orange tree, which was damaged last year, is dead. I think in the spring I will have to have it felled, as it is no longer safe. The tree means so much to me, to us, that this will be difficult. I am so happy that Celeste painted it, at least I will have that memory. I don't see the painting that often since I moved into the sitting room, but this room suit's us just right. But it is a comfort to know it's there. Christmas was a quiet affair, my grandmother came to see the children, and even my parents sent good wishes, but will not visit here.

9th January 1912

Annabela, celebrated her birthday this week, she is beginning to speak just a few words. Luis is rebelling a little about his lessons, the teacher comes in every day now, and I think he resents the loss of freedom. But I know you would want him educated, but it seems that he prefers to be doing things rather than book learning. Joao shows him how to make things in his workshop. Last week he came in with a toy sword he had made from wood, and he tells me that he is making something for Annabela.

23ʳᵈ February 1912
I have at last summoned up the energy to write in the diary. We have all been ill my love, the influenza epidemic has hit the local community, and I have been so poorly. Isabel and Joao took the children to stay with them, to keep them safe, but then Luis and Joao caught it. Luis has been so sick, but like me he is now recovering, only Isabel and Annabela escaped the illness. Joao though was hit hard and unfortunately died last week. Isabel is distraught as is Luis, who had become very fond of him. I will have to find another man to help out around the estate and quickly, even though Isabel will not want it. But I know you have kept your word about us being able to stay here supported by the estate, so I must ensure that it is maintained.

1ˢᵗ April 1912
My love, I have found a new man to help out, Casimiro is strong and healthy, and best of all a cousin of Isabel, and so she has accepted the news without rancour. Luis is a little wary of him as yet, but Annabela who is now walking has attached herself to him, and she follows him around the gardens when he is working. I think Luis may be a little jealous. Still it is good to have a young man around, and he seems quite taken with Isabel.

16ᵗʰ June 1912
Oh my dearest love, I am feeling such misery and pain I don't know how I shall bear it. Our darling Annabela is dead, and I have been so wretched. Weeks have gone by and it's only now that I have found the strength and courage to write about it. In truth I am far from certain how it happened, but it seems that somehow, she slipped through the door from the parterre

321

garden to the lake, fell in and drowned. Luis, who was fishing on the far
side of the lake, managed to tell me that whilst he was concentrating on the
fishing line, out of the corner of his eye he saw a movement, and looked up
to see Annabela toddling on to the jetty. He dropped his line and stood up
calling at her to go back, but on hearing his raised voice, she looked up then
tripped and fell in. Luis got up and ran towards her shouting for help,
Casimiro heard him and came running and stopped him from jumping in,
Luis yelled at him that Annabela had fallen in the water, and even though
she was nowhere to be seen he didn't hesitate from jumping straight in.
Isabel told me afterwards that he dived into the water coming up for air
several times before he eventually found her and pulled her out. Gasping for
breath and holding Annabel he told Luis to run and fetch Isabel, so he ran
off, then when she heard what had happened she fetched me, and we ran
together to the edge of the lake. Casimiro was trying to get her to breathe.
Luis was crying, and Isabel was trying to comfort him. Eventually
Casimiro shook his head, 'she has gone he said, there is nothing else I can
do.' I screamed at him to keep trying, but it was no use, she simply had
been in the water too long. I cradled her in my arms, but it was like she
was asleep, her hair was full of waterweeds and streaks of black mud were
smeared all over her tiny face, and her little lips were blue. I carried her
back to the house and someone I guess Isabel, called the doctor and the
priest. My grandmother came and took control I was beside myself with
grief, I couldn't accept let alone believe she was gone. I just kept holding
her, close to me. Isabel tells me that the priest eventually persuaded me to
give her up to god, but I didn't want to let her go. Luis who was standing
nearby seemed very frightened of me, and kept saying that it wasn't his
fault. The doctor gave me some medicine and I slept, until they told me it
was time for Annabela to be buried, I vaguely remember being in the church
and then we came to bury her. I couldn't take it in, her coffin so small and
white, Luis held my hand and was very quiet but didn't cry unlike me, in
the end it was my grandmother who whom once again handled it all. Then
I found myself at her graveside, and saw her beautiful face for the last time,
I asked for a lock of her hair, and my grandmother knelt down and cut me
one, then I bent down and kissed her forehead for the final time before I

322

fainted and had to be taken inside. Isabel tells me that they were really worried about me, I refused to eat, and cried all the time. Luis continued to be frightened of me, and it was for his sake alone that I eventually rallied, and came back to the world.

18th June 1912
Luis is very quiet, we have told him it is not his fault that Annabela fell into the lake, but I think he blames himself, he says if he hadn't shouted at her she might not have fallen. I have tried to tell him that he was trying to stop her from being in danger and he couldn't have known she would trip and fall. But I am not sure I am getting through. I have had the door to the lake closed for good, and Luis will not be allowed to go there either, I can't afford to take the risk. But I am angry, angry with everyone, especially god. I am even angry with you for not being here, for not knowing of your child's conception, birth and death, for being ignorant, but most of all I am angry with myself. I was her mother, and I let her die.

14th September 1912
I have some of the lock of Annabela's hair in a necklace around my neck in the locket you gave me on your last visit, I will wear it always, that way she will always be with me. Today, we planted a young orange tree to grow over her, slightly further back from the space where the old tree grew. I know it will protect Annabela forever, and as it grows, as she never can, it will spread its branches over her. The priest consecrated the ground, so she lies in a place where you and I were most happy, protected forever from the pain of life. But for Luis and me that pain will continue, and I have come to believe that we need to leave here, if we are to begin to live again. But where to go?

5th December 1912
My dearest love, despite my love for this place, and with some misgivings, I have decided that Luis and I will set sail for a new life in New York in the spring of next year. With the tension in Europe growing, we might also be able to avoid any problems here, but most importantly it will I believe, help Luis to put Annabela's death behind him. You would not recognise your son

now, he is so quiet, and he has lost all of his former spirit. He behaves well, but I know being here just reminds him of that terrible day, my heart breaks when I see him so sad. For myself I long to stay, simply to be close to Annabela, but what good would that do?

And even if I did stay I really do fear it may harm our son. I have prayed for guidance, and I am sure that god would prefer me to do whatever I can for Luis, who still lives and will, one day become a man. I saw in the newspaper that your commission came through, I hope this gives you the satisfaction that your marriage cannot, but my darling please keep safe. I have booked us on a steamship, and we will use your money to support us for the first months when we arrive. I am hopeful that I can get a job as a governess, with a good Portuguese family. I am assured that there is a small but growing community who will be able help us to adjust.

January 1913

What a sombre Christmas, the weather during December has been terrible, with much too much rain, everywhere one looks it is damp and depressing oh how I long to see the sun. The only bright spot is that Annabela's orange tree flourishes, when I can I take a chair, sit out next to it and tell her about what has been happening. I have also told her we are leaving, but she will be with me wherever I go, and that one day perhaps I may come back. I have had some positive news, after writing to a family friend, she has been able to secure for me a post as a governess, and I will be able to join the family immediately. I hope you don't mind but I have put your money to one side to be used for Luis's education, and to buy an indenture. He wants to work with wood he tells me, and I have no doubt he will be a good carpenter. I wrote to your lawyer today to notify him of my plans to vacate The Quinta in March, I hope this will ensure he can make what arrangements he needs. I am assuming that Casimiro and Isabel will need to stay on to maintain the estate.

March 1913

Tomorrow we leave for Lisbon, to be sure we are ready for our crossing. I have said goodbye to Annabela, and I noticed Luis sat there for a while as well yesterday. I placed some forget-me-knots by the base of the tree. I was overcome by such a wave of sadness, first I had lost you and now our only daughter. But then the tree's branches quivered a little even though there was no wind, and I knew that at least Annabela was giving me her blessing. I will take the diary and place it in our cottage safely hidden away, one day you may decide to visit, and I hope you find it and know what happened here and why I left. My love for you is undiminished, but I have to do what is right for Luis, and so my love we go to a new life. I will pray every day that yours is happy and fulfilled until we meet again.......

Helena, having read these last two entries to her father wiped a tear from her eye. In the days that followed, many things Helena knew and some that she guessed began to make sense, and although at first, she and everyone else was rather spooked by knowing that a child was buried in the grounds that initial anguish had now passed. In the immediate aftermath she had telephoned Marco, who on hearing what she had discovered, offered straightaway to visit the next day. And whilst he too was taken aback by the revelations, he assumed a practical approach advising Helena to speak to the local parish priest, he offered to call him for her. An appointment was secured for the following afternoon, at three o'clock. Helena, Marco and her father drove to Cováo and waited for him outside the church. He was as astonished as they by what he heard, and went to fetch the local parish records, where to his amazement he found clear evidence that the ground had been consecrated by the then Bishop, and that the local priest conducted the burial service. He was a good listener, and very empathetic, and recommended that if the remains could be found, Helena could have them blessed, and then cremated and spread around the tree if that made it easier for her. Helena however said that given the tree was almost dead, she felt deeply that when the trees

325

protection was over, then this action might be appropriate. The priest nodded sagely, and agreed with her, making it clear that he would be ready to help whenever she was ready, and so they headed back home, quiet and thoughtful.

Over the next few days' things slowly got back to normal, and Helena's thoughts began to turn to the future, both hers and the Quinta's. With the mystery solved it felt right to move on.

Helena's appointment to meet Carolina Alencar was fast
approaching. It had been delayed by a several weeks
due to Carolina contracting the flu. Mid July was hot, with
clear skies, and warm winds blowing in from Spain. In a
couple of days she would travel to Porto with Marco and
visit the home of the current Count, where the meeting
was scheduled to take place.

Once there, she hoped to be able to see some family
papers relevant to Rafael and Sofia. Although she wasn't
sure that Carolina would want to read Sofia's diary she
had already decided to take it with her just in case.
Carolina might after all this time be curious to know about
this new side to her family, and to do that it had to begin
with Sofia.

Helena acknowledged to herself that she was quite
anxious about the visit, how would she be received,
coolly, warmly, or perhaps worst of all with complete
indifference? She hoped that she would be kind to her,
and she tried to put herself in the family's shoes and think
what it must have been like for them to suddenly find a
branch of the family you never knew you had, and
moreover one whose beginnings were not legitimate.
Today's world was much more liberal about births out of
wedlock, in fact it was even fashionable in some circles.
Even so she knew that Portugal was a more conservative
and catholic country, and perhaps at the higher end of
society, this might still be frowned upon. Well she would
find out shortly, so she would have to handle whatever
came, and Marco would be with her, and that made it
easier, and she had to move on in any case.

The process of restoring the Quinta was gaining a little
momentum

327

Carlos and Manuel continued to handle the builder's enquiries, and they were quite engrossed with the project to sort out the barn, she loved the way it all continued around her. They had purchased a number of mobile phones, and a couple of lap tops with a 4G cards and this was proving useful. Her father was an immense help, and despite his rudimentary but improving Portuguese, he somehow managed to keep things ticking along between him, the trades people and Carlos. The plumber Senhor Dias had called in to say he would be quoting for the work, he had found some plumbers, who had just come off a big job, who were available, and he thought he would give it a shot. Helena was particularly pleased by this turn of events, and it seemed word had spread as when on the previous Sunday she and her father had called in café central for a coffee, they were warmly greeted by a growing number of people. Louisa's mother seemed particularly pleased to see them, and was much more talkative, than at Helena's first encounter with her. On the day agreed for the visit to Porto Helena drove to Serta, where she had arranged to leave her car and meet up with Marco. They would travel onwards together. When she arrived at the meeting place he was already waiting for her, they greeted each other with pleasure, and the usual welcome kisses on the cheek. Helena thought he smelt divine, and despite his casual dress managed to look every bit like a film star, as they settled into the car Marco was the first to speak.

'Well shall we get on, I expect your keen to get to Porto and meet your family?'

'I feel some trepidations, if the truth be known, this could be a disaster, what if she doesn't like me, or even want me there?'

'I think your worrying unnecessarily, Carolina Alencar and her cousin wouldn't have agreed that you should go to

the house, if they were uncertain. Of course, they haven't met you yet, and I can appreciate that both you and Carolina will be anxious.' he gave her a warm smile.
'It is a shame that Felipe and his family are in Brazil, but he was very supportive of Carolina meeting you in his house, that's a good sign. If they had any doubts, they would have arranged everything through their solicitors, I am sure it will be fine, so don't worry. Shall we go?'
'Yes of course let's do this.'
They drove in comparative silence for about fifteen minutes, before Marco broke the brooding silence.
'How are things with you now Helena, have you got over the initial shock of finding out about Annabela and her burial in the grounds?'
Helena thought about his words for a few moments before replying.
'You know I think I am almost reconciled to it, partly because so many things make sense now, and as for her remains as the Priest explained, in this climate little is likely to have endured other than some bones, so I think once the tree finally dies, it will be an opportunity to handle it then, he has offered to be present if and when we do, and that is a comfort. In the interim we will re-position the seats and put up the plaque that Sofia made.'
'It is good to hear that, it is an unusual situation, but many large estates have a small family cemetery, much like in England I think.'
'Yes, your right, but this is a bit different!'
Marco laughed it was rich and throaty.
'Yes, it is isn't it.'
After this short exchange they chatted about his work and the works at the Quinta, before lapsing once more into a contented silence. Marco concentrated on driving whilst Helena looked out of the window at the passing countryside. A little later Helena said

329

'You know something, while I am a little anxious about the meeting at the same time part of me is looking forward to it, do you think Carolina feels the same about meeting me?'

'I imagine Carolina is more than a little curious, your descended from an illegitimate branch of the family, but your still blood related.'

'Well that is true of course, but I would like to think that a hundred or more years since my great grandfather was born, attitudes have changed. I know Portugal is still a catholic country, but divorce happens here, as elsewhere despite the doctrine.'

'True, though you have an inheritance that would have passed to her cousin and her, if you had not come forward to claim it. She of course is wealthy in her own right, so I don't think that is likely to be an influence on her thoughts at all, well you will find out soon enough.'

They settled back into silent mode once more until once again Helena broke the reverie by asking,

'How old is she, Carolina I mean.'

'I think 55, she is not married, and has no children.'

'Okay, that means there is only one branch of the Alencar line left?'

'Yes, Rafael's younger brother who inherited the defunct title and property after Rafael's death, was married and had children, so there is a line of descendants through him. The youngest of which are three siblings, and the elder will inherit the families remaining estate. Carolina is a direct descendent of Rafael's sister Isabella's line, she is an only child, that branch hasn't been very lucky, so Carolina is the sole heir on that branch, I assume when she dies Felipe will inherit her estate. Carolina's family has always taken responsibility for the family archives. So currently with Felipe and his family in Brazil for a few months overseeing the coffee plantations she is staying there. It's where the archive is kept, so they were the instigators of the idea that we meet there.'

'I see, well that's interesting and positive, I think.'

'It is, so don't look so worried, we are about twenty minutes away, but be prepared it is a large place.'

'Thanks for that Marco, if I wasn't nervous before I am now!'

Helena straightened herself up, took her compact out of her handbag and searched around for her lipstick and applied a little. She had decided to wear a pair of plain black Channel trousers and a soft pale green, loose fitting cashmere top, combined with a pair of Jimmy Choo kitten heeled pumps, she now wished she had worn a suit, still it was too late for that. Out of the corner of her eye she could see Marco glancing occasionally at her, and she felt a little self-conscious. She closed the lipstick and the compact and placed them back in her bag.

'Do I look okay, should I have worn a suit or a dress?'

'You look fine, very refined and casual, and I think Carolina will be more interested in you than your clothes.' He gave her encouraging smile and that seemed to settle her nerves.

They were now driving through the outskirts of Porto, and the traffic was heavy, much more like she would have experienced at home. Marco was driving with all the sureness she would have expected of him, a little while later he turned into an entrance drive, between large walls that sailed away into the distance on either side. He stopped at the gates left the car, and walked to an entrance buzzer on the wall. Helena could see him speaking towards it, and a few seconds later he returned to the car, as the gates slowly swung open.

'Okay we are here, are you ready for this?'

'As ready as I will ever be,' said Helena controlling her voice, whilst her stomach was doing cartwheels.

The driveway was lined with tall Beech trees which seemed to go on forever, it twisted to the left then the right before the house came into view. It was quite amazing, an exuberant façade of bright white painted render, the top of the house was surmounted with cupolas, and round bell towers reaching up towards the sky. Matching pairs of tall windows with Baroque Pediments of triangular shape, gave the house a beautiful symmetry. The entrance doors to the Manor House were via a grand staircase, with a white marble balustrade that rose simultaneously left and right, before returning to meet itself in front of another gorgeously Baroque pediment over the double wooden doors.

As they drove round the large drive towards the staircase, a gentleman who was waiting at the bottom of the staircase moved towards the car. Marco pulled up the car, turned off the engine and got out first, he spoke with the gentleman, and then said to Helena,

'We are expected if you're ready he will take us in, then he is going to park the car around the back.

Helena got out of the car, picked up her handbag, and walked around to join Marco, she looked all around, gulped, and thought to herself she was entering another world, and suddenly she wondered if she had to curtsey, but almost immediately she dismissed it, that was just being silly!

The gentleman who was waiting wished her good afternoon, and motioned towards the house.

'Please follow me.'

Helena was suddenly stricken by panic and became rooted to the gravel where she stood, she very much wanted to hold Marco's hand, and he must have sensed her unease, as he very gently put his hand on her back to propel her forward.

'Don't worry,' he whispered, 'I am here.'

Helena muttered to him,

'Thank goodness for that, do you mind if I put my arm through yours because I don't think my legs will move otherwise!'

He lifted his arm, so she could link hers through his, and joined together thus, they walked up the staircase to the door. Helena felt very comfortable with her arm linked through his, and stepped forward trying not to show that her knees were wobbling, and she reflected she was pleased she hadn't worn high heels.

On opening the door, the gentleman moved to one side to allow them both to pass through into an entrance hall which was spectacular, in every sense. Here Baroque architecture had been allowed to run amok. Everywhere Helena turned she saw beauty, the floor patterned in bi-coloured marble, statuary, and paintings in gold rococo style frames. Around the top of the walls was a frieze of intricate plasterwork, with vines, flowers and grapes in abundance. Helena found herself absolutely speechless, so when an elegant woman descended from the staircase, she only just managed to stop herself from curtsying. As the elegant woman approached Helena could see that she was a similar age to her mum somewhere in her mid-fifties. Her auburn hair was piled on top of her head in a chignon bun, and she was wearing a pair of blue slacks, and a white silk blouse, around her neck she had a double string of pearls, that matched the earrings she wore. Her makeup was understated, but she was undoubtedly beautiful. Carolina turned to Marco gave him the customary two kisses on the cheek before saying in Portuguese.

'Marco it's lovely to see you, how are your parents?'

'They are fine Carolina, they send their best wishes.'

Carolina turned away from him and moved a couple of steps towards Helena holding out her arms in front of her,

'And you must be Helena.'

She then placed her own hands on Helena's upper arms, and bent forward and kissed her on both cheeks.

'I am so pleased to meet you at last, you can't believe how surprised we were to find that Uncle Rafael had had a son, and now we have a new line in the family.'

Helena, who was still reeling from the beauty of the entrance hall, and the knowledge that Marco's family knew Carolina, pulled herself together before responding in Portuguese with

'I am happy to meet you too, and to be here in this lovely house, and whilst it has been more than a bit of a shock, I am delighted to discover I have more of a family in Portugal than I could ever have expected.'

Carolina gave her a dazzling smile, and then turned to the gentleman who had shown them in and who was silently waiting nearby, and she said very quietly,

'Jacomo, would you mind asking Monica if we could have coffee and lunch in the drawing room? Thank you.'

As he turned away to carry out the request, Carolina unexpectedly put her arm through Helena's.

'Come on Helena, let's go and have some coffee, and you can fill me in. Marco has of course given me the basics, but I would love to hear the story from you.'

Carolina gently ushered Helena towards a door which she opened, and they all went into the splendidly furnished Drawing Room. Once inside she propelled Helena towards a sofa close to the fire, which despite the heat outside was burning low in the hearth. Marco sat on a sofa opposite, and waited until Carolina had sat down too before saying.

'So are you staying here Carolina or just visiting to show Helena the archive?'

'Ah, well I am staying for a few days, Filipe as you know is in Brazil with the family, and he likes me to stay, but it's so large and draughty that a few days at any one time is all I can cope with!'

Turning her head to Helena she said

'Filipe sends his best wishes Helena, and says he is sorry he is not here to welcome you into the family, but he is looking forward to meeting you later in the summer, he always returns in mid-August, as we normally have a house party in late August and if you and your father are free he would wish you to be here for that.'

Pointing around the room, she said,

'Parts of the house are not as old as you may think Helena. It had to be largely rebuilt in the late 1930/40's. As I am sure Marco has already told you, as a family we lost a lot of money in the depression, and the old house fell into a state of disrepair. Happily for us, our investments in Brazil, eventually restored most of the family's fortunes, and we were able to rebuild in the same style.'

Helena who had been taking in the room and its paintings said,

'It looks like a beautiful house, I thought the Quinta was large but obviously it pales in comparison to this.'

Carolina smiled broadly.

'Well perhaps one day I could visit and see it for myself, I have only ever seen the plans, and I admit to a large degree of curiosity about what he built.'

'Well I think it's beautiful of course, it is in the art nouveau style, though it needs a lot of work to modernise it, and that might take many months. But please, your welcome to visit anytime you like. I would love to show you around.'

Marco looked meaningfully at Carolina.

'Helena has decided to stay here in Portugal, and already she has been busy.' He smiled, and Helena's heart fluttered, he went on,

335

'She has already started to meet tradesmen and has received quotes, she is determined though to use only local people, and she was telling me last week that she has seen an interesting set of people, including a one-handed plumber!'

Helena interjected,

'Well he may be one handed, but he has the skill and he can manage others, I want to be able to be part of the community and to do that, I need to make us of local skills.'

'I am only teasing Helena, I think your very far sighted, and I am sure the Quinta will flourish under your hands.'

Carolina, who had been observing Marco's attention to Helena, raised an eyebrow and said,

'Well, that's a good first step, and I am sure that you're a good judge of character, by the way do you have a boyfriend Helena.'

Helena was a bit disconcerted by the sudden change of direction, but rallied quickly.

'No not any more, my partner decided that we were not compatible after five years together in California.'

Surprisingly she found that she could not keep the bitterness out of her voice.

'He behaved disgracefully after my mother was diagnosed, and soon after she died he telephoned me to tell me it was all over. Even though I had no idea he felt like that I am glad now, I have other things to occupy me.'

Carolina smiled and looked at Marco, before saying to Helena

'Well it sounds like you're better off without him, did he know about your inheritance before he made his decision?'

'Well he knew about my granddads letter to my mum, but he just wasn't interested enough to ask me about it, or what it might mean, then a couple of weeks later he

336

ended our relationship. So, no he didn't know the full extent.'

Just then came a knock on the door, Jacomo entered with the coffee, followed by a woman Helena assumed was Monica, who was carrying a tray of sandwiches and cakes.

They placed them down set out some china and napkins, and then discreetly left.

Carolina said to Helena, tea or coffee?

'Tea would be great thank you.'

'Please help yourself to whatever you would like, I guessed you might be hungry after your journey, so I asked Maria to prepare us a light lunch.'

With tea and coffee dispensed, they ate and made small talk, Helena explained about the finding of the letter, and the subsequent revelations about Annabela, which judging by Carolina's face had truly astonished her, once Helena had finished, Carolina spoke very softly,

'So Rafael had two children with Sofia, I am sure he didn't know about her, how terrible for Sofia to have had to cope with that on her own. The archive has some letters that Rafael wrote to Sofia, and some she wrote to him. Obviously, they loved each other very much, but circumstances and society then being what they were, the relationship was always doomed, and in the end as you know he was pressured into marriage with Christina, but that turned out to be a disaster for both of them almost from the start, as you will see in the archives. In the end Rafael's clearly acknowledges Luis, but there is no mention of a second child. Look, how long do you both have, because if you're not in a hurry I could show you around before we look at the archive?'

Marco was the one to reply.

'We are staying overnight in the Pousada, as I didn't want Helena to feel rushed, so we have plenty of time.'

Helena meanwhile looked at her hostess and said
'Thank you Carolina I would love to see the house, if it's
no trouble.'
'Of course not, come on the pair of you, let's see what I
can find to interest you.'
For the next hour or so Carolina, showed them the major
rooms in the house, pointed out paintings of Rafael, and
his father, mother, and Rafael's siblings, before they went
out into the gardens. It was some time later that they
returned to the house, and once inside Carolina led them
both to the Library.
'The family archive is kept in here, it's quite extensive so I
have taken out some items that I think you might like to
see, they are set out over on the library desk, in date
order. Whilst you are looking through them Marco and I
will go and catch up, I am sure you would prefer to be on
your own to do this. We will be in the Drawing Room
when you want us. With that they left closing the door
gently behind them.
Helena glanced around, it was a lovely room, not overly
large for a library, everywhere was wooden panelled, a
small fireplace sat in once corner, and Helena thought it
odd for a Library to have a fireplace. All of these books
would go up very quickly with only one loose spark, then
she noted the chain mail fireguard which was stretched
across the front, and which would have proved a more
than effective blanket. She walked towards the library
desk and sat down.
In front of her were laid out several files, on top of which
sat files of correspondence. The first file was headed
'Rafael to Sofia' on second file were a larger number of
letters from 'Sofia to Rafael.' On a third file were a small
amount of correspondence labelled Christina and Rafael,
and on a forth file was a heading Rafael and family.
Helena did not know where to start.

So she picked up the sheet of paper that identified each letter by date, and decided to tackle them in date order. The first was from Sofia to Rafael.

July 1901

My Dearest Love,

How much I enjoyed our weekend together, try as I might I cannot hope to be able to explain to you how much I think of you and dream of our future together. I still find it hard to believe that you love me, let alone come to terms with your exciting news that you are going to build a Quinta here, so we can be together. I keep expecting my happiness to burst, but it thrives. The land upon which the Quinta will be built is beautiful, we will be able to keep our Orange Tree won't we? It means so much to me and I hope to you too. I know that even when it is finished, your duties to the family and your business means that will not be here all the time, but I promise that I will not turn into a scold, even though my heart will break when you leave me. Do you remember the day we met? I think of it with such pleasure. When our eyes met it was such a shock; I felt I had known you forever, and I knew without a shadow of a doubt that I loved you. If Estrela had not gone lame as you toured your land here, I shudder to think how my life would be now. How much luck came our way the day you entered my father's forge and asked him to fit a new shoe. My mother asked me to fetch my father for lunch and there you were, holding on to your horse's bridle, whilst my father fitted the new shoe. I had no idea who you were, but when you couldn't break contact with my eyes, I knew you felt the same way. You asked me to walk with you to show me the way to the high road, which of course you knew very well, but on that short walk we knew that we had both found our love. I am smiling to myself as I write this, so hurry back to me, I ache to be close to you once more.

Your loving Sofia

September 1902

339

Darling Sofia,

It has been far too long since I was with you. My wretched commitments keep me firmly tied to Porto, though I am beginning to think my parents guess that I have interests in the country, which are not entirely commercial, and they conspire to keep me close. But I have good news, Jorge tells me that the Quinta will be sufficiently advanced in its construction and furnishing for me to occupy it in December. Having a few business interests in the area will give me a legitimate reason to visit, and so my love we can be with each other as often as can be legitimately managed. I intend to visit for a couple of weeks at least in early December, but unfortunately, I will have to return to Porto for Christmas. Since I received Jorge's letter, I have been giving some thought to how we can legitimately be in the house together without causing social scandal. For me it is of no importance, but for your reputations sake we must maintain a degree of social propriety. It seems sensible for me to simply employ you as the Quinta's housekeeper, in this way you will receive an income, and additional funds for you to employ a couple to cook and maintain the gardens. They can stay in the cottage in the grounds. I hope you find this solution acceptable, for I can think of no other. I know you will not want the income, but you must to maintain appearances. In any case you will have sole charge of the house and grounds, whilst also having the majority of your time at leisure. I cannot tell you how important it is to me that the outside world knows you have a legitimate role. You can employ help as you see fit in the house, my men will oversee the farm itself, does this sound workable to you? I am overjoyed that we will be able to spend more time together, even though we cannot live openly together, and the marriage that we both desire cannot be. This arrangement is this is the best I can do for you my love, barring leaving you to make a life without me, and I confess that I cannot bring myself to do that. Do let me know if this is acceptable to you. I am intending to be back sometime in late November.

Your Rafael

During the next six months or so the correspondence continued, and Helena read how in late January of 1903 Sofia duly took up the post of housekeeper, and they spent as much time together at the Quinta as they could given Rafael's commitments. They would write to each other sparingly but increasingly the letters showed a level of frustration on both sides. They were so clearly in love it was difficult to read them without feeling voyeuristic. A change occurred in late October 1903, when Sofia wrote the following short letter to Rafael.

My dearest love,

I am in such a fluster, and I cannot wait until you come in December, so I must tell you by way of this letter that we are going to have a child. I saw the doctor yesterday and he confirmed that our baby will be born in early June next year. Oh my love, I have never been so sick and so happy at the same time. I am sure it is a boy and he will be as handsome as you, please hurry back my darling we have much to talk about. Where shall we have the nursery? What will we call our son, how will we handle this news as my condition cannot be hidden for long. I have so many questions and so few answers. I ache to see you and feel your touch.

Your loving Sofia.

Helena read the short reply from Rafael, and whilst she did so she realised she was holding her breath.

My darling Sofia,

Your letter filled me with such joy, and anguish in equal measure. We are to be parents, at my age I never thought this would happen to me and it is such a blessing, and I hope it is not too much of a strain for you. I don't want to sound too dramatic, but at the same time as feeling such joy, I was plunged into the depths of despair. I cannot acknowledge my child, and I cannot give it a name. I so long to do that but my family would never condone such an action and the scandal would be very damaging, especially now when our investments are not doing as well as we hoped, and it is our

reputation alone that keeps the worst news from leaking into high society. I have managed to find a pretence to visit the area soon, so I will be with you before the month is out.
Rafael.

Helena was saddened, Rafael's response was so muted, almost matter of fact, and the words on the page were so stark. She knew her reaction was rooted in her own more liberal twenty first century morality. Intellectually she also realised that Rafael had written, and expressed himself within the social mores and context of the time, which was one she couldn't possibly hope to understand. Nonetheless it still made her feel ridiculously outraged on Sofia's behalf, and also sad. Had Sofia more compassion than Helena was able to find? Was her recent betrayal by Tom clouding her judgement? Had she ever been in love with Tom? For the first time, she acknowledged that perhaps not, maybe what they had was a poor facsimile of what Rafael and Sofia had experienced. Helena suddenly felt a lightness in her heart, maybe true love was out there waiting for her, and she involuntarily thought of Marco and smiled. Turning back to her reflections on the relationship her great-great grandparents had had, certainly all she now knew seemed to confirm that Sofia have accepted the situation she found herself in, and nothing Helena had learned since reading these letters indicated that she was unhappy with it, far from it. Thinking about it Helena could only conclude that the love they had for each other sustained them despite the immense social barriers they faced. This love, a deep and abiding true love was never broken, it endured. Even when Rafael married, Sofia's love remained firm, though it did change the social situation dramatically. Helena continued to read their letters in turn, they were few in number, and she was

342

frustrated that she had no idea what had happened to them both in the weeks and months between writing and receiving a response. Rafael had visited Helena more than once between her October letter and March 1904. She writes to Rafael about how much she has enjoyed his visit's, and that she remains well, the morning sickness has lessened, she felt strong and the baby was kicking. She told him that the nursery was being prepared, and that she has brought some items for it herself with her own income. Rafael wrote in April that sadly he was unable to come in early May as he wished, but he would be with her later in the month and he hoped to remain at the Quinta until the baby was born. The next letter from Sofia was dated October 1904.

My dearest love,
Luis is such a good baby, you should see him now, he is growing so quickly, he recognises me I am sure he does, when he is in my arms he is content and so am I. I have so much to thank god for, it has been a lovely couple of months here, the weather has been hot, but it has meant we have been able to sit out under the orange tree. I paint a little now that my strength has returned, and Luis lies in his perambulator, sleeping mostly. Our cottage is nearly completed, and I know it will afford you the privacy you require for us.
Hurry back home my love. Luis longs to see you.

Your loving Sofia.

The letters continued in the same vein, right until 1909, Rafael visited many times, Luis grew into a small boy, and Sofia wrote of his exploit's. Rafael instructed a teacher for him when he was six, and he began to be educated at home. Everything in the letters she read confirmed the strength of the love they had, and it wasn't until 1909 that Helena detected, and perhaps only then, with the hindsight of knowing what happened subsequently a slight detachment and sadness in Rafael's letters. They were still caring, but she felt there were hints in them that his situation might be changing. In May 1909 the first part of Rafael's May letter intimated just such a change.

May 19, 1909

My darling Sofia,
Your last letter made me laugh, I can imagine Luis's fierce little face as he climbed the orange tree, only to have got stuck, and had to call for help. It shows some character, how I envy him the freedom to play and to be and do what he wants. It makes me melancholy to know that this is something that at 43 years of age I can never do. Let him be free my love, I rejoice in the fact he will never be tethered and bound as I am…

Sofia's letters in reply were always positive, and if she felt his growing anxiety she never mentioned it. She contented herself to telling him of the Quinta and its tales, keeping it light and playful, she always told him how much she loved and missed him, but she never reproached him when he had to put off his visit's. There was an underlying sense of frustration in all of Rafael's letters of 1909, the reason for which Helena knew was made clear in his letter to Sofia in June 1910.
Sofia must have sensed the impending change, and Helena could only marvel at how she handled herself during those last months of 1909 and early 1910. The archives contained no more letters, between them. Helena was reminded once more of the bunch of

344

envelopes she had found which contained nothing inside, what happened to the contents? She would mention this to Carolina. Meanwhile she picked up a letter written from Rafael to his wife dated December 1910.

Christina,
My mother has been speaking to me yet again, she tells me you are unhappy. I confess I do not understand why you complain so, you have my name my title, I am your husband and I visit your bed, yet you constantly complain about my attentiveness. You seem to have forgotten, perhaps conveniently, that I was honest with you from the beginning that I could never love you. I accepted the pressure from my family and yours to marry and I promised to do my duty by you, but no one could expect me to like it. You must recall that you told me you would be satisfied with a loveless marriage, so why so many grievances? I told you only the truth, if you ever thought that you could change me, well you know now that can never happen, my love lies elsewhere, and always will.
Rafael

The reply from Christina made difficult reading for Helena,

My husband,
You are making me a social pariah, will you not come with me to even the most ordinary events? If I go alone I am constantly whispered about, and some even dare to ask me where you are, of course they do it lightly and in passing, but I know I am the most talked about woman in Oporto. What am I supposed to say to those who ask; tell me that? Do I say that my husband of six months

345

abandons me for the love of a peasant girl? Whatever did I do to deserve such treatment at your hands. I fell in love with you and I now regret that bitterly, how can you demean me so much? How stupid was I to think this could work, your name means nothing without your presence beside me I know that now. Well I will not give you any satisfaction, you will keep to your part of the bargain and I will to mine. I will find some way of coping with your slights, and I demand that you continue to visit my bed weekly, perhaps once I am with child you will see the folly of your conduct and then behave appropriately for our children's sake. Until then if I must go out in society alone, I need a reason to do so, my father says you should consider taking a commission in the Navy, at least then I can go out in society alone without experiencing more ridicule.

I would implore you, but I know that it will not work. Isabella was right when she warned me that I was making a grave mistake; but I was young, and foolish enough to believe that I could bring you round, that our money and my beauty would be sufficient for you. Well we are where we are, we have entered into this marriage and now we must make the best of it. My father has spoken to yours and the sooner you gain your commission the better for us all.

Christina.

Helena read the letter with a sadness that threatened to overwhelm her, it was obvious to her that this love triangle could only ever end badly. But Rafael and Christina stayed married for ten years, no children were conceived, Rafael's commission came through and this seemed to have provided him with a reason for living. Christina however must have felt so humiliated, to find

346

her dreams shattered so shortly after her marriage, Helena couldn't help but feel sorry for her. No one had gained by this marriage, indeed all three of them had lost something precious. Sofia lost the love of her life, the father of her child, her home and ultimately her son. Christina, lost her innocence, her belief in love, and her status must have been diminished, and throughout those ten long years doubtless she become a bitter young woman.

Rafael, arguable lost the most, he not only lost his one true love and his only child, he also had a marriage which must have been torture for him, and even then, he had to leave his family home for a commission he probably never wanted. Helena put the letter back down on top of the file, and felt a pang of regret for a love that had been lost, demeaned and unrequited, it was a tragedy of epic proportions. The last document she picked up was Rafael's Will, in which he makes clear that now his marriage has been annulled, he recognises not only Luis as his only son but also Sofia. He did the only thing he could by bequeathing the Quinta to Sofia, along with an annuity for life, and a capital sum to Luis or his direct descendants.

Helena, had come almost full circle, however there was one other file on the desk, she opened it and inside she found an envelope, she picked it up and saw it was addressed to Sofia da Silva, Quinta das Laranjeiras, Ameixeira. On the back at the bottom edge was a further line which said, 'To be sent after my death.'

The envelope still contained its waxed seal, Helena shivered. It appeared that this letter had never been sent and therefore never opened, she didn't know what to think or to do, it was only then she saw the note which was lying next to the file. It read

347

Helena,

Rafael wrote this letter in the weeks before he passed away, it was found inside a small wooden box with an orange tree inlaid in the top. We came across the box along with some other items in a trunk. The trunk was discovered when a leak in the roof was investigated, and we had called workmen in to effect a repair. In the trunk we found the box, which contained seven letters from Rafael to Sofia in an envelope, and this one from him to her that after his death was never posted. I think it is only right that you as a direct descendent of Sofia should be the one to open it.
Carolina.

Helena found her hands were shaking as she picked up the unopened envelope once more. Carolina had thoughtfully provided her with a letter opener, and very gently she broke the seal, which disintegrated in her hands. She pulled out two sheets of fine writing paper, and looked on the familiar writing of her great-great grandfather.

My Darling Sofia,
I am ever hopeful that this letter reaches you and it is my greatest wish that you my darling are in good health and happy with your life. I have so much to say to you, but first, I must tell you that my marriage such as it was, ended over six years ago. Since then I have lived quietly here, with the company of my sister who when widowed came to care for me. I have visited our Quinta a few times, even though it pains me to see it empty and forlorn. Maybe it is fanciful of me, but I am certain I sensed your presence, especially when sitting underneath our orange tree, and I felt some comfort in that. In writing to you I am breaking the oath I swore to myself when I agreed to marry. I made that difficult decision because I couldn't in all conscience ask you to

348

be my mistress, to have stooped so low would have been demeaning to the most precious person in my life. Consequently, I made the intractable promise to myself that I must never contact you again, as to do so would have been a grand indulgence on my part. I break that vow now because I found out recently I am ill my love and cannot hope to live much longer even the doctors tell me to prepare for the worst; but I am content as I have made my peace with god and now I must do the same with you and Luis.

Before I leave this earth, it is important for you to know that I never stopped loving you or Luis, and I have made such provisions as I can to make amends for my unforgivable behaviour. I have something else to tell you too, and I hope in its telling you will have some peace. I shall begin with my last and what will have been my final visit to the Quinta.

It was a nice day. Jorge drove me, and I was pleased to have his company, which in the light of what I discovered proved most invaluable. When we arrived at the Quinta, Jorge left me to walk through the empty house alone, it's windows and doors had been opened for me, but inside all was covered and dusty. When I wandered into the drawing room my eyes fell upon our painting and I felt such a longing that I am not ashamed to say tears fell down my cheeks, I cried silently as I looked upon it. I stayed there some time remembering happier times and wished I could turn the clock back.

Eventually I left the house and visited the grounds, whilst walking in the gardens I met for the first and only time Casimiro who, Jorge told me, was charged with keeping the grounds tidy, the name was familiar, and I remembered my solicitors had written to me and told me about him being hired many years ago. He knew who I was of course because of Jorge accompanying me. After

349

I had been formally introduced, he respectfully asked if I had any news of you and Luis. I was not expecting so forthright a question and was a little taken aback, but after regaining my composure I told him the truth, which was that I had no idea. I let him know that I knew you had left for America, but we had not stayed in touch. He seemed disappointed in my response, and in truth I was saddened that even today I had no idea where you were or even if you were alive. An hour or so later our goodbyes had been made, and we left. I was very thoughtful and reflected once again on my actions, and my treatment of you and Luis. Because I had already decided to visit the church in Covão and leave a gift for the church's upkeep, Jorge drove on and before I knew it, we had pulled up outside the church. As I entered the local priest came to greet me, he was I think surprised to see me, though he knew who I was of course. We chatted for a short while and then on the spur of the moment I asked him if he would take my confession and he agreed. Following this solemn exchange where I bared my soul, I felt lighter of heart, and in this condition, I went to sit on the bench outside the church in the sun. After ten minutes or so the priest emerged and joined me on the bench, he looked deeply into my eyes for some time and he seemed to be making a decision. He then told me that he had something to tell me, he said he had searched his heart and had asked god for guidance, and he was sure that I should know about my daughter. I was completely at a loss, what daughter? I said to him. Then he began very gently to tell me about Annabela's accident and death. I listened to his gentle words in silence, my mind was in a turmoil, my daughter had been conceived, carried, born and died, she had been buried in the Quinta under the orange tree, and I was ignorant, I knew nothing. The damage I had done was far greater than anything I could have imagined. Half an hour later, the priest accompanied Jorge and I back to the Quinta, where together we sat quietly praying at Annabela' s grave. My darling how you must have suffered, and I had no idea, why didn't you tell me, I would have come, I owed you that and more. It is only now that I fully understand the reasons why and you and Luis left for America. You must have been distraught and at last I can fully understand your subsequent decision to leave for Luis's sake. When I was told by my factor that you had left the Quinta with Luis for America I was I admit stunned, but I never gave any real thought to why you left. I remember thinking it odd you should wait three years before doing so, and forgive me but I assumed you had met someone else and I couldn't begrudge you happiness even though my own heart was breaking. With what I know now, I cannot begin to imagine how you and he only a young boy must have suffered. Luis of will be a young man now, and I hope at some point he will come to know his heritage. Now down to the main purpose of this letter, I cannot hope to compensate you for the lack of care I have inflicted on you both, but I can acknowledge Luis as my first and only son, and I have done so publicly. Also, I have bequeathed to him a capital sum. To you my darling I have bequeathed our beloved Quinta, and an annual income for as long as you live, so you can ensure Annabela's remains can lay undisturbed.

I have never stopped loving you or Luis, even though I allowed my duty to my family to take precedent. Even now I feel a deep love for the daughter I never knew, and I bitterly regret my actions but what is done is done and I cannot change it. I am sorry that I never met our daughter who I imagine had your beauty, I will meet her soon. Think well of me my love.

Your Rafael.

Helena sat at the desk and tears that had been forming in the corners of her eyes escaped, large sobs shuddered through her and try as she might she couldn't stop them. Her thoughts were alternately happy and achingly sad as she reflected on life's cruelties. As she sat there trying to stem the tide of tears by wiping her eyes and blowing her nose, Carolina who had entered the library very quietly, gently but firmly put her own arms around her and held her whilst she continued to cry.

It was some time before Helena's breathing became more regular and when at last she was still, Carolina let go of her, and brushing damp hair from Helena's face said very gently.

'Come on Helena let's go back to the drawing room you need a brandy.'

Helena allowed herself to be led back to the drawing room, the letter was still in her hand, and she heard her shoes making little clicks on the marble floor. When she entered she looked up at Marco, and he immediately came towards her and took her into his arms. He held her close and whispered into her ear that it was okay, crying was good. Afterwards she had no idea how long she remained there in his arms, but he smelt good, his arms were strong, and he held her gently.

Finally, Helena lifted her head up and he let her go, she moved to the sofa and sat down, Carolina had poured her a large brandy and set it down on the coffee table in front of her, and she picked it up and took a large gulp.

Carolina and Marco were both looking at her with concern in their own eyes.

'I am sorry for all of this,' said Helena gesturing at her face and her sodden handkerchief.

'I must look a fright, but you should both read this.'

She handed them the letter and remained seated clutching the brandy glass as if it were a good luck talisman. She watched them both as they slowly read down the pages, and she could see that they too were moved by its contents. Once they had finished it Carolina put it down and once more came over to Helena and gave her a hug. When she let her go Helena was surprised by how it made her feel, it was protective and supportive, like one that her mum might have given her, and much to her embarrassment tears started to fall silently once more. Marco picked up her hand and held it until she stopped, then Helena glanced over at Carolina and said,

'May I use the bathroom?'

'Of course, of course come with me,' and Carolina led her to a room on the first floor, and said with a gentle smile on her face.

'Please feel free to use whatever you need from in here and take your time, we will wait until you're ready to join us again.'

Helena looked at her and the mascara streaks on Carolina's blouse and said,

'I am so sorry I have ruined your blouse, with my crying.'

'It's nothing, don't even think about it, just take your time and come down when you're ready' and with that she left her alone and shut the bedroom door.

Helena walked around the large four poster bed to the door on the right-hand side which she assumed led into a en-suite bathroom. On entering she found herself in a sumptuous room, and she went over to the double his and her sinks, and stared at her face in the mirror. Her hair was damp, and her face red and blotchy, her eyes were puffy, and her mascara had run. Picking up a flannel she turned on the cold tap until the water ran cold, then she put the flannel into the stream of water. When it was saturated she leant over the bowl and lifted it up to her face holding it there for a few seconds before repeating the manoeuvre several times more. Eventually she saw it was having the required impact, and she turned on the hot tap, and washed the makeup from her face and then dried it. She was still a little puffy and blotchy, but she felt calmer, she saw a pot of moisturiser and applied a little, before using a cotton wool pad to dab more cold water under her eyes. Ten minutes later she made her way down to the drawing room, and as she approached the hum of conversation rang out. Just outside the door she hesitated, straightening her clothes before entering. Carolina saw her first and smiled broadly.

'There you are Helena, come and have some tea, they tell me that tea to the British is a universal panacea, I hope this is how you like it.'

Helena sat down, and Carolina poured tea from an elegant teapot into an equally elegant teacup, before adding some milk, Marco was no longer in the room and Carolina on seeing her glance around said,

'Marco will be back soon, he has just gone to return a call to his father apparently he wants his advice, before recommending an approach to his client.'

Helena nodded and took a sip of the tea.

'That's good thank you. What did you make of the letter Carolina?'

'I thought it was very sad and in those days, it must have been for him anyway, a difficult letter to write. But the worst part is that having written it to Sofia, we know she never received it, and as Annabela wasn't mentioned in the will, I guess she couldn't have known that Rafael knew about his daughter. We know from the date of the Will that he had already bequeathed the Quinta to Sofia and the capital sum for Luis six months before he visited the Quinta for the last time. I suppose he either didn't get around to, or didn't see the need for acknowledging Annabela in a codicil to the Will certainly no additions, or changes were made. I can only imagine that he assumed that the letter would explain everything to Sofia, if she ever returned. In the end it was never sent, and I have no idea why not. But he had already ensured via Jorge and his solicitor, that Sofia's solicitor, who would have handled the paperwork that transferred to Sofia's her grandmother's house, knew what to do in the event that Sofia or Luis returned to claim it.

'I agree with that. Given that Rafael had no knowledge of Sofia's whereabouts, he certainly did all he could to ensure that if either of them did return to the area they would learn of their good fortune.'

Helena forced a smile brighter than how she felt, and then said

'I suppose I should feel happier now that the story is complete, but there still feels some unfinished business. I wonder why Rafael kept seven letters that he had written to Sofia?'

'I think I know the answer to that and I think you will too once you have read them as I have. They are basically love letters, he wrote to her spilling out his heart, but I believe he never intended to send the letters, so he simply posted the envelopes. This to him probably didn't feel like he was breaking his promise to himself. I think he just needed the solace of from time to time saying what was in his heart. And it maybe that Sofia was consoled by receiving the empty envelopes. Perhaps for her they represented the knowledge that he still loved her, she more than any other person would have understood him not breaking his pact. Rafael was after all in a loveless marriage, he spent ten years married to Christina, and it must have been torture for him. We know that Christina

355

herself started to take lovers, discreetly of course, and eventually it was to marry one of these that made her finally agree to the annulment. Rafael spent many years away from home in the Navy, and he must have been a lonely man.'

'I can see that he must have been wretched, and funnily enough I understand, because I have a diary that Sofia wrote, it feels to me like a series of letters that she wanted to send to him but knew she shouldn't. So instead she put her thoughts in a diary, I have it here, I would like it if you read it, but only if you want too.'

'Well why don't we swap the diary for the letters and we can exchange them tomorrow before you leave, as long as Marco doesn't mind dropping you back in.'

'Thanks Carolina that would be fantastic.'

'What would be fantastic?' said Marco who had just entered through the door. Carolina patted the seat next to her and beckoned him to sit down, whilst she filled him in. Helena continued drinking her tea, occasionally she looked up at Marco and smiled, he smiled back. Her tummy did little flutters, and she found she was really looking forward to the evening head.

Half an hour later with diary swapped for the letters, Marco and Helena bade Carolina goodbye and agreed to call in the next day.

Once down the drive and out on the open road to the Pousada, Marco said,

'You have had a quite a day, are you sure that you don't want to be on your own this evening?'

'No absolutely not, I am looking forward to a nice glass of wine and to talking about something other than Sofia and Rafael. To be honest, I would love just to chill out, maybe listen to some music, if that is alright with you.'

'Whatever you wish, I am looking forward to it too.'

Helena who felt slightly mischievous and wanted to understand more about this man said quite casually, 'Perhaps you can tell me about yourself, I don't normally let strangers hold me tightly in their arms whilst I cry all over them.'

Marco briefly looked over at her.

'Well perhaps you could tell me more about you, as I don't normally hold strange women in my arms crying or not!'

They both laughed, and Marco reached over with his right hand and squeezed hers briefly, before returning his hand to the steering wheel.

Helena, felt the same fluttering as she always did when they had accidently touched, and she knew that Marco felt something too. They continued to drive in silence, the road wound slowly upward, and she could see the lights of the Pousada ahead. Once the car had been parked, Marco picked up both bags and they went inside, once they had checked in and been given their room keys Marco said

'What time shall we meet Helena?'

'How about seven fifteen? That should give us plenty of time to relax, shower and change.'

'Fine, seven fifteen it is, in the bar. I have booked the restaurant for eight thirty, so the taxi will pick us up at eight fifteen is that good for you?'

'Perfect, see you later then.'

Helena put the key in the door and walked into her room. Along the corridor Marco had also entered his room, and as he put his small case on the luggage stand he regretted not kissing her. He had wanted too earlier when she was crying, and again in the car but his natural reserve for a client had held him back. He walked into the bathroom picked up the bathrobe, and turned on the taps over the enormous bathtub, before returning to the

357

bedroom where he opened the wardrobe to check that his suit had been delivered. It was hanging up. He undressed folding up his clothes and placing them on the chair. He put on the bathrobe and sat lightly on the edge of the bed. He pushed his hands through his hair, and knew that for the first time in his life he was falling in love. He had had a few relationships in his thirty-four years. As a successful solicitor from a well-known family he knew he was considered a catch. Isabella had made it clear that she wanted more from him, but he was clear that he didn't feel for her in the same way. Alex had lasted the longest at almost two years, but she too in the end wanted marriage and children, and as he was only 26 at the time he wasn't ready to settle down.

Besides he now knew beyond a shadow of a doubt that he hadn't loved her. How he felt about Helena though was a new and unsettling experience for him, put simply she made him feel good in a way he had never known before. She knew nothing about him of course, other than he was her solicitor, but Portugal has many solicitors it wasn't a unique occupation.

Marco reflected on his own family's position, he was descended from a former minor aristocratic family, but he was also heir to quite a family fortune; and whilst he was under no pressure to marry yet, his parents particularly his mother had been dropping hints recently about it being time for her to become a grandmother. Helena, came with a simplicity that entranced him, right from that first day when he could sense her building annoyance at being kept waiting, and then realising she was being ridiculous, she had simply treated him like any other man. She liked him he knew that, he could tell by the way she felt against him and he had seen the sudden change in her behaviour if they touched. He had fallen in love with her and he wanted her, it was as simple as that, with that decision made he picked up his mobile and phoned his father, fifteen minutes later he put down the phone, smiled to himself and was looking forward to the night ahead.

At seven fifteen prompt, Helena left her hotel room and made her way to the staircase, she had on a red sleeveless shot silk shift dress, red sandals and a cream pashmina was draped over her arm. Her clutch bag contained a lipstick, her compact and some money. She hoped her outfit was classy enough for the restaurant without being over the top. She had fretted for days over what to wear, it wasn't a date after all, but she had dreamt that it might be many times. As she walked down the staircase she thought to herself, that surely after today they couldn't ignore the attraction that existed between them, one of them had to say something if only to clear the air. At the bottom of the stairs, was a discreet sign that signalled the way to the bar and restaurant, with her eyes she followed the arrow and then turned walked in the direction it pointed to. As she crossed the threshold her breath caught in her throat, Marco was standing by the bar, dressed in a deep navy blue well cut suit, over a pale blue shirt open at the neck, she could detect the hint of dark hair where his shirt opened at the top of his chest and neck, her tummy did a delicious little roll and she realised that her fingers itched to coil themselves in the dark curls. Just at that moment he looked up and saw her and waved to her, at that she walked unsteadily forward. Marco looked up and saw Helena in the doorway, though he knew she was there before he looked up, he sensed her presence. She was quite beautiful, and he didn't think she knew quite how much. The red dress showed off her eyes, his heart which was already beating a little fast now began to boom in his ears. He put down his glass and walked towards her, when he reached her, he bent down

359

and kissed her cheeks, before propelling her gently to the sofa nearest the bar.

'I've taken the liberty of opening some wine, I hope you like it.'

If Helena was a little disappointed by the chaste welcome it quickly vanished as he smelt divine, and she couldn't stop the involuntary shiver that she felt as his lips touched her cheeks. She allowed herself to be propelled to the sofa and sat down before accepting the glass of wine he offered. Taking a sip her eyes flew open, it was gorgeous, deep black in colour but fruity with a hint of liquorice and black pepper.

'Wow this is fantastic,' she said.

'May I see the bottle?'

Marco picked up the bottle and gave it to her.

After a few seconds Helena gave it him back and said 'This is a superb wine though myself I prefer the 1957 vintage.'

He cocked his head at her raising his eyebrow, and she couldn't contain herself anymore and gave him a small laugh.

'I am sorry I couldn't resist that, you looked so smug.'

'Smug, what is this word smug what does it mean he said with a hurt expression on his face.'

During the next few minutes Helena tried to explain, but in vain and finally she gave up and said

'I was joking it's a fabulous wine, a super choice you have a good palate, though I am surprised they have this in the cellar here.'

'They don't, my father just sent it over for me to share with you tonight.'

'He did but why? it must have been expensive to buy, he should have kept it for a special occasion.'

Marco gave her a wry smile.

'I really have no idea of its price, my father is the wine connoisseur, I like it but it's not one of my areas of interest.'

He sat down on the chair next to the sofa, Helena felt his proximity affecting her equilibrium, she was behaving like a giddy schoolgirl, and she told herself to pull herself together and grow up. In order to break the tension Helena said slightly mischievously,

'So what are your areas of interest? Do you keep bees or grow Bonsai?'

'No none of those, but as a boy we did have hives in the garden, and Senhor Gomes used to come every other week in the summer, and take the honey off. I loved watching him, lifting out the frames and checking it was full. If I was well behaved he used to give me a chunk of honeycomb, I loved it, still do as a matter of fact, but these days I buy it from the supermarket.'

'I see, well we need bees more than ever these days, I plan to put many hives on the land at the Quinta. If I develop the wine business we will need them. My grandfather had a hive and I used to help him. I think it was his love of nature that gave me the idea to study horticulture. So what made you choose to study law?'

'It's a good question. I think it was decided before I was born, I just grew up knowing I would follow my father and grandfather into the family business. My younger sister also studied law, but she went into the business side and is a corporate lawyer currently in New York, very high powered and driven like you can't imagine.'

'Does that mean you're not so driven then?'

Marco thought about this for a moment and then said 'No, I don't think I am, don't get me wrong I love my job, but I am not consumed by it. I saw what it did to my grandfather and to my father to some extent, and realised I wanted something different. It was never in any doubt I

361

would join the family firm, but I don't want to run it, my sister can do that when the time comes. She is much more suited to it than I.'

'What's her name?'

'Vitoria, she is 31 and single before you ask.'

'I am sorry I am a bit nosey, but I like people they interest me.'

'Do they? Do I interest you then?'

Helena was a little surprised by the obvious forthrightness of the question, but looking into his eyes she said,

'Truthfully?'

He returned her look.

'Truthfully.'

Helena who had put her glass down on the coffee table, stood up, and took the three steps to the sofa where he was sitting and sat down beside him. She looked up into his eyes, and lifting up her right hand to touch his cheek said in an almost inaudible voice

'Yes, yes you do very much.'

Marco put his hand over hers and leant in towards.

'That makes me very happy, as I am very interested in you.'

Then tilting her chin upward, he lowered his head, and very gently kissed her on the lips. The touch only lasted a second or two, but Helena felt such a jolt of electricity that she almost jumped backwards, and it took all of her will power not to return the kiss more strongly.

Marco then held her hands in his.

'This is neither the time, nor the place, to kiss you the way I want to kiss you right now, but rest assured that before the night is out that this time will come and when it does I doubt that I will be able to stop at just a kiss.'

Helena looked into his eyes and simply said

'I know, I feel the same too.'

After few seconds, which felt like minutes to Helena, Marco let go of her hands.

'Perhaps now would be a good time to drink our wine, I wouldn't want to waste it, my father would be most unhappy.'

With a nod in the direction of the door he continued with, 'And we are no longer alone.'

Helena who had been oblivious to anyone or anything else that was happening in the room, shook herself and went to move back to the chair, but Marco held on to her and whispered,

'No please sit here next to me, I want you as close to me as I can achieve.' He then gave her a look that melted her insides, and she sat back down. Marco smiled and handed Helena her wine glass, then gently touched his own glass against hers in a toast.

'To life, to love, to us.'

Helena her own heart beating much faster than it should have been looked up into his eyes and simply said.

'Igualmente.'

In the second book Helena and Marco's relationship blossoms, and the work on the Quinta gets underway in earnest causing interesting situations to arise. But expected and unexpected visitors cloud the horizon, so join us to see how Helena and the characters of the local villages grow and become part of the fabric of the Quinta das Laranjeiras.

Printed in Poland
by Amazon Fulfillment
Poland Sp. z o.o., Wrocław